UNDENIABLY ASHER

THE COLLOWAY BROTHERS #2

K.L. KREIG

COPYRIGHT

DEDICATION

For my brother, Rodney, and all those who have suffered from the pain and loss of suicide. Please know that you are not alone. You are never alone.

PROLOGUE

ALYSE

Eight years earlier...

"Slow down, Beck." I know my news is shocking, but I had no idea he would react so badly. I thought we were in love. We've even talked about getting married after I graduate this spring.

"I can't fucking believe you let this happen, Alyse!" His hand slams the steering wheel so hard you'd think it would break.

"*I* let this happen? I don't understand why you're reacting this way. I know it wasn't planned, but..."

I'm cut off when Beck takes a corner too fast, throwing me into the passenger door, tires squealing their protest. My head bounces off the window and my elbow now throbs where it slammed into the metal handle.

After I broke my news over dinner, Beck threw three twenties down on the table and stormed out of the restaurant. I barely had time to hop into the vehicle, let alone put my seatbelt on, before he took off at warp speed, no doubt leaving fresh black rubber marks on the pavement.

"Beck, slow down. Please. You're scaring me." But he doesn't. He punches the gas even harder, lurching the car forward. I fumble for my seatbelt, frantic to get it on before we crash. The dark, desolate road we're flying down—at speeds that would rival a cop chase—is winding and treacherous, especially with the slight sheen of December frost that's now covering it. There is more than one makeshift cross that lines its deadly path. I don't want one to be mine.

"This can't be happening," he mumbles to no one in particular. He seems lost within himself, which confuses me even more. This news isn't the end of the world; it only accelerates our plans to be together, just as we'd talked about many times over.

"I'm sure they'll understand, Beck. I know I haven't met your parents yet, but you're a grown man for God's sake."

My eyes flick between the speedometer and his angry, clenched face and my heart races. We're now going over sixty miles per hour in a forty-five zone. He takes another bend too fast and his truck fish-tails. The tires spit gravel when he overcorrects, landing the passenger side wheels on the shoulder. We narrowly miss a speed limit sign that's mocking us to slow down before he finally regains control.

I brace my arms against the door and the armrest to my left, my long fingernails embedded in the leather fabric. Every muscle in my body is coiled and taut, ready for the inevitable collision. Fear courses through my bloodstream, nearly paralyzing me.

"You're going to kill us if you don't stop this!" I scream.

For the first time in nearly twenty minutes, he looks at me, and I see a man I am not at all familiar with. Pure panic is written on every inch of his handsome face. I shrink into my seat, wondering what alternate universe I have just slipped into.

"Trust me. I'm better off dead." His soft voice is thick with fear and sadness and suddenly I'm truly terrified. The man sitting to my left is

2

not at all the man I fell in love with. It's like he's been possessed by a demon or the devil, and he's taking me on the fast, fiery ride to hell with him.

I don't get a chance to respond to his confusing words before I register we're quickly approaching a particularly wicked curve nick-named the Widowmaker. The speed limit here drops to thirty, because it's deceptively sharp and steep and many people have lost their lives by not adhering to the slower speeds. Taking this curve at forty-five miles per hour is reckless. Taking it at seventy is nothing short of suicidal.

You've heard people say that your life flashes before your eyes in the seconds before a near-death experience, right? That they are filled with regret for that degree they didn't finish, harsh words they wish they could take back, or letting *The One* get away?

Well, that's not what's happening with me. The only thing clouding my mind at the moment before impact with a grove of thick, life-ending oak trees is anger.

Anger at my naiveté.

Anger at my judge of character.

Anger that I let myself trust someone else who would fail me.

And anger that my life is going to end at the tender age of eighteen at the hands of a man who claimed to love me.

Metal crunches.

Glass shatters.

My screams echo in the blackness.

Then...*nothing*.

CHAPTER 1

ALYSE

I STARE AT THE STACK OF BILLS ON MY DESK AND SIGH HEAVILY, MY stomach churning.

They taunt me. Remind me that unless we pull in a large client and fast, this business that I rushed to open is about one month from total, epic failure and not only will I be out of a job, my three employees will be as well. I'm almost a month behind on the loan payment and our electricity is pretty close to being turned off.

I'm not bragging, but I'm pretty damn brilliant when it comes to numbers. Not much in my twenty-five years has been easy, but school always was. It's difficult for me to wrap my head around why someone can't understand math. Numbers are simple. Numbers make sense. Numbers are to me what a piano is to an accomplished pianist. They are my home. My love. My passion.

"You have a gift," my teachers said. And let's face it; it's a statistical fact that men clearly dominate the mathematics field of study. It's a hard road for a woman to pave and be successful in, but I was very bound and determined. I still am; no white flags are being thrown down yet.

I graduated with an accounting degree from the University of Michigan at the top of my class and a year and a half earlier than others my age. I had my master's under my belt shortly before my twenty-second birthday. Last year, I opened ARK Consulting, my own small auditing firm, where I employ two other auditors and an office manager slash receptionist slash marketing director slash assistant slash...well, you get the picture.

But for all my brilliance, the one thing I didn't fully consider was how my young age and worldly inexperience would impact my business model.

Turns out companies are loath to hire a young, newly opened firm with not a lot of references. Not to say that our clients aren't reference worthy. The ones that have given us a chance are more than happy with our work, but as a company, we are young.

Six months ago when I hired Al, a seasoned forensic accountant of forty-four, I found that we became slightly more successful at pulling in clients than when I walked into a meeting by myself. That stung. My pride takes a small hit every time they look to him as the more senior person, simply because he has a pot belly, an Adam's apple, and a dick.

"Alyse, call on line one. It's the bank." Heather's soft voice carries through the speakerphone, echoing off the walls of my small, windowless office. Heather, my all-around keeps-the-office-running assistant is not dumb. She knows we're in some financial trouble, but she's also told me she'd stick it out until the end, because she believes in me. I'm glad someone does. I doubt myself daily, especially lately. Not my ability, not my intelligence, but my decision to jump into a small business with both feet, eyes wide shut. It's not the first time my naiveté has gotten me into trouble.

"Tell them I'm in a meeting, Heather." This is the third call this week. And the third call I'll be avoiding.

"Yes, of course."

I take inventory of our projects, current and potential. Al is working on a breach of contract audit that will be done by mid-next week. Tabitha just started an audit for a bar, where the new manager is suspected of skimming funds, and I'm putting the finishing touches on a large burglary claim that was submitted to an insurance company and is believed to be fraudulent. Turns out it's valid, just not for as much as the business claimed. I have two meetings with potential clients early next week, but even if we're awarded both jobs, it won't keep all three of us busy.

Damn it all to hell.

Needing to take my mind off my financial and business demise, I sit back in my secondhand rolling desk chair. My stare floats to the yellow-stained ceiling, watching the slow drip in the corner. My office is small, a bit rundown, and isn't in the nicest part of Detroit, but it's cheap and close to home. A small, eleven hundred-square-foot home that I'm the proud owner of.

I let my mind wander back to two months ago when the sexiest man ever created by God's hand cornered me in his mom's kitchen during a family dinner I was attending, because my sister is now engaged to his brother, Gray.

"What the fuck happened to your arm?" His insinuation pisses me off, even if it is somewhat true. Finn and I were arguing yesterday and he grabbed me a little too hard, leaving several dark bruises on my bicep that were clearly finger marks. It's the first time it's happened and it will be the last. I meant to throw on a long-sleeved shirt to avoid questions and speculation, but we were already running late and I forgot.

"None of your goddamn business."

He steps closer, clearly not understanding the rules of one's personal space and I have nowhere to escape. I crane my neck at his six-foot-plus height, glaring into his stormy and mesmerizing blue eyes. They remind me of dark pools of warm water. With every inhalation, my lungs fill with his manly scent and citrusy cologne and my mouth waters remembering what his skin tasted like, how his lips felt on mine.

"I don't like him, Alyse," he growls.

7

I would laugh at his bold and unsolicited declaration, but I'm too shocked.
"Then lucky for me I don't really care what you think," I retort smartly. I had
not laid eyes on the enigmatic Asher Colloway in years, so how dare he judge
my boyfriend. Only I get to call him a douchebag loser.

"If he hurts you, I'll fucking kill him."

"What? Asher, it's not like that." And why do you care? I want to ask, but
don't.

"Then what is it like?"

"Why do you care?" Whoops, guess it slipped out.

His heated eyes roam my face. His perfect pink lips part as though he's
about to speak but doesn't. He's so close now, I can feel every hot breath wash
over my face and the warmth from his body soaking into mine. I inwardly
groan. While my boyfriend is outside smoking God knows what, I'm getting
impossibly turned on by another man. I haven't been this wet for Finn in
months, despite his best efforts.

Asher slowly runs the back of his index finger down my bare arm, gently
circling my bruises. Chills and fire break out in its wake. My mind swirls
with confusion at both this conversation and my body's involuntary reaction
to this man after all these years. I can see the mature Alyse is just as affected
by him as the immature one. "Because I hate to see a beautiful woman get
abused," he finally replies in a low, raspy voice.

Scarlet curtains descend. Maybe his concern should make me feel good
or cared for, but all it does is send hot rage firing through my veins. It's
clear to me that Asher thinks I'm letting myself be used as a punching bag
by some asshole and that's the furthest thing from the truth. I am nobody's
bitch.

"Fuck you. You don't own me," I spit.

A slow, sexy smirk spreads his lips as he leans close. His lips brush
against the shell of my ear when he speaks. I'm unable to hide the shiver that
his scorching words produce. "Not yet I don't, sweet Alyse."

Pulling back, he pins me with a smoldering, hungry stare that feels like a
sweet breath against my wet sex. I have to bite my lip hard to keep from
moaning. Leaning in again, I think he may kiss me and I haven't made up
my mind if I will give him my mouth or a swift knee to the jewels, but just as
he's a hairsbreadth away, he reaches behind me, grabs his beer off the

counter, and turns, walking away. I stare after him, practically panting like a crazy bitch in heat.

"Egotistical asshole," I mutter under my breath. *Apparently not quiet enough, though, because I hear him laugh as he enters the living room.*

I broke up with Finn later that night. Something that was long overdue, despite what I'd led everyone else to believe. It was a bad decision to let him move in with me in the first place, but he'd just lost his job and couldn't afford his rent, so I caved. Chalk that relationship up to another grand failure, but it had absolutely nothing to do with Asher Colloway and his whispered promise that went to that dark place between my thighs.

Nope. Nothing at all.

Hearing my cell buzz, I look down to see it's my sister, Livia, and hesitate. Despite the fact that we're slowly mending our relationship, I can admit I still have a fair amount of resentment toward her. She up and abandoned everyone she loved when she disappeared without being seen or barely heard from for over three years. Livia was my rock. I still feel enormously betrayed that she left me, just as everyone else has in my life, especially when I needed her most.

"Hi Libs. How are you?" I say, right before the call rolls to voice mail. It's rhetorical, because I know exactly how my sister is. Giddy, madly in love, and still battling morning sickness.

"Hey, Lysee. Better, actually. You?"

"Great," I inject with as much enthusiasm as possible. *Juuuust great.*

Livia's expecting twins in a little over six months and is engaged to the love of her life, Gray Colloway, who also happens to be Asher's older brother. I'm happy for her, but I'm also admittedly a teensy bit jealous. At one time long ago, I thought I had what Livia now has with Gray. Oh, how very wrong I was.

"How are my nephews?" I ask, trying to get out of my own head.

"And why do you think I'm having boys?" she laughs.

My laughter joins hers. "Look at our families, Libs. Twin boys are practically a pandemic." Livia's husband-to-be is a twin, along with his younger brothers, Asher and Connelly, plus Livia said that Frank Colloway was an identical twin. And though I didn't know her well, our grandmother was a twin. Basically anytime Livia gets pregnant, she'd better watch out.

"Well, I'm still a few weeks away from being able to tell yet."

"So you're going to find out?"

"Yes. Both Gray and I want to know. Planners that we are and all."

Wanting to get off the subject of babies and the twins she's having, I ask, "So how are the wedding plans coming?"

"Funny you should ask," she hedges.

"Uh oh...did you guys decide to elope?" When Livia first called to tell me about her engagement and pregnancy, I asked if they were going to fly to Vegas, but she was adamant she wanted an actual wedding. Small, but complete with the works. Dress, cake, dancing, family, and friends, and they wanted to get married before the babies arrived.

"No. But we did set a date."

"Oh my God, that's great!" I can practically hear Livia's smile. For the first time since she told me she was getting married, I feel a twinge of real excitement for my sister. *About time, you selfish bitch.*

"You may not think so when I tell you. I'm really going to need your help to pull it off."

"Oookay."

"December twenty-seventh."

My stomach drops. "Livia! That's in five weeks!" *The worst day of my life*, I think.

"I know, I know, but...I just want to get married before I get too fat. Despite the morning sickness, I already can't fit into my jeans. You'll be my maid of honor, right?"

My head is reeling at the date Livia's chosen for her wedding, so when I don't respond immediately, I hear her calling my name. "Yes, of course I'll be your maid of honor, Livia," I mumble.

Livia's silent for a few beats. "Alyse...I understand if—"

"It's okay, Livia," I interrupt. "It will be a good distraction." Ever since the accident eight years ago this December twenty-seventh, I take that day off and wallow.

I cry too much.

I drink too much.

I remember too much.

I'm surprised to find that I'm actually sincere when I say it may be a good distraction. Eight years is long enough to mourn. I need to move on. Maybe a good memory on that day to replace the bad is exactly what I need.

"I wanted to pick a different date, but this worked best with Gray's schedule and—"

"Stop. It's fine. It's your day and I'll do everything I can to make it special for you. I promise."

"Thanks, Lysee."

We spend the next twenty minutes talking about wedding details and splitting up duties. Livia's two friends, Addy and Kamryn, will also be helping with the planning, so no one person becomes too overwhelmed with all the tasks that need to be completed in such a short period of time. The wedding will be small: only family and a few very close friends. Regardless of the wedding size, there is an overwhelming amount of detail that needs to be considered.

"So...who is standing up for Gray?" I ask. Livia told me each of them would have only one attendant.

"Asher."

My stomach flutters. I'm ashamed at the rush of desire flowing thickly through my body at the mere mention of his name. "Really? I would have thought Luke would have that role."

For as long as I've known the Colloways, we all thought Gray's twin, Luke, was dead. Turns out he was just disowned for some unsavory life choices, but now he's back in the family fold, somewhat. I think. It's all very confusing.

"It's...complicated. Gray and Luke are slowly working things out, but it will take a while. Gray had a hard time choosing between Asher and Conn, but Conn insisted it be Asher."

I'm glad he did.

We hang up a few minutes later, after I agree to Thanksgiving dinner at the Colloway house next week. It's not like I have anything else to do. I had planned to spend the day in ratty sweats, curled up on the couch, watching football and drinking wine. Guess I'll be doing all of those with the Colloways instead. Minus the ratty sweats. Luckily for me, it's here in Detroit and only a thirty-minute drive from my house.

Looks like I'll be seeing quite a bit of the sexy, irresistible Asher Colloway over the next several weeks. And I'm not sure if I'm excited or nervous.

Both, I think. Definitely both.

I pull myself from my daydreams and back to the problems at hand—getting more clients so I can stay in business past year-end.

CHAPTER 2

ASHER

"So how was your *date* last night?" I ask my fraternal twin, Connelly, breathing hard from my physical exertion. I'm bent over, arms on my thighs, winded from our quick five-mile run. It's early in the morning and the traffic in the gym we offer as a perk to our employees is pretty light. Exactly how I like it. The fewer people around, the better. Actually, I prefer to take my runs outdoors, regardless of the weather, but the half inch of ice and three inches of snow on the Chicago sidewalks overnight make for treacherous conditions, even for the most skilled outdoor runner.

His mouth quirks up on one side. "Satisfying."

"You're such a manwhore."

"We're cut from the same cloth, brother," Conn replies darkly, wiping the sweat collected on his forehead with his drenched shirt. Heading over to the free weights, Conn grabs a pair of fifty-pound dumbbells and begins his bicep curls. I grab the eighty-fives, laying down on the bench for chest presses.

"What about you?" he grunts, rapidly curling the weights up to his shoulders, alternating one after the other, muscles bulging with each stroke. "Haven't bragged about any conquests lately. Why is that?" Conn looks down to where I'm lying and gives me a knowing wink.

Apparently my *feigned* nonchalance about a certain dark-haired, brown-eyed petite beauty who is consuming my every single waking thought is just that. Of course, my twin knows me better than anyone. I've not been this enthralled by a single woman since Natalie, and I don't even think I was this way with her. That scares the fuck out of me.

"Fuck off. I entertained Gabriella recently." And by recently, I mean more than a month ago, which is like a drought for me. I'm surprised my dick hasn't fallen off for lack of use. But the problem is, the entire time I was inside another woman, I thought of Alyse's caramel eyes glazing over with pure ecstasy as I pushed her body to the very limit. Christ, just thinking of the pleasure that would etch on her beautiful face as I force her to give me orgasm after orgasm gets me hard, which won't go unnoticed by my brother, even in my baggy gym shorts.

If I thought my attraction to her at twenty-one was intense, it's a blip on the radar compared to what I'm feeling now. It's been two long months since I've last set eyes on Alyse. I'm trying to figure out how the hell I can see her again before my brother's wedding when Conn drops a gift in my lap.

"You know she's coming to Thanksgiving dinner on Thursday."

No. No I did not.

I struggle with my last two reps, my shaking muscles protesting the heavy weight I've intentionally chosen. "Who?" I pretend to have no idea what he's talking about, but at the inference that I'm finally going to set my starved eyes on Alyse again my dick twitches involuntarily and, noticing, Conn barks a laugh.

Fucker.

Conn racks his weights. Leaning against the mirrored wall, he gauges my every reaction. "I haven't seen you act this way about a woman since…"

"Don't," I snap.

I let my weights drop to the floor and sit up, suddenly feeling too vulnerable with where this conversation is going. I don't talk about Natalie. Ever. Conn knows this. I keep that young and foolish part of my life close to the forefront of my mind so I don't make those same mistakes again. Since the woman I'd planned on marrying crushed my very heart underneath her five-inch cheating stilettos four years ago, I don't let women into that exposed space, choosing to take Conn's route of moving from one willing bed to the next.

So manwhore is a pretty apt title for me, too, as much as I'd like to argue otherwise.

But somehow I find myself thinking that if I ever *would* let a woman worm her way into that dark, broken space again, it would be Alyse Kingsley. Same as it was years ago, there's just something about her innocence that inexplicably draws me to her like a moth to an open flame.

Innocence I want to corrupt.

Badly.

And repeatedly.

Her innocence is about as compelling as her fire and tenacity and intelligence. Add to that the whole outer beauty with her insanely sexy and fit body and drop-dead-gorgeous face, and she really is the whole package. She's grown into an incredible woman. I find myself wondering why someone hasn't married her yet, but at the same time I'm glad they haven't. Because I want her like I haven't wanted another woman in a very, very long time. I have to wonder if I've ever wanted a woman as badly as I want Alyse.

As I've *always* wanted her.

I've known Alyse since my older brother, Gray, started dating her sister, Livia, over eight years ago. Even then I was irrationally attracted to her. I shouldn't have been. She was seventeen, in high school. I was twenty-one, in college. She was jailbait, but that didn't stop me from having a brief summer fling with her. I've had a lot of women over the years, too many, in fact, and I've pretty much forgotten all of them.

Except Alyse Kingsley.

She's simply unforgettable, as is that Fourth of July where we almost made the biggest mistake of my young adult life. Being attracted to Alyse was one thing. Actually acting on it was something else entirely. Except we did. Had my twin not caught us in the boathouse at that moment, I don't think anything would have stopped me from taking her that night. Right or wrong.

I saw her briefly a couple of times after that, but we never acted on our attraction again. Ever since I saw her just two months ago at a family dinner in Detroit, I haven't been able to stop thinking about Livia's baby sister. Or the fact that she's no longer a baby, but a twenty-five-year-old fucking hottie that my cock is begging me to take on a long, sweaty ride.

When I saw the bruises on her arm, I about lost it and pounded her meathead boyfriend's face into the concrete. Just thinking about it now makes my blood boil with rage. I wasn't kidding when I told Alyse I'd kill the fucker if he ever put his hands on her again. If I so much as glimpse one mark next time I see her, I'm sure my brother Luke can hook me up with someone who would be all too happy to make that happen.

Knowing that both the Natalie and Alyse discussions are closed, Conn's quiet as we finish our weight training. Forty-five minutes later we're showered and enter the elevator.

I punch the button for the thirty-fourth floor harder than I mean to, frustration still coursing heavily through my system. By now, I'm not actually sure what I'm frustrated about most. Natalie, for fucking up my life; Alyse, for driving me batshit crazy with a voracious craving I need to quench; or meathead, for putting his...*anything* on the woman I want.

Or it could be my lack of getting laid in weeks, because all I can think of is sinking into what I know will be the best pussy I've ever had. I just don't know what I want beyond that. In my gut, however, I know it will be more. I'm already almost savagely possessive of her and she's not even mine. *Yet.* I'm very worried that once I have Alyse, I'll never want to give her up. I'm not sure I'm capable of giving her everything she deserves either.

The elevator doors open. It's not even seven yet, so the floor is quiet and most of the assistants haven't arrived yet, except mine. As the CEO of CFC, Colloway Financial Consultants, I usually split my time between the branch in Detroit and our headquarters in downtown Chicago. When I'm in the Chicago office, my assistant, Tara, puts in long hours, always making sure to arrive by six-thirty. CFC is one of the three companies my brothers and I own together under GRASCO Holdings and since I'm also on the board, I tend to put in long, grueling hours.

"Any news on the audit?" Conn asks, as we exit the steel cage.

"I have a meeting with Sheila Willis today at three. They're supposed to finally have a full report after two goddamn months." A few months ago, an accounting discrepancy of over a half million dollars was brought to my attention. Though I have my suspicions about what's happening, I've kept them to myself. Keep your friends close, but your enemies closer, a wise person once said. In business, I have found that's some very sound advice. Someone's going to jail over this, and it's not going to be me.

"Good. I'm off to Cincinnati later for a meeting tomorrow, then headed to Mom's on Wednesday morning. See you there?"

"Yes. It will probably be late when I get there, though."

We part ways and I spend the majority of the day on phone calls and in back-to-back meetings. I barely have time to wolf down the roast beef sandwich Tara ordered for me from my favorite deli down the street. I ate it so fast, I now have indigestion. At three, there's a soft knock on my door before it opens.

"Your three o'clock is here, Asher," Tara announces. I don't know Tara's exact age, because I've never asked, but if I had to guess, I would put her in her late forties. She's soft-spoken, has three grown children, and has been married for almost twenty-five years. After all these years, her husband still does romantic, off-the-cuff little gestures that light her face aglow. For the first time in years, I find

K.L. KREIG

myself a little envious that I don't have that kind of love, but since seeing Alyse again I wonder if it's possible to find that. I think maybe it is, if I just open myself up to the option that not every woman out there is a two-timing, cheating whore who's only after my money. This wispy, feisty little twenty-five-year-old woman has me actually thinking of possibilities, and I haven't done that since Natalie.

"Thanks, Tara." I smile, steeling myself for a rough meeting with Sheila Willis. We've used Willis's auditing services for over twenty years. Hank Willis was an old friend of my dad's. Sheila, Hank's daughter, is only a year younger than my twenty-nine years and she's *always* had a thing for me.

Unfortunately for *her*, the feeling is not mutual.

Unfortunately for *me*, one alcohol-hazed night changed everything.

My father had just passed away two months before and we were holding our annual Christmas party, to which we routinely invited some of our closest vendor partners. Hank's wife had recently passed away as well, so he brought Sheila as his plus one.

Grief plus alcohol…bad fucking combo.

In a very weak moment, I ended up banging Sheila against the women's bathroom door. To me it was a quick fuck and a much-needed stress reliever; to her it meant a diamond, a honeymoon in France, and happy-fucking-ever-after.

Before that night, I tolerated her failed attempts to trap me. After that night…well, let's just say if she could cut off my dick and get away with it, she would. I slept with one eye open for months afterward, worried she'd break in and make good on her threat.

Luckily, I didn't work with Sheila often over the years. But if I could have predicted Hank would die just a few short months ago, Sheila would take over his business, and I would have to be constantly subjected to her, I would have found another audit firm before that fateful day. We have three months left on our current contract and then it's buh-bye Sheila. Until then, I have to deal.

Tara steps aside and Sheila walks into my office, her attitude cocked and her feathers on full display. But like a female peacock, hers

18

are dull and drab. They don't attract the opposite sex. Only, because she can't look behind her strut, she can't see it like everyone else.

I contain my eye roll as she strolls in.

"Sheila, nice to see you again." I wave for her to take a seat.

"Save it, *Asher*. We both know that's not true." She walks by me with barely contained disdain. I follow her, taking a seat behind my desk. Jesus, this is bound to be a painful meeting.

"Have it your way. What did you find?" I ask, leaning back in my chair, trying my best to intimidate her. She just shakes her head.

Bitch.

"Slightly over half a million dollars is unaccounted for. I suspect misappropriation of funds, but as you know, we don't have that auditing expertise in our small firm, so you will need to hire a forensic auditor."

Fuck. This was exactly my fear. We have an embezzler in our ranks and I need to find out who it is and stop them. They've already stolen over half a mil of my company's money. Probably more by now.

"Can you tell how long this has been going on?"

"Sometime within the last twelve months since our last audit. I went back and checked the work papers from last year to ensure we didn't miss anything, but that audit is clean."

So sometime within the last twelve months. This has been going on under my nose for up to a whole year and I was none the wiser? Ouch. That stings. Some motherfucking heads are going to roll, the first being my CFO. How the hell did he not know about this for a goddamn year? Either he's incompetent or he's the culprit. I'd bet money on the latter.

"Anything else?" I want to get this meeting over with so I can formulate my next steps. And they happen to involve a chocolate-eyed beauty that I've been wanting to spend some quality time with. Now I have a valid reason.

Sheila pulls out a couple of papers from her folder, laying them on my desk. "I have a few recommendations for forensic audit firms. Ones we've used in the past that produce solid work. They're reputable."

The one thing I would not do is take any of Sheila's recommendations. I'd just as soon scour the damn phone book, picking one blindfolded. Besides, I already know exactly who I'm going to hire.

"Thank you. I'll call you if I have questions after I read your report."

She rises, not acknowledging I said a damn thing, throws her briefcase over her shoulder, and turns to leave. *Three months*, I tell myself. Just three more fucking months.

After she exits, I quickly pull up the Internet and type in "ARK Consulting," the name of Alyse's auditing firm, which I remember from our family dinner. Her *forensic* auditing firm. Exactly what I now need.

After several minutes of perusing her website and reading client testimonials, I call her office and talk to a lovely woman named Heather. I find out that Alyse will be in on Wednesday, so I ask Heather to send me client reference phone numbers and to block the afternoon for me, starting at noon. I schedule the meeting under the name GRASCO, as I don't think Alyse is familiar with our holding company name. For now, I want to keep my identity under wraps. I don't want to give the lovely Alyse time to formulate reasons why she should deny my proposal.

Thanking Heather, I hang up and ponder how my impending discussion with the stubborn Alyse will go the day after tomorrow. Her clients seem relatively small, so I have no doubt this will be a big job for her tiny firm, but if you listen to Livia talk, she's as brilliant as she is beautiful. I also overheard enough of her conversations a couple months ago with my mom to know she's extremely passionate about what she does.

In the end, I have to make a business decision to hire the best auditor. I have every confidence that after I check references at the end of our meeting on Wednesday, the firm awarded that job will be ARK Consulting.

"Tara," I call through my open door.

"Yes," she yells back.

"Clear my calendar on Wednesday. I have a last-minute business meeting in Detroit that came up."

"Will do."

I smile to myself as I sit back and stare at the picture Alyse has posted of herself and her team on her website.

So professional.

So prim.

So proper.

But I know something kinky and adventurous lurks beneath the straitlaced persona she puts on for everyone else. That side is something I have a visceral need to explore, expose, and exploit.

I didn't miss her sharp intake of breath when I told her I meant to own her. I didn't miss the quick flutter of her pulse in the slim column of her neck when my mouth was at her ear. And I most certainly did not mistake the scent of her desire as I stood within an inch of her supple lips, wanting desperately to capture them with mine, making good on my promise to own her right then and there.

Remembering all of these things, as though they happened yesterday, it's not surprising that my cock jerks at the thought of being buried inside her slick, velvety warmth. What *is* surprising, however, is the strange and foreign sensation I feel in the middle of my chest at the thought of simply having her in my bed and holding her in my arms.

Somewhere in the back of my mind, I've never been able to forget her. I'm beginning to think that Ms. Alyse Kingsley may be a game changer. I have to wonder, though...am I ready for the game to change?

I think the answer to that finally is...*yes.*

Yes, I am.

CHAPTER 3

ALYSE

A QUICK GLANCE AT THE CLOCK SHOWS IT'S ALMOST NOON. I READY myself for my next meeting, wondering what the hell Asher Colloway thinks he's trying to pull and why he didn't just put his name on my calendar instead of his holding company. Clearly he's trying to surprise me.

Well, the surprise is on him. Not only do I know it's him I'm meeting with, I know that he asked for client references, and I know he's already called each and every one of them. We're a small office and Heather keeps nothing from me, not to mention we like to give our clients a heads up when we know they'll be called by a potential customer.

The thing is, I have no idea what he would possibly want to hire my small firm for, but since I'm desperate for revenue, I can't *not* take the meeting. I have more to think about now than just my pride. I have three employees counting on me to feed and clothe themselves and their families. That's a heavy burden.

I thought about having Al sit in, but decided against it. I already know Asher and he knows me, so having another male in the room isn't a necessity. Besides, a little part of me is thrilled to spend a few hours alone with him, even if we are just discussing business. *Okay, a* big *part of me.*

I managed to close one deal earlier this week and am waiting to hear back from the other client, hopefully by the end of the day. That one doesn't look too promising as we're a bit apart on pricing for our services. I have a small office and can't afford to be quite as flexible as other, larger firms that have more capital to work with. Another thing I did not take into consideration when I jumped into this dream of mine headfirst. *Ugh.*

My speakerphone squawks, and Heather's voice floats through. Her normally quiet, soft demeanor has clearly been ratcheted up a few degrees, because she actually sounds excited. I can hear the smile in her voice. Yes, Asher Colloway will do that to a woman, at least any straight one. "Ms. Kingsley, your noon appointment is here."

Ms. Kingsley? Heather hasn't addressed me as Ms. Kingsley since our first interview, and even at the end of that meeting she was calling me Alyse. I keep the laugh from my voice as I respond, "Thank you, Heather. Please send Mr. Colloway in." Once I disconnect I do chuckle. Heather usually has me on speakerphone when she buzzes my appointments in, so Asher's little surprise has just been turned around. *Ha! Boo-yaa!*

I'm still laughing when Asher opens my door. The moment my eyes land on him, though, it stutters a slow death. My gaze slowly travels down his insanely fit body and I realize he's watching me watch him, but I don't care enough to stop.

He's absolutely breathtaking in his fitted charcoal suit and crisp white shirt, which he's left open at the throat, sans tie. And the tiny bit of chest hair I see peeking through against his golden skin makes me water in more than one place. I've never seen him in anything but jeans and henleys or polo shirts, but *hot damn* if he doesn't look even

23

K.L. KREIG

more mouthwatering when he's dressed up. My entire body feels warm and tingly, inside and out.

I gravitate toward men with dark looks.

Dark hair.

Dark whiskers.

Dark eyes.

Dark personality.

Asher Colloway fits that bill to a perfect "T". At a little over six feet, he's tall, at least for me since I hover around the five-foot-four mark, give or take a half inch on a good day. And he's downright beautiful. All of the Colloway brothers could effortlessly grace the cover of a magazine, but Asher is different. He's a guy you could easily get lost in before your brain catches up to remind you why you shouldn't. He has an aura about him that's nothing short of magical and when you look at him, a spell is woven that you can't escape. You don't want to.

When I met him for the first time at seventeen, I thought he was the best thing since sliced bread. I even thought I was in love with him, but we were in very different places in our lives. Then I met Beck and I moved forward instead of looking back. Now, though…now, I can honestly say that at twenty-nine, Asher *is* the sexiest man I have ever laid eyes on, hands down.

I want him. Desperately.

And desperation makes you do stupid, stupid things.

"Get your fill yet?" A smug smirk turns up one corner of his kissable mouth.

Damn him. I have absolutely no snarky comeback to that, because I've been openly ogling. I only hope I don't have drool dripping down my chin. I nonchalantly reach up to check, faking a cough.

"Why the secrecy?" I ask, changing subjects, not taking my eyes from him.

He closes the door before taking a seat in the chair across from my metal desk, throwing one foot onto the opposite knee. He steeples his fingers in front of his chin. The arrogant glint in his dark eyes makes me want to drop to my knees in front of him, unzip his pants, and wipe it off.

24

"You knew it was me."

I knew Asher had taken over as CEO for his father's company—I *may* have asked Livia what the Colloway brothers were up to after she'd reunited with Gray. In preparation for this meeting, when I researched GRASCO Holdings and found that CFC fell under them, I was irritated at first that Asher wanted to catch me cold. I never attend a client meeting without doing my homework first, especially since I'm fighting for the very existence of ARK Consulting. But then I quickly decided to turn the tables on the self-assured SOB.

Knowing that I would be meeting with Asher today, I've dressed particularly sexy in a short nude pencil skirt paired with a sheer royal-blue blouse and a matching low-cut cami underneath. Definitely not how I would dress for a normal client meeting, but I went all out for Asher. I let a slow smile turn my lips as I sit back in my black vinyl chair and casually cross my legs.

Asher's eyes follow my leisurely movements and widen at the expanse of bare thigh I'm now showing. He may have even seen a flash of the nude thong I'm wearing from his position. His heated gaze rises, capturing mine, and I have to actually talk myself into breathing, trying to remain unaffected by the intense desire he clearly wants me to see. It's not working too well.

"It may surprise you to know that I do know how to use the Internet," I finally manage to bite sarcastically.

"You haven't changed a bit, Alyse."

"I beg to differ," I retort, knowing full well life has made me more cynical and closed off.

He rewards me with a small smile, which almost melts me on the spot. He's like the sun. Warm. Inviting. Only more deadly if you spend too much time in his presence. He's quiet for several beats, his eyes assessing me deliberately. "I like a woman with fire."

"Do you?" I cross my arms, unsure where this conversation is headed, but it's not about business anymore. I don't miss how his eyes linger too long on my now-exposed cleavage.

"Yes." He uncrosses his leg and leans forward, elbows on spread knees, hands clasped. His want-filled gaze burns my cocky attitude to ashes. "It makes her complete submission all the sweeter."

A flash fire of heat scorches my lady parts. My mouth drops open temporarily before I think to close it. Asher is so good, so smooth, and I am *waaaay* out of my league trying to trade barbs with him.

"What are you doing here, Asher?"

He leans back again, resuming a casual position, a slight smirk on his face. His eyes twinkle like stars and I find myself getting lost in them again. "Besides getting you wet?" he drawls roughly. Even though he's spot on, his assumption angers me. I open my mouth to protest when he interrupts. "You still with Popeye?"

Huh? It takes me a minute to figure out what he means. *Finn.* I stare at him in complete and utter shock for several moments. Then, I can't help it. I laugh. I've never been around a man who has kahunas as big as Asher Colloway. He was always direct, but in the years since I've seen him, he's sharpened it considerably. It's refreshing and unsettling at the same time.

I shake my head, still chuckling, but he's stony silent. His desire has now clearly morphed into annoyance, which makes me laugh even harder. "And if I say yes?"

"Are you?"

I almost decide to lie just to see how he'll react. Anger isn't the type of response I want from Asher, though. I'm not really sure what I do want, but I know it's not that. "No."

As fast as his annoyance came, it went with my admission.

"Did you come here to question my relationship status? You could have just hopped on Facebook for that, saved yourself the drive." I uncross my legs and lean on my forearms, the coldness from the steel desk seeping into my exposed pores through the thin fabric. It's November in Detroit and very cold, but I still can't regret my choice of wardrobe after seeing the appreciation in both Asher's eyes and slacks.

"Because it's not official until it's Facebook official, right?"

"Right," I drawl. "So, back to my original question. Why are you here?"

"I want to hire you."

I assumed when he was calling references that was his angle. I'm thrilled, but at the same time, disappointed. I need this job, but I also want Asher, even though that's not the best of ideas. And I can't have both.

*Why?...*a little voice whispers.

Because it's kind of a faux pas to sleep with your clients, I tell that little slut.

"For?"

"There's someone embezzling within my company. I want them found and stopped and prosecuted." He pulls an envelope out of a folder he set down on the edge of my desk earlier. "Our outside audit firm completed our annual audit and found a discrepancy in the books, but they aren't equipped to take it further. We need someone who has expertise in ferreting out things like this, whose techniques will hold up in a court of law. I know you've worked on cases before where your work has supported a legal case."

True. I live to bring down white-collar thieves. My dad was a thief; he just stole our childhood from my sister and me instead of a corporation or business. I think that's one of the reasons I went into this field to begin with. "Is this a past or ongoing issue?"

"I have reason to believe it's ongoing, but of course I can't be sure."

"Do you have any suspicions?"

"Yes. Unfortunately nothing solid, though."

I look down, unsure of how I should approach this. I don't want to talk myself out of a job, but I want to be up front as well. I don't doubt my ability in the slightest, but CFC would be, by far, the biggest client I've worked on, and this project could possibly take months, given my small staff depending on how deep the embezzlement is buried. "You do know I haven't worked on a project for a company your size yet, correct?"

He nods, staying quiet.

"Okay. Let me look this over and work up a proposal and a time-line for your review. I can have it to you by mid-next week. Then we can meet again, discuss any questions you might have, and negotiate terms."

"No."

My brows draw together in confusion. "No, what?"

"No. I told you I want to hire you. *You.* I've already done my research. I don't need to review anything."

I'm taken aback for a moment. "I could rob you blind. My fee may not even be competitive with the other firms you're considering."

"I'm already being robbed blind. And you won't. Whatever your fees, whatever your terms, I'll agree to them. I want the best, Alyse." He pauses before he adds, "I hear that's you."

Huh? This is by far the weirdest client prospect meeting I've ever had. I have to wonder what the catch is, because this seems too good to be true. "Uh, oookay."

"I want you to start on Monday."

It's the Wednesday before Thanksgiving. I think for a minute, cataloging our current projects. I was planning to take this new client I just secured, but I can give that to Al. Tabitha still has at least two weeks on her current project, and I'll have to come in now on Friday to wrap up a few loose ends and do some paperwork. "I can make that work."

He's silent, studying me. "One more thing. And it's non-negotiable."

I smirk. "I'm not sleeping with you." *Even though right now I can think of nothing else but your hot, wet tongue worshipping every inch of me.*

Laughing, he leans forward, his forearms on my desk, his face mere inches from mine. I want to lean back, yet not at the same time, so I don't. Once again, Asher invades my personal space. I can't stop the big breath I take, inhaling his manly, spicy scent. It's all I can do to keep my eyes from rolling back in my head.

He doesn't miss it either. I'm getting the distinct feeling he doesn't miss any of my bodily reactions to his inebriating presence. When he finally speaks, his voice drops several octaves to panty-melting sexy. "Good. Because I'm looking forward to fucking you instead."

Holy balls. His blistering stare and egotistical words light a blaze deep within my belly. If I was wet before, I'm positively drenched now. And mute. Very, very mute. On account of the fact that my mouth is now bone dry and all thought has fled my desire-clouded brain.

His next words pull me out of the sexual haze he has trapped us in. It's a place I could imagine myself staying. Forever. "I need you at headquarters during the audit. In Chicago."

I blink a few times to clear my mental fog, letting his words register. Being onsite during an audit is pretty standard, as least part of the time, but this will be a big audit and could take months. I bill for lodging and meal expenses, but the thought of spending months in a hotel and shuttling back and forth on the weekends to Detroit is less than appealing. On the other hand, it gets me closer to Livia. Hell, who am I kidding? I'd shuttle back and forth to San Francisco if there were a paying client there.

"You have offices here in Detroit, right?"

"Yes, but I need to keep this as quiet as possible. CFC is not all that big, so the fewer people who know about you, the better. I need you in Chicago. There's a secluded office available on my floor."

The thought of being near Asher daily does funny things to my insides. More than it should. More than I want. "That's going to be pretty costly for you," I murmur. *And me,* I think, in more ways than one.

He leans back slightly and I'm able to take a deep breath for the first time in long minutes without inhaling him. His unique fragrance is clouding my mind, my judgment.

"I have another proposal."

I roll my eyes, leaning back in my chair. His magnetic pull makes it hard to do even that.

I am in so much trouble.

"I'm not staying with you, either."

"Now, Alyse, why do you insist on ruining all my fun?" he quips, winking.

I smile, but remain quiet. Even if he would be so bold to suggest it, he would have to know I'd never accept.

"Okay. If you won't stay with me, then we have an executive apartment that's not being used. It's fully furnished and close to the office. The building has a nice gym and a couple of restaurants. It's not terribly fancy, but it's better than a hotel."

"I—I don't know, Asher." I'm hedging, but the second his proposal left his mouth I already made up my mind. If I had a place that felt like my own, I could stay there most weekends instead of driving back to Detroit, where there was really nothing left for me except bad memories and ghosts from my past that won't seem to let me out of their unyielding grip.

He gets comfortable again before continuing his sales pitch. "It's in the same building as Livia and Gray, so you'll also be close to your sister. I know you're helping with their shotgun wedding and wouldn't it be convenient to be able to hop in the elevator and pop in on her? Of course, I would probably call ahead first, because..."

He leaves his insinuation hanging and we both laugh, lightening the mood.

As I pretend to think about it for a couple of minutes, his intense gaze never leaves mine. I can feel him willing me into acquiescence. I almost break a smile, but that would be giving him too much and right now I need to hold parts of me back, because I can already tell Asher will demand everything from me. And then some. Certain girlie parts are already begging me to submit, submit, submit.

Seeing Asher again a couple of months ago triggered something inside me. Made me remember my girlish dreams when I was eighteen and in love with Beck. Dreams that have been too painful to remember, but now that I do, I want them desperately. To be honest, it made me remember what I felt when I almost gave myself to a young Asher Colloway.

I want bone-deep love, a family, happiness, and a man that will worship me. I thought Beck was the man who would give me everything, but he's dead and apparently wasn't the man I thought he was at all.

Finn certainly wasn't that man.

And I don't think Asher Colloway can give me any of those things either. I'm not sure he can give *any* woman that.

Pleasure? No doubt.

A future? Not likely.

He's nearly thirty, never been married, and is clearly a player. I want more than that now. God knows I *deserve* more than that. As much as I'm attracted to him, sleeping with him is probably the dumbest idea to ever cross my mind, yet my conviction not to needs a lot of reinforcement.

I refocus on the reason we're having this discussion in the first place. Keeping my business afloat. "Okay. I accept your terms."

His smile blinds me, and all thoughts I just had about why I should stay away from this man float out of the room on a cloud of pure lust.

Yep, my conviction needs a lot of work.

A. Lot.

CHAPTER 4

ASHER

"Have you had lunch yet?" Now that she's agreed to my terms, I want to get to the fun part. Getting to know this grown-up Alyse who has me mesmerized. Who's been overshadowing my every thought for weeks. The fact that her asshole boyfriend is out of the picture is that much better. Because one way or another, he was gonna be gone.

"Yes. I ate a quick bite before you arrived."

I can't tell if she's telling the truth or not, so I change tactics. "Dinner, then."

"I don't know, Asher. It's probably best if we don't."

Bullshit.

"I have a few more things I'd like to discuss. Get you up to speed on CFC before Monday." I don't, because I'd planned on doing that Monday morning, but she doesn't have to know that. Besides, if it makes her say yes, then I'll spend some of the precious personal time I get with her on business.

She smirks and her eyes twinkle. I guess I'm not as smooth as I think. That, or she sees right through me, which is the more disconcerting of the two.

"Well, since it's only a little after one o'clock and you blocked the entire afternoon, we have time now."

"Yes, I did," I reply slowly, trying to think how I'm going to get her to agree. "However, another urgent matter came up on the way here and I'm afraid I have an important call in an hour." It didn't and I don't. "I'll pick you up at seven," I say as I begin to rise. I can see asking Alyse will get me nowhere, so demand it will be. That's my usual MO anyway and what I'm far more comfortable with.

"I'm going to see you tomorrow at your mom's for Thanksgiving. We can just talk then."

I turn, my hand gripping the doorknob. I surprise myself by telling the truth instead of being flippant. "I don't want to spend a holiday talking about business, Alyse. That's one of the few days I get away from it and I just want to enjoy spending time with my family."

Her face falls and I know I have her, but I wonder why it doesn't make me as happy as it should. Maybe because I want Alyse to *want* to be with me, not coerced to be with me.

"Yes, I'm sorry. Okay."

I nod, open the door, and walk through, calling over my shoulder, "See you at seven."

Half an hour later, I walk through the front door of my family home, surprised to see Gray and Livia there already, but happy nonetheless. Things are finally getting back to normal between Gray and myself after the whole firing *misunderstanding* with Livia.

At the time, I truly thought it was best for both of them. Although it's hard, even I can admit when I've royally fucked up. I guess I should have discussed my decision with Gray before sending Camille to Livia's apartment with severance papers. In retrospect, I can see how very uncool and unprofessional it was, but I was also trying to avoid another debacle like the one five years ago.

Gray was destroyed when Livia left him, and although neither will tell me the whole story, Gray has assured me it wasn't because she wanted to. Whatever that means. All I know is if she hurts him again, I will stop at nothing to keep her out of his life, underhanded or not. Although with twins on the way, keeping her out of his life will be that much harder.

But at the moment I don't have to worry about that, because they seem genuinely happy and are to be married in just a few short weeks. For both of their sakes, I hope it works out. I know how devastating it can be to have the woman you love crush you. It's something I still haven't fully recovered from. I'm beginning to wonder if I ever will.

"Hi," I say, grabbing a beer from the fridge.

"Starting a little early, aren't you?" Gray responds. He's sitting at the island with his arms wrapped around Livia from behind, who's standing between his legs thumbing through a wedding magazine. I don't want to examine too closely why that intimate gesture causes me a little pang of envy.

I ignore his jab. I only plan on having a couple of brews before I spend the rest of the afternoon catching up on some work. Then I want to spend the evening and all day tomorrow just enjoying Alyse's company. I need time to break down her defenses before Monday. I already know she's trying to ignore what's sizzling hot between us, and in some ways I have to respect that. She's professional, she's trying to run a business, and she doesn't want to fraternize with clients. I get that. Hell, I *agree* with that. But I plan on being more than just a client to her.

"Where's Mom?" Usually she would be running around the kitchen like a chicken with her head cut off by now.

"She needed a few things from the store. She'll be back shortly," Gray replies.

"Why are you guys here so early?" I ask after taking a nice long drink of the cold, tasty liquid. Mom doesn't normally drink, except for an occasional glass of wine, but she always has each of my brothers' favorite beers on hand when we come home.

"I wanted to help your mom with the cooking," Livia says, looking up from the wedding dresses she's perusing.

"That's nice, Livia." I smile and she returns it. Livia and I are also trying to mend things, although that's taking a little bit longer. One of my biggest personality flaws is the ability to forgive and forget. I'm not good at either, especially when it comes to someone hurting the people I love.

"Why are *you* here so early?" Gray eyes me suspiciously. I haven't told him about my intent to hire Alyse yet, but he's no fool. He spent an hour lecturing me weeks ago on why I needed to stay away from her.

She's like family.

Don't use her.

Awkwardness.

Blah blah blah. But I'm a grown fucking man. I make my own decisions and I almost always get what I want. I want Alyse. Surprisingly for more than just sex, because if that's all it was, I *would* stay away from her. Or I'd try my level best, for to some degree I agree with Gray.

Livia is all Alyse has and now that she's marrying my brother, we're bound to see a lot of each other at family functions. So if I use her, as I have every other woman for the last four years, yes, I would be a rat bastard. Thing is, I don't want to *use* her. I like her. A *lot.*

I need to change the subject. The last thing I want to do is get into a conversation about Alyse in front of her sister. "Is Luke coming?" I ask.

Gray shakes his head disapprovingly. He knows exactly what I'm up to. Bastard. "He said he would try. I'm not holding my breath." He sounds rather caustic and I see a look of hurt pass over Livia's face before Gray spins her in his arms so she's facing him. He cups her face. "I'm sorry, angel."

"Try to be nice to him. For me," she replies softly.

"You know I will." When he brings her mouth to his, I feel like I'm intruding on a private moment, so I turn and leave, heading to my bedroom. I have no idea how Livia knows Luke, all I know is that she does. Another one of the little mysteries that surrounds Livia's disappearance and Luke's long absence.

Since Luke has resurfaced and apparently cleaned up his shit, we've talked a few times, but it's strained—on both sides. Last time I talked to him, he told me he's in the process of relocating his PI business from Dayton to Chicago so he can be closer to family. Having been out of our lives for over ten years, he's almost like a stranger to me and I'm not sure how I feel about that, but I think I'd like to have my big brother back.

I spend the next few hours catching up on emails and making a few phone calls before taking a shower to get ready for my date with Alyse. I have a lovely little Italian restaurant picked out. It's a hole in the wall, but it's quiet and romantic and their chicken cannelloni is to die for.

Alyse didn't give me her address, but I know where she lives. I've driven by her house a couple of times over the last few months to see if I can catch a glimpse of her. About a month ago I saw her in the living room windows. I stopped on the street, drinking in the sight of her for several minutes.

She was cleaning and singing. She looked so goddamn carefree and happy. Even then the thought crossed my mind that *I* wanted to be the one to put that smile on her face. I quickly put the car into gear and got the hell out of there before I did something even more stupid than stalking, like walking up to her door and demanding that she let me fuck her against the closest wall.

At five-thirty, dressed in dark jeans and a black wool sweater, I head downstairs to visit with my family a bit before I head out. When I hit the landing, the noise from the kitchen draws me in that direction. I don't know if it's like this with every other family, but in our house the kitchen is the hot spot. I've spent more than one night standing around the island, drinking and laughing with my brothers, my mom, and my dad when he was alive. That kitchen is full of dozens of good and bad memories, but I cherish each and every one. Even though I've not lived at home since I went away to college, every time I'm back here it feels like where I should be.

"Hey Mom." I kiss her on the cheek before I grab a piece of cheese from the charcuterie platter. One thing I'll say about my mom...we'll never starve when we're home. By the time I leave on Saturday, I'll probably have gained five pounds.

"Hi, sweetie. What have you had your head down doing?"

I pull her into a hug. "Just some work things to finish up. I promise I'm yours the next two days." Mom worries about Gray, Conn, and me working too much. She's probably right to worry, but it takes dedication, hard work, and a lot of hours to be successful. Yet the only thing she sees is a husband taken from her too early because he dedicated his life to his company. A company that I now run.

"Promise?"

"Promise." Kissing her head, I release her. Grabbing a cold one from the fridge, I twist off the top and take a long pull.

"Anyone special snag your attention yet, Asher?" she asks.

Why are mothers always trying to marry you off? I'll tell you why in one word: grandchildren.

I look around to see if anyone else heard her question and it doesn't appear they did. "Possibly," I reply softly, not wanting anyone else to hear. "But keep it on the down low, okay?"

She winks and I smile. I fucking *love* my mother.

I notice Gray and Livia sitting at the kitchen table. They appear to be going over a checklist of sorts. Probably more wedding shit. I don't know how he has the patience to go through all that crap. When I get married, whatever my wife wants, she'll get. Wait...did I just think *when*?

"You look nice, brother," Conn quips, a smug smirk on his face. I mouth, "fuck you" while throwing up my middle finger. Behind my mother's back, of course.

"I'm meeting some of the guys at Stubby's later. You coming?"

"Who?" I ask, just to be conversational. I have no intention of going. I plan on spending the whole evening with Alyse. If she'll let me. Even if she doesn't, I don't really have any desire to spend an evening with a bunch of old high school people who I couldn't care less about. Everything I care about is in this room right here. With the exception of one person. I find myself mulling over that thought when Conn answers.

"Alan, Bud, Mark. The usual."

"I have plans." At that declaration, Gray's head snaps in my direction. The withering look he gives does the opposite of what it's supposed to do. I laugh. He whispers something to Livia, then stands, making his way to me.

"Can I talk to you for a second? Alone?"

I roll my eyes, but follow him into the darkened sunroom anyway, far away from the prying ears of others.

"What the fuck are you doing?" he hisses.

"I have no idea what you're talking about."

"I told you to stay away from Alyse."

I just chuckle. "Yes, you did."

"Then what do you think you're doing? That's Livvy's sister you're fucking with."

Amusement is quickly replaced by anger. "First of all, this is none of your goddamn business, Gray. Second of all, I would never hurt Alyse. I *like* her."

"Yes, Asher. I'm familiar with your definition of 'like'. Can't you find someone else to wet the wick in besides her?"

I get right in my brother's angry face, mine a perfect mirror. My voice comes out low and threatening, which is exactly how I feel. My older brother may be bigger and can likely to beat me in a fight, but I'll get in a few good hits before I go down. If he's lucky, his face will be healed before his wedding day. "You'd better watch how you talk about her."

Surprise quickly flashes in his eyes. He takes a deep breath, slowly letting it out. "I don't want Alyse to get hurt."

While I somewhat deserve that jab, it stings nonetheless. I admit that since Natalie, I haven't been willing to give a woman more than one or two dates—*fucks, whatever*—but Alyse is different. I know that already. Trust me, I've been struggling with it for two long months, warring with myself on how, or if, I pursue this intense attraction I have for her.

But no matter what I do, I *cannot* get her out of my head. She's like a fucking magnet and I'm inexplicably drawn to her, exactly as I was so many years ago. I like her. I don't want to hurt her. And for the first time since Natalie, I find myself wanting someone to like me back. That's some scary shit.

"And what about me?" I ask quietly.

"What about you?"

"What about *me* getting hurt? Do you care about that?" I sit heavily on the couch behind me and drop my gaze from Gray's. I have no idea how Alyse feels about me. After today, there's no doubt she's attracted to me, but does it go beyond physical? After two months of doing nothing but thinking about her, now that I've seen her again today, I know it's more than physical for me.

So me getting hurt is a very real possibility here. I'm scared shitless to make myself any more emotionally vulnerable than I already have been. Even *thinking* that Alyse could be something long-term makes my lungs seize up. But not enough to want to stop.

"Wow. I had no idea," he says, taking a seat beside me.

I don't respond, because there's nothing really to say.

"Of course I don't want to see you hurt, Ash. Do you...do you think Alyse could?" What he's actually asking is, do I like her enough to open myself up to even getting hurt?

I fucking hate feeling this exposed. "Yes," I answer quietly. "I've always had a thing for her."

"I remember. I thought I was going to have take you down on the Fourth that one year."

I laugh sardonically. I didn't think I did a very good job of hiding my unholy attraction to her back then. "I didn't know you knew about that."

"Yeah, well, it was hard not to notice how you two disappeared for a while. Then you all showed back up, you and Conn pissed and Alyse embarrassed. Didn't take a genius to put it all together. I never missed the way you looked at her that summer. You're lucky I down-played it with Livvy or I would have been required to beat the shit out of you."

"Nothing happened," I say quietly. *But it certainly wasn't for lack of trying.*

"Nothing?"

"Connelly and his big fucking mouth," I mumble.

Gray chuckles lightly and we fall into silence, allowing that day's events from long ago to roll through my mind.

"Jesus, asshole, put your tongue back in your mouth before someone catches you."

"Fuck off," I tell my twin, unable to tear my eyes away from the ethereal vision in a white-string, barely there bikini currently floating on top of the pool. Her eyes are squeezed shut against the sun's bright rays. Her hands are stretched out, gently pushing the pool water back and forth. Her nipples poke against the thin fabric of her suit, making my mouth hurt with the need to taste them.

"She's jailbait, brother."

That she may be, but it doesn't stop me from liking her more than I should or wanting her anyway. Alyse and I have been apparently not so subtly dancing around each other for the last two months now, ever since I came home from college for the summer.

I'd met Alyse a couple of times last summer, but dismissed her because of her age. She may now only be seventeen, almost eighteen, but. Hot. Damn. What a difference a year makes. There's not one red-blooded male who wouldn't be attracted to her. I've had the fortune to be able to spend quite a bit of time with her these past two months since she and Livia have frequented our new in-ground pool. In addition to being stunning, she's also smart and funny and more mature than girls my age, let alone hers. I look forward to spending time with her more than any other girl I've ever known.

"Thanks, but I don't need your two fucking cents." I slam my beer and throw the empty in the trash before jumping in the pool close to her, enjoying her screams as my splash drenches her.

"Hey!" she laughs, splashing me back once she gets her footing.

I circle her like prey and she pivots with me, following my every move, smiling flirtatiously.

"You look fucking hot, Alyse," I whisper, edging closer to her, but not close enough to touch. My hands itch to pull her into me so she can feel just how

hard she's making me. When she was here last weekend, we had a few stolen minutes where I made it to second base and the only thing I've been able to think about all week is getting my hands and mouth back on her. That, and the possibility of rounding home plate.

"Actually, the pool cooled me off," she responds flippantly.

"Yes, I can tell." My gaze drops to her dark, beaded nipples. When I finally look back at her face, she's bright red, but lust swims in her golden eyes.

"Oh," is all she says.

"I want to kiss you, Alyse," I growl lowly. I flick my eyes over to Conn who is watching my every action intently. Fucker. Quickly glancing around, I see that Gray and Livia must have gone inside, so at least they're not witness to my lack of restraint.

"You do, huh?" She's acting coy, but there's no mistaking how her breaths have picked up.

"Fuck yes."

She starts swimming around me, teasing, "Is that all you want to do?"

Fuck Conn. I couldn't care less about his disapproval. I firmly plant my feet on the pool floor, reach out, and grab her waist, yanking her flush to me, our bodies now touching from knee to chest. There's no way she can miss my desire for her. "No. Not even close."

She swallows hard and doesn't speak, but she doesn't need to. I can see the longing mirrored in her innocent eyes. Jesus, she's still in high school and I'm a bastard of epic proportions for wanting her like I do, but I can't make myself stop. There is just something about this girl that I'm unable to resist, no matter how hard I've been trying.

"Wanna get out of here for a while?" She's young, she's innocent, and I have no doubt she's a virgin. Plus I'm going back to college next month, so I know what I'm proposing may send me straight to hell, but a stampede of wild animals couldn't make me take it back.

Yep. Asshole-of-the-year award winner, right here.

"And do what?" she asks nervously, chewing her bottom lip adoringly.

My hand drifts down to cup her firm ass, tugging her lower half closer. I let my fingers slide underneath her teeny bottoms. Her slight moan and hand tightly gripping my hip only make my cock throb harder, causing the palm sitting on her ass to start kneading unconsciously. "Whatever you want, Alyse. No pressure here, but you have to know if it were up to me, I'd be sliding my dick inside you within the next five minutes, tops."

Her eyes never leave mine, searching for what, I don't know. But she must find it, because when she finally responds, I can honestly say I haven't been more excited at the prospect of being with a woman. Ever. And even at the young age of twenty-one, my portfolio is broad.

"Okay."

"Everything all right in here?" a female voice cuts in, causing the vision of Alyse coming all over my fingers not five minutes later to dissolve.

Fuck. I've never forgotten a single minute of that summer with her.

Not one.

I look up to see Alyse's older sister standing in the doorway, looking back and forth between Gray and me, brows creased. Even in the dark, I see her belly is starting to swell. Of course, Livia's pretty slight and with twins it probably doesn't take long to show.

Once again, I have to tamp down that little green monster.

Jesus, I'm acting like a pussy instead of the confident, successful businessman that could have any woman he wants.

Except now you don't just want any woman. You want one. Alyse.

"Fine." Rising from my seat, I give her a quick hug on my way out. "See you all later."

When my mom asks where I'm going as I pass by, I simply say, "Out." I'm sure one of my brothers will fill her in that I won't be home for the rest of the evening, but I know neither will say I'm with Alyse.

As I get in my car and back out of the driveway for my short drive to pick Alyse up, I try to snap that cocky, confident mask I wear firmly back into place. Gray's and my discussion has shaken me up more than I want to admit. I could fall hard and deep for this woman, but I have to know where she stands first. Because it's not too late to rein my feelings back in and just move on to the next warm body.

Right, Ash. You just keep telling yourself that.

CHAPTER 5

ALYSE

EVEN THOUGH I HAVE NO INTENTION OF INVITING ASHER IN, I RUN around my tiny house making sure it's tidy.

Looking at the clock, I see it's still only twenty to seven, so I pull a Coors Light from the fridge to calm my nerves while I wait. I don't know where we are going to dinner, so I've decided to go with a navy-and-cream-striped sweater dress, paired with tights and dark brown knee-high boots. It's dressy enough for a nice restaurant, but casual enough to get by at a bar if that's where we're headed. I could see Ash fitting in easily in either place. He may be somewhat cocky and arrogant, but he's not pretentious in the least. I think that's one of the things that draws me to him.

His dominance excites me.

His passion ignites me.

His magnetism simply captivates me.

Pacing the small floor of the kitchen, I mentally tick off the reasons why this dinner slash date is a very bad idea. Because despite what Asher tried to lead me into believing, this is absolutely a date. One that I agreed to without much arm-twisting, hussy that I am.

One: He's a playboy. He can't commit. I've heard stories about him for years from Livia.

Two: He'll be like family soon. God, I will see him *all* the time.

Three: You're going to be employed by this man. For months!

Four: I can't think of a fourth, but I'm sure it's there. Oh yes...the most important one. *He'll break your heart, Alyse, because of reason number one.*

I tip the brown bottle to my mouth. It's empty and I still have ten minutes left. I head to the fridge to grab another, trying to think of the reasons why this may *not* be such a bad idea.

One: Your whole body lights up like the Fourth of July around him.

Two: You've been half in love with him for eight years.

Three: You feel alive for the first time since Beck.

Four: It's time. It's time to let yourself be vulnerable again. And why not with him?

Shit.

I'm a very big list person. Always have been as long as I can remember. I make lists for everything. Groceries, to-dos, books I own, books I want, short- and long-term goals I want to accomplish. You name it, I have a list for it. And before I make any big decision, I make a very comprehensive pros and cons list, even before dating a man. I don't even realize I'm doing it half the time.

So before I started my business, of course I made a list. The cons far outweighed the pros, but I went for my dreams anyway, because if you don't go for your dreams you're just left with regret. And I've lived with enough regret to fill up my small house two times over. But even if my business fails, at least I can say I gave it my all. My blood, sweat, and tears will be soaked into the matted, dirty carpet before I close the doors. I think that's why I stayed with Finn so long. When I go for something, I'm all in and I don't like to admit failure. Who does?

As I think about my pros and cons list for Asher Colloway, I know there are so many more things I can add to the cons column if I give it some thought. That little number three on the pros list is what has me hesitating, though. *You feel alive for the first time since Beck.* Asher sets my very blood on fire and no one, not even Beck, has done that.

When Asher had me cornered in the kitchen of his mom's house, I'd forgotten what it was to genuinely be turned on by a man from the top of my head to the tips of my toes. I realize now that I've only been going through the motions all these years in my pathetic attempt to move forward, not look back.

His eyes and words challenge me. A man hasn't challenged me in, well, ever. Even Beck didn't challenge me. Until that December night so many years ago when he did a one-eighty, he was warm, compassionate, and loving. But never challenging.

How odd. I didn't know what I was missing until I had a taste of it.

I absently shake my Magic 8 Ball, the one I've had since I was four years old, silently asking the same question over and over. Magic 8 is ever the optimist.

Me: Is this a smart idea?

Magic 8: Signs point to yes...You may rely on it...It is certain.

Hand to God, if it gave me even one negative answer, I'd be calling Asher to cancel.

It may look to the outside world that I've moved past the darkest time in my life, but I know the truth. I haven't. Not really. I'm stuck in quicksand, fighting daily to not let myself be sucked completely into its dark, grainy nothingness.

Until I set eyes again on Asher Colloway, that is, and I felt my heart *really* beat.

God, I'm so scared to make the wrong decision. I know beyond a shadow of a doubt that Asher Colloway could hurt me. Badly. Probably even ruin me permanently for any other man.

But...

It's the *'but'* that has me wavering. Actually contemplating. It's the *'but'* that had me agreeing to this faux business meeting, against the stronger need for self-preservation.

But...he could be your salvation.

The doorbell rings and I quickly finish the last of my beer, dropping the empties into the recycling bin. I take a deep breath and head to the door, wondering to myself what lies on the other side.

My salvation...or my destruction.

CHAPTER 6

ASHER

"I'M SORRY TO HEAR ABOUT YOUR DAD," SHE SAYS.

"Thanks." I look down, trying to not let this subject ruin the great evening I've had with Alyse. "It's always hard at holidays, especially on my mom."

She nods. "I can relate. Even though my dad wouldn't have won any father-of-the-year awards, he was still my dad, you know? He did the best he could given his...sickness."

I don't know what to say that won't be perceived as mean. I hate how Livia and Alyse's father used to put his own selfish desires ahead of his children. I could never understand how parents do that. It's obvious that Alyse loved her dad, despite all his faults, and that only makes me like her all the more.

"We can't choose our family."

"True."

"Do you want dessert?" I ask, trying to lighten the mood.

"God no. I'll save my food coma for tomorrow," she laughs.

Success.

"Do you want another beer?"

She hesitates for a moment before declining. Damn. It's only a little after ten and I'm not ready to call it a night. I can't remember when I've enjoyed myself more on a date when I knew beforehand I wasn't going to get laid at the end of it. As much as I'd like to make a move on her, I won't, because strangely enough, I want that even more. I want the *anticipation* of claiming her for the very first time. More and more I think that's exactly what this is.

I want her to be mine.

When Alyse opened the door earlier, I nearly stopped breathing. Vibrant chocolate eyes that glimmered slightly with sparkly makeup gauged my every reaction. I couldn't have stopped my eyes from traveling the length of her if you held a gun to my head with the trigger cocked.

Her dark, shiny hair was in loose waves down her back. All I could think of is how it would look against her fair, naked skin as her head was thrown back in ecstasy. The sweater-like form-fitting dress she wore hugged her every curve like a gentle lover. I've never wanted to know what lay underneath a woman's clothing so badly.

When I got to the high-heeled boots...*fuck*. I could imagine her in those and nothing else while she was bent over my desk as I watched my cock slide in and out of her slick pussy. And her glossy red lips? Jesus, I couldn't decide if I wanted to kiss them or have them wrapped around my cock. I spent the whole drive to dinner willing my dick back to at least a semi-hard state, reminding him of our end goal here.

Get the girl, not just the fuck.

I don't want to follow my usual and very-well-treaded path with this woman, which would include dinner, a few after-dinner drinks, and a hard fuck over the back of the couch. Preferably hers so I could leave afterward. It would make her like all the others, and she's so not. Don't get me wrong, I want all of those things with Alyse, especially the hard fuck...just at a slower pace.

The talking to I gave my cock all the way here didn't work and he's been pounding against his metal prison ever since. He's mighty pissed he won't be let out until I jerk him in the shower when I get home, because that's gonna happen. You can bet your sweet ass the entire time, I will be imagining it's Alyse's hot mouth bringing me to the edge and over.

I knew Alyse had grown into an incredible woman when I listened to her talk my mom's ear off about her business a few weeks ago. Spending the last three hours in comfortable conversation, I have learned that Alyse is not only an extremely intelligent woman, she's passionate, fiercely dedicated, independent, and a little broken, just like me. She didn't say so, but I can see it every time I stare into her dark eyes.

No woman has ever made me feel this way, not even Natalie. I'm completely at ease with Alyse. Like I can be the truest form of myself. It's comfortable, but not in a boring way. More in an I-finally-feel-like-I'm-home way.

I reach across the table, taking her hand in mine. It feels natural. Right. God, it feels so fucking good. "Are you ready to go?" I ask quietly, hoping that the answer is no, but fearing it's yes.

She looks between our entwined hands and my face repeatedly. I watch the pink flush that starts right above her firm breasts creep into her face, just as if someone's pulling a curtain from the ground up instead of the opposite. All through dinner I've felt her attraction as much as I've felt her fighting it, but her body doesn't lie. *Can't* lie. My dick jumps at the thought of being inside her, of having that flush come from the multiple orgasms I will demand of her, instead of the valiant, but fruitless fight she's trying to put up.

Her mouth says yes, but her eyes say the opposite.

Jesus, Alyse, please don't make this so hard on me. I'm not that fucking honorable.

Minutes later, the bill is paid and we're silently driving back to her house. Now that I've held her hand in mine, I can't *not* reach for it. So I do. She lets me take it. I hear her quickened breaths as loudly as if she'd just run a marathon and I wonder how I'm going to simply walk her to her door then turn around, climb back into my car, and leave.

I may have to pull over to the side of the road before I get home and relieve this ache deep in my balls. I'm not sure the hard-on I'm sporting will go away any other way. And the last thing I need to do is walk into my house and have my brothers and my *mother* see this giant bulge in my jeans. Although at least Gray will be assured that Alyse's virtue remains intact.

For now. Because it won't for much longer.

Fifteen minutes later we pull into Alyse's driveway. I turn the car off. She waits for me to run around and open the door for her. Somehow this little 'business dinner' ruse has turned quite nicely into a real date. I can't help the smile that takes over my face.

Taking her hand, I walk her to the front door where we stand, awkwardly. I can honestly say I've never been in this position before, so I have no clue what to do. Every time I've walked a woman to her door for the last seven years, I knew what followed, even on my first date with Natalie. Hot, sweaty, dirty sex. I'm truly in foreign territory here, so I have to follow my gut for the first time in…ever.

"I'll pick you up tomorrow at eleven," I tell her as I raise my hand to cup her cheek, my thumb stroking her silky skin. I can't seem to keep my hands off her. Jesus, maybe hiring her *was* a bad idea. I don't know how I'm going to be around her day in and day out, without wanting her underneath me all the time.

"No. I can drive," she answers. Breathlessly. I understand the feeling. I can hardly breathe myself. I want to devour her right here on her front step; fuck anybody who may be watching. I'm not shy. I don't mind.

"No arguing." I take a step closer, putting my entire body almost flush with hers. I have to give her credit, she doesn't step back. She swallows hard and her pink, glossy lips part ever so slightly, teasing me to kiss them. "Thank you for going to dinner with me."

"I enjoyed it," she responds quietly. This is as hard for her as it is for me. Good. At least I won't be the only one suffering tonight. Then she totally takes me by surprise. "Come in."

I groan.

Fuck. Me. I'm trying to do the right thing here and she's a temptress. Holding water just out of reach to someone who's been in the desert for a week without it. Except in my case, it's been over a goddamn month. I want to be buried in her pussy so fucking bad.

All.

Night.

Long.

And if I step foot through that door, that's exactly what will end up happening.

"I shouldn't," I finally manage to say. Jesus. That physically hurt, like the words were tugged right from my balls.

I see the hurt in her eyes and it guts me that she thinks I'm rejecting her, so I do the only thing I can to reassure her of my insane, burning desire. Backing her up against the house, I palm her face and eat at her mouth like the famished man I am.

We moan. We paw. Our bodies writhe as we taste each other's unique flavor for the first time in eight years. My cock is raving mad with the need to get inside her, except I won't let this go any further.

Not tonight.

With great effort, I pull back, drawing her forehead to mine. We're both panting, our breaths ragged. Her eyes are closed tightly, like she's afraid to open them and look at me for fear she'll be lost. I know I will be. And I know if she does, I'll be walking through that door with her, throwing away all my good intentions.

I take her hand, placing it over my throbbing cock. And he is throbbing. Angrily. When her hand makes contact, I hiss, feeling him twitch, and she can't hold in her own groan. I torture myself by moving our hands up and down my stiff shaft, slowly, my hips pumping involuntarily. I let my lips trail to her ear so I'm sure she hears every word I'm about to say.

"I want you so fucking bad, Alyse. You have no idea the restraint I'm using here to not pull down those sexy tights and claim you right here. Right now. In front of anyone who cares to watch. But you deserve more than a quick fuck. I want, no...I *need* to do this right. I want you desperate for me, because when I do finally take you, you're going to be mine. *Only* mine."

I suddenly wonder how I ever managed to stay away from this incredible woman for eight long years and why it took me that long to find my way back to her.

With a nip on her earlobe and a quick peck to her lips, I release our hands and walk to my car before I can't. Before my little head takes over the big one, which is about two point five seconds away from happening.

"Be ready by eleven," I call as I slip into my pearly white Range Rover, my voice thick with lust.

As I back out of the driveway, I turn, taking one last glance at her. She's watching me leave, her fingertips brushing against her lips like she's trying to remember what mine felt like there.

Fuck. It's going to be a long night.

CHAPTER 7

ALYSE

WINE IN HAND, I SIT IN THE QUIET GLASS-LINED SUNROOM LOST IN MY own thoughts. I watch Maxwell, the Colloway's goldendoodle, tootle around out back, sniffing the dead grass for God knows what.

It's an unusually warm day for November in Detroit, the temperature hovering in the mid-fifties. Asher, Conn, and Luke have moseyed outside to shoot some hoops and Gray is upstairs lying down with Livia, who needed a post-meal nap.

I hear Barb Colloway busying herself in the kitchen, no doubt setting out more food. I've never seen a woman with more energy than she. I don't think she's sat down once since I arrived this morning, except for our meal.

While I've enjoyed being at the Colloway's today, and it's certainly better than spending Thanksgiving alone, I can't help the melancholy mood I find myself in. I need some alone time and this quiet, serene room is the perfect reflective spot.

When I'm in this home, I feel like an outsider looking in. A welcomed interloper, if that makes any sense. This family is so tight, so full of love and happiness that it makes me ache for all that I don't have, for all I never had, and for all that's been taken from me. I try to stay away from these dark cracks in my head. If I let myself wallow there too long I know I'll accidentally slip into one, unable to get back out of the thin crevice.

As I listened to Barb say grace before our meal, I almost burst into tears. Growing up, I don't remember very many family meals and we certainly never prayed, unless it was that the electricity would be turned back on or that we wouldn't lose the house that was days away from foreclosure.

As a gambling addict, my father was an absent parent for the most part, and my mother walked out on us when I was just four and a half years old. I don't even think I remember what she looks like anymore, my childhood memories long faded.

But I do remember her voice. I remember the way she used to sing softly to me at night when I couldn't get to sleep. I remember the way she'd stroke my hair as she held me on the couch when we'd watch Disney movies. I remember how safe she made me feel when she'd scour under my bed and in my closet for monsters. I remember feeling that she loved me, so I never understood why she left me. When she abandoned us, Livia took over those duties, even though she was only eight. Livia was more of a mother to me than my own.

Then Livia left me too. She left everyone without any reason, without any forewarning, and without any explanation. Just like our mother did. It was a heart-crushing, devastating blow. To this day I still don't know why, even though I talked to her several times during her absence. All I know is her story about needing some time away was pure bullshit.

Livia was always a caretaker. What she did was completely out of character for her. It's a secret between us that has caused a huge rift, one that I'm trying to let go, because after her three-year absence, I'm simply glad to have her back in my life, but some days it's difficult.

Like today.

I see how happy she and Gray are and obviously he has fully forgiven her, so why can't I? I see acceptance in the actions and words of the Colloway family, so what's wrong with *me*?

In one way or another, everyone I have ever loved has deserted or betrayed me.

My mother.

My father.

My sister.

My lover.

So is it any wonder that with every relationship I have, I'm always waiting for the other shoe to drop? Is it any wonder I don't let myself fully love another person?

I've never let anyone see one hundred percent of Alyse Kingsley. Not one. I've had secrets from *every single person* in my life. Even Livia. I show people what I want, keeping the rest hidden, protected. Never putting myself completely out there. Never really exposing my thin skin, my inner brokenness. I excel at appearing open, while keeping people firmly at arm's length. It's just easier that way. It hurts less. I was with Finn for almost a year and it was a fight that we had constantly. He wanted in, I pushed him out. I was never in love with him. I was just lonely.

If I let Asher into my life, I can't help but wonder if he'll be next in a long line of people who have been unreliable. Will he dump me on the side of the road like a pile of trash and drive away without a second thought, without a look back?

Why wouldn't he? Everyone else has.

I'm honestly not even sure I have the ability to let him into my heart.

My body? *Yes.* I have a feeling that's inevitable, but my heart? *I simply don't know.* Though if I could see anybody there, I think maybe it would be him. I often think back to that day at the boathouse so long ago. I almost gave myself to Asher that day without a second thought and I wonder if our lives would have been different if Conn hadn't interrupted just in the nick of time.

Taking a sip of my Chardonnay, I think back to last night when I foolishly asked Asher to come in. It's almost as if I become someone entirely different when he's staring into my eyes, stealing my thoughts. His intense gaze burns my barriers to ash like they're made of nothing but tissue paper. It's like he sees me. The *real* me. The one I've kept hidden away from any other human being. And that's highly unnerving, because I've never felt more vulnerable around another person as I do Asher. Which means he has all the power to hurt me, to destroy me. Irrevocably.

In hindsight, I'm glad he declined my foolish proposal. For so many reasons I never should have asked in the first place, but I can't find it within myself to truly regret it either. I think I would do it again, given the chance. My feelings are on a goddamn seesaw, bouncing erratically from one side to the other. One minute I want him. The next, I want to forget I ever met him.

He makes me *feel*. And that's not an easy feat.

God, and his wicked words…I haven't stopped replaying them ever since. I think I remember them verbatim. I've not had any other man ever speak to me like that. I liked it. *More* than liked it. After I watched him drive away, I barely made it inside before my hand was down my tights, bringing myself to orgasm after orgasm against the closed front door until my legs were like jelly. It was empty and unsatisfying, and even today I still ache for his touch, though he's had his hands all over me all day in one way, shape, or form. Just not in the way I want or need.

His attention has not gone unnoticed by the entire Colloway family, either. Livia cornered me in the bathroom earlier asking me what was going on between us. I had to tell her the truth.

I don't know. But something is, and as much as I need to I'm not sure how to stop it. I don't think I can. He is a mystery that I want to solve. Or maybe it's simply just the girlish instinct to corner the untamed boy and make him fall in love with her. Everyone wants to attain the unattainable.

"Need some time away from my handsy brother?" a low voice penetrates my rampant thoughts. I look up to see Conn walk in, taking a seat in the cream-colored chair across from me.

"Something like that," I reply with a forced smile. If he senses my Debbie Downer mood, he's gentleman enough not to mention it.

"You having a good time?"

"Yes." I smile, because despite my glumness at the moment, it's honestly been a great day. Watching the Colloway brothers banter is like reality TV, only ten times better.

"So, did Asher tell you about the Colloway Thanksgiving tradition?"

Tucking my right foot under my left leg, I set down my wine and shift my complete attention to Asher's twin brother. Conn is devastatingly handsome, like all of the Colloways. He is definitely the most laid back of the four brothers, but I can also see he's an instigator. And I have a hunch he can easily manipulate any situation to his advantage.

"No. He failed to mention it."

"Probably didn't want to scare you." He winks, a broad smile lighting up his gorgeous face, which I return. If there's one thing I've learned about Conn, it's that he's an incorrigible flirt. More than one innuendo has been thrown down today, and at one point I thought Asher and Conn were going to come to blows. "In case you couldn't figure it out, we're all pretty competitive."

"Really?" I laugh. "I hadn't caught onto that at dinner when you challenged everyone to a timed pie-eating contest. Or when you put two hundred bucks on the line for whoever won at HORSE. So what's your tradition?" And why do I even care? I had planned on asking Asher to take me home shortly anyway. All of a sudden I don't feel like I'm very good company.

"Bowling, followed by a wicked game of laser tag."

"Laser tag? Aren't you boys a little old for that?" The look on Conn's face is so serious, I can't help but laugh.

"Who are you calling old, babe? I'm the reigning champ, five years running."

"Yeah, because you cheat," a velvety deep rumble calls from the other side of the room. It's a voice that goes straight to my sex every time I hear it. "And she's not your babe," Asher growls, taking a seat next to me on the couch.

He puts a possessive arm around my waist, pulling me close to his side. I turn my head, glaring daggers at his clear statement of owner-ship, but all he does is wag his eyebrows and wink.

"Has Asher told you about his performing arts days yet, Alyse?"

"Conn," Asher growls in warning.

"No really, it was practically Tony worthy," Conn quips on a bark. Yep, definitely an instigator.

"Shut the fuck up, Connolly."

He doesn't. "Yeah, he played Putzie, one of the lesser known members of the T-Birds in the ninth grade musical *Grease*. You should ask him to sing 'Summer Nights' for you sometime. Epic." Conn can barely get the last part out because he's laughing so hard, as am I.

The only one not laughing is Asher.

"Wow, I didn't know you had so many hidden talents. I'd like a performance."

Asher looks at me and I expect anger, but all I see is heat. And hunger. "I'd be happy to give you a performance. A private one."

I make an embarrassing noise that's somewhere between a huff and a laugh. He continually throws me off my game.

"Well, you boys have fun. I think it's probably time for me to go home. I don't want to overstay my welcome." I wiggle my way out of Asher's ironclad grip. He frowns, which makes the inner girl that's been crushing on this guy for years giddy as hell.

Pulling me back to him, he cups one cheek with his free hand. It's intimate. It's intoxicating, and the temperature in this cool windowed room has suddenly risen a dozen scorching degrees. Once again, I'm lost.

Out of my peripheral I see Conn stand and exit the room, quietly chuckling.

"You're going with us."

The effect Asher has on all of my senses is confusing. Every single time he touches me my pulse races. I have a hard time remembering to breathe. I have no idea what we're doing here and I have to start working for this man in just a few short days, yet he's almost acting like we're a couple. I need to get myself together or I'm going to be completely lost to him.

"Why?" I breathe.

"Alyse," he moans, his eyes searching mine. They penetrate my soul, pilfering a little bit of it into him. "Because I'm not ready to let you go yet."

I watch him lower his lips to mine, the whole scene playing in slow motion. Jesus, I shouldn't let him do this, but I'm going to anyway.

When his mouth touches mine, sparklers ignite behind my eyelids. Low-current voltage flows slowly through my body, lighting me up from the inside. I think it's spilling out of my pores, like sunbeams.

This is exactly the way it felt last night. This is a million times more intense than it felt eight years ago. My blood literally flares to life with his simple touch, his passionate kiss. It's dizzying. It's exhilarating. What the hell will having sex with him make me feel like?

Completely consumed, Alyse. Utterly lost.

Groaning, Asher deepens the kiss, his tongue demanding entry, which I give. Lips never leaving mine, he pulls me astride his lap. I helplessly comply. Both hands now cup my face and I hand over complete control to him. Or he takes it. I'm not sure which and I'm not sure I care as I feel his thick, pulsing want for me in exactly the right spot.

My denim-covered pelvis involuntarily rocks against his hard length. His grip tightens and a low, guttural growl comes from deep within him as his kiss becomes more feverish. My God, the man knows how to use his mouth. I can only imagine how much experience he has with his cock.

Suddenly he's pulling away, holding me far enough back that I can't reach his lips. It takes a few seconds to force my eyelids open, but when I do and meet his dark blues, they're hazy and dilated with lust. His jaw ticks with restraint. Our chests heave with want and exertion. We stare at each other for long moments. I feel the heat in my face and know I'm flushed from head to toe.

I'm fully aware anyone could walk into the room at any second, catching us in this compromising position, but I can't make myself move or look away. He's a sorcerer; I'm completely enthralled in his magical spell.

When Asher finally speaks, it's barely above a whisper and the sincere words he utters make me foolishly want to give myself to him. Every broken, ragged edge of me. "I'm not sure I will ever be ready to let you go, Alyse."

"Asher…" I close my eyes, trying to get my violent hormones and riotous emotions under control. When I open them, his hunger hasn't abated a single bit. "What are we doing here?"

A small smile tips his lips. "I don't honestly know, but I can't seem to stop. Hell, I don't *want* to stop." He pauses, his eyes sweeping to my swollen lips before lifting to capture mine again. "There's something different about you, Alyse. There always has been. Even when I shouldn't have been attracted to you all those years ago, I was. And now that I've found you again, I need to know what it is. See if we have something else here besides the intense need to fuck each other."

I suck in a sharp breath, his unfiltered words catching me off guard once again. But for the first time since I met Asher Colloway so very many years ago, his cocky attitude is shed and I see vulnerability in its place. It's probably the most endearing side of him he's shown me yet. It makes me want to agree to anything he'll ask of me, which I'm one breath away from doing. He pulls me to his waiting mouth once again.

"Thoughts of you have utterly consumed me for weeks," he whispers against my lips before kissing me softly. His kiss is reverent, worshipping. Sweet.

So damn perfect.

Every word he's spoken is what any woman wants to hear from a man who's interested in her, but still I hesitate, trying to make one last lame, admittedly *very* lame, effort. "But I'm going to work for you," I manage to say when he lets me pull back.

"No, you're going to work on a project for my company."

"But you own the company."

"Technically, my brothers and I own the company. I can keep my professional and personal lives separate, Alyse."

"I don't sleep with my clients, Asher."

He sighs, leaning his head back against the couch, eyes going to the ceiling. "Fine, I'll hire a different audit firm."

"What?" Shit, now I've done talked myself out of a job. "No...I didn't mean *that*."

"If it means you'll consider dating me, then that's what I'll do."

"Asher..." I hesitate, not sure I should confess so much, especially to someone who will be almost single-handedly keeping my company afloat. It will make me look desperate.

Aren't you?

Shit, not only do I need the money, having CFC as a reference would be a huge coup for me. Maybe I'd be able to actually execute some of the long-term business plans I put together so long ago now. "I want the job." *I* need *the damn job.*

He lifts his head and pins me with his beguiling eyes. "And I want *you*, Alyse. I want you so fucking much I can hardly think straight. I've thought of nothing else but you for the last two goddamn months." God. His words steal the very breath from my lungs. Lungs that have been oxygen starved since he walked into my office yesterday.

"What if this doesn't work?" I respond quietly, nervously. Christ on a cracker. *Why are you even considering this, Alyse?* This could be emotional *and* professional suicide.

Grabbing my face again, he replies passionately, "What if it does? There's something here. I *know* you feel it, too, Alyse. Give me a chance. Give *us* a chance."

I can't think when he's touching me, so I stand and walk to the bay of windows, my back to him. I stare into the tree-lined estate, watching two squirrels pillage for food, taking advantage of the warm weather to tuck away more nuts before the snow falls.

I try to recall my pros and cons list that I created last night, but all I keep remembering is number three on my pros list. *He makes you feel alive.* Everything else seems to be quickly fading away, like it was written in disappearing ink. I'm at the edge of a cliff getting ready to jump. No parachute. No harness.

I'm tumbling headlong into a complete free fall.

Dammit.

I feel his heat at my back and watch his reflection in the glass as he moves my long hair off of the right side of my neck. The graze of his fingertips makes me shiver, my eyes falling involuntarily closed. I've worn a tank underneath a lavender cardigan sweater and the unfettered access he has to the sensitive flesh on my neck has my body on high alert.

"I've never had to work this hard to convince a woman to go out with me," he says roughly against my ear. His lips on my skin make me moan. Lithe fingers trace the exposed flesh against the trim of my cardigan, edging downward toward the top of my low-cut tank. I wish like hell we were alone so he could push it off me and take me right against this damn window.

His presence alone spins me completely off balance. His touch, though...it totally obliterates every last trace of common sense I possess.

"Maybe it's good for your ego to be denied once in a while," I pant as his lips travel down the expanse of my throat. Teeth nip gently and my breath hitches. The air thickens impossibly with desire and I'm lost to everything he's doing to my mind, my senses, my body. "Asher...you're not playing fair," I breathe, trying to protest. It sounds more like a plea to continue instead.

"No point playing unless you play to win. Say yes, Alyse," he demands against my heated flesh.

His left hand has hooked around my waist, pulling me flush against his erection. By now my head is leaning back against his broad shoulders and the fingers of his right hand dip into the top of my cami, brushing against the lacy cup of my bra, while the thumb on his left has worked its way under the hem, circling the sensitive flesh underneath.

Oh God. I can't form a coherent thought. This is so inappropriate. I'm in Asher's mother's house, for the love. I'll never be asked back.

"Say yes."

"Yes to what?" I have no idea what he's talking about. I just need him to continue putting his hands and lips all over me.

He stills, then spins me so my back is pressed against the cold glass and my front is pressed against one hundred-ninety-plus pounds of taut, toned, virile man. My face is once again in his hands. I've quickly determined this is a position of dominance for him.

"Possibilities, Alyse. Say yes to possibilities." His eyes plead with me to agree. Without even thinking, I find myself nodding before his lips are once again on mine, our tongues dueling wildly. I wrap my arms around his waist and pull him close. My resolve slips, and I finally give in to what I've wanted since I laid eyes on Asher Colloway over eight years ago.

Him.

Moments later a throat clearing in the background freezes us. I would have jumped a mile away from Asher given the chance, but he has me pinned in place. He doesn't move a muscle, except to slowly pull his mouth from mine. Heated eyes bore into my panicked ones like he doesn't have a care in the world.

There is so much he's trying to convey to me in that moment, but the only thing I hear is *you're mine now.* The thought makes my core practically weep with joy and my heart race in sheer terror.

"Everyone's ready to go," Conn jibes in almost a singsong voice. "You two lovebirds coming or you going to pussy out on me this year, Ash?"

Asher's eyes never leave mine when he leans in for a final quick peck before turning toward his twin. "Game on, little brother."

"By four minutes. Jesus H, are you ever going to let that go?"

"You know I'm not." Asher laughs.

I'm so incredibly embarrassed to be caught making out that I can't even look Conn in the eyes, my gaze falling anywhere but on him. I have no doubt in less than a minute Asher's hand would have been down my pants, and, *oh God,* I would have let him. I only hope no one else has walked by this secluded part of the house, especially my sister. I roll my eyes in disgust, unable to believe I'm acting so wanton in someone else's home.

"You goin', babe?" Conn asks me, forcing me to look at him. The smirk on his face almost makes me laugh. He's enjoying goading Asher. Immensely.

Asher pulls me to his side, growling at his brother. "Call her that again and I'm going to fuck up that pretty face of yours." Conn laughs loudly at that, but Asher is not amused.

My mind is a jumble of racing thoughts. It feels like it's been stuck in a blender and someone has pushed the pulse button. I need to go home and take a cold shower...or a dozen of them. Or maybe an ice bath. I need time to breathe, think, pound my head against the wall so I knock some sense into my stupid self. I need time to work on my pros and cons. Correction, I need time to work on my cons. Why does it seem like I've made a deal with the devil? Surely I can still change my mind. I start to answer that no, I'm absolutely not coming, when Asher interrupts.

"Yes, she's going."

Caveman much?

"Hey, shouldn't *I* get to decide?"

He turns, pressing me against the glass once more, completely indifferent to the fact that his brother's watching every move, listening to every word. "You said yes."

"I—are you delusional? You don't own me. I make my own decisions." Jesus, this man infuriates me as much as he sexes me up.

His eyes glitter with mirth. "You remember what I said last time you said those words to me?"

"Fuck you. You don't own me."

"Not yet I don't, sweet Alyse."

I could only nod. Not only did I remember, I replayed those six words constantly, especially in the dark of night when I used my vibrator. We're becoming besties lately. I may have even named him AJ when I found that Asher's middle name is James. Pathetic? *Maybe.*

But I'm not ashamed, though I wouldn't go around renting a billboard advertising it either.

"Are you always so disagreeable, Alyse?"

"Are you always so dominating, Asher?"

Leaning toward my ear, he lowers his voice so only we can hear. Hot breath tickles my lobe and travels downward between my thighs. "Yes, I am. You love it, Alyse. Your eyes dilate and your breath hitches with every dirty, demanding word. And the thought of owning every inch of not only your gorgeous body, but your heart and soul has me so fucking hard, I'm having to fight myself not to make you mine right here."

"Asher..." My voice is barely audible. My pussy now has its own heartbeat. I have no idea if Conn is still standing there, watching the show we're putting on, but he could sell tickets and I don't think I'd protest, because I don't want this fluttery feeling in the pit of my stomach to stop. God, I have never felt like this before.

"Tell me you're wet."

"Asher, God." My eyes drift shut. All I want is for cool glass to be pressing against my flushed naked skin while he moves inside of me.

"Tell me." His tongue darts out to trace the shell of my ear. I have to bite my lip not to voice the moan hovering in the back of my throat. I think I actually draw blood I bite so hard. "Tell me, Alyse. Fuck, tell me how soaked you are right now for me."

I can't deny it. I can't deny *him*. "I am." Pulling me flush to him, he curses low in my ear and it jumps straight to my sex. I've never wanted to strip my clothes in front of an audience before, but damn if that thought isn't just running wild through my fuzzy, sex-addled head. Damn, he is good.

"Come."

Oh God, I *could* come. If I just rub my thighs together a little bit, I could be moaning his name so loud the whole house would hear it, but then I realize that's not what he meant. I somehow find my voice. It's squeaky when I force it out.

"Why, so you have someone to beat? I suck at bowling and I've never played laser tag."

He takes a step back, finally letting the oxygen that was sucked out by our sexual vortex circulate back in. I gasp for the breath I don't feel I've taken in long minutes.

"You can be on my team."

I think about it for a moment, but I'm really trying to push every second of the last ten minutes into my memory bank so I can pull it out later when I'm alone. Ultimately, I give in, as I knew I would the second his lips met mine, begging. Deciding to play with him a bit, however, since he's coerced me into embarrassing myself even further today, I finally respond.

"Okay, but I think I want to be on Conn's team."

"Like hell," Asher practically yells.

"I'll take her."

Well, that question's answered. Conn has apparently been intently watching our little carnal interlude. I wonder if he could hear me panting all the way across the room. *God.* Kill me now.

"Well Conn *is* the five-time reigning champ," I tease. My breathing is finally starting to calm slightly, but I'm sure my face is as red as a beet. Asher is still blocking my view of Conn. For that, I'm grateful.

"Alyse." His voice is rough and growly and while I've kept a straight face until now, I can't any longer. I start laughing.

"Fine, you big baby. I'll go. I'll be on your team. I'll do whatever you want."

The fierce look of lust on Asher's face at my last comment makes the laughter die in my throat. "I'll remember you said that."

"Can we get going now or are you guys going to eye-fuck each other some more." *Oh. My. God.*

"Connelly James Colloway! Watch your language!" I hear Barb Colloway yell.

Unnngh. This is seriously worse than death.

Minutes later as we all funnel out the front door, I ask myself for the hundredth time in the last twenty-four hours: *Just what in the hell do you think you're doing, Alyse?* And each time I come up with the same answer.

I don't have a goddamn clue.

CHAPTER 8

ALYSE

IT'S SUNDAY NIGHT AND I WALK INTO THE QUIET RESTAURANT ASKING for Livia at the hostess desk. I'm the first one to arrive so she takes me back to a table for four, leaving menus, along with a wine list, around the square glazed oak top.

Finally deciding on a glass of house Zinfandel, I've just placed my order when I see Livia walking toward me, being directed by the cute young blonde working the front. My sister has an armful of magazines and folders along with an iPad.

"Hi," she says, setting everything down just to my right.

"Hi. That's a lot of stuff," I reply, eyeing the three-inch thick stack she's trying to keep from spilling all over the floor.

She laughs. "Well, we have a lot of stuff to get done. The wedding is in four weeks now." The waitress comes over to take Livia's order and she sticks with water.

"How are you feeling?" I ask. She looks good. *Really* good. Deliriously happy. I haven't seen or talked to her since Thursday night—the same night Asher took me home directly from the bowling alley and kissed me senseless on my front porch before he drove away, leaving us both aching.

I can still feel his lips imprinted on mine, and his hard, sinewy body pressing me against the wood siding. I didn't ask him to come in this time and he didn't push for it either. Though the racy texts he sent me later, and all weekend long for that matter, left no doubt we both want to be in each other's pants. Big time.

"I feel really good today. I was only nauseous this morning and I've actually had an appetite."

"I'm glad."

After she gets organized, she turns her piercing gaze to me. If there's one thing that hasn't changed about Livia and me, it's that she can read me like a damn good book. I wish I didn't have these feelings of lingering bitterness toward her. I so want to let them go, but I just...can't. I want to let her in, but I don't know how.

I've spent so much of my life keeping people out, I'm not sure I know *how* to let them in. I'm hoping that spending some quality time with her over these next couple months will allow me to finally forgive her. Maybe she'll even tell me the truth about what actually happened.

A little hypocritical, aren't you, Alyse? There's so much about your own past you haven't even told your own sister.

Fuck off, I tell my conscience. That's different. Right?

"So, are you settling in?"

Livia was very supportive when I told her Asher hired me for this audit, and she was excited that I'd be temporarily relocating here so we could spend more time together. But I breathe a sigh of relief that she doesn't ask me about Asher, because I don't know if she approves of our personal relationship and quite frankly, I still need some time to get my head on straight about where it is I think I'm headed with him. Other than his bed. After these past few days, we both know that's inevitable.

"Yes, I guess so. I just brought a couple of suitcases and spent the afternoon getting unpacked and picking up a few groceries at the corner market, so it was pretty easy. I start on the project tomorrow."

I don't tell her that there was a huge bouquet of wild flowers waiting for me, courtesy of the man I can't get out of my head for a single solitary second. Or the bottle of champagne I found in the fridge, along with a note that was clearly not business related. Unless that business included getting me underneath him in short order. His romantic side is equally as endearing as his domineering one.

"Are your friends coming?"

"Yeah, they're running late. They will both be late to their own funerals." She pauses and I can tell she has something more to say so I wait patiently. "I'm glad you're here, Alyse."

"Me too, Libs." I grab her hand and smile.

Livia looks down like she's nervous. "Alyse, can I ask you something?"

Uh oh. "Sure," I respond slowly, drawing out the word. *I can't guarantee you I'll answer honestly, though.*

"Are you doing all right? I mean...*really* all right? With the breakup with Finn and all?"

Ah, Livia. Always worried about my mental health.

I take a deep breath, followed by a deep drink of my wine. I'm not sure why I can't just tell her no. I'm not doing all right, and it has nothing at all to do with Finn. I haven't been doing all right for the last eight years since my boyfriend and the father of my baby went apeshit behind the wheel of a car, trying to kill us, apparently thinking he was better off dead than having a family with me.

Because she doesn't know about Beck, at least not that he was my boyfriend. She thinks he was a friend's brother giving me a ride home. And she certainly didn't know I was pregnant.

My dad was so caught up in his own world, he didn't give two shits what I did; however, Livia would have never approved of me dating someone who was twenty-two when I was only eighteen. But she wasn't home much. She worked or went to college and whenever

Gray came home, they were inseparable. I didn't exist. In some ways I feel like Livia deserted me well before she physically left.

So she has no idea why I sank into a deep depression after the accident or why I tried to take my own life not just once, but twice. I lost everything that day and I still don't understand why. I think that's the hardest part. Not knowing. I've replayed that day hundreds upon hundreds of times, trying to figure out what I missed. Every single time I come up blank.

I absently rub the scar low on my breastbone where the surgeons had to remove my ruptured spleen. In some ways I was lucky that day. I sustained relatively minor injuries. A few lacerations on my face and body, a broken ankle, a ruptured spleen, and of course, a miscarriage because the trauma was likely too great for the baby to handle, they said.

Outwardly, all I have left of that horrific day are a few silvery, ragged scars marring my once-perfect skin. Inwardly, however…those wounds are the most severe. They run far and deep. On some days I feel like they're still bleeding out. Sometimes I think it's impossible for the scars on your heart and mind to scab over. They're the most fragile ones, easy to rip open, so they constantly remain fresh and raw.

Then instead of vomiting everything that I should, I smile and do what I always do.

Lie.

"Yes, I'm really good, Livia. Truly." I feel my nose grow just a bit and guilt stabs me for the fact that I'm what I hate the most. A hypocrite.

I'm saved from any further probing when I hear laughter at the far end of the restaurant and see two stunningly beautiful women approach us. Livia jumps up and runs to meet them. They hug and giggle. I'm surprised at the tinge of envy I feel. Heather is the closest person I have to a friend. Or Finn. *How sad.* I'm suddenly consumed by an almost overwhelming sense of loneliness I haven't felt in a very long time. I don't like it.

And I vow to find a way to fix it.

"Alyse, this Addy and Kamryn. Guys, this is my sister, Alyse." I stand and try to shake their hands, but they both race around the table and hug me instead, telling me how happy they are to finally meet me, how much Livia talks about me, how happy they are that I'll be here for a while. They both go on for what seems like minutes. I can't help but smile and laugh with them. I can see why Livia likes them.

An hour later, after we've chatted and eaten a light dinner, Livia drags out her iPad, pulling up a spreadsheet she's created. We're different in so many ways, but the one thing Livia and I always did have in common was the obsessive need to be organized.

"Okay, Kam, were you able to find a venue yet?" Livia asks, feverishly typing on her little keyboard. With such short notice, that was one of the things bound to be difficult. That, and the fact that it's the holidays in the city, and every hotel ballroom will no doubt already be reserved with holiday parties and other events.

"Jesus, Livia. You owe me big time for this. I must have called a hundred hotels, but you're in luck. Yes, just on the way over here I heard from the Palmer House. They have one of their smaller ballrooms available, but the wedding rooms are booked and we'll have to work around the chapel's availability because there is another wedding that day. I think if you shift the time of the ceremony from five to six o'clock, we could make everything work. And they have a wedding coordinator who can help you manage a lot of the details, like catering, flowers, cake and such."

"Well, I'm going to have to be as flexible as a gymnast to pull this off."

"Good, I'm glad you said that, because I gave her my credit card to hold it. She said she had another inquiry just hours ago."

A look of relief crosses Livia's face. "Thanks, Kam."

"Welcome, babe."

Addy speaks up. "We have appointments on Saturday at two different bridal stores, Livia. You'll need to buy something off the rack, but the two shops I booked have quite a bit of inventory to choose from, so hopefully you'll walk away on Saturday with your wedding dress!" Addy squeals, causing the few other patrons in the restaurant to look our way.

"Thanks Addy. I'm sure it will need some alternations with my rapidly growing belly, though. And Lysee," she says, looking at me, "I'm thinking something simple for you in navy. Your pick. Whatever you like. My treat."

"Sounds good," I reply, feeling bad for taking the charity, but grateful I won't have to find the money for a dress I can't afford.

Livia bites her lip, running her eyes over the spreadsheet. "Invitations?" She looks at me. Whoops, that was my task and I haven't even started.

"Sorry, with trying to get everything ready to move here on such short notice, I haven't had time to start. But I'll get try to something done by the end of the week." I'm not sure why I'm tasked with invitations. I don't have a creative bone in my body and the thought of having to come up with something worthy of Livia's wedding is freaking me the hell out.

"I would love to do that," Addy pipes up. "I mean, if that's okay, Alyse. I really love that stuff. Maybe we could swap and you could take the task of finding a photographer instead. Plus, you're good at negotiating. I'm good at design. There are only a couple that are still available that day so all you need to do is maybe meet with a each one and pick the best."

"Sure," I reply, relieved. "That sounds great. You okay with that Libs?"

"Of course. We have the same tastes. I trust you."

"Thanks." Those simple words slice me like a hot knife through butter. At least she trusts me with something.

We spend another hour going through wedding minutia. By the time we're finished and I head back up to my apartment, I'm bone tired. I spent long hours Friday and Saturday trying to get everything in the office and at home pulled together for my absence. I told Heather I'd be back once every two weeks or so for a day or two, though. I just can't disappear when I have a business to run and I can't run it all remotely. I was thrilled that we did land that other new client, but that meant I had to work up a contract, timeline, and details for that audit before handing it over to Tabitha.

I need a drink and a bath, in that exact order.

WHEN I OPEN the front door, I'm met with the fragrance of lavender from the candle I left burning on the counter. Other than the small light that I left on over the stovetop, that's the only light that spills through the dark room.

I walk over to the counter and drop my purse and keys down, spotting the card Asher personally wrote for me, tacked to the champagne. Picking it up, I read his innuendo-filled words and once again grow wet. That seems to be my perpetual state of late.

My sweet Alyse,
Welcome to Chicago. I very much look
forward to collecting on my bet. Soon.
Yours,
~ Asher

After pouring myself a flute of bubbly, I head into the bathroom, run a bath, and a few minutes later I'm sinking into the pool of heated goodness with a sigh. Leaning back, I take a sip of the smooth, fruity wine and remember the side bet Asher and I made during the most competitive game of laser tag I'm sure was ever played by a group of twenty-nine and thirty-year-old men.

"We betting the same thing?" Conn asks, smugly. I'm not sure I've seen another look on him besides cocky. I wonder how many women he's both sucked in and turned off with that arrogance.

"Always," Asher responds. "Gray, you in?" he yells across the small room where we were all putting on vests of some sort. I can't get mine figured out, so Asher turns to help me.

"Hell yes," Gray replies. Even Livia is playing. She's paired up with Gray,

as I am with Asher, but she clearly knows how to use these things that I imagine might feel like a bulletproof vest.

"What about you, Luke? You game?" Asher asks, turning to his older brother.

"You're going down, little brother." Luke smirks, his dark, unruly hair tucked behind his ears. God, Luke is sexy with his brow piercing and tats. Every time I look around at these men who are the epitome of raw masculinity and sexuality, it's as if I've been dropped into some type of erotic fantasy. The only thing that could be better is if they all ran around shirtless. Or naked. I don't judge.

"I don't think so," Asher coos.

As they trash talk, I can't help but smile at their excitement. They're like a bunch of ten-year-olds getting ready to skim through their first Playboy. *It's hilarious, actually.*

"What's the bet?" I ask, looking up into Asher's face, which is now so close I could reach up on my tiptoes and capture his mouth with mine. I mentally clip the wings of the butterflies in my stomach so they'll settle down.

"We have a family house on Mackinac Island. Whoever wins gets it over New Year's Eve."

"Isn't it big enough for all of you to go?"

"Yeah, but..."

"Ah, say no more." I laugh. Privacy and all that.

"It's a great place to be. No matter the weather, Main Street is always hopping and, of course, they have their famous Great Turtle Drop at midnight. When we were kids, we used to go there almost every single year." He smiles and gets a faraway look in his eyes, as though he's recalling a particular happy memory.

"What's the Great Turtle Drop?"

"It's like the ball drop in Times Square, just with an ugly lighted turtle instead. Not a real one, of course. Very popular with the tourists."

"Sounds fun," I reply quietly. My melancholy returns with a vengeance. I wish I had good memories like that. Sadly, the only vacation I took as a child was the one time we went to Cedar Point amusement park in Sandusky, Ohio when I was nine. I got sick on a rickety wooden roller coaster and we had to come home early.

He finally has me all buckled in when he pulls me close, smashing the little plastic thingies on the front of our vests together. Those damn butterflies take flight again, the clipping apparently failing. Leaning down, he asks quietly, "Wanna make a side bet?"

I'm breathless. "Like what?"

"Yes or no, Alyse?" Oh my God, his bossiness zips straight to my pussy every single time.

"Okay."

He palms my neck, pulling my ear to his mouth. "When we win, you'll let me do anything I want to that sexy body. Whenever. Wherever."

Oh. My. "That..." I swallow thickly. "...leaves things pretty wide open." My mind is racing a hundred miles an hour trying to picture the carnal ways he'll play my body when I least expect it.

"Anticipation heightens the senses, Alyse." His lips graze the sensitive skin underneath my ear as he speaks. He could get me to do anything when he does that and I think he already knows it. I've decided there must be a yes button implanted along the column of my throat, the secret switch only responds to him. Dull teeth nip my lobe and I suck in a breath. "Say yes."

I'm weak. Oh so very weak.

"Okay. But we won't win. Conn has beat you five years in a row and now you're stuck with dead weight." Why does it disappoint me to think that Asher won't have the chance to make good on his promise?

Pulling back, I see the smugness has now spread from Conn to Asher like a virus. "Oh, we'll win, baby. I've never had so much incentive in my entire fucking life as I do this year." He winks, kissing me quickly on the lips.

And with that, the tall, lanky, pimply teenager manning the game glides into the small dark space, gives us instructions, makes sure we all know how to use our guns, and sets us loose in a darkened room that reminds me of a cheap western movie set, complete with painted pressed wood and glow paint.

I've never seen someone so focused on winning before and I never really understood true sibling rivalry until I saw the four of them in action. They all even brought their own black facemasks, which made them look like a bunch of bank robbers. About halfway through our allotted time, Livia and I hunkered down in a corner and tried to stay out of the melee. They all came out with a few scratches, but Asher could've cared less.

He won.

By ten points.

My cell, which I've laid on the side of the tub, begins to ring. I practically squeal when I see it's Asher. I have no freaking idea why I'm acting like a besotted teenager around him and how I so quickly went from trying to fight this to caving in like wet sand.

"Hi," I answer breathlessly.

"Hi yourself." His voice sounds sweet, decadent. Like warm melted dark chocolate over sea-salted caramel. "Just wanted to see if you you've settled in okay."

"I did. Thanks for the flowers. And the champagne." *And the reminder that at some unknown point in the near future you're going to be doing some unknown wicked things to me.*

"You're welcome, gorgeous."

"Do you do that for everyone who stays here?"

"Only the hot ones," he chuckles.

"Wow. I feel special."

"You are, Alyse," he says quietly, sincerely.

Swoon.

"I should have called or texted earlier, but I had to unpack and get some food and meet Livia and her friends for dinner and wedding planning and time just slipped away from me, so..." I'm rambling, stupidly. I always ramble when I get nervous.

He laughs. "It's fine." Pausing, he adds, "Is it wrong that I miss you so much and it's only been three days?"

I sigh and smile, my insides quivering. My nipples have hardened to sharp points. "You miss me?"

"Yes. Very much," he rasps. Clearing his throat, he says, "So...what are you up to now?"

"I'm not sure I should tell you," I tease.

"Oooohhh. Do tell. Are you doing something naughty?"

"Ah, not at the moment." Unless the fact my free hand is now slinking underneath the water to the juncture of my thighs counts.

"Are you naked?" His raspy voice drops an octave and it feels like he just rubbed his whiskers over my clit.

I hesitate for several moments before responding. "Yes," I whisper.

"Fucking hell, Alyse," he groans, lust thickening his voice. "Are you in bed, baby?"

"No. Bath." I close my eyes, wondering what the hell I'm doing. I could have just as easily told him I was sitting on the couch in mismatched pajamas with my glasses on and my hair in a messy bun, but nooooo...

"Christ, baby." He sounds in physical pain. I don't know why, but it makes me smile. And the fact that he's used endearments several times has not gone by without notice. "Is your hand on your pussy?"

"Asher..."

"Yes or no?"

Damn, he's bossy. And it's so fucking hot.

"Yes," I barely mutter.

"Are you thinking of me?"

"Yes," I admit.

"Make yourself come. I want to hear you."

Why does he make me crave following every single command, like I'd drop dead on the spot if I disappointed him? "Asher, I—"

"Alyse, you said yes."

"I didn't know saying yes would mean I'd have to follow your every whim," I snip with more ire than I'm feeling. I want to do this probably more than he wants me to, but I also need him to know he doesn't control me.

"You should have asked more questions then, I guess." I hear the smile in his voice.

"You were stealing my thoughts."

"Now you know what I've been going through," he replies. Softly. Earnestly. And suddenly my lust is back with full force. "Now, put me on speaker so you don't drop your phone in the water."

I do. Silently.

"You there, baby?"

"Yes."

"Touch yourself, Alyse. I want to hear your voice hitch when you come. Fuck, I want to hear you moan my name when you fall apart."

My eyes tumble closed as my hand once again reaches my clit. Even though I'm in the bath, I feel my arousal, thick and silky. My body instinctually responds to Asher's voice, his dirty words. *Him.*

"Pinch your nipple," he demands. I do.

"Tell me how it feels." I hear his breathing speed up, becoming choppy.

"Good. So good," I whisper.

"Imagine I'm sitting behind you and it's me fingering you. I'm thrusting one, now two fingers inside your tight, wet pussy, Alyse. My cock is pressing between your ass cheeks, wanting inside. Fucking hell, I want you."

"Jesus, Asher..." My breaths are now coming in shallow gasps at the sound of his barely restrained voice. My touch brings me closer to the high I need to reach, like an addict. Normally it would take me several minutes and many dirty fantasies to make myself come, but I was already halfway there before I even laid a finger to my aching flesh.

"Tell me you're close, baby. I want to come together," he pants.

I whimper. *Oh God.* That's all I needed to hear. Imagining Asher on the other end of this phone firmly grasping his thick cock while listening to me get myself off throws me headfirst into an intense climax. I cry out his name as hot sparks shoot from the center of my body outward, heating each limb, flooding my body with pure euphoria.

"Fuck, fuck, fuck," his low curses and guttural cries join mine until finally we're both spent and grow silent, except for our ragged breathing. I've sat in the bath so long the water is now chilling. Once the heat from my orgasm abates, I'll be shivering.

"Alyse." His rough, gravely voice wraps around me, providing me much-needed warmth.

It takes several moments before I'm able to physically respond. "Hmmm," is all I can manage.

"Why did it take me so long to find you again?"

My heart stutters and my eyes fly open. I think I felt a little part of my soul pass through the phone line into him. I don't know how he keeps doing that. A simple word here, a reverent look there. Pretty soon I won't have any of myself left to hold back, because he'll have it all. Why *him*? Out of all the men I've dated since Beck, how can Asher Colloway do this to me?

"I wish it didn't." That's probably the most honest thing I've said to anyone in a very long time. I've often thought of the day I almost lost my virginity to Asher. Instead it was Beck.

"God, I wish I was there with you."

"Me too," I tell him softly.

We're quiet for a minute or two, but it's comfortable. Relaxing. "You should get out of the bath before you get too cold. I'll see you tomorrow, baby."

I want to say so much in response to that. Like, am I really your baby? Don't you think this is moving way too fast? Are you freaking the fuck out like I am? But I don't. Instead I say, "Okay."

"Sleep tight, my sweet Alyse."

"You too."

Sitting in the now-cool water, I'm cloaked in goose bumps, but with my body sated and my brain in a whirl, I can't seem to make myself move. This feels like it's moving too fast, but at the same time it has been a long time coming. With each passing day and every interaction, Asher burrows further and deeper into my mind and my heart and I have no idea how to stop him.

I don't even think I want to anymore.

CHAPTER 9

ASHER

I WANTED TO BE IN THE OFFICE WHEN ALYSE ARRIVED THIS MORNING FOR her first day, but I have a standing monthly breakfast with my brothers the last Monday of the month that none of us likes to miss unless absolutely necessary. I'd completely forgotten about it until reviewing my weekly calendar last night after what was undoubtedly the hottest phone sex I've ever had. Alyse surprised me. And it takes a lot to surprise me. I knew she had a hidden sex kitten underneath that perfectly proper persona.

I intend to explore that further.

Much, much further.

So as much as I wanted to be there with her, I also couldn't skip tradition. We're all so consumed with our own lives and our own work that, besides the time I spend with Conn in the gym, this is one of the few times we have uninterrupted brother time together. This is one time we try to keep our discussions personal, leaving work at the door.

For the first time, Luke has joined us.

"Hey, Luke," I say as he takes a seat. Conn, Gray, and I have been here for at least fifteen minutes. I guess as much as things change, they also stay the same. Luke was always perpetually late. I have to wonder what else about Luke is the same or if his rough life has changed him into a person I'd no longer recognize. He arrived just before dinner on Thanksgiving and took off after I beat everyone's ass at laser tag. The only time we really got to talk was when we were shooting baskets. Even then it was only surface discussion. He spent quite a bit of time with Mom though, and she was beaming ear to ear until I left on Saturday.

Molly, our regular waitress, sees another person has joined us and heads over to take Luke's order. But instead of talking, she stands there looking at Luke before looking around at the three of us. I understand why. I almost laugh when I remember the *Sesame Street* song that I used to be so fond of when I was a kid—*Silence, haters.*

Luke is definitely the one thing here that doesn't look like the others. He's dressed in black from head to toe, complete with well-worn black boots and a leather jacket. Hell, he looks like he belongs with an MC versus sitting with three businessmen dressed in tailor-made suits. The only thing he's missing is a patch and the name of his club on the back of his bomber. He fits *Sons of Anarchy* to a fucking "T."

"Hi, darlin'," Luke drawls, winking and placing a hand at the small of her back. "I'll take a coffee, black. And bring the pot. Come back in a few and I'll be ready to order."

"Uh, okay." She slowly turns and walks away, but looks back several times, brows drawn, trying to figure out this conundrum. For the year we've been coming to this little hole-in-the-wall diner on the corner, down the block from our office building, Molly has never seen us with a fourth to our little party. She knows we're all brothers and knows we own GRASCO Holdings. Hell, she even knows Gray is engaged. She should probably be invited to the fucking wedding. She's practically family. I've not spent as much time with one single woman since I kicked Natalie's ass out as I have with Molly. I'm hoping to change that with Alyse, though.

"Luke, how's the relo going?" Conn asks.

"It's coming. I found some cheap office space on the south side of town. I need to hire another guy because Johnny doesn't want to relocate from Dayton to Chicago. Then need to figure out a place to stay. It'll be a while yet before I make the move official."

"I thought Livvy's portion of the lease was in your name?" Gray asks, taking a sip of his coffee. "You just renewed it a couple months ago. Why don't you stay there? You're responsible for the rent on it anyway, unless you sublease it."

Huh? Something else I didn't know. How many ways is Luke tied up with Livia, soon-to-be Mrs. Gray Colloway? Gray seems completely neutral on the issue, like we're talking about paint color or something. I wish I knew what the hell happened with those three.

Luke shrugs noncommittally. "Been thinking about it, but I'm not sure I want to room with a chick. Especially that one. She's a little high strung."

Gray laughs. "She is that. But she's also pretty hot."

Luke smirks. "Don't get me wrong. I'd worship at her church any Sunday. I'm just not sure I want to *live* in the temple full-time."

"Mmmhmm," Gray hums, eyeing Luke like he knows he's full of shit. Luke flips him the finger and I almost sigh because things seem to be getting back to normal slowly but surely between the four of us. It's nice.

Molly comes back with Luke's coffee and we place our orders. Most of our breakfasts here are spent in harmless flirty banter with Molly. She's a cute enough blonde, probably mid-forties. Never been married. We tip her well and she takes good care of us. This time, however, it's almost like Conn, Gray, and I don't even exist. She cannot tear her eyes away from Luke. He's playing her like an expert bassist as we all watch and laugh and learn.

"Wow. You're smooth," I tell him when Molly finally leaves.

His face turns serious. "Had to be in my line of work." That's the first time Luke has said anything about his past and suddenly the mood at the table takes a sharp dip.

"So," Conn starts, looking at me. "You'll never believe who I saw Saturday night."

"Who?" I ask, trying to lighten the mood. "That little redhead that you've been trying to deny you're dating?" Not since Nora Cantres, the redheaded beauty that Conn had a thing for in high school, have I ever seen him settle down with one woman. She broke his fucking heart our senior year when her family moved and she broke it off. I'm pretty sure he liked her more than he tried to let on and she jaded him for a future Mrs. Conn Colloway. Which is too bad, because Conn would be a great husband and father. If he'd just let himself find the right woman.

You should take your own advice, Ash.

"I'm not dating her. I fucked her. You know my rule, Ash. In and out. Anyway..." He pauses, looking at me pointedly. My senses are now flashing bat-phone red, because I know that look. I know what he's going to say, but I have no idea how it can be as she doesn't even live in Chicago. To my knowledge she still lives in Detroit and Conn came back to the city on Friday.

"Natalie."

"Fucker," I mutter under my breath. "Why do you insist on bringing her up when I continually ask you not to?"

"Because you need closure."

I look away from Conn to Luke and Gray who are raptly watching our little exchange. I want to tell them both to fuck off. Luke has no idea who Natalie is—*was*—to me and the last thing I want to get into before I see my sweet Alyse for the first time in days is fucking Natalie. Her very name is associated with heart-wrenching agony. Hell, when we first moved to Chicago and I had to hire an assistant, one of the most qualified applicants was named Natalie. I burned her resume. No fucking way am I going to be surrounded day after day by someone who has a name that reminds me of the woman who blew shards of adulterer straight into the center of my heart.

I shift my gaze back to Conn. "I have all the closure I need."

His lips thin and he shakes his head. "She said you were having an affair."

"Are you fucking kidding me here? *She's* the cheating whore." My voice rises, causing several sets of eyes around us to turn our way, but I hardly notice. I'm only staring into the traitorous ones of my twin, who it feels an awful lot went Robert The Bruce on me. "I'm not sure how I could possibly misconstrue the fact that she had her legs spread for another man in our bed. It was pretty fucking clear."

It was classic Natalie to try to deflect her adultery back on me. She repeatedly accused me of cheating, and I never understood it. I never gave her any reason to think that.

What Conn doesn't know is there were definite red flags that I simply ignored, so I was far less than inclined to believe a fucking lying word that came out of her mouth. Conn doesn't know a lot of things about Natalie. They are things I'll never tell another soul. I lost my entire future because of that woman and her selfishness and lies. Always with the lies. I was a patsy and I'm ashamed I ever thought of making her my wife.

"She claims they never had sex. She just wants a chance to talk to you and make things right."

Why, after all this time, does she even care what I think?

"I'm sorry, Conn, but regardless of what happened after I left, having her pussy eaten out by another man is sex. At least in my book. She was committed to me. She should never have let another man lay a finger on her. Nothing happened that she didn't want."

I shake my head and stand, throwing my napkin on my unfinished plate. I skirt around the table, intent on leaving before my fist lands in my brother's face, which will fucking happen if I stay here five seconds longer, but his words stop me cold, making me fume with rage. I have to hand it to Conn. He blindsided me in a public place so he would lessen his chances of ending up with a black eye and swollen lip.

"Your reaction proves my point. You'll never be able to give Alyse what she needs if you don't put this behind you, Asher. What happened with Natalie keeps you bound to the past. Cut her loose, man. Move forward."

I feel something being pushed into my hand. I look down to see a scrap of paper with a phone number on it.

"Call her. Free the chains."

I should drop it to the floor, but Conn will just take another opportunity to sabotage me, so I shove the conniving bitch's number in my pants pocket and leave without saying a word or looking back.

I have every intention of watching it burn later. Maybe I'll even toast marshmallows over the roaring fire.

CHAPTER 10

ASHER

IT'S AFTER NINE BEFORE I MAKE IT TO MY OFFICE. I'M STILL FUMING mad. What I would normally do is head to my office, close the door, and spend a couple of hours getting lost in work so I could rein in my temper. Instead all I can think of is tracking down Alyse and pulling her into my arms.

I emailed Tara last night, asking her to greet Alyse, get her settled in her office, and set up a meeting first thing this morning with Sheila and my director of accounting, Aaron Hinton, so she could hit the ground running. I'm sure Alyse could have busied herself, but the fact of the matter is, the sooner she gets started, the sooner we can stop this thief. I've already wasted so much time. In retrospect, I should have followed my gut sooner and hired her weeks ago. Not only would we be closer to finding the culprit, I'd already have her in my bed.

"Hi, Tara," I snip.

"Uh, hi. Bad morning, Asher?"

I grunt. "Where's Ms. Kingsley?"

"She's down on twenty-eight with Sheila and Aaron."

Aaron. He's a couple of years older than me, very good-looking, and if rumors are true, he'd give Conn a run for his money in the ladies department. I'm already irrationally jealous at the thought of her talking to another man. I realize I set this whole meeting up, but that does little to calm the absurd envy I'm suddenly feeling.

She's not Natalie, I remind myself. Fucking Conn. Now he's all up in my head. Christ. I need Alyse.

"Do you know when she'll be back?" My voice sounds strained and Tara's forehead creases.

"I don't know, Asher. Would you like me to call down to Aaron's office and ask?" She's talking to me like she would a cornered animal. Slow and soft.

I open my mouth intending to say fuck yes, but at the last minute change to the more professional response. Alyse is here to do a job, not cater to my every whim, as much as I wish it were different. She seems to put up with the domineering side of my personality outside of work, but if I start pulling that shit here, I may just lose her before I have her. Damn if that thought terrifies me.

"No. When she returns, though, please send her to my office. It doesn't matter what I'm doing."

"Of course. Uh, everything okay, Asher?"

"Fucking golden," I mutter as I turn away. I spend the next hour and a half pretending to work, when all I'm doing is watching the clock. And my closed door.

Waiting.

Fuming.

Remembering.

Finally, I give up and turn my chair toward the window, watching the contrast of white billowy clouds floating by against a blue sky that looks like crystal-clear water today. I want to think about the future, which I'm hoping is Alyse. But instead I find myself remembering the past. And the woman who ruined me.

I remember the heaviness of the ring in my pocket as I caught an early flight home.

I remember pulling into the driveway and knowing when I saw a strange car that as soon as I walked through the front door, my entire life was about to change.

I remember feeling sicker and sicker with each step I took toward my bedroom, the low moans tethered to my feet. They felt heavy, weighted, like I was wading through a swamp, the thick muck threatening to suck me under if I stayed in one position too long.

And I remember the look of pure and utter euphoria on Natalie's face as her coworker, Rick, knelt on my bed, his face buried between her naked thighs.

But try as I might, I don't remember much about what happened after that. I was simply numb. Without a word to either of them, I turned and left. I don't even think they saw me. I know I ended up at Conn's house and stayed there until I went to work on Monday. I still had clothes and toiletries from my trip, so I didn't need to go home until I could make sure every part of her there was erased.

Natalie called me repeatedly on Sunday. I ignored her. She showed up at my office on Monday afternoon and with just one look at me, she knew she was busted. It was almost entertaining watching her try to come up with a lie on the spot. When she refused to leave, I called security. I then called a locksmith and met him at my house later that day so he could change all the locks. I had her stuff couriered to her house with a note to never contact me again.

She tried, numerous times, and after one gut-wrenching text two months later, I haven't heard from her since.

I don't think I can adequately explain the soul-destroying agony you go through when you find out the one person who is supposed to be your everything throws it all away for the sins of the flesh. It bruises your ego. It forces a lot of tough soul-searching. It makes you reevaluate every single aspect of your failed relationship and how you contributed to it. And it closes you off from making the same mistake again.

Conn's words nag at me. *"Free the chains."* But he's wrong. I did free the chains when I cut her cheating ass loose. I realize we're all human beings and we make mistakes. I've made my fair share, but I'm not at all tolerant when it comes to deceit and as I've stated before, I am not the forgive-and-forget type of guy. I will neither forgive Natalie for what she's done, nor forget it.

I think that's what Conn means, asshole.

The paper tucked away in my pocket feels like it's burning my thigh. I'm just reaching in to pull it out and throw it in the trash, where it belongs, when I hear a soft knock at my door. Tara pops her head in. "Ms. Kingsley is back. Okay to send her in?"

Relief hits me like a ton of bricks. My salvation has finally arrived. I have no idea how this one woman has become so important to me in such a short period of time, but damn...she has.

And I'm done waiting to have her.

"Yes. Send her in. And, Tara." Tara pauses, waiting for further instruction. "Make sure we're not disturbed."

CHAPTER 11

ALYSE

THREE SECONDS AFTER I WALK THROUGH ASHER'S DOOR, I'M ENGULFED in his arms.

Four seconds later, his lips are on mine.

Six seconds in, my back is up against the closest wall as he ravages me like he needs my kiss to breathe, to live. One strong arm bands around my waist, while the other palms my neck, holding me in position so his mouth fits perfectly to mine.

Something is wrong. Something more than the fact that he missed me. This feels like desperation. It feels like deflection and I'm the person he needs to get lost in.

"Asher," I gasp when he breaks the kiss, feathering his lips down my neck. "What's wrong?"

He captures my mouth again without a word. Picking me up, he walks backward until I'm seated on what I think must be his desk.

I want to pull him into me as much as I need to push him away, because this is so many shades of wrong. I can't have sex with Asher in his office, for God's sake. But it's as if he's trying to tell me something with his body that he can't with words.

And Jesus, I can relate to that on so many levels, so I tell my goody-two-shoes bitch to back off and give in to the moment. The second I do, his kisses slow, his breathing starts to calm, and his grip loosens slightly.

Reaching up, I palm his face and take over. He lets me. I place soft kisses to the corners of his lips, his cheeks, letting my mouth travel over his clean-shaven jaw. I like the whiskers so much better.

"I'm sorry," he murmurs.

"Is everything okay?" I ask, finally leaning back. I search his eyes and find anger and pain fighting for dominance. He pulls me to him, holding tightly.

"It is now," he whispers against my hair. He takes several deep breaths and I wait for him to explain, but he doesn't. I don't know why that hurts more than it should. I don't even know what we are to each other yet, but it's something. That much I already know. And I want him to trust me, to feel like he can tell me anything, even though I don't know if I can give him the same in return.

"Have dinner with me tonight."

"Yes," I reply without hesitation.

"My place."

I know exactly what that means and, remembering our wicked phone call last night, I feel my body readying itself for him. "Okay."

"I'll pick you up at seven."

"Okay."

Sighing heavily, he unwraps his arms and takes a step back. The immediate loss of his body warmth is startling and chills run the length of my spine. Scrubbing his hand down his face, he walks back over to his desk chair, sitting. His erection is evident through his thin slacks and I want nothing more than to kneel down in front of him and take care of it. He watches me. As our eyes connect, I swear he knows what I am thinking.

"If I don't stop touching you now, Alyse, I'm going to end up fucking you on my desk. That *will* happen, just not today."

"Asher—"

"How was your meeting with Sheila and Aaron?"

"So it's like that, huh?"

"Did Aaron hit on you?"

Laughing, I shake my head, hoping he takes that as a no. Aaron did, but by the tone of Asher's voice, I am *not* about to reveal that little factoid. Something tells me Aaron Hinton will be escorted out by security in about six-and-a-half minutes if I say yes.

His jaw ticks and he pierces me with a hard glare, which I stubbornly return. His voice is low and gravelly when he speaks, like he swallowed broken glass. "Do you want me to fuck you on my desk, Alyse? Is that what you want?"

I didn't, until he just challenged me. I hadn't moved from the edge of his desk where he placed me earlier, but now I stand and make my way in front of him. I sit back on the desk again so my feet dangle, spreading my legs ever so slightly. Gripping the edges, I lean forward toward him.

Today I've worn a simple, short black A-line dress with three-inch nude peep-toe shoes. It's cold, but I didn't wear tights or hose, so my legs are bare and the chilly desk gives me goose bumps.

"And if I said yes?" I have no idea what creature just took over my mind or my mouth, but at this second, I can't even care.

Asher's hooded, lusty eyes haven't moved from mine. The sheer hunger I see in them slays me. He's probably trying to gauge whether I'm serious or a tease, but God help me, I mean every single word I'm saying. I want him to fuck me. *Now.* I don't want to wait another second. One week ago if you told me I'd be in a client's office offering my body for his pleasure, I would have said enjoy your one-way free trip on the crazy train.

Now I'm afraid it's me that's hopped on and the train seems to have jumped the tracks.

Rolling his chair closer, a slow, devious smile curves his full lips as his hands make their way to my bare thighs. Firmly grasping them, he runs his palms up until he reaches the juncture of my aching flesh. Thumbs tease the edges of my panties, slipping slightly underneath. Teasing, but not touching where I need. A low moan escapes my throat and suddenly my head is far too heavy for my neck to support, so it falls back as my eyes drift shut.

"Eight years," he whispers so soft it takes a minute to register.

Then his hands are on my ass, pulling me toward him. His mouth against my inner thigh startles me. It's soft. Too soft. I want hard. I want rough. I want wild. I'm like a caged animal and if he doesn't fuck me hard soon I think I might attack.

"Jesus, Alyse. So wet," he rasps, dipping a finger fully inside my panties.

"Asher..." His name comes out on a breathy exhale.

Hot kisses are scattered up one inner thigh and down the other before he takes my cloth-covered clit in his mouth and sucks. I barely catch the cry his wicked move forced from my lungs. "So fucking tempting," he rumbles right before he scoops me off his desk and onto his lap, holding me tight.

Confusion rattles my brain and embarrassment tightens my skin. This is the second time in just days I've practically thrown myself at him and the second time I've been gently let down. That is definitely not good for my fragile feminine ego.

Ugh.

"Hey." His finger hooks under my chin, forcing me to look at him. I shift my eyes. "Alyse, look at me," he demands. Reluctantly, I do, because as with every other time he gets that bossy tone, I want to comply. I want to please him.

God, I hate myself. I am *not* this weak woman who wants to do a man's bidding. I've been nothing but strong my entire fucking life. I've suffered heartbreak, death, abandonment. I survived my own debilitating depression, twice. I started my own business right before my twenty-fourth birthday, for Christ's sake.

I am woman. Hear me roar.

But around Asher, I just want to let it all go. Around him, I can set my heavy burdens down and take a much-needed rest for the first time in my entire life. I don't feel like I have to be that strong woman I pretend to be with everyone else.

"Do not doubt how much I want you. I'm in utter misery with want. But, *God*, I have to do this right. For the first time ever with a woman, I need this to be right."

Leaning down, he snares my lips in a gentle kiss and just like that, my awkwardness dissolves in a cloud of mist, replaced strangely enough with peace.

I try to sit up and gain some distance, but his arms tighten. "I— This is not who I am, Asher. I'm like a completely different person around you."

Cupping my cheek so I can't look away, he shakes his head, a smile tugging on his lips. "This is exactly who you are, Alyse. I don't know how you keep the real you hidden from everyone else, including Livia, but you do. You're very good at it; I'll give you that. Even better than the last time I last saw you.

"But I saw into your soul the very first time I looked into your eyes eight years ago and I still see it now. It's darker, worn around the edges, but Jesus, it's brilliant. It's magnetic. I see my reflection in it. This is exactly who you are, Alyse, because with me, you can let your guard down and just be you."

I'm captivated. Every word is a warm ray of sunshine that settles on my skin and seeps into my pours. It fills those lonely parts of me I don't like to acknowledge. It makes me feel lighter. Happier. Greedily, I want more of it.

"How do you know?" I'm not even sure what I'm asking, but Asher does.

Smiling gently, he pecks the tip of my nose. "I know, because that's exactly how you make me feel."

"Asher." I let his name linger, because I don't know what to say. I've known him for so many years. I know so many things about him, yet I don't know him at all. Except I can't help but feel that it doesn't really matter, because I do. It's like my soul recognizes him as mine. It's confusing and may not make a lot of sense to anyone else, but it makes perfect sense to me. Everything he's said is true. I can be myself with him. I always have. It almost feels like my person, the one I've been looking for my whole life, has been under my nose the entire time.

"Let me in, sweet Alyse," he tells me softly.

I swallow hard. Unwelcome tears prick and a traitorous one escapes, rolling slowly down my cheek. "I'm not sure I know how." My voice is quiet and it cracks upon my weighty confession. I wasn't even this truthful with Finn and I was with him for a year. It gives me hope that maybe I'm not a lost cause after all.

Asher's smile puts me at ease. His thumb wipes away evidence of my vulnerability, which is making me nauseous. "I have my own issues, Alyse. My own trouble letting a woman close. But I can honestly say I've never wanted to try more than I do with you."

I'm quiet, absorbing his confession. "Okay."

He nods, pressing a prolonged kiss to my hair. "Okay."

I take this as my cue to leave, but he pulls me back into his lap and settles my head on his shoulder. "I'm not ready to let you go yet."

Good. I'm not ready to be let go. I don't think I ever will be.

After a couple beats, he asks, "How was your meeting? Did you get what you need to start?"

"This doesn't feel very businesslike," I tease, running my fingers up and down the buttons of his grey dress shirt, unable to stop myself from touching him.

"You are far more than business to me, Alyse Kingsley."

Good answer.

I finally grasp the courage to ask him a question that's been plaguing me since last Monday when I figured out Asher was coming to see me. "Did you hire me because you wanted to sleep with me?"

He laughs. Not the response I was expecting.

"I'd be lying if I didn't say yes, but that's not the only reason I hired you." He sits me up so we're looking eye to eye. "Nothing I said in our meeting last week was untrue. I did do my homework and I've heard nothing but rave reviews about you and your company. I've never wanted to get a woman in my bed as much as I do you, Alyse, but I would never put my company in jeopardy to do that."

"Thank you. It means a lot that you put your trust in me."

"You have no idea," he mutters right before he kisses me again. Just as Asher deepens it, his assistant's voice echoes through the speakerphone.

"Asher, Mr. Grandy is here for your lunch appointment."

He sighs. "Give me five minutes, Tara."

"Yes, sir."

I glance at the clock to see that it's already almost noon. I've spent nearly an hour in Asher's office doing nothing but flirting. The sweet ache between my thighs will have to wait until later to be assuaged, I guess.

Helping me off his lap, he tells me, "I'll be tied up for the rest of the day. Is there anything you need from me?"

"Ah, no. I have what I need to start." I run my hands through my long hair and underneath my eyes, trying to make sure I don't look like I've just almost been fucked before walking out of the boss's office.

"You look gorgeous, Alyse." He leans down to my ear. "Desire is a good look on you. The flush of an orgasm will look even better."

"Oh God," I groan, unsure if I'm embarrassed or turned on.

"Seven," he says with a peck to my lips.

"Seven."

I'm about halfway to the door when he calls, "And, Alyse, to be clear, you will be in my bed tonight."

My steps falter, but I don't turn and I don't reply. He doesn't expect one.

God he's bossy.

Why do I like that so much?

CHAPTER 12

ASHER

"I can't believe you live in this building and didn't tell me."

That's because you probably would have said no to my proposal. "You didn't ask," I reply, putting the finishing touches on the salad. I could give a fuck about dinner; what I'd rather be eating is her. I spent the entire rest of the day in a state of semi-hardness, which did not go unnoticed by Phil Grandy. And since he plays for the other team that was one awkward lunch.

"Are you sure I can't help?"

"No, baby. This is my treat."

I can't believe how easily that endearment just rolls off my tongue with her. Even more, how she lets me say it without putting up a protest. Besides Natalie, I haven't used an endearment on another woman. And I wish I could stop comparing every fucking thing I do with Alyse to Natalie, because she is not her. She could never *be* her.

K.L. KREIG

I already see that Alyse is trustworthy. Maybe I'm a fool, but I can't imagine she's the type of woman who would ever cheat. I had my doubts about Natalie from the very beginning, but I was in love with her. And love truly does blind. I ignored all the signs, all the warnings, all the neon fucking flashing lights. I made excuses. I rationalized.

I was stupid.

"Okay, soup's on. I hope you like chicken. I should have asked."

"I do." She smiles. "I'm not terribly picky."

I set two plates containing chicken piccata over brown rice and fresh green beans on the table, along with a loaf of sliced multigrain bread and arugula salad. Two glasses of my favorite Chardonnay await our consumption. I've set the mood, going all out. Candles, low lights, some sultry music playing softly in the background. I don't need it, because we both know where tonight will end, but I *wanted* to do it.

I want to fuck Alyse. Badly. The need to take her in a hundred different ways is almost animalistic. The things I want to do to her would scare her if she knew. I am demanding and I am adventurous. There are certain things I enjoy that not just any woman would go for and I want them with her. I want her to *want* them. At the same time I'm terrified she won't.

I can't believe I denied her earlier today, but the first time I'm inside of her is not going to be on my desk. As much as I want to ravage her, I also want to romance her. I don't want her to think I'm only in this for sex, because while I can't wait to get her underneath me, I want so much more from her than just her body. I want her heart.

It makes mine palpitate a bit when I think about how much I *really* genuinely like this woman already. The more time I spend with her, the more I know I could easily, so very easily, fall in love with her. Hell, if I'm honest with myself, I'm already falling.

"Where did you learn to cook?" she asks, taking the seat I've pulled out for her.

"My mom," I reply, taking my own chair.

"Really? You actually spent time in the kitchen with your mother learning to cook?"

"Didn't have a choice." I sip the buttery wine before cutting into my chicken. "She made all of us learn. We each had to help with one meal during the week."

"Really?" She's smiling, but it's sad. I don't know much about Alyse's childhood, but I do know Alyse and Livia's mother walked out on them, leaving them with a deadbeat, gambling addict father to raise them.

I can't imagine growing up without my mom, who taught me so much that I'm still only realizing it now as an adult. Knowing Alyse didn't have one to teach her to do simple things like cook or ride a bike, let alone do the more important stuff like build her self-esteem or handle conflict makes me ache for her. I, on the other hand, had an idyllic childhood, at least until Luke started with all his bullshit.

My brothers and I were raised by great parents who loved us and had morals and a great marriage. We went to church, we gave back to the community, and we were a tight family unit. Still are today.

As much as I want to talk about Alyse's upbringing, I want tonight to be about beginnings, not sadness. I try to lighten the mood. "Really. Of course, we all hated it at the time, except for Luke. Luke loved to cook. And he was good." I laugh remembering some of the inventive meals he and my mom came up with.

"Well, I'd say she taught you very well, too, because this is excellent."

"Thanks." I smile. "My mom always said a woman loves a man who knows what he's doing in the kitchen."

"Well I would agree with your mother." Her eyes drop shyly down to her plate. "What's your specialty? Your favorite thing to make?"

"Lasagna. Or anything pasta, really. Whenever it was my turn to cook, I always wanted to make spaghetti, but my mom made me branch out into other food groups." She nods, but doesn't respond. "Can you cook, Alyse, or am I going to have to do all the cooking in this relationship?"

She studies me for a few heartbeats like she's trying to dissect my question. "Is that what this is? A relationship?"

"Is that what you want?" *Jesus, please say yes.* I have spent the last four years trying to avoid relationships of any kind. One or two "dates" was all I would allow, then I'd move onto the next one. I think I took one woman out three times, and when she asked if I wanted to go away for a weekend…well, I made sure she saw me out with someone else. So the fact that I'm sitting here silently begging her to say yes is not lost on me. I want from her what I've denied anyone else for years.

And Christ…I want it badly.

I watch her struggle to speak and I don't realize I'm holding my breath until after she quietly says, "Yes."

I nod. We're silent for a couple of minutes while we enjoy the meal I cooked especially with her in mind.

"Do you?" she asks softly.

"Do I, what?"

"Want a relationship?"

I think about how to respond without scaring her. I want so much more than *just* a relationship. I want *her*. All of her. Every fucking part of her.

Every thought.

Every memory.

Every secret.

Every dream.

Every fantasy.

Every breath.

I want every waking and sleeping minute to belong only to me. I want her heart, her very fucking soul. I want it all.

Never in my life have I wanted someone to be wholly mine more than Alyse.

"Yes."

Her smile is magnificent. Like a thousand brilliant suns raining down on me at once. My cock is stone hard at the thought I will be inside her within the hour. I didn't prepare dessert, because I plan on that being Alyse. Spread out on this very table. I want to reach out and touch the silky skin of her face. Only if I do that I won't stop, and for now, I want to talk. I want to know everything about her.

"You never answered me. Can you cook?"

She laughs. "Somewhat. I can follow a recipe, but I have no creativity when it comes to the kitchen. I make a mean Rice Krispies treat, though."

"Do tell? I'm a sucker for those."

"I'll remember that." She winks. "Do you like living in Chicago?"

"God, yes. I love it. I work so much, I don't have a lot of time to do as many extracurricular activities as I would like, but the food here is second to none, they have great running trails right along the lake, and everything I need is within a five-mile radius from here. Add to that a great, centrally located airport and there's nothing else I need. Almost," I add, winking, pulling the smile out of her I long to see.

Yes, the only thing missing is sitting right across from me.

"Have you spent much time here?" I ask.

"I've been a couple of times, but I'm not too familiar with the city."

"Well, I look forward to showing you around."

"Me too." She smiles.

"So, tell me about your business."

She nervously pushes the food around on her plate. I suddenly feel like I've asked a taboo question. "What do you want to know?"

"Anything you want to tell me," I confess. Because at this point, I'll take anything Alyse will give me. I have a feeling I'm going to have to pull every shred of information I want to know from her. If I thought I felt exposed with this scary, dark, curvy road we're headed down, it's nothing compared to the vulnerability that wafts off her in crashing waves. Fuck if I ever thought *I'd* be the one driving a relationship forward, but here I am.

And I'd floor the gas if I didn't think it would scare her away.

We spend the next twenty minutes talking about ARK Consulting. I learn Alyse's middle name is Renee, after her mother, hence her firm's name. I learn Alyse has had this idea since her first year in college and by the time she graduated, nearly two years early, she already had a solid business plan written and reviewed by a couple of her professors.

By the time she obtained her master's, she had secured a small business loan, with the backing of her previous employer. But what I was most impressed with was the long-term business plan she created. Within one year, she's doubled her staff, and within five, she plans to have at least a dozen auditors and to triple her profits. That's pretty damn impressive for a twenty-five-year-old who grew up basically without parents.

"And are you on track to meet your long-term goal?" I'm genuinely interested, but I've also been exploring adding an audit firm to the CFC portfolio of services. Suddenly, I'm wondering if Alyse's diamond-in-the-rough firm is possibly what I've been looking for. I've evaluated two or three companies over the last few months, but none of them fit our organization for one reason or another.

I wonder, after this project is over, if I should consider discussing this possibility with her, or if she'll take it as a slight. Or, God forbid, a failure on her part. I would never want to make her feel that way, but I'm also still a businessman and this smells like it may be a ripe opportunity. And a very good fit in more ways than one.

"Well, this job certainly helps."

Hmmm, there's a story there, but one that I don't want to pursue tonight.

"You done?" I ask. She's eaten most of her meal, which I appreciate. I hate a woman who doesn't feel like she can eat in front of a man and then goes home to scarf an entire carton of ice cream. It's fake and I detest fakery.

"Yes, but I can get it. You cooked."

She stands, trying to take the plates, but I grab them from her. "No. Sit. I've got it."

But she doesn't. She grabs the breadbasket and the salad bowl, following me into the kitchen. We quietly busy ourselves cleaning up, and it feels very domestic. Comfortable. I like it.

Immensely.

Taking her hand, I lead her into the living room, sit on the chaise part of the sectional, and settle her by my side. She hooks a leg over mine and our eyes are drawn to the fire roaring away behind the thin protective glass. Orange, red, and yellow flames throw shadows that dance seductively in the dark, taunting us to join them in writhing on the floor.

As if by divine intervention, Adele's gravelly voice starts to croon "One and Only." I've never really stopped to listen to the words before, but now that I do, I think each feels like they were meant for us in this very moment in time.

Alyse's head is on my shoulder and she tilts it up, our eyes locking as the song encourages us to forget the past and take a chance on love. I see every emotion pass through her eyes as clear as day. Apprehension and anxiety, surrender and desire. But most of all, I see her plea. I can almost hear her begging me not to hurt her. It wraps around my heart squeezing like a fist. It pains me physically to know that someone in her past has made her so skittish.

Just like you.

We are two lost souls looking for redemption, a second chance, but scared as hell to let our protective barriers fall for fear we may not recover this time.

I already know I won't.

"Don't break me," she whispers before closing the inches between us.

Ditto, I think, right before I cup her face and take everything she's offering me, but giving equally of myself in return.

CHAPTER 13

ALYSE

BEFORE HIS LIPS TOUCH MINE, I SEE MY PLEA REFLECTED. ASHER HAS A past, maybe as painful as mine, maybe not, but a past nonetheless. We all do. We all walk with our own story, our own secrets, our own damage, our own scars. Internal and external. Some of us just carry them better than others.

It's apparent someone hurt him, broke his trust. Broke his heart, even. And I want to know about her. I want to know who turned such a caring, romantic, handsome man who could have any woman he wants into someone who can't commit.

But can he commit now?

Can I?

As Asher kisses me long and deep, the questions and doubt fade into nothingness, powerful lust and longing easily taking their place.

Just like every other time he touches me. Nothing feels more right than when his lips are on mine.

He's like gravity.

He keeps me grounded in the present and out of my own head, where my personal demons try to torment me.

Mouth never leaving mine, Asher pulls me across his lap and suddenly I wished I'd worn a skirt for easy access, because I desperately need his hands on me. Instead I have dark, tight jeans and a clingy, black long-sleeved blouse, which shows off the swell of my breasts, courtesy of the deep purple push-up bra I'm wearing.

"Alyse," he mumbles against my goose-pebbled flesh. "Tell me what you like, what you want." His hands tightly grip my waist, hot tongue traveling slowly down to the base of my throat. His rock-hard erection pulses beneath me, throbbing, keeping time with my own beats.

What do I want? So many things. So many dirty, wicked things. Things I've never wanted with anyone else. I know Asher can show me. I've been with several men, but I almost feel like a virgin with him. Not in the physical sense, but the emotional one. I believed him when he said he would own me. God help me, I want that. I've thought of nothing else than what it would be like to be completely and wholly his in every sense of the word.

I will the chains I've secured tightly around my heart to loosen. I imagine the lock clicking open and slack taking up the links I'd wound so tightly, so securely that no one could penetrate them. It's terrifying. It feels foreign, naked, like taking off a piece of jewelry you've not removed for years, the imprint of the precious metal leaving a visible mark behind.

And then I do the one thing that feels right in this moment, but goes against all that I've tried to protect myself from over the last eight years.

I submit.

"I want you to own me," I beseech. Beg. Implore.

All of me. Not just my body.

My voice echoes loudly in the darkened room, like I've yelled those six words at the top of my lungs for the whole world to hear and judge versus barely uttered so that they sound distant, even to my own ears. I'm not even sure Asher heard me.

But he did.

His lips still, his body tenses, and his grasp becomes almost painfully tight. When he pulls back, the insatiable lust swirling in the depths of his striking blues causes my stomach to drop like I've just been tossed off a five-story building.

Burning eyes never leaving mine, one hand pushes underneath my blouse, traveling up to palm my breast. He pulls down the cup, his nimble fingers tweaking my hardened nipple. Pleasure ricochets off every cell like a pinball machine, landing squarely between my pounding thighs. My eyes drift closed on a moan until I hear his dark command.

"Look at me, baby." His fingers never stop pulling and pinching and twisting, each movement sending another sharp zing on a fast track south of the border.

I finally comply, but my blinks are long and heavy.

"Fuck, I want to corrupt you in the wickedest of ways and completely ruin you in the best possible ones."

He's asking for permission, even though I already gave it.

He's asking for trust, when it's already his.

He's asking me to be sure.

I am.

Letting a small smile tug the corners of my lips, I reassure him.

"Promise?"

CHAPTER 14

Asher

"Promise?" her sultry voice whispers.

Fuck. Me.

I think I may have fallen a bit more in love with her.

Despite what my brothers may think, I'm not into BDSM, but I do have a certain type of kinkery about me, like I imagine most people really do if they're totally honest with themselves. I obviously haven't shared any of this with Alyse, so I'm not sure she knows fully what she's doing, but I'm not going to look a gift horse in the mouth. I won't take advantage of her unwavering trust either, because I already know she does not give that lightly. It blows me away that she's giving it so freely to me. I can't wait to push her to her very limits.

Holding my smoldering gaze, she climbs off my lap and reaches for the hem of her clingy shirt. The one that's been mocking me all fucking night. I could barely resist the urge at dinner to reach over and pull down the low-cut top a couple of inches, exposing the fantastic bra that I can now see is cupping her perfectly formed breasts. Ones that I will be sinking my cock between sometime very, very soon.

She shimmies out of her tight jeans that mold to the shapeliest ass I have ever laid eyes on. Alyse is perfectly proportioned with full breasts, a waist that curves in, and hips that flare. Perfect for holding onto when I'm fucking her blind from behind. Her stomach is just slightly rounded and her thighs are trim and toned.

She is utter, sheer flawlessness, right down to her pinky toe. In the glow of the firelight, one side of perfection is illuminated like a golden angel rising from the white-hot flames. The other side is dark, shadowed. Shrouded in mystery. It's a perfect reflection of who Alyse Kingsley is.

She shows people the shiny, untainted surface.

I want the murky, damaged depth. The shadows.

I want in all the way.

I want the *real* Alyse, to solve the mystery that is *her*.

And *that's* the one who will be mine.

The one I'm sure no one else has ever had.

I'm still reclining, hand behind my head, as I hungrily watch her slowly bend down to step out of her denim, foot by foot, and I am entranced. Wrapped up in everything that is Alyse. I'm so enthralled I almost don't realize she's starting to remove her bra, but I want that pleasure of completely unwrapping her for the first time.

"Stop." I hold out my hand, which she takes. "Let me," I rasp. Sitting up straight, I pull her to stand between my legs. My hands wrap around the back of her knees and move slowly upward as my lips find her heated flesh, placing scattered wet kisses right above her panty line. She sucks in a sharp, ragged breath. The sting of her grip in my hair causes an involuntary smile that I know she has to feel.

My palms itch with the need to redden her ass, but I won't do that tonight. There are so many things I want to do with her that I won't do tonight, but you can bet I am plotting every fucking one of them out in agonizing detail in my head.

When my hands reach her purple lacy panties, I tug them down, helping her step out of them. My face is just above eye level with her nearly bare mound. I want to take my time with her almost as much as I want to strip and just pound into her like a madman. But I want to worship her like she deserves. I'm so hard with the need to be inside her, my balls ache and I am suffering big time, but ladies first, as my mother taught me. Although I'm quite sure this wasn't what she had in mind when she said it.

Running my thumbs along her smooth, sensitive, womanly flesh, she exhales in a rush when I dip a finger inside, feeling her intense want for me.

"God, you're beautiful," I murmur against her naked flesh. "So damn beautiful, Alyse."

And mine, I think.

Mine.

Because after tonight, I don't think I'll be able to let her go.

I force my lips from her skin, but am still slowly pumping that single finger in and out, and when I glance up her body, she's raptly watching every move I make with hooded, smoky eyes, and fuck if that doesn't turn me on even more.

"Does that feel good, my sweet Alyse?"

"Yes," she breathes before her head falls back.

I insert another finger, then a third, before feathering my thumb over her hard clit. I keep my rhythm slow, my touch light, teasing, and even then her tight walls clench around me as she nears her release.

"Asher, God, yes."

Placing her hands on my shoulders, she steadies herself. When she starts moving her hips, fucking my fingers it's the most glorious sight I have ever seen, but suddenly I can't wait a second longer. I need my mouth on her, in her, all over her.

I lie back on the wide couch and pull her over me so her knees are on either side of my head and, grabbing her hips, I slam her glistening, aroused pussy to my lips, groaning at my first taste.

Her body falls slightly forward as she props herself up on the back of the couch, holding on against my assault. I'm relentless, needing to devour every inch of her. I hold her open, my tongue darting in her slick channel before I flatten it, dragging it up to circle her clit, which is so fucking hard. Her cries and moans and breathless hitches spur me on. I thrust two fingers inside her tight, dripping sex and hook them, pumping my hand as furiously as I'm lashing my tongue.

She rides my face with complete and utter abandon and I love every fucking uninhibited second of it.

Then I tighten my grip on her hips, take her swollen clit between my teeth and bite while still flicking my tongue on the very tip. Her whole body shakes as she explodes, my name bouncing off the walls.

From beneath, I watch her fall apart.

I watch her lips part slightly.

I watch her eyes roll back before they fall closed.

I watch her back arch when she cries out.

I watch the pink flush of satisfaction creep up her fair skin.

In that moment, I watch myself lose my very heart and soul to her.

I force her to ride wave after wave, bringing her to ecstasy again and again until she's begging me to stop. After the very last tremble fades, I pull her down my prone body, releasing her bra clasp in one smooth move. I push aside the loosened cup and take a dusky stiff nub in my mouth and suck.

Hard.

"Ahhh..." she breathes.

Flipping our positions so she's on her back, I rip the bra from her arms and fling it across the room, my lips now traveling back and forth between her two tight nipples, biting, sucking, laving as my hands knead and twist. I feel the flesh pucker on my tongue and I am completely lost in her. *To* her.

"Asher—"

"What do you need, baby?" I ask before I capture her lips, making her taste herself on me. She can't answer because her mouth is busy dueling with mine, but her hands do. She reaches between us, unbuckles my belt, and unbuttons my jeans before reaching inside to grab my throbbing cock.

When her tiny, warm hand wraps around my dick, I snap. I've

waited eight fucking years to be inside of her.

I'm done waiting.

Pushing myself off her, I strip, letting my pure, raw lust for her bleed thick and hot. Grabbing my wallet, I pull out a condom. This will be the one and only time I use one with her. I'm clean and tested and once I confirm she is, we will never need one again. I already know she's the last woman I'll be with.

"Put it on me," I command, handing her the foil packet as she sits up. I need immediate relief as I wait, so I fist my cock and pump.

Hard.

Fast.

Swirling when I get to the head, I groan at how fucking good I know it will feel to finally sink home.

She fumbles with the packet, distracted by my self-pleasure.

"Baby, do it now or I'm going to come all over your perfect tits and I don't want to do that. Not the first time at least."

Her eyes darken. She licks her lips and I immediately know I've found my soul mate.

Sexually.

Emotionally.

Spiritually.

Jesus, I've found my wife. And the fact that thought doesn't freak me the fuck out means every cell in my body knows it too. Her soul has called to me for eight years. I just wasn't listening.

She wraps her palm around my cock, right over mine, our hands moving together in tandem for a few strokes. It feels so goddamn good I almost don't stop her. If she puts her mouth on me, I'm done. There will be no going back. The first time I come with her, I want to buried so deep we both forget our names, so I force her to stop, take the condom from her other hand, and roll it on myself.

My only goal is to get inside her as fast as possible.

I sit down beside her and pull her astride me. She hovers right above my stiff erection, like she's waiting for permission. *Or direction.*

Which I'm more than happy to give.

"Guide me inside you, Alyse. Now, baby."

CHAPTER 15

ALYSE

HOLY HELL. I HAVE *NEVER* IN MY LIFE HAD A SEXUAL EXPERIENCE LIKE this. Yes, mouths, fingers, and cock have pleasured me—or in some cases, *attempted* to—but I've never been worshipped with a man's eyes the way Asher is doing to me now.

Exalted.

Revered.

Like I am the only thing that has or will ever matter to him.

That's a stupid, foolish thing to think so early on, but I know what I'm feeling. I know what I see. I *know* what he's silently telling me.

His eyes have mine snared. Helpless. I'm unable to do anything but fall further and deeper within their warm, bottomless pools as I follow his command, guiding him to my opening. I sink down slowly and we both groan. It's exquisite. My lids feel heavy, but our eye contact never breaks.

He's big.

He's thick.

He stretches me to my limits.

But I've never felt anything more perfect in my life.

He grabs my face between his strong hands, holding me tight as he thrusts into me, my multiple orgasms making his drive easy and smooth. My breath hitches and my body burns. I need him to move more than I've needed anything. Ever.

"Alyse. Jesus…you feel too damn good. So fucking perfect."

He withdraws slowly, pushing back in slowly. He does this over and over again until I am crazy with want.

Delirious with need.

Frantic with the desire for him to possess me.

He never lets my face go. Never lets my eyes leave his.

"Fuck me harder, Asher."

"No, baby. I've never felt anything like this in my entire life. I need to savor you."

"Please," I pant. "Possess me. Own me."

"I am, Alyse. I am. You're mine now."

"Possess me faster," I beg.

But he doesn't. He just continues his methodical pace, pleasure etched over every inch of his face. I'm on fire. I need to come. My hand snakes between us, but he grabs it, pinning it behind my back.

"Asher, please."

"Your orgasms are mine, Alyse. Mine to give. Mine to withhold. They all belong to me now."

A long moan leaves me, a cross between intense euphoria at how right he feels and sheer frustration because I need more.

Jesus, this is like deliberate torture.

I want hard.

Rough.

Messy.

I don't want tender. It's suddenly making me feel too vulnerable. Now, my earlier thoughts about being completely consumed by him are suffocating me. Like a weight that's slowly pressing me into the ground. Asher's slowly been taking pieces of me day after day; some I freely give, some I'm trying to hold back, but it's like they're drawn to him.

Like they're *his* already and they're finally being called home.

I feel the chains tightening. I feel the lock trying to slam back together. Inside I'm having a slight panic attack and I'm trying to keep it from showing, forcing him to take me like I need instead. This is exactly what I do when people get too close. I try to shut them out. God, I could win a Pulitzer, I'm so damn good at it.

But Asher's perception about my inner struggle doesn't go unnoticed.

His hips halt. "Stop."

"Stop what?" I roll my hips, causing us both to moan. I need to get him back on task so I can get the hell out of here and back to the safety of my self-imposed lonely prison. Why do I have to be so fucking screwed up? I almost want to cry.

One hand leaves my face, palming my hip instead, but the other holds me steady, so I'm forced to watch him. Just when I think he may end this, trying to have a heart-to-heart instead, he takes a different tactic. He resumes his slow, methodical plunges, causing my eyes to roll back before refocusing on him.

"Do you know there are different forms of possession, Alyse?"

I don't answer. I'm in such excruciating pleasure I can't string vowels and consonants together, let alone instruct my tongue and lips to make sentences.

"Quick. Fast. Brutal." He punctuates his words with vicious thrusts. I nearly come from the pleasure his movements stir in every sensitive, swollen nerve ending. I'm so damn close, a couple more pumps and I'll be flying.

But he doesn't give it to me.

"Surrender is inevitable, but it's messy. It's fleeting. It doesn't last." Pulling me to his mouth, he takes my lips in a hard, deep, almost-savage kiss that's completely contradictory to the way he's now slowly pushing into me again.

"Slow. Methodical. Deliberate," he whispers against my kiss-

114

swollen lips. "That possession, Alyse, that surrender is beautiful. It's transcendent. It's eternal." Pulling me back down, his lips brush against my lobe as he whispers, "And that's what I want from you."

What if I can't give you that?

As if he reads my mind, he murmurs right before taking my mouth again, "You will give it to me, Alyse."

Asher takes his sweet time, making me come twice more. He only picks up the pace at the very end, seconds before he climaxes, finally tensing and releasing on a roar. Our bodies are covered in a fine layer of moisture, our breathing is ragged, and as we sit here wrapped in each other's arms, my emotions are all over the goddamn board.

I've never felt so raw.

I've never felt so exposed.

I've never felt so consumed.

I've never felt so wholly *loved* by anyone.

And I've never felt so damn scared in my life that someone is about to see the real Alyse for the first time.

But my real fear is: *what if he doesn't like her?*

CHAPTER 16

ALYSE

SIPPING MY BELGIAN CRAFT BEER, I'M LOST IN MY OWN LITTLE WORLD thinking of a certain dark-haired, blue-eyed sexpot. Asher and I haven't been able to spend much time together since Monday night. The night he took complete and total possession of both my body and mind. And another little piece of my heart.

I'm still reeling from that night.

The mind-bending sex that I feel days later.

His soul-piercing words went straight to the center of my very being. They still echoed loudly inside me.

And the fact that he wanted me to spend the night? Asher doesn't seem like the kind of man who regularly welcomes a woman into his bed. When he picked me up and carried me into his bedroom, still inside me, I had a little mental tug-of-war. I had an almost irresistible need to escape back to my safe little apartment, but, just like when I nearly had a meltdown during sex, he wouldn't let me retreat within myself. I have a feeling that Asher will be challenging me at every corner.

Isn't that one of the things that drew you to him in the first place?

Even though I've been a bit grateful for the space this week, I find I'm missing him terribly. More than I should this early in a relationship. He was out of town on Tuesday and Wednesday. Thursday nights are poker night with Conn and some other friends. Tonight he has a business dinner with Conn and Gray, so I'm having dinner with Livia when I'm done with this meeting. I've seen him periodically in the office for a stolen kiss here or there, but it's not the same.

It's not enough.

I need him inside me. I have never had this visceral physical need for a man. Remember when you were in love for the first time and you couldn't keep your hands off each other? This is different; it's more than that. This is…soul destroying. In either the best possible or worst possible way.

I just don't know which way it will end.

Annihilation or salvation.

Mine or his.

Or both.

"Ms. Kingsley?"

I look up to see an extremely attractive man looking down at me. I have to blink a few times to make sure I'm not hallucinating. When I realize I'm not, I am momentarily yanked back in time.

He walks through the door and I try to pay attention to the woman with three rowdy, unruly kids currently ordering six drinks. I feel like it takes forever to make her four strawberry smoothies, hazelnut blender, extra whip, and double-shot espresso. We're shorthanded today, so it's just Anna and me behind the counter. The line this morning is long and people are getting irritated.

By the time he reaches the counter, I'm flustered and short-tempered.

"Hi, I'm Beck," he says. His smile disarms me, totally taking me off guard.

"Uh, hi."

The runway model chuckles darkly. I've seen him in here a few times, but

117

he's never spoken to me other than to place his order. I already know he's not a creature of habit, because his order varies every single time, as does the time he comes in. Coffee, black, one day. Caramel macchiato the next. Vanilla latte, nonfat, please, another time. Not that I've been paying attention or anything.

"Do you have a name, beautiful?"

"Yes," I whisper, my mind racing a million miles an hour that this beautiful creature thinks I'm beautiful.

He leans against the high counter, like he has all the time in the world and doesn't care about the line behind him impatiently waiting for their morning caffeine fix. "And do you plan on telling me, or do I have to guess?"

We're usually supposed to wear nametags, but I was dragging ass today and it's still sitting at home on my dresser. I'm glad I'm behind the counter, because even my socks don't match. One is black and one's navy blue.

"It's okay. I don't bite. Much," he says with a flirty wink.

Oh. Too bad. I blink a few times, trying to remember my name. "Uh. Alyse. My name is Alyse."

Reaching across the strip of laminated wood separating us, he grabs my hand, bringing it to his soft lips. "Well, Alyse, now I can finally put a name with the girl I can't stop thinking about."

"Wow, that's quite a pickup line," I reply, chuckling.

He smiles sheepishly. It's adorable and accomplishes its intent. "Did it work?"

"Yes." I laugh, knowing I'm being way too easy. "It did."

"Good."

Five minutes later I watch his fine, tight ass walk out the door of Esse's Coffeehouse with a plain vanilla coffee and my phone number, which he used later that day. That's how my whirlwind love affair with Beck Mercado began.

The man looking at me now bears a striking resemblance to Beck. His sandy-blonde hair, strong chiseled face, and brilliant green eyes are nearly an exact replica of Beck's. They could be twins, but I know Beck didn't have a brother. He was an only child.

I don't know how long I just stare at him, a barrage of unwanted memories slamming into the front of my brain at a hundred miles per hour.

Picnics by the beach.

Stargazing.

Banana splits on a Sunday afternoon.

Making out in the back alley behind Esse's during a break.

Proclamations of love and stability and a future.

All shattered.

"Are you okay, miss?" Beck's doppelganger asks, concern wrinkling his forehead.

"Yes. Yes, sorry. Mr. Jensen?" I ask, standing to shake his hand.

He smiles. If he was attractive before, he is simply breathtaking now. I can hardly pull my eyes away from him. My stomach flutters. This is one of the reasons I'm stuck and can't make myself move on with someone else. A part of me is still in love with a dead man, despite what he did. I don't want to be, but I just can't seem to let it go.

Maybe part of letting it go is letting it out, Alyse.

"Please, call me Cooper." He winks.

"Then by all means, call me Alyse."

Grinning again, he takes a seat at the restaurant we've chosen to meet at and, pushing aside the fact that he looks like Beck, we spend the next half hour going through his portfolio. He's edgy and creative. I think he's absolutely the perfect photographer for Livia and Gray's wedding. I met with the other photographer yesterday, but I already know I'm going to pick Cooper.

"I know CB29 Studios hasn't been in business long, but I personally have over a dozen years of experience shooting weddings and our clients have been very happy." He pulls out a list, dropping it in front of me. "Here are some references if you'd like to call them."

"Thanks," I say, folding the paper and tucking it into my purse. I have no intention of calling references. I'm a big believer in first impressions and I have a very good first impression of Cooper Jensen. "So, your price is five thousand?"

"Yes. That includes rights to all digital pictures and six continuous hours of my time, along with an assistant."

"Wow, eight hundred thirty-three dollars an hour? Do attorneys even get paid that much?" I laugh.

He leans forward, a slight smirk on his face. "The good ones do. Did I mention the tens of hours that it would take me to retouch the photos?"

"How about four thousand?"

"Wow? You want me to take a twenty percent haircut?"

"Correct me if I'm wrong, Mr. Jensen, but you are free that evening, right? So, a twenty percent *haircut* is certainly better than a complete shave. Besides, having Gray and Livia Colloway as a reference would be a big boost to your new company. Trust me on that. Think of it as an *investment* in your future."

He leans back, crossing his arms. I find myself wondering how many women have gone missing in his smile. We silently stare at each for a few moments before he answers.

"Okay."

Our gazes never break and I realize we are smiling goofily at each other. I break eye contact, shaking my internal head at the way I'm acting. "So, you require a deposit, I suppose?" I reach back into my purse to pull out the blank check Livia's given me to secure the photographer once I've made a decision.

"You're giving me the job? Without calling references?"

I look back up. "Yes."

"Wow. That's great. A thousand-dollar deposit today is sufficient."

As I'm making out the check, I feel his eyes on me. Watching. Assessing. Wondering if I'm interested in him, which I'm not. Not in the way he's probably hoping, but I know that's not the vibe I'm throwing off, because he's caught me staring at him several times. I can't help it. I cannot seem to get over the uncanny way he resembles my dead boyfriend. It's eerie. And a little unsettling.

"So, Alyse," he starts after I hand over the check. I cringe at what I know is coming. "I'd love to take you out sometime."

"I'm flattered, Cooper, but…I'm actually seeing someone." I look down, ashamed at myself that I've led this nice guy on.

"Is it serious?"

When my eyes draw back up, he's leaning forward on the table, hands clasped. Usually when you tell a man you're dating someone, he responds with *"That's too bad,"* or *"Sorry to hear that,"* or *"Here's my number if it doesn't work out."* But after spending the last forty-five minutes with Cooper, I already know he's not like most men.

Just like Asher.

I don't hesitate to respond, because as attractive as I think Cooper is, I like Asher. A lot. More than a lot. It's very possible he could even be *The One*. So I have too much to lose to screw it up by thinking of another man. Especially one that looks like my first love.

"Yes."

"Well, maybe we can be friends then."

I'm drawn to this man for reasons I can't understand or explain and not on a sexual level. I think on his proposal for a few seconds, something that would be easy for anyone else to jump on, but for me it's not. And I decide that if I can let Asher Colloway in a little bit, maybe I also have room for a friend. A *real* one.

"I think I'd like that."

Maybe I'm turning over a new leaf after all.

"Come in!" Livia yells.

Opening the front door to Livia's penthouse apartment, I'm immediately hit with the heavenly smell of pizza, one of my all-time favorite indulgences. Livia and I ate a lot of frozen pizza when we were kids. Totino's. It was cheap and quick and surprisingly good. You'd think with as much pizza as I ate when I was young that I'd hate it, but you'd be wrong. Livia even worked in a pizza joint. She still loves pizza to this day.

"How was the meeting?" she asks excitedly when I walk into the kitchen.

"Good," I reply, throwing Cooper's business card on the counter. "I hired this guy. He's really good. Very creative. I think you'll like him." Picking up a celery stick from a veggie platter, I take a bite and add, "And I saved you a thousand bucks."

She stops cutting a red pepper that she's going to add to a platter big enough to feed ten people. "Really? How'd you do that?"

I shrug. "I used my stellar negotiation skills."

"Thanks. It just makes me sick that this wedding is so expensive. If I would have known how much things were going to cost, I may have reconsidered eloping."

"Livia, you deserve the wedding of your dreams. And I think Gray can afford it."

"I know. It's not that. It's just...I...we never had much growing up, Lys, and even though I know all of this," she waves the hand that's still wielding the knife around the massively eloquent apartment, "is going to be mine, it doesn't seem right to spend money foolishly. I think I'll always be pragmatic, and spending tens of thousands of dollars on one day just feels...wrong. And stupid." She shakes her head, going back to her chopping.

"Libs. Your wedding is not foolish or wrong or stupid. It's special. I know you. It's the one and only time you'll be married and you deserve to have everything you've ever dreamed of."

Her eyes snap up and I see something undefined in them before they well with tears.

"Oh God, I'm sorry. What did I say?" I round the counter and hug her. Her shoulders shake, but she says nothing. "Livia, what is it?"

She pulls back, wiping her tears. "Nothing. Hormones. Everything makes me cry these days." She won't look at me when she answers. That's a telltale sign Livia's lying. My heart hurts that she won't trust me with the truth.

Hypocrite, my conscience whispers.

We're silent for a few uncomfortable minutes. It's like there's this big swirling cloud of secrets and distrust between us. I hate it. And I can't even blame it all on her.

She turns to grab the pizza that's warming in the oven and sets it on the counter. "I have beer or wine. Which would you prefer?"

"Beer, but I'll get it."

"No. I've got it. I sit around all day doing nothing. I'm going absolutely stir-crazy now that I'm starting to feel better."

I watch her busy herself for a couple minutes. "Do you ever think about Mom?" I blurt. I don't know why I'm asking, because we haven't talked about our mother in years. It's not really a taboo subject, just more of a painful one that we both try to avoid.

She sets a Dark Side Porter down in front of me and I take a big, unladylike swallow.

"Sometimes. I wonder if she's still alive."

"Me too. Will you miss her being at your wedding?"

Contemplating my question, she finally answers, "I think it's hard to miss someone you don't even really know. I'll miss the *idea* of her, but I can't say I'll miss *her*, per se. Make sense?"

"Yes." I pick at the label, making a confession. "I used to fantasize that she sat outside the house and watched us play in the yard, or that she snuck in at night and tucked us in. I swear I used to smell her perfume lingering in my room some nights or feel the light press of a kiss on my cheek. I used to tell myself she had no choice but to go away and that the only way she'd stay away was if it were against her will."

Livia's lips thin. "The older I get the more I realize we don't always have a choice in a lot of things in life, Alyse. Sometimes choices are made for us and we just have to go along for the ride."

I nod, not knowing exactly how to respond. I happen to think there's always a choice. Maybe they're not good ones, but there are options. Luckily Livia changes subject to something lighter, more neutral.

"So, how's your project at CFC going?"

Getting settled, I moan at the first bite of the deep-dish cheesy goodness that will go straight to my ass, but I do not care.

"It's good. I've had a lot of meetings this week and just started really digging into the books these past couple of days. I wish I could hit the

123

ground running, but it takes a few days to get acclimated to a company's systems, culture, and processes. But everyone is very nice and helpful so far, so that's a plus. That's not always the case when an auditor walks through the door. We're just about as welcome as the IRS."

"That's true," she says, chuckling.

My cell buzzes, which is sitting on the table beside me. It's a text from Asher. I quickly pick it up before Livia sees.

Asher: miss u, baby

I miss you too. I can't help the smile that eats up my face.

Me: thought u were eating dinner

He responds immediately.

Asher: i'd rather b eating u

I hope to hell Livia is too busy eating her pizza to notice I've turned twenty hues of pink.

Me: me too

Asher: i'm going to feast on u ltr, alyse

God.

Me: i'm not sure i'm on the menu tonite

I set the phone in my lap while waiting for a reply. It takes all of two seconds, but I can't look because Livia's watching me like a hawk.

"I can tell by the look on your face that's Asher," she smirks.

I ignore her jibe because the suspense is too much. I have to look down at the dirty words that I know await me. I may not have been able to spend a lot of time with Asher this week, but we've certainly kept a string of raunchy texts alive and breathing. I've been in a constant sexual haze since the day before Thanksgiving when he sauntered into my office looking so goddamn edible I could barely concentrate on the words falling from his lips.

Asher: i'm going to fuck that sass right out of u later

I type a quick reply.

Me: promises promises

I lift my eyes, trying to pay attention to my sister. "And you know that how?"

"Because you're all flush and giddy." Damn. I look away, embarrassed, but my head snaps back up when she adds, "And I'm not sure I've ever seen you so happy."

She's wrong. I was very happy once upon a time. I feel another buzz, but decide to give my attention to Livia.

"Spending a lot of time with him this week?"

"A little. We've both been busy."

"Are you?" she asks.

"Am I what?"

"Happy?"

I take my time answering, because I'm afraid to jinx things.

Yes, I'm insanely happy. Happier than I've been in a very long time, but I don't have any idea where this is going. We're clearly in lust, but is there more? Can there be more? Asher wants me to submit to him in every way, and Monday night felt more like lovemaking than a good fucking, and that both thrills and scares me.

But my fucked-up mind still waffles dozens of times a day. So much so, I'm giving myself motion sickness. One minute I think I can go all in, leaving the past behind, the next I'm sure this is probably the biggest mistake I've ever made, because against my better judgment,

I'm invested emotionally already. I haven't been emotionally invested in a man since Beck.

"Yes," I finally answer. "But I just don't know where it's headed."

"Where do you want it to go?"

"I—" I want to lie and say I don't know, but that's not true. I do know. I am already half in love with Asher. He's had a part of me since I was seventeen years old. But the other half is mired deep in the past. "I really like him," I settle for. It feels too early to think about long-term, even though I can't stop my foolish female mind from going there.

"But..."

"But, I don't know, Libs. We're insanely attracted to each other, but I just, I don't know what he wants beyond sex." And I'm reluctant to put myself out there completely until I do. Asher's a player. I've known that since the moment I met him eight years ago. So what if he's just playing me now? His words, and even his actions say otherwise, but I don't know. My life, my business...they are all in Detroit. Not Chicago. This is only temporary.

Why does that thought make me so sad?

She studies me for a few moments. "You know, I probably shouldn't tell you this, but Gray talked to Asher the night before Thanksgiving about you."

That perks me up. That was the night we had our "date" slash fake business meeting. "He did?"

"Yeah. Asher hasn't been serious about a woman in a very long time, and Gray knew back at that family dinner a couple months ago that he took an interest in you. He's been trying to warn him off ever since, because he was worried about him hurting you."

Interesting.

Livia continues. "And Asher asked if Gray cared about *him* getting hurt." She reaches across the table, taking my hand; sincerity oozes from her. "He likes you, Alyse. A lot, from what I can tell. A woman in his past hurt him badly, but Gray doesn't talk about it and Asher and I aren't exactly buddy-buddy, so I don't know the specifics, but Gray says he hasn't taken an interest in a single woman since then. Until you."

My body tingles at her revelation and all those stupid elementary school girl fantasies about Barbie and Ken living happily ever after in their Barbie Dreamhouse try to take hold.

Then a sudden, sick feeling hits me in the pit of my stomach, making me break out into a sweat. "Does Asher know about...you know?"

After Beck's death, I couldn't date again until I was a sophomore in college. Nearly two years. His name was Jedd. Even though he was the polar opposite of Beck, I really liked him. Unfortunately I made the relationship-ending mistake of telling him about my little thirty-day vaca in the psych ward because I foolishly wanted to be honest. Once he found out, he didn't return my calls for a week, and when he broke it off, his bullshit excuse was "It's not you, it's me." Riiiight. So if Asher already knows...

"No, Alyse. He doesn't know. Gray swore he wouldn't tell another soul and he never has."

My relief is palpable. I'm not ready for Asher to know. In fact, I'm not sure I ever will be ready.

I think about how Asher's worried I may hurt him. He's not wrong with his concern. "With my track record, Livia, I think maybe *I'll* end up being the one to hurt *him*."

"I don't know, Alyse. I see the way your eyes light up when he's in the room or when he touches you or even when his name is mentioned. I know I missed a lot these past few years..." The last several words are choked. I sense a sadness in Livia I haven't seen before and I wonder why I haven't noticed.

Maybe because you've been steeped in resentment, you selfish B.

"...but I've never seen you look at someone like you do Asher."

Guilt stabs me, because I *have* felt this way before. With Beck. I genuinely loved him. I'm hiding so many secrets from Livia. What would be gained by telling her?

Peace? Maybe.

Freedom from the past? I don't know.

"I'm scared, Libs. I'm scared I'll get hurt."

"So is he," she replies, smiling gently. "No risk, no reward. Right?"

"Right," I mumble, not at all convinced. *No risk, no rejection* has always been my pathetic mantra instead.

How do you persuade your mind to free your heart so it can soar high and free, grabbing that happiness that evades you? I wish I knew the answer. I could bottle it and sell it and become a billionaire.

I chance a look down at the texts that have been sublimely whispering my name and smile. No matter the unwelcome ping-pong game my emotions seem to be playing, there is no denying how I feel about this man. *God, I like him.* So *very* much. But liking him isn't the real issue. Letting him in is.

Asher: do not touch urself

Asher: ur ass will b a pretty shade of red if u disobey me

Asher: alyse, answer me. now

There's no way I can leave Asher's bossiness unchecked. Somehow I think he'd tire quickly if he had a meek woman he thought he could push around.

Me: too late. moan...god that feels sooooo good

Setting the phone back down, I try to turn my attention back to my plate, but suddenly my physical appetite is gone, replaced instead by a sexual one so intense that I'm definitely going to be taking the edge off later. Maybe even now. In Livia's bathroom. My phone buzzes again and my breath hitches. I can practically hear the growl in his written words.

Asher: ur orgasms belong to me, beautiful

Me: why r u so damn bossy

Asher: cuz it makes u so wet

Damn. Yes it does. Just as I'm about to reply with something snarky, I hear the door open. Male laughter carries into the kitchen where Livia and I sit.

Seconds later, Gray and Asher walk in. The minute they spot us, their laughter stops, replaced by looks that can be mistaken for nothing but hunger. And not for cooked dough topped with hot cheese and pepperoni.

Holy shit, they both look like male gods dropped down from heaven above dressed in their fitted suits. Asher's is charcoal grey with a deep purple shirt underneath, the top two buttons undone. He looks so fucking sexy, my mouth actually hurts with the need to taste him.

I'm instantly wet. Well...wetter.

Gray hastily makes his way to Livia, tugging her to him for a hard kiss. When he whispers something in Livia's ear, her face turns red.

Strong arms band around me from behind. Asher's desire presses hard against my lower back. A rough, raspy voice rumbles in my ear, "Are you ready, baby?"

"For what?" I mumble, just as low.

"Promises."

How does he always know the right thing to say?

CHAPTER 17

ASHER

THE SECOND WE WALK OVER THE THRESHOLD OF MY APARTMENT, I HAVE Alyse pinned up against the wall, my mouth on hers, my hands frantically searching to find naked skin. I kick the door shut on a slam, not quite ready to share her with the rest of the world yet. I have that planned for later.

Four fucking days since I've been inside of my woman is too goddamn long and that's not going to happen again. I've thought of nothing else all week. I almost ditched dinner tonight to be with Alyse, but I couldn't. We're in the final stages of a major acquisition under GRASCO Holdings that we need financial backing for. Although I should have pulled a Gray and brought Alyse with me. Only she had other plans.

"I need to fuck you, baby. Hard. Now." My teeth nip the delicate flesh along her neck. My tongue laves the tiny hurts I'm leaving behind. Her choppy gasps and breathy moans ignite a raging inferno inside my groin that can only be put out by the silky wetness I know is waiting for me between her toned thighs.

Quickly I pull the baby blue sweater over her head, dropping it on the cold tile beside me. Her jeans and panties are gone in a flash and she's managed to push off my suit jacket, but I can't wait a second longer.

I yank down the cups that are keeping her pert nipples from my view so I can watch them bounce up and down while I fuck her, and as I pull one into my mouth, I reach between us to free my straining cock. Then I'm pushing inside her in one hard stab. She's wet, but not enough, because I was too impatient to prepare her properly. It takes two more thrusts before I hit the end of her womb, going as deep as her body will allow.

My eyes roll back at the feel of her bare skin on mine.

Fucking. Nirvana.

"Alyse, baby. So tight. Fuck, your pussy's scorching me, it's so hot."

I have jacked off to thoughts of her every single night this week, fantasizing about being inside her raw, but it's like I haven't come in days, because within seconds of immersing myself in her snug heat, I'm about to blow. I haven't been inside a woman without a rubber since Natalie, but absolutely *nothing* compares to the feel of Alyse's tight, wet, velvety pussy hugging my dick.

Nothing.

Being inside her, skin on skin, is like I've reached the pearly gates early.

"Hard, Asher. I want hard."

"Beg. Beg me to fuck you harder."

I expect words. What I get instead is a sharp tug as she jerks me to her mouth in an explosive, aggressive, demanding kiss. Dragging my bottom lip between her teeth, she bites so hard I taste blood. When she finally pulls back, her smoky eyes don't beg.

They challenge.

And I fucking love a good challenge.

"Palms against the wall. Keep them there," I growl. Jesus, it makes me swell even more when she readily complies, and by the gush of wetness I feel at my command, she loves it when I control her like this.

Smirking, I withdraw slowly until just the tip remains inside. "All right, baby. You want hard, you'll get hard. Hang on."

Hands underneath her bare ass for support, I grip tight and slam her down on my straining dick.

Hard.

Filthy.

Rough.

Her breath rushes out on an exhale and I watch a small smile of satisfaction break through the hazy lust.

"Tell me this is okay," I demand gruffly as I withdraw fully and pound into her again and again. My hips are like pistons and if she says no, I'll stop, but fuck...it will take a giant feat of willpower, and I left that at the front door.

"Don't...stop..." she gasps.

That's all I need. As tightly as I'm gripping her, she'll probably end up with bruises, but damn if I'm not dying to give her everything she wants. Everything I *need* her to have. The thought of leaving my marks of passion on the woman I'm falling in love with hits me someplace deep and primal.

As impossible as it seems, I think I've already fallen. I have to push that thought to the back of my head. All I can concentrate on right now is bringing us to the brink of rapture so we tumble over together.

I hold her tight, setting a fast, brutal pace and within only minutes, her walls clench moments before she closes her eyes and her body convulses in pure bliss. I watch her unravel and I'm thoroughly, hopelessly lost. She's so damn beautiful my breath stops. My legs shake from my effort as I continue to pound into her, not slowing a bit. I stave off my own climax so I can watch the waves of euphoria wash over her gorgeous, flushed face.

I don't think I'll ever tire of the light blush that takes over her fair skin when she orgasms at my hand. It's quickly becoming my favorite color.

"Baby, I'm going to come," I rasp. Finally, unable to last any longer, I let the last of her orgasm milk me. I throw my head back and with a howl follow her into the Promised Land.

I empty everything I have into her.

My seed.

My love.

My very fucking essence.

It's official. Somehow within a matter of what seems like only days or months, but what has really been years in the making, I have found the one woman who has the power to outright decimate me. I was wrong before. It wasn't Natalie.

It was Alyse.

It's *always* been Alyse.

And I've just handed her the golden keys, whether she realizes it or not.

CHAPTER 18

ALYSE

"Tell me something about your childhood I don't know."

It's dark, it's late, and I'm exhausted. Asher's fingers lightly trailing up and down my spine have me nearly lulled to sleep when he quietly asks his question. We haven't been able to get enough of each other and spent the last three hours indulging everywhere in Asher's apartment. He may be almost thirty, but the man doesn't seem to need much recovery time, that's for damn sure. I'm deliciously sore and unbelievably sated, but I need the healing effects of sleep now.

Once again he's insisted I stay and sleep in his bed. This time I don't argue. He's sexed the fight right out of me. In truth I really *want* to stay.

"What do you want to know?" I ask groggily, trying to blink away the mist of unconsciousness that's almost claimed me.

"Anything. Everything. The good, the bad, the ugly. I want it all, Alyse." His soft words almost undo me. I tilt my head from its resting place in the crook of his muscular arm and even in the dark, I see him looking at me. *Into* me. I want to close my eyes to keep him out almost as much as I want to invite him in. I want to let him root around and find all my hiding places so I don't have to reveal them on my own.

I'm finding I want Asher to know everything about me, because somehow I think he'll accept the bruised parts of me. Wanting it and getting the words out, however, are two completely different things. That's the hard part. That's always been the hard part. I don't know where I inherited my inability to let people all the way in, but I hate it.

And somehow Asher seems to know this about me.

"Let's start with an easy one. Tell me a story about you and Livia."

I smile when I remember a particularly funny story. "Okay, well one summer when I was ten and Libs was fourteen we went to a park about a mile away from our house. My bike had a flat tire, so we took Livia's, riding together. But we weren't supposed to do that, because we had crashed before and if Dad caught us, we would have been in big trouble.

"Riding to the park, I sat on the seat and Livia stood, peddling the entire way herself. We must have stayed at the park for hours. Getting out of the house was not only an escape, but a necessity sometimes." I sigh heavily, wishing my childhood was different. Happy. Like Asher's. Rubbing my back gently he's silent, letting me continue at my own pace.

"Anyway, it was starting to get dark and we decided we needed to head home, but this time instead of sitting on the seat, I rode on the handlebars."

"Uh oh." He laughs and I join him.

"Yeah, uh oh. So there was this pretty steep hill. We walked it on the way there, but on the way back, we decided to ride it instead. We flew down that thing going probably twenty miles an hour and Libs lost control after catching some gravel. I had on a sundress. Dresses and gravel do not mix, let me tell you."

"Ouch." He's laughing harder and louder, which makes me do the same.

"Livia only had a few scrapes, but I filleted the skin from the right side of my ass, like literally took the first two layers right off. I couldn't sit down for days and I had to wear thongs for what seemed like a month at the time, but was probably only a few days, because regular underwear stuck to the wound and our neighbor, who's a nurse, insisted that it 'get some air' to heal properly. No ten-year-old should be forced to wear thongs. It's damage I can't undo to this day."

Asher's entire body is now shaking.

"Do you know what it's like to have your dad see your bare butt at age ten? It's humiliating. I still have scars from that incident, physical *and* mental."

"Stop, stop." He can barely catch his breath, he's laughing so hard. After a few seconds, he manages to ask, "Did you get in trouble?"

"No. We told Dad we collided on swings at the playground. He never knew we'd crashed on Livia's bike, or if he did, he never let on."

"You collided on swings?" he asks incredulously.

"It was the best lie we could come up with on our long hobble home."

We laugh for a few more minutes, before he wipes the tears from his eyes. "Oh my God. That's a great story, Alyse."

Now I'm wide-awake. "Your turn." I prop up on my elbow and gaze down at him. Even in no light he is simply beautiful. His raw masculinity is hypnotizing. I trace the black Chinese tats he has running down the outside of his bulky left bicep.

"Tell me about these," I say softly. "They're very sexy." I think back to just an hour ago when I was tracing each pattern with my tongue and impossibly, I feel myself getting wet again.

He brushes aside a stray hair that's fallen in my eyes, tucking it behind my ear. The move is soft and seductive. Loving. He treats me like blown glass one minute and a raunchy sex toy the next. I love it.

"The first one means family. The next two stand for older brother, one each for Gray and Luke, and the last stands for younger brother, Conn."

I laugh. "Oh, I bet Connelly loved it when you got that."

"Pitched a hissy fit like a little bitch."

That makes me laugh harder. "I love that you have a great relationship with your family, Asher. It's very...endearing. And refreshing."

"I'm lucky, I guess. We have our issues, like any other family, but... yeah. I have a great family. The best parents and brothers a guy could ask for." He pauses. "I'm sorry you didn't have that, Alyse."

I'm sure Asher knows the basics, but I wonder how much he actually knows. His family was idyllic. Mine was...dysfunctional to the nth degree. Our voices soften. It feels like story time has given way to confession. And confession is something I am not good at. It takes me a minute to answer. "Me too."

"Do you miss your dad?"

Do I?

"He had a sickness, you know, a disease, but he tried his best when he wasn't sucked into his gambling so deep. When he managed to stay away, he was actually a good dad." I thought maybe he had finally beaten it, until a few months before Livia disappeared, when he seemed to fall back into it. He was at his worst then.

"When Livia was gone for those few years, he was honestly the best he'd ever been and then he got cancer. I wish she could have seen him then. Until he became so sick and weak, those were probably some of the best times I remember with him. But at the same time it made me angry, because I had a glimpse of what it could have been like if he wasn't an addict."

"I'm sorry, baby." His soft lips touch my temple. "Have you told her that?"

"No. Livia has her own jaded views of our father. I mean, I can see where she's coming from to some degree. He was imperfect. We all are. But I think it's interesting how two people can grow up in the same house and view their parents in such a different light. He hated the way he was. He just...couldn't help it. I think Livia saw it as a weakness, but I viewed it more as a sickness. One he just couldn't find the cure for."

"I think I know what you mean. I feel that way about Luke. The way he talks, you would think we had different fathers. My parents weren't perfect, but they were pretty damn close, and I never understood how Luke could feel that way about our dad." He pauses briefly. "You seem to have a pretty good relationship with your sister."

I'm not really sure how to answer that. I *want* to have a good relationship with her. Another thing I can't let go. I hate that about myself. The inability to forgive and forget. "I—It's complicated."

"Most relationships are. How did you get this?" he asks, tracing the scar just below my sternum.

"What is this? Twenty questions?"

Laughing, he pulls me tight. "I have hundreds of questions, Alyse. Thousands. I told you I want to know everything about you. Every scar, every wound, every hurt. I'm going to heal each and every one of them."

I smile. "Wow. Theatre *and* medicinal prowess? Who knew you were so talented?"

"Oh, baby. You have no idea the things I'm capable of." His fingers tickle my sides and I giggle. "Now, the scar."

I sigh. I hate talking about that day. I hate thinking about that day. I hate remembering that day even happened. But I figure since Livia was dating Gray at the time, he probably already knows I was in an accident, so I can at least talk about that without revealing the whole sordid story.

"I was in a car accident my senior year. They had to remove my spleen."

"Yes, I remember. I tried to come see you and your father wouldn't let me up. Then I had to get back to school so I couldn't come back."

"Really?" I ask, surprised. "I never knew that."

"Yes, really. I would have at least thought he'd tell you."

"He didn't," I mumble. He was probably too distraught that he had to sit in a hospital chair versus a poker one.

"You were in the hospital for a few days right?"

"Yes."

"Didn't the driver die in that accident?" he asks quietly.

I stiffen and he pulls me tighter. "Yes," I answer on a choke.

"A friend?"

"I don't like talking about it," I say softly. Tears prick over another man that are most unwelcome in this moment with Asher. A reminder of no matter how much I try to put that part of my life behind me, I just can't seem to cut the cord and leave it there.

"I'm sorry, baby." I feel his lips on the top of my head. I'm surprised at how much they comfort me.

He doesn't ask any more questions. I don't offer any more information. We've gone silent again, but it's not uncomfortable.

"Tell me what *your* tattoo means."

Wow, he's really going for the jugular and he doesn't even know it. I was grateful that we'd moved off the topic of the accident, but this one isn't much safer. I hadn't even realized he'd seen the small tattoo on the inside of my ankle. He hasn't mentioned it once.

"What do you *believe* in so much that you had that word inked on your body?" he prods.

It's so simple, but often the simplest words mean the most. It's a reminder that my life is worth so much more than I thought it was at my lowest point. The day I got it is a day I'll never forget.

It's life.

It's hope.

It's second chances.

It's a future that I almost selfishly deprived myself of because I was too depressed to realize that my emotional agony would eventually become bearable.

But I don't say any of those things. Instead, I settle for my usual MO. Being vague. It requires a lot less explaining.

"A lot of things and sometimes nothing at all."

"That's pretty cryptic, baby."

"Yes, it is."

"Alyse...I want in."

"I know," I whisper. "I'm trying. It may not seem like it, but I am. I've never shared with anyone what I just shared about my father."

I'm back to lying in the crook of his arm, but he rolls me over so I'm now pinned underneath his heavy weight. He takes my face in his strong hands, eyes searching mine, thumb stroking my bottom lip.

"I want every single part of you."

Breathing becomes difficult and not because he's heavy, but because the conversation now is. I know exactly what he's asking. I want to give it, but I'm terrified that he'll look at me differently once he knows my dirty, dark secrets. I can't expose myself like that without knowing where this is headed.

Those damn tears return. "What if you don't like them?"

"Alyse, there's nothing you could tell me that would scare me away. I'll love every part of you."

Doubtful. "I don't want to be just a fling," I respond instead. I won't survive it. I'm already too invested in him.

His eyes soften. "This is so much more than just sex to me, Alyse. I was kind of hoping this would turn into forever."

The pathways from my brain to my lungs are singed by those romantic words, rendering me breathless. "I—I don't want to get hurt, Asher."

"Neither do I, baby. And with the way I'm feeling about you, if you don't feel the same, I... Jesus, I like you, Alyse. A helluva lot. *More* than a lot."

"Me too." I confess through the lump in my throat. I'm falling so hard and fast for him, I'm freaking out. My insides are quaking so much that all thoughts about why this was ever a bad idea are crushed to dust under the heavy weight of the emotional avalanche.

"Alyse," he whispers reverently before taking my mouth in a soft, slow kiss. I expect him to deepen it, I expect him to ravage me, but he doesn't. He worships my mouth, my body, and my soul.

Slowly.

Passionately.

Thoroughly.

He makes unmistakable love to me, telling me with unsaid words what we both feel, but what is probably too early to voice.

I am undeniably in love with Asher Colloway. If I hadn't admitted it to myself before tonight, there's no refuting it now, just like there's no refuting the love pouring from Asher into me with each reverent touch or each slow thrust of his hips.

I've given him my body.

I can't keep him out of my heart.

But I have to wonder…once I let him into my mind and he sees the real me, will he want to stay?

CHAPTER 19

ALYSE

"I'M GLAD YOU SAID YES," COOPER SAYS BEFORE TAKING ANOTHER BITE of his bison burger.

"Me too," I reply, looking longingly at his burger as I stuff some bland lettuce into my mouth. With Livia's wedding just a few short weeks away, I have the requisite five pounds to lose. Or...at least not gain.

"I'm sorry, I forgot to bring the contract I need signed."

"Really? Are you sure you didn't just want an excuse to see me again?" I tease.

His smile is contagious. "Caught me. I'll check my calendar and see when I'll be back in the city and give you a call."

"You can just email it, you know."

"But this is a lot more fun." He winks. "So how long have you lived in Chicago?"

"Oh, I don't live here. I'm just on assignment for a few months."

That piques his interest. "Doing?"

"An audit. I'm a forensic auditor."

"Really? A woman with beauty *and* intellect. I like it."

I smile at his compliment. When Cooper called earlier this week asking me to join him for lunch, I almost declined, but there's something about him that I really do like, so I agreed. Now I'm glad I did. It would be nice to have another friend.

"So, where do you hail from if not Chicago?"

"Detroit."

"Ah…Motor City. Nice. My cousin spent some time there a few years back. What firm do you work for?" He pops a fry in his mouth and with a smirk hands me one off his plate. I look at it only a couple of seconds before I snag it and devour it before he changes his mind. He winks and I cock a brow, giggling.

"I work for me. I opened my own company last year. ARK Consulting."

"Wow. That's great, Alyse."

"Thanks. What about you? How did you come up with the name of your studio, CB29? I love it. Coming up with a name was probably one of the hardest things when I opened my business."

His face lights up.

"I actually co-own the studio with my cousin. We had a dream of opening our own photography studio when we were younger, so it's named after our first two initials and we were both twenty-nine when we opened it."

"I like it. Very creative."

Half an hour later, after talking about the challenges of being small business owners, Cooper and I part ways, agreeing to meet for lunch again sometime soon.

Wrapping my scarf around me in a lame attempt to protect against the bitter winter winds and swirling snow that started coming down five minutes into lunch, I walk faster, wishing the four blocks back to CFC weren't so damn long and definitely wishing I'd worn anything other than a skirt and heels today.

Once inside the building, I'm shaking the snow that's collected on my hair when I hear my name.

"Alyse, hi."

I look up to see the head of CFC security, whom I met in the cafeteria earlier this week, talking to a guard at the front desk. What's his name again? Casey? No. Craig? No. Conner? Hell, I don't know, so I settle for a generic, "Hi."

I make polite chitchat with someone whose name starts with a "C" for a couple minutes before I beg my leave. He's a nice enough man, but I'm a little uncomfortable around him.

It's after one before I finally reach my temporary office on the thirty-fourth floor. I sit behind my desk with a sigh, still chilled from my short walk but glad I took the much-needed break.

I've spent the last two weeks looking at ledgers and balance sheets and bank statements until my eyes are crossed. With a little over a thousand employees, CFC isn't that big of a company, but big enough this audit could take me well until January or even February.

So far, I've not uncovered anything that looks suspicious, but I have yet to really dig into the accounting system or start validating vendors against invoices, which is my next project. With the hundreds of third parties that CFC works with, that alone could take me weeks.

Because of the nature of CFC's business, I will also need to look at each client account and review billing practices. I may need to pull in Al to help with this after he's done with his current audit or I could be here for months. Not that I would mind. The more time I spend with Asher, the more I can't fathom not being able to see him every day.

I've spent every night at his apartment this week. Regardless of my own emotional reservations, I can't deny that's where I want to be too. I've been trying to keep a little bit of distance, trying to protect my heart, but Asher sees right through me and he's very convincing. I can see why he's been so successful in his career. He's tenacious, like a bulldog.

Pushing aside thoughts of Asher from my head, so I can get some actual work done, I turn to my laptop and log onto the SAP accounting system that CFC uses. Last week when I met with Aaron

Hinton, the director of finance, and one of his analysts, Amanda, they gave me a cheat sheet to understand the vendor and banking codes within the system. As I search my desk for it, though, I'm unable to put my hands on it.

After ten minutes of hunting, I decide I must have accidentally thrown it away. Picking up the phone, I ring Amanda's extension first. For one, she's a little lower level and I don't want to bother Aaron if I don't need to for something so inconsequential. For another, I want to limit my time with Aaron. I've seen him a couple of times these past two weeks. Both times he's asked me out for drinks, regardless of the fact that I told him I'm seeing someone.

Of course, I haven't told him it's his boss's boss's boss, because, well, that's just not good for either Asher or me. I need to at least give the appearance that I'm being professional, although Asher makes that as difficult as possible at every turn. Yesterday he found me in the copy room and shoved me against the wall, kissing me passionately for a full minute. Thank God there aren't that many people on this floor, although I'm quite sure his assistant knows something is up by now. He may not care, but I certainly do.

Unfortunately, Amanda doesn't answer and this is the next thing on my list. Because I like to obsessively follow my lists, I'm kind of at a standstill. So reluctantly, I dial the extension Aaron gave me. *Lucky* me, he answers.

"Aaron, sorry to bother you. It's Alyse Kingsley."

"Alyse, well it's no bother at all." He's smooth. I'll give him that. And handsome. On the hot-o-meter, Aaron is about an eight. He meets my tall, dark, and handsome requirements, but he just doesn't make any of my bells ring. I think Asher's permanently silenced those for any other man.

"I apologize, but I seem to have misplaced the legend you gave me for the accounting system. Could you email me another copy?"

"I'll just run it up to you."

"No need to trouble yourself. Email is fine."

"Nonsense. I need to get out of my office for a bit anyway. See you in a few minutes."

"Sure," I mumble before hanging up.

A couple minutes later a light knock comes at my door before it opens. Aaron peaks his head in. "Knock, knock. Okay to come in?"

Why wouldn't it be? "Yes," I reply as I stand.

"Hi. Wow, you look great today, Alyse."

I'm wearing a simple white silk blouse tucked into my black pencil skirt. A clear-and-black silver-beaded necklace complements my very simple outfit. I wouldn't say I look great, but I don't look too shabby either.

His eyes slowly rake down my body and when they finally reach mine again, they are full of appreciation. He gives me a panty-dropping smile. I have to admit it's charming. I find myself smiling back.

"Thank you. Sorry to trouble you."

He walks all the way in, leaving the door open, for which I'm grateful. "No trouble at all. I'm happy to be of help *however* you need."

I don't miss the underlying innuendo of his thinly veiled attempt at being professional. Smirking, I hold out my hand for the paper he's now holding hostage in his. "Ah, sorry."

"No problem," I say, taking the document and setting it by my computer screen. "Well, that's really all I need so I won't waste any more of your time."

"Actually, I was wondering if Amanda showed you some of the shortcuts in SAP to make your job a little easier. Faster."

I spent an hour with Amanda earlier in the week, but she just went over some of the basics. I'm fairly familiar with SAP, but CFC has put their own homegrown spin on it, so it's a little different than what I'm used to. "No, she didn't."

"Well if you have a few minutes, I have some time now to show you."

"Sure," I reply.

"It may be easier if I come over there and sit with you, if that's okay?"

I inwardly groan, wondering if this is some ploy for him to get closer to me, but anything that can shave time off my research will be helpful, so I can't turn him down either. Damn that Amanda.

"Yes, fine."

For the next forty minutes he walks me through some of the nuances of their accounting system. He even shows me how to run a few simple reports that I can download into Excel for easy filtering and sorting, so I don't have to wait for someone else to do it. I find Aaron is very intelligent and funny. If I wasn't head over heels for Asher, I might actually entertain the idea of a date.

"Thanks, Aaron. This was very helpful." I smile, turning toward him.

"My pleasure." He reaches up and brushes his thumb against the fullest part of my bottom lip, startling me. I try to pull back, but he curls his fingers around my neck, holding me in place. "You have a crumb here that's been driving me mad," he tells me in a low voice.

"Oh," is all I can manage, remembering that I had a few crackers with my salad at lunch.

His fingers don't move and I swear his face just came closer to mine. "Do you know what else is driving me crazy, Alyse?"

I swallow hard and shake my head. My brain has clearly not caught up to what's going on here or otherwise he would have a fist in his face by now.

His eyes have darkened, now flitting back and forth to my mouth. "Your perfume. Jesus, you smell good."

I start to pull my head out of his grip and open my mouth to tell him how highly inappropriate this is when I hear a throat clear. A deep, male one that does not belong to Aaron.

Oh. Shit.

I can tell by the look in Aaron's eyes as they leave me and look toward my door that he's thinking the same exact thing. He drops his hand from my face so fast, it's like my body is now a conductor for ten thousand volts of electricity.

"Uh, Mr. Colloway, hi," he bumbles. Pushing his chair back quickly, he stands and starts to walk around my desk. I'm still looking the other way. Knowing exactly how Asher will react to what he thinks he just saw, I bend my head and close my eyes, taking a deep breath to steel myself for when I turn around to see the blazing fury in his.

When I do finally look at Asher, I stifle a sigh. I've never seen a man look like he literally wants to commit murder before, but there's no mistaking he wants to do just that. I'm surprised that his eyes aren't flashing red and he's not wielding a bloody scythe with Aaron's head already rolling out my office door.

"It's time for you to go," he grits, punctuating each word slowly. Even through Asher's tailored suit, I notice his muscles are rippling. He's fighting to physically restrain himself from hurting Aaron.

This time I don't even hide the shake of my head at his ridiculous reaction. I have to bite my tongue not to chew his ass up one side and down the other. Mind you, I'll do that, just not in front of Aaron.

Asher's one of the most possessive men I have ever known, and while that should be a total turnoff for me, it's not. Most of the time I find it exhilarating. Today it's just irritating. And embarrassing.

"I was just showing Alyse some things in the accounting system she needs for the audit." Aaron's brows are drawn together in confusion, probably wondering what kind of crazy his CEO just turned into. Asher's practically morphing into a wild, frothing animal right before our eyes. Aaron apparently has no self-preservation skills or he would have been out of here the second he looked up and saw Asher ready to rip out his jugular.

I rise and make my way around the desk, standing between them. I'm not sure if I'm protecting Aaron or saving Asher from himself. Probably both. "Aaron, thanks for your help. I appreciate it. I'll call you if I need anything else."

"The hell you will," I hear Asher reply under his breath.

Jesus, I hope Aaron didn't hear that. I do sigh now. Rather loudly. I want to glare at Asher, but I don't dare look at him or I'll either kick him square in the little boys or burst out laughing at his utter absurdity.

"Yeah, sure. Glad I could help." His puzzled eyes dart back and forth between Asher and me. I can tell he's trying to quickly piece this jagged brainteaser together. He makes his way toward the door, but Asher is still blocking it, not looking like he's going to move.

Grabbing Asher by the elbow, I gently nudge him into the room and out of Aaron's way. "Mr. Colloway, please come in and have a seat. I'll be right with you." Asher silently walks forward, but I can actually feel his body shaking with rage.

I smile, hoping to hell it looks relaxed and professional, not like I'm about to have Asher's balls twisted firmly in my palms in about five seconds.

"Thanks again, Aaron." I quickly usher him out and shut the door. "What the fuck was that?" I hiss, spinning around to face my utterly ridiculous...lover? Boyfriend? *Whateverheis?*

"You're kidding me, right? That's my line, sweetheart. The guy practically had his tongue down your throat and you were just sitting there letting him do it!"

Taking a deep breath, I lean against the door and cross my arms. It's obvious that one of us needs to remain calm. It's also obvious it's not going to be him. I lower my voice, trying to gain control of a situation that's close to exploding into a hurtful verbal war any second.

"Asher, it wasn't what it looked like."

"Really?" he sneers, leaning against the front of my desk, mirroring my stance. "Because what I *saw* was his hand touching your skin. What I *saw* was his face about two inches from yours. What I *saw* was a man who was looking at my woman like he wanted to throw her down on her desk and fuck her into tomorrow. And what I *heard* was him tell you how fucking good you smell. So, please...explain to me what I misconstrued."

Okay, so it was *exactly what it looked like.*

Crap.

I want to break our gaze, but I can't because then I'll look guilty. And I'm *not* guilty. I did nothing wrong, but when he puts it like that, I *feel* guilty. Damn him for making me feel like I did something behind his back.

"I did nothing wrong here. I didn't lead him on. I've told him

149

repeatedly I'm involved with someone. Nothing happened, and I wouldn't have let anything happen. You're overreacting."

"It didn't look like nothing was happening to me."

"Dammit, Asher. You got here about two seconds before I was about to tell him to back the fuck off."

"Two more seconds and his mouth would have been on yours."

"Damn you! Nothing happened. Nothing *would* have happened. I'm *not* attracted to Aaron."

"He wants you."

I shake my head. "Well, I don't want him," I retort. "I only want you."

His eyes bore into me, as if trying to ferret out a lie. I wonder who hurt Asher so badly that he doubts me when I've given him no reason to. I'm disappointed and offended that he thinks I would do that to him. To *us*.

"I may have a lot of personality flaws, Asher, but adulterer is not one of them. I have never cheated on a man in my entire life. I wouldn't do it."

"I won't share what's mine, Alyse. That's a deal breaker."

"It is for me, too."

We stand there, eyes locked for several tense minutes, neither of us moving. The five feet that separate us may as well be the goddamn Pacific Ocean. As hard as I've fallen for Asher, I don't know if we're going to make it if he freaks out like a rabid animal every time a man shows any hint of interest in me.

Possessive is one thing.

Irrational psychotic jealousy? No. I won't subject myself to that for any man. Not even Asher.

A knock breaks us out of our strained standoff. I open the door to find a sheepish Tara standing outside. *Lovely.* She's probably heard half of our fight; maybe she's even transcribed it for our reading pleasure later.

"I'm really sorry to interrupt, but your two o'clock is here, Asher." Tara spins, quickly walking away without waiting for a response. I don't blame her. The tension swirling in this office is now so thick it's suffocating me with every shallow, harsh breath.

Without a word, Asher pushes off my desk and starts to walk out. Grabbing his arm, I stop him, but he doesn't look at me. "You need to trust me."

If you break down his three-word response, each word is innocuous and harmless all on its own, but the way he strung them together hurts as much as being stabbed slowly with the end of a spoon. In fact, I'm not sure any other man has ever hurt me as deeply as the pain those three little words inflict.

"Trust is earned."

CHAPTER 20

ASHER

"I'M OUT." I TURN OVER MY CARDS, INCLUDING MY PATHETIC PAIR OF twos, throwing them down in disgust. As I attempt to watch the rest of the hand play out, I pick up my Jameson, neat. Taking a long swallow, I savor the slow burn spreading in my nostrils, down my esophagus, and into my stomach.

I deserve it. I need it.

I want it to sweep through my bloodstream quickly and numb my brain, erasing my entire day.

My entire shitty day.

The potential acquisition we've been working on for months was flushed down the shitter today because of a huge unfunded pension liability we found during our due diligence. Thank God we found it, because after the HMT patent debacle and the current embezzlement mess we're in with CFC, the last thing we need is to inherit another pile of financial crap, but we were literally just two weeks away from closing that deal. Months of work, wasted.

Then Tara told me she needs six weeks off at the first of the year because she's having "female" surgery. Tara's like my fucking right arm. Without her I'll be lost, even if it is just for a short period of time. I couldn't be an asshole and tell her she couldn't have time off, even though those words were on the tip of my tongue. I wanted to ask if she could work from bed, but I figured I'd probably be violating all kinds of employment laws with that request, so I smiled politely and kept my mouth shut. She assured me she knew of a couple good temps that would work "so well I wouldn't even know she was gone." Not highly likely.

And then of course there's the way I handled the situation with Alyse. I'd gone to find her in hopes of spending a few stolen minutes selfishly getting lost in her, only to find that fuckhead, Aaron, hitting on her.

I handled the situation poorly. I know that. I knew it at the time, but it was like having an out-of-body experience. My body and my mouth had been taken over by some unknown force. I hovered ten feet above, watching it play out like a bad fucking movie that I couldn't pause or rewind.

I could anticipate the next assholeish thing I was going to say, only I couldn't stop myself from opening my mouth and vomiting the hurtful words. They were sharp and caustic and not at all the way I felt. The only thing I could envision was Natalie all over again and the certain agony I would feel at Alyse's betrayal.

Alyse is not Natalie.

Free the chains.

Fuck.

"Hey, asshole. You in or not?" Conn asks.

"Why wouldn't I be?" I snip.

"Oh, I don't know. Maybe because I've taken you five out of the last six hands and three of those you should have won. Head in the game, brother, or I'll clean you out."

Damn Conn. He's right. "You can try."

I'm down five hundred already tonight, so at the rate I'm going, it actually won't take him long to take the rest. Shit, I should just hand it over and be done so I can go grovel at the feet of the woman who's been ignoring my calls and text messages all damn evening. By the time the red haze faded so I could actually think clearly, Alyse had already left for the day. I haven't seen her since I was the Prince of all Jackasses walking out of her office while spouting some bullshit that was completely untrue.

I *trust* Alyse. I just don't trust anyone with a dick to get within ten feet of her. She has no fucking idea the innate magnetism she exudes. She draws people to her without even trying. I don't know if it's her inner beauty or some goddamn scent she emits or the shimmery aura surrounding her that everyone unconsciously sees, but whatever it is, people are powerless to resist.

Especially men.

"You start, Ash." Conn is leaning back in his chair. By the smirk on his face, he's clearly enjoying watching my inner turmoil.

Without a word, I throw in a twenty-five-dollar chip before Conn deals the next hand.

We play our regular Thursday poker games with two of our board members, Graham Billowy and Marcus Hemsley, and our Vice President of Security, Carey Christensen.

I usually enjoy our Thursday nights. I rarely skip, unless I'm traveling for business. Whenever I'm in town, I make it a priority to attend. Except these last few weeks the only thing I've wanted to do is spend my Thursday evening with Alyse instead. I want to spend every single free minute with her. Now I understand why Gray bailed on us. Until he reunited with Livia, he was our sixth.

After the flop, I throw in another twenty-five.

"Shit luck on the Willow acquisition," Graham says, chewing on his cinnamon toothpick. Outside of board meetings, I'm not sure I've ever seen the guy without a piece of wood in his mouth. He has to have splinters lining his entire GI tract.

"Better we find out now," I reply brusquely. I really don't want to discuss business. I don't want make idle chitchat about anything, actually. I just want to be buried inside Alyse, whispering my apologies until she forgives me.

When the turn comes, I look at my pocket aces and up the bet to a hundred. I've already lost five hundred tonight. The maximum I let myself lose in an evening is a grand, and with the way I'm carelessly throwing money into the pot, maybe this will be my last hand. One can only hope. I risk a look up at Conn to see him smiling and shaking his head at my bet. He knows exactly what I'm doing.

"By the way, I think I'm in love," Carey quips, calling my bet.

"What else is new?" Conn replies, also calling. Carey is thirty-five and divorced and, at five feet nine inches, is probably about thirty pounds overweight.

"No, this time I mean it. She's absolutely stunning. I think it was love at first sight."

I've lost count at how many times he's sat here telling us he was 'in love.'

"Have you even talked to her this time or are you just stalking her?" I ask. Carey is a great guy. Smart. Loyal. And a heart as big and deep as the ocean, but because his wife left him for another man, he lacks confidence. Hell, that's probably why she left him in the first place, so he has a very difficult time actually approaching women. He tends to stalk them from afar instead. It's actually kinda creepy. Will probably land him in jail someday.

Once the river is laid, I see I have three of a kind, so I throw in another hundred-dollar chip. This time Conn laughs out loud.

Fucker.

"No. I talked to her. Bumped into her in the cafeteria earlier this week actually. She's working on some sort of short-term project for CFC, but wouldn't say what."

My head snaps to my left, which is where Carey is sitting. In about sixty seconds, he's gonna wish he was sitting across from me instead, because at this angle, it would be all too easy to wrap my hands around his throat and squeeze the ever-lovin' life right out of his pudgy little body. I feel the haze that clouded my vision and judgment earlier return with sweet vengeance.

155

He can't be talking about anybody else but *my Alyse*.

"Really? What'd she look like?" I try to sound nonchalant, but with my jaw clamped so tight, it comes out more like a hiss. If Carey was smarter, he'd catch on and shut his big fucking mouth before he digs himself further into his own grave.

"Oh man. Gorgeous. Couple inches shorter than me. Long, dark wavy hair. Eyes the color of melted caramel. Killer curves. And she actually has a personality. She was sweet, smart, and funny. Literally the whole package wrapped up in one tight little beautiful body. And her name was just as beautiful. Alyse." The way he draws out Alyse's name, letting it reverently roll off his tongue as if he'd like to savor it on his taste buds first, is the final trigger.

Remember that haze that I said was clouding my vision? Well now it's turned thick and sticky and dark.

Red.

Blood red.

The exact color of the very liquid pumping through Carey's veins, which is just about to be spilled all over Conn's off-white carpet, permanently staining it a dark pink, forever marking the day that I killed my friend because of the way he's talking and thinking about my woman.

I throw my cards on the table, pushing my chair back so hard it flies across the room. Before I can even lay a hand on Carey, who now looks in fear for his life as he damn well should, a pair of strong arms wrap around me from behind, pinning mine down.

"Have you lost your fucking mind?" Conn hisses in my ear. "Sorry, guys. Asher's off his meds today."

Dragging me into the kitchen of his apartment, which is in the same building as Gray's and mine, he finally lets me go with a shove, blocking my exit with his bulk.

"What the hell is wrong with you?"

Leaning against the fridge, I grab my head in my hands, pressing my skull between them hard. I have no fucking idea what's wrong with me, other than the fact that I've fallen madly and deeply in love with Alyse Kingsley and it's completely fucking me up. I don't want to share her with another single soul. It's selfish and controlling and completely unrealistic, but I don't want another set of male eyes to even graze over her. Ever.

She's mine.

Christ. I've completely lost my shit.

"Nothing," I finally grate. "Bad day."

"Like hell. It's Alyse, isn't it? What happened?"

Sometimes it's great to have a twin. They think like you, they generally like the same things you do. A twin is a built-in best friend. But other times, like now, it's fucking irritating, because they know you just as well as you know yourself. It's almost impossible to bull-shit them.

"You mean other than the fact that every single male within a five-mile radius wants to fuck her? Not a goddamn thing."

Conn laughs. Actually has the balls to stand there and laugh at me. "Well, she is smokin'."

I push off the fridge, intent on raining a world of pain down on my brother in the next five seconds when he throws up his hands in mock surrender, taking a couple steps backward. "Just kidding, Ash. Well, not really, but I have no interest in Alyse. She's not my type."

"Right, because your type is five foot seven, curvy, and redheaded."

Conn's playfulness suddenly evaporates and his jaw ticks with anger. It was a low blow to bring up Nora, but I'm feeling pretty fucking low at the moment. I need to drag someone down into the bowels of the gutter with me.

I think we've made it clear I'm a jackass sometimes.

"Sorry," I mumble. Conn likes to hear about Nora just about as much as I like him to bring up Natalie.

He simply nods and his anger vanishes. That's probably the thing I admire most about him. He bounces back like a rubber ball and has the biggest capacity to forgive of anyone I've ever known outside of our mother. That, and his ability to detach himself emotionally from a situation, evaluating it thoughtfully from all angles. I jump to the worst possible conclusion while Conn sees the best in people until proven otherwise.

"What has she done to get you so twisted? You're acting like a goddamn lunatic."

I sigh, taking a seat at the kitchen table. "She hasn't done a damn thing. It's all me. Men flock to her like flies on shit and I can't stand it. I'm irrationally jealous, like on the verge of spending the next ten to twenty in cell block ten of the Illinois State Pen for attempted murder."

Conn takes the chair across from me. "Jesus, you're in love with her," he says incredulously.

I laugh, because it feels like so much more than love. I suddenly wonder if I ever loved Natalie at all. The feelings I have for Alyse are so different, so intense, so consuming, they almost border on obsession. And the thought of losing her to someone else makes me fucking homicidal.

"I am," I sigh, scrubbing my hand over my face.

"How does she feel?"

God, I wish I knew. "Not sure, but after today, she may never talk to me again. I fucked up big time."

"What'd you do?"

I stand and pour myself another whiskey in a fresh glass, taking a healthy gulp before answering. "I walked in on my director of finance with his hands all over her, just seconds away from kissing her. Jesus, I could see the lust in his eyes. I have never felt such rage, even when I walked in on Natalie that night. I wanted to kill him with my bare hands, Conn."

"Oh boy. What happened?"

"He left, unfortunately unscathed. Alyse and I had words. She told me she wasn't attracted to him and said I could trust her."

"Oh Christ, Ash. Tell me you didn't."

He doesn't need to ask. He knows exactly what I said, but he's going to make me speak the words anyway. I look down at my caramel-colored whiskey, which reminds me of Alyse's eyes.

Warm. Deep. Beautiful.

And full of unknowns that could hurt me.

"I told her trust is earned."

"Jesus, Asher. You fucking asshole."

"I know. Trust me. I know."

"You need to make this right," he replies adamantly.

"I've been trying. She won't answer my calls or texts." And part of me even wonders if she'll show up in the office tomorrow. Hell, she's probably halfway back to Detroit by now, making arrangements for one of her other auditors to take her place.

Dammit.

"You're probably one of the most tenacious people I know, Asher. Get on the damn elevator and go down the five floors to her apartment. Make her listen to you."

"I don't even know what to say."

"Tell her the truth."

Taking another drink, I savor the bite. "And what's that?"

"That some other woman permanently fucked you in the head." I half expect him to laugh, but he doesn't. He is serious.

"That's not true."

"Yeah. It is," he chuckles. "Look, I know you don't like me to bring up her name, but Jesus, Natalie did a number on you and I told you last week that you can't be what Alyse needs until you let that shit go. I know you don't want to hear it and you may not even believe it's true, but sometimes you can't see the forest through the trees, brother. The fact that you just about assaulted a good friend of ours in the other room ten minutes ago says it all."

I'm silent, which is apparently Conn's clue to keep talking, even though I wish he'd shut up.

"You have it all backward. Guilty until proven innocent is fucked up and a lonely way to live. Listen, I don't claim to know exactly how you feel, having the woman you love cheat on you, but not every woman is Natalie. Alyse *isn't* Natalie. And you can't put Natalie's shit on Alyse like you did today. She's an attractive woman, Asher, and you're going to have to deal with that better than trying to take out any guy who looks at her with a little appreciation or you're gonna find yourself blowing in the wind. Alone.

"I don't know Alyse all that well, but she doesn't seem like the kind of woman who would put up with that possessive jealousy bullshit. And in all of my twenty-nine years, I've *never* seen you act like this over a woman, not even when Natalie screwed you over. Alyse is the real deal, Ash. Don't fuck it up and let the best thing that ever walked into your life walk back out because you can't get out of your own way."

I listen to his insightful words and I know he's right. Then I decide to tell him the other thing that's bothering me. Hell, I might as well peel all my skin off at once. "She doesn't know about my...*preferences*." That was always an issue with Natalie, even though she pretended to like it at the beginning. Natalie pretended to be a lot of things she wasn't.

"And you still want that even though it makes you homicidal if another man looks at her? That makes no sense, man."

I shake my head, because he's right. It's a complete contradiction, but it doesn't change how I feel about either thing. "Yes."

"I'll believe it when I see it."

"You're not going to see shit, brother. Ever." My glare pulls a laugh from him.

"You know I didn't trust Natalie from the very beginning, Asher. Everything she did had an ulterior motive. Alyse is not like that. Alyse is real and honest and sincere. If it's not her thing, I think she'll tell you."

I nod, hoping he's right. "Why do you want me to talk to Natalie so damn bad if you never even liked her?"

"I told you, you need closure. I could give two shits about her. It's *you* I care about." Maybe he's right. I file that away in my 'I'll think about it later' pile.

"She's hiding something. Alyse. I just don't know what."

"Aren't we all? Maybe if you open up, she will too."

"It was a hell of a lot easier when I didn't have to worry about what a woman thought."

"Maybe. But nothing truly worth having comes easy."

True that. And Alyse is absolutely worth having.

Throwing back the rest of my whiskey, I stand, as does Conn. Pulling him in for a quick hug, I can only say, "Thanks, brother."

And then I'm out the door, but instead of waiting for the elevator, I head toward the stairs, intent on getting to my woman as fast as possible so I can right this wrong that I've created.

Conn's right. My past is fucking up my future.

I can't let that happen.

CHAPTER 21

ASHER

I RING THE BELL.

No answer.

I knock on her door.

No answer.

I try her cell phone again.

No goddamn answer.

I could turn around and go back to my apartment, forgetting that everything I want and more importantly, *need* and *crave* down to the marrow filling my bones is right behind this two-and-a-half-inch piece of locked wood, to which I have the key.

I could turn and walk away, waiting for her to come to me.

I could do a lot of things besides what I'm about to do.

But fuck that.

My entire future is contained within the four walls standing before me. I won't let it slip away without a fight.

I slide the extra key I have for our executive apartment from my pocket, glide it in the lock, and open the door to complete silence and near total darkness.

The only light in the entire apartment comes from the hot flames being thrown by the gas fireplace, which appears to be going at full blast. My relief is palpable. Alyse must still be here. Certainly she wouldn't have left town with a raging fire going.

Looking for her, I take a quick sweep of the room, which is relatively small, but about average size for a downtown high-rise apartment in Chicago. The main area is an open floor plan with the kitchen to the right and the main living area straight in from the front door. Through the main room to the left is a short hallway that has a common bathroom, a master bedroom at the end with an en suite bath, and another small bedroom. We have the entire apartment decorated warmly with neutral colors and high-end furniture.

The whole space is not much more than twelve hundred square feet. It rarely gets used. When it does, it's sufficient enough for a short stay until our executives find permanent housing. That's one of the reasons I suggested it to Alyse, but the real reason was I wanted her just steps away from me at all times.

Not seeing her in either the kitchen or living room, I deduce she must be in bed, even though it's relatively early at only ten o'clock. I quietly close the door and have taken only three steps before I freeze.

My cock is instantly so hard I could jackhammer concrete.

Lying on the plush white area rug in front of the raging fireplace is Alyse. Even though it's a chilly twenty-two degrees outside, the heat from the fireplace has quickly warmed this small space. Alyse has taken full advantage of it.

She's wearing an almost sheer white tank and black lacy panties that look like little boy shorts from the side, but you know once you get a glimpse of them from the back, they will be those cheeky kind that frame a woman's heart-shaped ass to perfection. Goddamn genius invention, those.

Her attire alone is a man's walking wet dream and is sexier than almost any lingerie I've ever seen, but it's what she's doing that has me nearly whipping out my dick right here, right now, and following her lead.

From my angle, I can't see her face because the loveseat is in the way. I can only see her body. And sweet baby Jesus, I've never seen anything as hot as what I'm currently witnessing.

Fuck.

Me.

This moment will be singed into my corneas for the rest of my days.

She has her top pulled up on one side, palming a breast, tweaking her nipple. The other mound is still covered by the thin white cloth, but because of the firelight, I can see the outline of her dark areola, and I can definitely see her pebbled nub trying to poke through.

But the thing that has my rapt attention is the fact that she has her panties pushed aside while she fucks herself with a vibrator. And not just any vibrator. It's the kind that massages the clit at the same time. I'm not sure I've ever been this jealous of an inanimate object in my entire life.

As she works herself into a frenzy, her breathy moans mix with the low noise of the fireplace fan. After only three weeks, I know Alyse's body intimately. We are in tune like we've been together our entire lives.

I know the exact spot on her neck that will convince her to acquiesce to my every sinful desire.

I know exactly how hard to suck her nipples, delivering just the right amount of pain to mix exquisitely with the pleasure I'm lavishing on other body parts.

I know the precise amount of pressure she needs on her clit to unravel and come repeatedly all over my fingers, my tongue, or my cock.

And I can tell when she's getting close to climax by the flush on her skin, the change in her breathing, and the little hitch in the back of her throat. By her current level of breathlessness, I'd say she's getting pretty damn close to flying.

I unconsciously reach down to stroke my pulsing cock through my jeans. I think it's highly possible I could embarrass myself and come in about five pulls. I'm not at all sure I even care.

I want to move and watch her face as she falls headfirst into what I can tell will be one intense orgasm, but I don't want her to stop. She obviously doesn't know I'm here and I don't want her to. I need to watch her through completion.

Once I hear low curses, I have to force my hand down to my side or I won't be able to stop myself from coming with her. And when she finally falls over that elusive ledge, crying *my* name, I can't help but move a few steps to the right, embracing the voyeur in me.

My favorite part of making love with Alyse is watching her face when she comes. Her pleasure becomes my own, especially when it's me forcing her body to places I know she hasn't been before.

When I finally get a glimpse of her pleasure-laden face, I suck in a breath. Christ almighty, she is absolutely magnificent. I have never seen a single thing more beautiful than Alyse in the throes of orgasm. I want nothing more than to bury my face between her legs and lap up every drop of her release. It belongs to me. I crave it on some primal level that I can't even explain.

I shamelessly watch her come down. Her body slowly stops shuddering and she works to control her breaths as she withdraws her little pleasure wand, now coated with her juices, and drops it with a heavy thud to the floor.

Alyse's eyes are tightly closed, but if she opens them at all, she'll see me blatantly staring at her, ravenous hunger etched over every inch of me. It's taking all my willpower to not scoop her into my arms and fuck her against the closest object.

Chancing it anyway, I move quietly forward and take a seat on the couch, letting my legs fall open. I have to carefully adjust my cock. He's throbbing and on edge. One wrong move and he'll erupt. The need to palm myself is powerful, but I won't. The need to just sit here and drink in the sight of the woman who has become my entire world wins out over releasing the agony that's drawn my balls tight.

I savor each second, because I fear once she realizes I'm here, she'll kick my ass out.

So I sit.

I watch.

I wait.

And about fifteen seconds later, my visual worshipping is shattered when she opens her eyes.

CHAPTER 22

ALYSE

"WHAT THE FUCK, ASHER!" I SCREAM, SCRAMBLING TO SIT UP. I PULL MY ear buds out and climb to my feet, but my legs are wobbly, both from my recent orgasm and the anger now coursing wildly through my bloodstream. "How the hell did you get in here?"

A slow smile eats his face. He proudly holds up something gold and shiny between two deft fingers, waving it idly back and forth. "Extra key."

I am completely mortified at the thought that he just sat there and watched me masturbate. And the fact that I practically yelled his name?

Oh.

My.

God.

How dare he.

"Get out." I stab my finger toward the door. I wish to hell I was wearing something that covered more. I'm also wishing I hadn't played Enigma on my Pandora app, which caused me to get so goddamn worked up I had no choice but to relieve the building pressure or I wouldn't be able to sleep. Asher has gotten my body so attuned to sex every damn day that, even through my hurt and anger, all I can think of is how much I miss the press of his perfectly honed, masculine body against mine.

"No."

"No?"

"That would be correct."

Like a petulant child, I huff angrily and make my way to my bedroom, trying to slam and lock the door, but a well-placed foot thwarts that idea. I sigh and keep heading toward the bathroom, so I can at least grab a robe to cover up. But he's on my heels and grabs it out of my hand as I go to put it on.

"Asher, stop. Just leave. Please." The last word comes out soft and weak. I'm a little buzzed, emotionally drained, and I'm just not up for a verbal sparring match tonight.

After he crushed me with his three little words, I couldn't concentrate. I tried to work, but finally gave up at four and left for the day. For about half a second, I briefly considered calling Al and swapping jobs with him, but I'm no quitter. I took this job, I committed to it, and no matter what happens with Asher and me personally, I will not shirk my professional responsibilities. I can't do that to myself, my employees, or my business.

So I came home, took a bath, had a bottle of wine, and shed just a few tears. My anger has mostly dissipated, but the hurt lingers. Words are powerful. Too easily thrown around. I have to believe that Asher didn't really mean them, but it doesn't remove the sting they left behind either.

Playing his dominance card, he frames my face in his hands. "When I saw his hands on you, I lost my mind. I do trust you. I'm so sorry, Alyse."

"Okay."

"Okay? Just okay?"

I shrug. "What do you want me to say, Asher?"

"Yell, scream, hit me. Do whatever you need to do. I deserve it. I was an ass. I overreacted. I'm so sorry. But I want you to tell me you forgive me."

"All right. I forgive you," I tell him, my voice monotone. And I do. *Mostly.*

He drops his hands and takes a step back, staring at me for an eternity. Then he does something unexpected. He walks to the shower and turns it on. When he draws his shirt over his head, my mouth waters against my will.

Asher has just a smattering of dark hair over his toned pecs. His abs are so damn cut, you could hold water in the grooves for later consumption. And the "V" that disappears under the waistband of his jeans? Jesus H. Don't even get me started.

"What—what are you doing?"

"I need a shower," he replies, shoving his unbuckled jeans down his trim hips. Roped muscles ripple enticingly with every movement, making my sex throb in anticipation. His grey boxer briefs, which frame his fine package perfectly, quickly follow. Christ, he's so thick and long and hard I have to lock my knees to stop from dropping and sucking him until he's mindless with pleasure.

I'm trying hard to remember why I was mad.

"Uh, you have a shower in your apartment," I manage to say, after I peel the tongue from the roof of my mouth.

"But you're here."

"Asher—" He sets a finger to my lips, silencing me. He quietly strips me of my skimpy clothes and leads me under the hot spray, remorseful eyes never leaving mine.

I let him.

Against my better judgment, I let him wet and shampoo my hair, while I close my eyes and silently relish his gentle touch.

I let him tenderly wash my body, even though this is the third time I've been cleaned today and my skin will be as dry as the Sahara.

I let him trail his lips over every part of me while his sincerely and earnestly mumbled *sorrys* sink through my skin and into my battered soul, healing the tiny wounds he inflicted earlier.

And then I *beg* him to take me as he slowly slips into my impossibly wet sex and spends long, languid minutes making sweet love to me against the cool glass wall, solidifying our connection once again.

As he usually does when he's inside me, his eyes lock with mine. I've never known anyone who likes eye contact more than Asher. It's like he needs that connection so he can bore past my defenses, which are at their weakest when he's taking everything I physically have to give.

We are so attuned to each other already, words aren't necessary.

I feel his sincerity.

I feel his relief.

I feel his love.

And when we drop into bed, sated and happy, I curl my naked form around his and feel the day melt away like it never happened.

Only it did. And I may no longer be angry, but I still need to know why.

CHAPTER 23

ALYSE

MY EYES SLOWLY OPEN, BRINGING ME OUT OF THE DARK RECESSES OF slumber. I vaguely note it's still dark outside. A warm, hard body spoons me from behind. It takes me a minute to remember where I am and who I'm with.

Friday.

Chicago.

Asher.

I look at the digital clock, noticing it's early. Only six o'clock. Asher's usually up before now, running off to the gym or to an early morning meeting, but by the even, shallow breaths and steady rise and fall of his chest, I can tell he's still in a deep sleep.

I'm grateful, because I need a few moments to digest the dream I just had about Beck. I haven't dreamed about him in years and I have to wonder why I'm doing it now. Is it because I've fallen in love with

Asher and Beck's now haunting me or because I met a man who is almost his spitting image?

"What time do you get off, babe?"

"Three. Why?" I haven't seen Beck for a week. We've barely spoken during that time. After only three months, I've fallen hopelessly in love with him, but when he disappears for days at a time without a word, it hurts and pisses me off. During those times, he's distant and every single time I feel like he's trying to break things off. But then he comes back and is his usual charming, irresistible, attentive self and I forgive him again.

He says it's family stuff, but he won't tell me anything else. He's always so secretive about them, I'm beginning to think he's trying to hide me, although I'm doing the same exact thing with him, because I know neither my father nor Livia would approve. That makes me frown.

"Don't plan anything. I'll pick you up at your house at three-thirty. Pack a change of clothes and tell your dad you're spending the night at Ali's."

I'm instantly aroused and scared as hell. We've done a lot of making out, tons of heavy petting, but we haven't had sex yet. I've wanted to, only Beck's been the one to stop us from going further every single time. If we're spending the night together, that can only mean one thing. "What are we doing?"

"It's a surprise. God, I've missed you, babe."

Well that's your own damn fault, I think. "Okay. Three-thirty."

A little before five, we're pulling up outside a small, secluded cabin on the outskirts of Monroe, Michigan.

"Where are we?" I ask, looking around. There's a tiny lake with a small forest-green rowboat attached to a weathered wooden dock. Evergreen trees line the horizon as far as the eye can see. I don't notice another cabin or any other signs of human life besides us.

"My dad's cabin," he replies matter-of-factly. Turning off the engine, he opens his door. Before he gets out, he leans over and takes my mouth in a greedy kiss. Grabbing our duffels from the back, he exits. I guess that's my cue to follow, so I do.

The place is as rustic on the inside as it is on the outside. Puke green must have been the decorating theme. It's everywhere. The appliances, the pilled couch, and even one of the stucco walls carries the putrid color. The main area houses a small table and three chairs, a couch, and one armchair.

No TV. I notice an open door to the left and from this angle I see it's a bedroom.

My eyes wander, trying to glean any information about his family from the meager contents of the cabin, but it's generic, functional. No pictures, no knickknacks, no personality. Just the basic necessities for a weekend fishing getaway.

"What are we doing here?" I finally ask, admiring the view out the front window.

He comes up behind me, wrapping me in his arms. "Whatever we want," he whispers against the shell of my ear, before placing open-mouthed kisses along my exposed neck. Electric sparks ignite everywhere his body touches mine. You'd have to be ten shades of stupid not to get what he's saying, especially as his hand travels up to cover my breast.

"Beck." His name comes out on a breathless wave of desire.

Then his mouth is on mine and within minutes, our clothes are on the floor, we're lying naked on the double bed, and he's pushing into me slowly. The pain of my womanhood being breached is unlike anything I was prepared for, but Beck takes it slow.

"I tried not to fall in love with you, Alyse. Fuck, I tried," he whispers against my neck as he pumps leisurely, taking the utmost care to attend to me. "I'm done fighting it. I love you. God, I love you so much."

My heart races and soars at the same time. This is the first time he's said those words. "I love you, too," I reply. I'm breathless. I'm giddy. I'm high on teenage love.

He tells me repeatedly how much he loves me, that he can't believe he found me, and that he wants to spend the rest of our lives together. My naïve eighteen-year-old self believes him.

As painful as it is to have sex the first time, I can't imagine anything more perfect than that day. I was in love with Beck, it felt right, and I never regretted it. But even when he was inside me I remember the guilt because I wondered what it would have been like to have that moment with Asher instead.

I still remember every detail of that day like it was yesterday. We made love, we hiked, we fished in the tiny rowboat, not catching damn a thing. Then we made love again before we spent our first night together in each other's arms. He was selfless and sensitive to my every need and regardless of the fact that I'd thought about Asher, it made me fall in love with Beck even more.

Beck was perfect in many ways, but he was also a complete enigma at the same time. I never felt like I knew someone so well but not at all. He was vague about his job, his family, his past. He would only say "it's complicated." I never even knew his parents' names. All I really knew about him personally was that he was an only child. I didn't even know what he did for work and he said he never went to college.

Whenever I'd ask a question about anything he didn't want to talk about, he'd hedge or evade or distract me with his body.

I know what you're thinking.

Stupid, naïve girl. And in retrospect, you'd be right. But I was blindly in love, so I overlooked things I shouldn't have. I figured once we were married, he'd have no choice but to let me all the way in, so I let it go.

Then one fateful night everything was taken away from me. And I was left with grief and nothing but a mountain of questions that I'll never get the answers to. I still feel tethered to the Widowmaker's curve, where two more sad, weathered wooden crosses mark untimely deaths.

One for Beck.

One for our baby.

I find it ironic now that I can't let people in and I ended up loving a man who was exactly the same as me. Had that horrible night not happened, I have no doubt we wouldn't have made it long-term. There were too many secrets between us. He knew my mom walked out on us, but I never talked about her. I didn't talk about Livia and my resentment that she was never around. And he never knew my dad was a gambling addict.

Now that I'm in love again, I don't want that secrecy, that barrier between Asher and me, because ultimately it will destroy us. Secrets are nothing more than lies of omission and I'm a big, black cavern of them. I don't want to be this person. I don't want to lose the best thing to happen to me in a very long time because I'm incapable of exposing my inner ugly scars. I'm starting to think I need professional help.

"What are you thinking so hard about over there, baby?" Asher's breath skates over my naked flesh and a wash of heat instantly settles over me, bringing me back from the past firmly into the present.

So much, I want to say, but instead of telling him everything I'm really thinking, I deflect, because I'm a fucking expert in that art. And we do need to talk through last night with words, instead of with our bodies.

I need to make sure this relationship isn't going down the same path as my last one. Because I don't think I can handle it if it is. I loved Beck and losing him was hard. But already my feelings are so much stronger for Asher, and losing him...I just don't know if I'm strong enough to survive it. The fact that I feel this way about him so early in our relationship is extremely disconcerting.

"Who was she?" I ask quietly.

He stiffens behind me. "Who was who?"

"The woman who made you so mistrustful."

I turn in his arms so our faces are just inches apart. Reaching up, I trace his thick brow, lightly dragging my finger down his scruffy jaw. I want to look into his eyes and have him tell me the truth.

"What makes you think it's a woman?" He's not sarcastic, but asking like he genuinely wants to know.

"A woman recognizes another woman's handiwork in the *wounds* left behind on her man."

He laughs. "Is that so?"

"Yes."

"What do you think this elusive woman did?" He brushes a piece of errant hair from my face and I'm not sure I could be any more in love with him than I am right now. The words are on the tip of my tongue, but once they're out, I need to be willing to be completely honest with him. About everything. And I just don't think I'm quite there yet. But I *want* to be. I want to get there.

"Hmmm...if I had to guess it would be that she cheated on you."

He gazes at me thoughtfully. I easily see the hurt flicker in his beautiful blues. It makes me sad. It hurts my heart.

We both have a past. We've both endured pain at the hands of another person who was supposed to love us, yet here we are, willing to try again. Trying hard to unlock the chains, to be vulnerable, to open up. We're both struggling with former demons that want to keep us shackled and unhappy, and somehow that makes it a little bit easier. At least for me.

"It was a long time ago," he replies quietly.

"But the wound still runs deep."

A sad smile curls his lip. "It sounds like you know all about it." His reply isn't accusatory or confrontational. It's fact. He sees more than I think I let on. He wants me to know it. No one has ever gotten me like Asher. No one.

"I have my own wounds, yes." He has no idea that even *that* small admittance is a very big step for me. I take great pains to make sure everyone around me thinks I'm hunky dory, but deep down I'm just...not.

"I know, baby. You can trust me." We both smile at the exact words that caused this mess to begin with.

"I think that's something we both need to work on," I tell him.

"Hmm," he says thoughtfully, almost like he's far away. "I guess so."

I don't want to lose what we're building here and I suddenly panic. What if he decides I'm just too much work? That my outer shell is too damn hard to crack before he can get to the gooey goodness inside? I need to start opening up, as hard and painful as it may be. Maybe if I open the door just a crack at a time, I can get through this.

"You're the only person that I've ever wanted to let all the way in, Asher. The only one. I'm trying. I want you to know that." Tears well and I blink fast, trying to willing them away.

His eyes soften. Palming my cheek, he runs a thumb across my lower lip. Tingles shoot like fireworks through my veins, warming me inside. "It doesn't have to be all at once. We can go slow."

I breathe a sigh of relief. "Okay."

"So, I'm your man, huh?"

I roll my eyes, pretending to think for a few seconds before answering. When his hand squeezes my side, I squeal, "Yes! Yes!"

He tickles me until I'm begging for him to stop through broken gasps. When I end up underneath him, his arousal presses against my opening, and all playfulness evaporates. His eyes pin mine, penetrating into the depths of my very being. "Alyse." He says my name with such quiet reverence my eyes sting again. "Christ, I'm falling so hard for you. So damn hard."

My eyes drift shut as my heart greedily sucks in his words. Then his soft lips touch mine. "Tell me you feel the same. *Please* feel the same," he begs between kisses that are getting more urgent.

"Yes," I mumble against his warm mouth. "Yes, yes, yes."

When my legs instinctually part and he slides in, I ask breathlessly, "Don't you have to get to work?"

"Fuck work," he mumbles against my mouth, shifting his hips so he's angled just right before he begins driving me quickly to the gates of heaven.

In that moment, I swear I feel our two souls merging into one. The only word running through my mind as we make love is: *beginning*. I finally feel like that's what I've been granted.

A new beginning.

CHAPTER 24

ASHER

"Did you follow my instructions?" I ask quietly against her ear while I help her on with her winter coat. It's long and ivory, with a belt that cinches her tiny waist snuggly. She looks like a snow princess. Jesus, I want to strip her and fuck her before we leave, but I need to savor her later.

"To the letter." She angles her head, capturing my lips in a heated kiss. "Are you going to tell me where we're going?"

"No. And if you don't stop looking at me like that, we're not going to make it out the front door."

"That wouldn't be so bad," she replies as she turns. Throwing her arms around my neck, she places a series of soft kisses on my neck, up my jaw.

Groaning, I force myself to grab her shoulders and push her back.

"Baby, we have dinner reservations at seven-thirty. We're going to be late if we don't leave now."

She pouts, but I clasp her protruding bottom lip between my finger and thumb and give it a good tug. We turned another corner in our relationship yesterday morning. I want to tell her I love her so badly my insides ache with it. Every time I look at her I have to eat the words. But after tonight she may decide I'm not the man for her. I've already exposed myself so damn much I just can't take that final leap until after I see her reaction to what I want from her.

One last peck and I lead her to the elevator, down to the Lincoln Town Car that Henry is driving for us tonight. I don't use our corporate driver, Henry, very often, but I want tonight to be special. Besides, if she decides to flee, at least I'll know she has a safe way home. When she sees the car and Henry standing outside holding the back door open, she slides me an amused look and smirks.

"Pulling out all the stops, huh?"

I guide her into the backseat. Henry shuts the door behind me. "You have no idea, Alyse," I reply, tugging her close to me, kissing the top of her head. Her hair smells like coconut and I have to restrain myself from doing even one of the dozen wicked things currently running through my head or Henry may as well turn around and take us back to my place. I won't be able to stop with a simple kiss or a light touch. I'll be taking her right here in the backseat, Henry be damned. And I may not mind a little exhibitionism once in a while, but I don't necessarily want my dead father's best friend to watch me fuck my woman into next week.

Even I have my limits.

Tonight's plan is a nice dinner at The Metropolitan Club, a downtown high-rise restaurant entirely encased in glass with a breathtaking view of Chicago. It's next to impossible to get into, especially on a Saturday night, but since GRASCO is a member, I was able to manage a last-minute reservation. But after dinner, I plan on taking Alyse to an exclusive club that caters to *particular* tastes.

I'm not scared to let people see this part of me, but I am selective about who I tell. With Alyse, however, I find I'm actually *afraid*. This isn't something I indulge in often or even *need* to have regularly, but this was a part of me that Natalie could never accept and it has weighed heavily on my mind for weeks. Ever since fate placed Alyse Kingsley in my sights again. It's one of the reasons I warred with myself on whether to pursue her or not, but I simply could not stay away.

She's my weakness.

My kryptonite.

Her acceptance of every facet of who I am is as imperative to me as the air I breathe.

Alyse is innocent and pure and my worst fear is that she'll judge me, condemn me...and then leave me. In retrospect, maybe I should have told her about this part of me initially when I knew I was interested in her. I could have gauged her reaction, maybe stopped myself from falling so head over heels in love with her before it was too late. But I was selfish. I wanted her like no other. Now if she bails, I'll be permanently ruined for any other woman.

Conn was wrong when he said Natalie permanently fucked with my head. She fucked me up, yes, but the only woman who has the power to *permanently* destroy me from the inside out is currently tucked under my arm, her hand twined with mine.

"Everything okay?" she asks, her thumb circling lightly on the top of my hand.

No. Everything is *not* okay. My stomach is in knots. My body is flooded with so much apprehension that cloying adrenaline flows like hot, scorching lava right underneath my skin. "Why wouldn't it be?"

She tilts her head up, catching my eyes in the darkened interior of the car. Hers sparkle brightly with each passing streetlight. She's so damn beautiful it hurts to look at her sometimes. For not the first time, I wonder why the hell I ever let her get away from me so long ago. "You're quiet. You seem distracted."

God, how does she know me so well already? *Maybe the same way you know her.* I've never met anyone more perfect for me than Alyse. I answer as truthfully as I can without giving anything away. "I just want tonight to be perfect."

Leaning down, I capture her mouth in what's meant to be a sweet, simple peck, but it quickly turns into more. Next thing I know her back is against the cool leather, with me on top. My hand is traveling down the length of her body, which has far too much clothing on. I finally find naked flesh and am working my way back up her thigh when I hear a throat clear. I realize that the car has stopped.

Damn.

I reluctantly push myself off her, both of us trying to catch our breaths. Before I can get too far, she grabs the lapels of my suit, bringing me back on top of her. "It will be. Perfect," she whispers before pulling me into another ravenous kiss.

Alyse and I spent all morning in bed, talking, laughing, and indulging in each other. I should be sated, but I'm far from it. Hell as much as I've had sex these last few weeks, my dick should be ready to fall off, but my intense need for her only seems to grow, not wane. Being with her is more than just mind-bending sex. It's a singular closeness I haven't experienced with another living soul. I hunger for it on both a conscious and subconscious level.

I think for the first time I truly understand how Gray feels about Livia and why he could never let her go, either in his heart or mind. She was in his blood.

Everything about Alyse has sunk into my very essence. I know I won't be able to get her out no matter how hard I try.

"Dinner," I tell her, pushing myself off and helping her from the car.

Placing my hand at the small of her back, I lead her into the office building and to the elevator. When we enter, I punch the button for the sixty-seventh floor. She reaches down and grabs my hand.

"Why do I feel like tonight is a very big deal?" she asks quietly, staring straight ahead. We watch our reflection in the shiny, silver doors, but her eyes don't meet mine. We're the only ones in the small steel box so she doesn't need to be so discreet, but it's like she has this sixth sense that this conversation should be muted somehow.

"I want to let you all the way in, too." Her dark pools now flick up to catch mine.

"I'd like that."

My smile is short, but I squeeze her hand in reassurance. "I hope so."

A few moments later the elevator opens. We make our way down a series of hallways until we reach the restaurant entrance.

When I see Trudy is the hostess, I cringe.

Gray, Conn, and I regularly frequent the club. They have impeccable food, top-notch service, and a kick-ass view. Plus we have a minimum we're required to spend monthly to maintain our membership, so I know Trudy.

Very well.

Too well, unfortunately.

This, right here, is the danger of bedding too many different women. Eventually you'll meet the one who sets your blood on fire and you know you'll never be able to take another deep breath without her. But as much as you want to, you can't keep her locked away in your bedroom indefinitely. You'll want to take her out, show her off, and make sure every man in the entire continent knows she belongs to you. And by doing that, you risk running into some of the very women you've been intimate with.

Women are catty. Possessive. Some are downright mean-ass bitches. That's the category Trudy falls into, so when she spots me with my arm around Alyse, I can already see the claws emerge and whites around her eyes turn a smoky green.

Like many women over the last four years, she wanted more than I would offer. She thought she'd change me. Catch me. She couldn't. None of them could. I now know why.

I was waiting for Alyse.

"Asher, how nice to see you again," Trudy's high, syrupy voice sings.

Quickly assessing the situation, her eyes bounce back and forth between Alyse and myself, whom I possessively have pulled into me. There's no doubt we're here on a date. And Trudy has never seen me here with another woman.

"Trudy." I nod politely. "Reservations for two."

"Sure, sweetie," she replies with such false sweetness it could cause an instant cavity. She snares two menus and the wine list before turning, expecting us to follow. I can only hope she leads us in silence to our table, but that would be far too much to ask because Trudy is both classless and a grade-A bitch. We had a quick fuck against the bathroom wall once in a moment of weakness, or should I say sheer idiocy. She's made me regret it ever since.

"So, Asher," she calls from ahead of us, "if you're not busy later, there's this quaint new club that just opened in Old Town."

Alyse's steps falter momentarily. Her eyes widen as she turns to look at me. I shake my head, speechless. I don't even dignify her disrespect of Alyse with a response, because I do not want to lower myself to her standards, and if I open my mouth right now, that's exactly what I'll do.

Once we reach a fairly secluded booth in the back of the restaurant, I help Alyse off with her coat, then take mine off and let her slide in first, with me right behind. I could sit on the other side, but I don't want to be that far away from her.

"It could be just like old times." She winks, handing us our menus, but never takes her eyes from me. "You're the only one that does that thing with your tongue I like. *You* know."

"That's enough," I growl. I've never had my tongue anywhere on or near that bitch.

"No, no. It's okay, Asher. I'd really like to hear more," Alyse says with a sweet smile pasted on her face. She scoots right next to me, placing her hand high on my thigh, a move that is not missed by Trudy. If she moves her pinky slightly she'll be touching my cock, which is now starting to harden at the thought. I put my arm around her, circling the bare skin of her shoulder lightly with my index finger.

Trudy stands there dumbfounded, not knowing exactly how to answer, and suddenly, instead of feeling nervous, I'm insanely proud. I relax, sit back, and enjoy the show. Alyse just checkmated Trudy, beating her at her own damn game. I have to hold back my laughter at the verbal lashing Alyse is about to rain down.

"Uh…"

"If you mean how he moves it in achingly slow circles, teasing, but *neeever* quite touching until you're mindless with the need to come, but then he flicks it so fast on the sweet spot you'd swear he just turned into a human vibrator, then, God yes, I've been on the receiving end of that. *Many* times. Honestly, his tongue is Olympic gold-medal worthy."

My hand tightens on Alyse's shoulder at her wicked diatribe. Trudy's face turns a progressively deeper shade of pink with every word.

"But if there's a new trick he hasn't tried on me yet, doubtful because I think we've even invented some new ones, I'd love to hear it so we can try it out later. Maybe even before we leave." Then Alyse's pinky snakes up and her nail scratches my stiff shaft, causing my entire body to jerk.

Trudy catches the movement and I swear her head is about to explode. She huffs and spins, muttering a string of curse words under her breath, which I don't all catch, but I clearly hear *motherfucker* and *cunt* mixed in. Yep. She's classy.

After she's out of earshot, Alyse starts to say something, but I'm on her in a flash, cutting her off.

With my mouth.

And my tongue.

And my moan.

I kiss her deep and long and passionately until we're both breathless. "You are extraordinary. I want to fuck you right here."

Her eyes flare, not with fear, but with desire. Just like that, my nervousness about the evening dissipates.

"Oh, baby. Hold that thought," I whisper, smiling lasciviously.

"Asher, so glad you could join us this evening," a male voice interrupts.

I break my gaze away from Alyse to look up at Miles, the manager of the restaurant. "Miles, nice to see you. How's Ellie?" I put my arm around Alyse again, pulling her close. I need to adjust my cock, which is now being bitten viciously by my zipper, but I don't dare.

Miles clears his throat. "She's hanging in there. Second to last chemo treatment on Tuesday."

"Glad to hear it. She's on my mom's prayer chain."

"Thank you, sir. That's very kind." Then he looks at Alyse. "Nice of you to join us..."

"Alyse," she offers. "Alyse Kingsley." She holds out her hand and like the smooth old Italian operator Miles is, he takes the opportunity to bring it to his lips, lightly running them across her knuckles. I bristle, but Alyse squeezes my thigh with her other hand.

"Pleasure, Alyse. I'm pleased Asher finally deemed us worthy of bringing someone special around." He winks.

"She's my girlfriend," I retort, pulling her hand away from his. She laughs and it's like a beautiful string symphony to my ears.

"Your usual?" Miles asks with a sly smile.

"Yes, two please. And a bottle of the Marcassin Estate Chardonnay, please."

"Is the two thousand and nine okay?"

"Yes, thank you."

"Of course." Miles winks at me, making a hasty exit.

"You're ordering for me now?" she mumbles under her breath as he's walking away.

"You'll love it, baby. Trust me. They make the best beef wellington in town here." She's silent for a moment and I can't tear my eyes away from her.

"Your girlfriend?" she asks softly, searching my eyes. "Is that what I am?"

I lean over, whispering in her ear, "Only until I make you my wife." It may be far too early in our relationship to say such things, but in my heart, I haven't meant any words more that those seven.

She sucks in a surprised breath. I wait with bated breath to hear her response. She doesn't disappoint. "Are you big into labels?"

"Only ones that actually mean something," I retort, kissing her neck.

"I wanted to claw her eyes out," she moans.

A smile tugs at my lips, but I try to keep it at bay. Glad to know I'm not the only one feeling rather possessive. Reluctantly, I force my lips from her neck. "I rather enjoyed your verbal exchange to a physical one. You were brilliant."

She rolls her eyes.

"Now you know a little bit of what I'm feeling."

"Except I didn't fuck Aaron."

There's no point denying the truth. "Touché. But it was just once and I didn't have my tongue anywhere near a single part of her body, just so you know."

"That doesn't make me feel any better."

Stroking her cheek, I confess, "If I could undo it, I would. If it's any consolation, I regret it."

She shakes her head. I wish I didn't cause the frown that's formed on her candy-apple-glazed lips. "I'm sorry. We all have a past."

I cup her face. "My past has completely faded. I see no one who came before you. You are all I see, Alyse. You are my future. Only you."

Her eyes twinkle with moisture and I don't think I could I love her any more than I do in this moment.

Before Alyse can answer, a waitress interrupts with our wine. After I sample and approve it, she pours two glasses and gives us privacy.

"To a perfect evening," I say, holding up my glass to hers.

"To a perfect evening," she parrots, clinking mine then taking a sip.

With Alyse by my side, I have no doubt it will be.

CHAPTER 25

ASHER

"WHAT KIND OF CLUB IS THIS?" SHE WHISPERS THE SECOND WE WALK through the red steel, nondescript door. It's unmarked and looks more like the entrance to an industrial building than to a club. Since it's for members only, they don't want flashing neon signs drawing the general public in.

"The private kind," I reply, giving my name to the receptionist behind the glass booth.

When you enter Curieux, you are enclosed in a small ten by ten brightly lit space and met by a beautiful, but usually conservatively dressed woman behind the protective barrier. Anyone who happens to stumble across this by accident is easily sent on their way or escorted by security if they prefer the hard one.

But when you are granted access into the club itself, the entire atmosphere changes.

It's dark.

It's seductive.

The vibe is intoxicating. Liberating. Decadent.

While I'm not a member of Curieux, I do know the owner. He's one of my most important clients and a good friend, so I have an open invitation. I don't like to take advantage of my friends, however, so I don't come here frequently. And now I'm glad I don't. I want to share some first-time experiences with Alyse. If the night goes well, maybe I'll even consider becoming a member.

"Mr. Colloway, you may place your personal effects in here." The hostess opens a small twelve-inch door to her right where she slides out an intricately designed wooden, plum velvet-lined box. Cameras are a big no-no, so everything, down to pens and lapel pins are locked safely away until you leave.

I remove my cell phone, wallet, and money clip. I signal for Alyse's small clutch, which she silently hands over, but I see the dozen questions written all over her face. I shut the lid and lock and pocket the small key. I also remove our coats, giving them to her.

"Thank you, sir. You and your guest are free to enter."

I hear a buzz and the latch of the door to our right unlocks, as it has no handle on this side. Placing my hand on the small of Alyse's back, I usher her forward and push the steel entrance open, holding my breath.

As soon as the door closes behind us, I pin Alyse to the wall, taking her mouth in a hungry kiss. She moans, twining her hands through my hair. Her bare leg winds around mine as I palm her ass through the short, sexy, brilliant blue dress she bought this afternoon after wedding dress shopping with her sister. I want nothing more than to fuck her right now.

I force myself back and search her eyes, hoping she'll see my appeal. "Before we go any further, I need you to be open-minded."

"Okay," she answers tentatively, drawing out the word into almost a question.

"This is me letting you in."

Her eyes soften and she reaches up to cup my cheek with one hand. "Judgment-free zone here. Promise."

I nod, hoping she feels that way in a few seconds. Kissing the tip of her nose, I grab her hand in mine. We make our way down a dimly lit hallway until it spills into the guts of the club. The pounding thump of the sultry bass thrums through our bodies, setting a new rhythm for our hearts. There is an unmistakable sensual vibe that permeates every one of your senses, erasing inhibitions. I swear pheromones are pumped through the ventilation system.

"Wow," Alyse breathes beside me. She grips my hand tighter probably without even realizing she's done it. The first time I saw this, I felt the same way.

The club has two levels and while I've been to the lower level, it's pretty hard-core exhibitionism and not really my thing. I'm more subtle about my taste, not minding if someone happens to see or watch, but I don't go out of my way to fuck women in front of a room full of people, either. That doesn't get me off; that just feels like a performance.

This level of the club is very open with a dance floor taking up the entire center. It's still fairly early in the evening, but there are several couples twined and grinding on each other. The one rule on this floor is any sexual activity has to take place in a booth, not out in the open.

The whole place is black. The walls, the tile floor, the leather booths, the bar stools. All black. The right wall houses the long black marble bar and is dimly lit with purple florescent lighting.

Two-dozen booths take up the remaining three walls. They vary in size, from those for more intimate encounters to others that can accommodate a larger group. Every booth is secluded with walls that round slightly in the front and go all the way to the ceiling.

Each contains the same soft ambient lighting as the bar, which can be turned off by the occupants if they would like additional privacy, and translucent curtains, which provide a modicum of discretion. Due to the placement and situation, some of the compartments offer more isolation than others, as everyone has a different level of comfort and desire.

Tonight I've requested a rather secluded area toward the back of the club, because while I want to be here, I don't want to share her with the entire place either. Maybe that's the natural possessiveness coming out, but regardless, I still have this pulsing need to show her this side of me.

As Alyse stands quietly beside me taking it all in, I spot John, the club's owner, headed our way.

"Asher, glad you could make it again." John shakes my hand, but his attention is all on Alyse. I can honestly say I don't blame him, but I still don't like it. Even though I realize I made her buy the sexy dress she's wearing today after she sent me a picture from the dressing room.

"And who do we have here?" John asks, turning his body toward Alyse.

I pull her closer. "She's mine," I warn. John's a good friend, but he's also a player. I would not put it past him to make a play for *her*.

"Asher, stop." Alyse slaps my chest. "Alyse Kingsley," she answers, holding out her hand. He takes it, bringing it to his lips. I growl and John laughs.

"John Weaver, owner of Curieux. I guess you're off-limits. Too bad." He winks at Alyse and I'm about one second away from knocking his ass into next week when Alyse wraps herself around me, hands roaming underneath my suit coat, up my back.

Her touch calms my raging jealousy. Maybe this was a bad idea after all. Maybe Conn was right.

"I'm yours," she whispers in my ear. When her lips touch my neck, those thoughts flee and I harden painfully, one hand snaking up to fist her hair, while the other pulls her flush against me.

"Looks like I need to get you both to a booth," John says wryly.

After a quick, hard kiss, we follow him to the back of the club. Alyse keeps her head forward, but I can tell she's scanning the place without trying to look too obvious. I'm dying to know what's rolling through that pretty little head. I'm about to find out as John stops at the furthest table in the far northwest corner. It's secluded, but still open to anyone who decides to walk by.

"Enjoy your evening." He nods and winks as he turns and leaves.

"Come here," I tell her gruffly. Sitting down, I hold out my hand. She stands there looking between my face and my hand and I anxiously wonder what her next move will be.

Will she accept me for who I am and stay?

Or will she tell me I'm a sick son of a bitch and flee?

Yes. I'm absolutely thinking I should have disclosed this aspect of myself before I fell hopelessly in love with Alyse Kingsley. In the next five seconds, I will either be the happiest man alive or I'll be emotionally annihilated with my heart bleeding out on the dark floor beneath me, which is pretty apropos, considering that's what will take up the space in my empty chest cavity if she leaves.

Eternal darkness.

CHAPTER 26

ALYSE

My mind has been racing for the last five minutes, trying to catch up to exactly what I'm witnessing. Asher told me this afternoon he was collecting on his bet tonight, but I had no idea it would be this. It *has* to be this.

"When we win, you'll let me do anything I want to that sexy body. Whenever. Wherever."

The few couples on the dance floor could seem to care less that anyone is watching. While none are outright having sex, their hands and mouths freely roam each other's bodies as if they are in the privacy of their own bedrooms.

From my angle, I can see clearly into one circular booth without the translucent curtain drawn. A woman, with her back to me, is on her knees giving a gorgeous man a blow job. And by the look of ecstasy on his face as he guides her bobbing head up and down, she's doing a bang-up job.

I've heard of sex clubs, of course, read about them, too, but honestly never thought they *really* existed. In looking around, however, I quickly deduce this can be nothing else but.

And I've never seen anything more erotic in my life. I mean, I've watched pornos before, who hasn't? But watching a D-grade porno is nothing like what I'm currently witnessing in real life. It's a sensual feast for the eyes. I find that I am impossibly turned on.

Now it's all making sense. Asher's nervousness tonight. His mysterious words about "letting me in." He's showing me a part of him that he's not sure I will accept.

Now I'm standing before him in a secluded, dimly lit booth in the back of the club. I recognize the fear and worry in his eyes as he holds out his hand for mine. I hesitate only momentarily before I take it, and once I do, I visibly see his entire body relax.

"Baby," he whispers in my ear when he pulls me down to his lap. He buries his face in my neck and I wrap my arms around his head, holding him tightly to me.

"I won't be shared," I say. I've never been to a place like this, done anything like this, and am not exactly sure what Asher's proclivities are or what he expects of me, but I feel like I need to state my limits up front. Being passed around to other men like some object is not something I would ever entertain.

He pulls back, his eyes burning into mine. "No one touches you but me. You're mine. And if this makes you uncomfortable, we can leave."

I don't want to leave. God help me, I want to stay and see where the night goes. My pussy has been throbbing since thirty seconds in the door. Actually, it's been pulsating constantly since he told me he wanted to fuck me at dinner. "What do we do?"

His smile is slow, impossibly sexy. He hasn't shaved for a couple of days and all I can think about is getting those whiskers to burn my most sensitive skin.

"We have a drink, we talk, we relax. We see where the night takes us. I don't want you to do anything you're not comfortable with."

I trace his hairline lightly, committing every one of his beautiful features to memory. "What do *you* want?" I ask softly. His dick twitches underneath my leg, causing a gush of wetness to seep from my core. At this rate, I'll be putting a very visible, very telling stain on my new dress.

"Everything you'll give me, Alyse."

I start to tell him everything I am already belongs to him, but a feminine voice interrupts.

"Two Jamesons on the rocks, courtesy of Mr. Weaver." A beautiful, scantily clad waitress whose low voice is as sultry as a sex phone operator sets two amber-filled glasses down on the small table in the center of our intimate space.

"Thank you," Asher replies, barely giving her a glance to which I'm secretly glad.

Feeling a bit nervous, I reach for a cup and bring it to my lips. Whiskey isn't generally my drink of choice, but I only had two glasses of wine with dinner so I could use some liquid courage about now.

"Do you remember the Fourth of July that year?" he asks.

How could I forget? I'm sure my cheeks are tinged in embarrassment. In all these years, we've never talked about that day. "Yes."

"Jesus, I wanted you so damn bad, Alyse. I wouldn't talk to Conn for days afterward."

"Really?"

"Really."

"Why?"

He draws a line from the edge of my eyebrow down the curve of my face, watching his finger descend. It's intimate. I like the way it makes my stomach flutter. "Because I selfishly wanted to be the first man you took inside you. I don't like that someone else has that part of you that was supposed to be mine."

Swallowing hard, I let his words sink into my skin, enjoying the tingle as they race through my veins straight to that dark, wet place in my core.

We never talked about whether I was a virgin or not, but like everything else about me, I guess Asher knew. I tried to be brave that day, tried to be grown-up. He was a man, after all, and I was just a silly teenager, but I wanted him so bad I'd ached for days afterward with unquenched lust. I had a giant crush on Asher, even thought I was in love with him.

Maybe I was. I think maybe I've been a little in love with Asher Colloway for the last eight years, a part of me still with him even when I was with Beck.

Silently, he positions me so my back is against his chest, draping my legs on the outside of his, which indecently opens me up. I don't protest. I can't. I want to wade into the warm, scandalous waters he's leading us to. I want Asher to own me completely. I want to please him.

I want this more than I ever thought possible.

Leaning forward, he snags his own cocktail, but instead of drinking, it hangs loosely from his deft fingers. His free hand crawls up my torso, cupping my aching breast. Short nails scrape across my hardened nipple and my head falls back, resting against his shoulder.

"Even back then you'd crawled under my skin, Alyse." His voice is soft, seductive, luring me to sinfully wicked places. "You were like a sliver, and I didn't realize until I saw you again that it had never come out. You've been buried inside me for years."

He pulls down the low neckline of my stretchy dress, exposing my breasts for anyone who cares to walk by and see. My stomach free falls, my eyes drift closed on a moan, and my pelvis starts to move against the raging hard-on twitching in the crack of my ass. I feel drunk on uncontrolled want that's burning like an inferno inside me.

Whoever thought I would want to be taken in a place where anyone could watch? The thought never crossed my mind. But that's all I can think about as Asher rolls his chilly glass against an uncovered erect nipple leaving its cold condensation behind, pulling a gasp from my parted lips.

His lips graze my ear as he speaks, creating a chill that runs down the length of my spine. "When I'm with you, inside of you, I know you were created just for me. You're a part of me I didn't know was missing until I had you again. I think even back then I recognized you were mine, but I was too young and foolish to understand. I should have never let you go, Alyse. I should have pursued you."

His low, raspy confession slowly unravels me, blowing down every last defense I've built to keep people out like a poorly constructed house of cards.

Setting his drink on the bench to the side of us, he runs his strong hands up my bare thighs, spreading his wider, which opens me further. He reaches the junction of my thighs, but stops.

I can just imagine what I look like.

My full breasts falling out over the top of my dress.

The hem pulled up practically to mid-hip, displaying my drenched pussy.

Passionate desire tightening every inch of my face.

"Tell me you want this." His choppy hot breath washes over the column of my neck. I feel his chest heave behind me.

I am nothing but a hot mess of coiled want and need.

My nipples burn.

My sex aches.

Every nerve ending is a live wire.

"God, yes. Yes," I beg. "Please, Asher."

"Somebody could walk by. See you splayed out for my pleasure."

"I don't care. Touch me."

"Fuck, baby. You're perfect. You're beautiful. You're *mine*."

"Yes."

"Say it." His thumbs have been slowly drawing circles on my inner thighs, driving me absolutely mad with longing, and no amount of squirming is moving them closer to ease my ache.

"So bossy."

"Your body loves it, baby. Say it."

"I'm yours. I'm yours. I think I've always been yours," I breathe.

His hand loosely grips my throat, thumb turning my head to face him. I blink fast, trying to clear the sexual thrall I'm drifting in. "I may not have been the first man inside of you, Alyse, but I damn well assure you I will be the last."

"Asher—"

"What we're doing here? It's part of who I am and I desperately want you to accept it. Accept every kinky, jealous, possessive part of me. But if you can't, I would give this up. For you."

"I don't want you to give up anything for me, Asher. I love every single part of you."

His eyes and nostrils flare at my indirect declaration, but he says nothing.

The hand next to my sex now moves and our moment of romance and emotional vulnerability morphs quickly back into a swirling ball of flaming desire.

I have to admit I haven't quite followed Asher's instructions to a "T" as I said I would. He told me not to wear any lingerie underneath my dress, so I skipped the bra, but I'm wearing a very special pair of panties, if you can even call them that. I think Asher will actually appreciate them.

With our eyes locked, I see surprise register when his finger finds the beads that run the length of my sex.

"What the hell?" he breathes, moving the hem of my dress out of the way so he can see what I'm wearing. "Fuck, Alyse. Where did you get these?" His fingers skim my hairless sex as he traces the two separate strands of black beads running between my cheeks attached to the skimpy thong. If he takes me wearing these, I know it will feel as good for him as they have on me all night.

Every step, every cross of my legs, practically every breath has rubbed these decadent panties against my clit, and Asher's dirty words heighten my sexual need to almost volcanic proportions. I'm so close to erupting it will only take a light touch to make me explode.

"My favorite part of today was lingerie shopping."

"Jesus Christ. I had no idea they made such sinful things. I'm going to buy you a whole drawer full."

I smile, closing the scant distance between our mouths. He has me pinned completely against him and the thread of control he's been exercising all night snaps. I hear it. I feel it.

Asher is as mindless with want as I am.

"I'm going to fuck you with these on," he mumbles against my mouth.

"It'd be a shame if you didn't."

He groans and thrusts his hips up. "Legs up, baby. Relax your knees so you're open to me."

Oh God. I have never done anything so hedonistic in my life.

When I'm in position, Asher turns my head back forward, so he can whisper seeds of iniquities in my ear. His finger traces around the beads, which are coated thickly with my arousal.

"Remember I said I was going to corrupt you in the wickedest of ways?"

"Oh God," I moan, trying to draw his wet digit inside me. I've never, *ever* been this turned on.

"Ruin you in the best possible ones," he rasps before biting my earlobe.

"Jesus, Asher. Touch me, please." He circles my clit, teasing, never touching, as if reminding me who is in charge.

"Tonight I'm going to do both, Alyse. I'm going to finger fuck you until you're begging me to quench your ache with my cock instead. Then I'm going to take you so hard, I'll be lodged inside your very soul for eternity."

"I think you're all talk," I breathe, tired of being taunted. I'm seconds away from forcibly pushing his fingers inside me, using them like I did the vibrator the other night.

"Oh baby," he chastises. "I know what you're doing and it's not gonna work. I'm the one pulling the strings here. I want you absolutely fucking blind with need." I curse under my breath.

I am. My world has gone completely black.

He's still holding my head with one hand, teasing my pussy relentlessly with the other. Forcing my chin up and to the left, he latches onto my neck, sucking hard. The sudden move causes my hips to buck, but the sadistic bastard anticipates that and moves his fingers back just in time before they're impaled inside me.

"Asher, please," I beg.

His hand briefly leaves my face and I gasp when I feel an icy cold cube circling my left nipple. The fiery cold wanes to numbness as he continues to circle the tightened bud, before moving to the other to give it the same treatment.

"Tell me I own you, Alyse."

"You know you do," I pant.

"Every single part of you." So many sensations are occurring at once, my brain is short-circuiting. Cool water drips down the inside of my dress from the melted cube. Fire rains in every nerve ending. My sex aches to the point I don't think a dozen orgasms will relieve it. And when Asher dips a finger shallowly inside, I swear I almost come instantly. I moan so loudly I know people have to hear it. "My God, I love how wet you get for me," he groans, running my arousal back and forth over my labia. "The words, baby."

My entire body is screaming for release. I'd say I was blue and hailed from Mars if it got him to do something. "Yes, every part of me. Please fuck me with something. Anything. I'm begging you."

"So perfect," he murmurs.

He must decide I've had enough sensual torture, because when his fingers finally enter me, they draw the pearls tight against my engorged clit, giving me exactly what I need. And with only three thrusts in and out, my world implodes into bright lights and falling stars.

His name drops like a prayer from my lips. I shudder uncontrollably in his arms, warmth and pleasure racing up my spine, down to my toes. I'm barely coming down from the first when another is upon me. Over the course of the next few minutes, Asher forces so many orgasms from me, each sharper and harder than the previous, I'm dotted in sweat and every limb is weak. My muscles feel almost atrophied I'm so wrung out.

As Asher shifts to unzip his pants, I faintly register voices getting closer. I should shut my legs, but I don't. I should jump up and close the curtain, but I can't. The only thing I can do is beg him to ease my internal ache with his cock, just as he vowed.

Now.

Voyeurs be damned.

Positioning us on our knees, he wraps my hands around the back of the wide leather bench for leverage, pulling my hips back so I'm completely open to him and anyone else who cares to walk by. My dress is pulled halfway up my back and my breasts are dangling free. "Whatever you do, baby, don't let go," he roughly commands in my ear.

Starting at my shoulders, he runs a hand all the way down the center of my spine, over my bare ass, lightly kneading. I can feel his eyes burning a path down my exposed flesh, heat seeping into each pore. I hear him whisper, "I love this perfect ass. Christ, you are an absolute vision like this."

When his touch leaves me, I expect him to spread me and slide in, so I am not at all prepared for that hand to come back down with a hard *thwack* on my right cheek, spreading fire directly to my already drenched core. I squeal and jump, but his other hand steadies me, fingers gripping tight.

"Hang on," his gravelly voice demands.

"Ahhh," I cry out as he does it again and again, never too soft, never too hard, striking a different spot every time, making sure to cover each cheek thoroughly. With each slap, I feel the beads running up my center shift, rubbing against my back entrance and engorged clit. The sensation is heady, like nothing else I've ever experienced.

The smacks he's raining stop suddenly and my entire body is on fire with want, all of it radiating from my middle. I have never been this turned on before. Who the hell knew a spanking could be so erotic?

He runs a single finger down the entire length of my spine, not stopping until he's reached my sopping pussy, pushing inside with embarrassing ease. My need is spread across my inner thighs, clearly evident.

"My God, you love this, Alyse. Don't you?"

"Yes," I moan. My hips are moving in time with the thrust of his finger, but it's not enough. I need him. All of him.

He withdraws his wet digit, feathering it slowly back up the path he took earlier, taking a slight detour to rim my puckered flesh before continuing, leaving behind my trail of desire.

"Shit," I curse low and long.

"I love your ass this shade of pink, baby. You ready to be fucked hard?"

"God, yes. Please. Now."

"Such sweet begging," he croons. "Makes me so damn hard."

He positions himself against my drenched opening, dick tugged snuggly between the twin strings of beads and roughly enters me. I cry out sharply with each pounding thrust as worshipping words pull me further and further under his sensual enchantment.

He leans into me, front flush with my back. Fingers of one hand fisting my hair, the others digging into my hip, he drives into me so brutally I'm lifted with each pump of his hips. The scrape of his pants only heightens my sensitivity more. When supple lips find the curve of my neck and sharp teeth bite, like he's marking me as his, I detonate.

"Fucking hell, Alyse. I've never felt anything like this. Like you." His hot, ragged breath brushes against the shell of my ear. The raw hunger I hear in his tone showers a mist of erotic chills down on me.

My slick walls clamp down on a loud, broken sob and Asher's fingers tighten almost painfully, a guttural "fuck yes" hissing in my ear repeatedly as he joins me in our place of pure, unadulterated ecstasy. It's a place I can no longer imagine being taken to by anyone but him.

"Alyse...I...wow," he exhales on a rush, holding me to him tightly. His body still trembles slightly in the aftermath of his powerful climax. *Ditto*, I think, but can't possibly voice, because all of my muscles are on lockdown. When our bodies sag in sated weakness, I know it's time.

Asher has let me into his world completely. I need to do the same. I just hope I can figure out how before it's too late.

CHAPTER 27

ASHER

"Thank you for tonight. For accepting me," I confess into the darkened room.

Alyse is sprawled over me, her leg pinning me to the bed. The feeling of having her in my arms and in my bed after the night we shared is nothing short of total and complete serenity. I've never been more at peace.

"You don't have to thank me, Asher. I—honestly, I wasn't sure what to think at first, but I'd be lying if I told you I wasn't turned on. I told you I wouldn't judge and I didn't. I enjoyed myself, actually."

"I'm glad."

"Do you think anyone...saw us?"

I laugh. "Doubtful, given where we were in the club, but it's the thought that they *could* that drives that need in me the most, I think.

I'm not a hard-core exhibitionist. Would you be embarrassed if they did?"

She's silent for a few beats. I pray she doesn't have any regrets. That would gut me. "I'm not sure. I don't want an audience standing there, clapping when we're done, throwing twenties, but I have to admit, the thought of someone seeing the wicked things you were doing to me from afar turned me on more. When we first came in, I watched this woman giving a guy a blow job and I..."

"You what," I prod when she goes silent for too long.

"I liked it," she whispers so low I almost can't hear.

I hook a finger under her chin, tilting her head up. "Alyse, there is nothing to be embarrassed about. Everyone there is either a member or an approved guest and they all have the same preferences."

"How can you want to share me like that, but you can't stand the thought of another man even looking at me? I can't reconcile that."

I sigh heavily, because I've been asking myself that same exact question for weeks. It makes no sense, but I'd repeat tonight again in a fucking heartbeat. It was the single hottest sexual experience of my life.

"I don't know, Alyse. I don't know exactly how to explain it. It's a part of me I never fully understood, just accepted. You may have noticed I took you to the most remote part of the club, so the risk was obviously still there, but the chance of getting a lot of attention was small. Maybe on some subconscious level, I don't want to share you as much as I thought I did."

"Do you want to go back?" she asks.

"Do you?"

"Yes," she whispers and I can't help but smile. She may have a kinky side, but this isn't engrained in her like it is me, so I have to think she'll always be embarrassed about the rush it gives her.

"Then we shall."

"Do you go there often?"

"No. That was only the third time I've been."

"Did you ever..."

"Have sex?" I finish for her.

She nods.

"No."

I feel her body relax. "I'm glad."

"Me too."

"Do you have sex in other public places?"

"Every chance I get," I joke and it makes her laugh. I love her laugh.

I love her eyes.

I love her intelligence.

Hell, I love everything about this woman.

My thumb traces the outline of her full, sexy lips and I know this is the right time to say the words bursting inside me.

"You are the most remarkable woman I've ever met, Alyse, and not just because of tonight. You're strong, yet vulnerable. You're innocent, but wild. You're like this multifaceted, multilayered puzzle. To get to the next level, I have to find the key to unlocking the first one. I can't tell you how desperately I want to unlock every single one of your layers until I'm at your very core."

"Asher—"

"Let me finish, baby. I know it may seem too early to say this, but I know deep in my very being you're mine. I'm in love with you, Alyse. I'm so fucking in love with you, I can't think straight. You don't have to say it back. You don't have to respond, but I need you to know how deep my feelings for you go and you should know I don't intend on ever letting you go."

She shifts, climbing on top of me, her nakedness arousing me all over again. It's dark and I can barely make out much beyond her shadow, but when she takes my face in her tiny hands, I know she's looking me in the eyes. "I'm fucked up." She pauses and her anxiety seeps into me. I slowly run my hands up and down her torso, patiently waiting for her to continue. "Every single person I've loved has left me, Asher. Every single one, including Livia. I want to give you every one of my keys, but I don't even know if I can remember where they're all hiding anymore."

"Then we'll look together until we find them all."

"Asher, I'm...scared to be hurt again."

"Me too, but I won't leave you." She leans down and I embrace her tightly. "I love you, Alyse. So, so much."

"I'm terrified of how much I love you, Asher."

"I'm your steady. I won't fail you. Ever," I tell her again, knowing now she needs this reassurance and probably will daily until she truly believes she can count on me to keep my promises.

"How do you know? How can you be sure?"

"My love," I whisper against the shell of her ear, threading my hand in her hair. "I know because I feel my heart truly beating for the very first time and leaving you is equivalent to ripping it out myself. I literally can't breathe with the thought of not having you in my life. It's simply unfathomable. Not even in the realm of possibility."

She's quiet for several seconds, before softly pleading with me, "Don't ruin me in the worst possible way. Please."

"Only the best, baby. I promise. Only the very best."

Alyse's few words have given me so much more insight into the real her than anything she's said in the last few weeks. She's been hurt repeatedly. I won't be one of those people. I know that no matter what happens, I will keep that promise I just made to her.

There is nothing in the world that would cause me to abandon the woman I love more than life itself like everyone else has.

Not a goddamn thing.

CHAPTER 28

ALYSE

"ALL BILLS ARE CAUGHT UP AND I RAN PAYROLL TODAY," HEATHER'S SOFT voice carries through the receiver.

"Good. Thanks," I reply, relieved to have enough money that we don't have to worry.

"I also received the quote from the web developer this morning on the enhancements you want done. I'll email that to you when we get off the phone."

"How much?" I ask, not able to wait.

"Five grand for full redevelopment, less than one for just some basic enhancements."

Five grand. Damn. When I started last year, I opted for an "almost free" version of a website. Unfortunately, it looks like it. Even with this job, I don't have an extra five grand to waste on my website, but I know it's a client's first impression of your organization's level of sophistication.

"Looks like we'll have to hold off on the redevelopment for a while then. Okay, what else?"

"When are you going to be back in the office? I have seven prospective client meetings I need to schedule. We've been inundated this week with RFPs."

"Seven?" What the hell? I haven't had this much interest in months. While I'm thrilled, I have a niggling feeling in the back of my brain that this can't be sheer coincidence. No, there's definitely somebody behind this. I'd bet my firstborn his name starts with the first letter of the alphabet. While I'm grateful for the help, I don't want Asher out drumming up business, using his influence to help me. I want to succeed on my own. I'll have to talk to him about this.

I glance at the calendar and realize I've been in Chicago for three full weeks now without making it back to Detroit. Tomorrow night is Livia's bachelorette party and the wedding is next weekend already. I don't have time to make a trip back, but I simply can't afford to lose any potential business. If I land all of these clients, I now have a new problem, a good problem, I guess. Staffing.

"Do you think Al could take any of the meetings?"

"Let me check. But one specifically asked for you."

I blow out a long breath. "Next week is tight with Christmas and the wedding. Can you get them scheduled for Tuesday morning or see who would be willing to have a phone or WebEx discussion? Or maybe they'd be willing to wait until the following week."

Shit, next week is Christmas already and I've done absolutely no shopping. Go me. Now I have the stress of presents to add to my pile.

"I'll see what I can do."

"Thanks."

"I kinda miss having you here," Heather admits.

"Really? You aren't happy to get a break from my neurotic tendencies?" Which she constantly complains about, by the way.

"Well, I admit it was nice for the first two weeks, but now I just miss you."

"Aw. I'll take that as a compliment. Miss you too, sweets." I look at the clock. It's almost three p.m. I have about three hours of work I want to finish before I call it a day. I was making good headway through the vendor matches. I found one that looks suspicious so far and I need to do a little more digging. Next I'm going to look at the various charities before I get into individual client account billings. "I gotta run. Let me know about those appointments, okay?"

"You got it, boss."

Boss. I definitely like the sound of that.

MAN I *LOVE* MY JOB! As weird as this sounds, when I find the smallest of threads that someone's tried to bury deep and I know that thread is going to lead to a big, twisted ball of beautiful yarn, that's almost tantamount to great sex.

Hot anticipation. That lovely little feeling is the one currently flowing rapidly through my body, pumping my adrenaline, fueling my desire.

My gut is screaming that I'm onto something. A new marketing supplier was set up nine months ago and I checked them out. They're the real deal. They have a valid website, tax identification number, and address, but something is very peculiar about the billing patterns. Marketing tends to be billed on a project or hourly rate, so pricing would vary, but all bills for this marketing company were exactly the same and that definitely feels wrong.

Also, each invoice is just below the amount required for two senior leader signatures, according to the process and procedure documents I reviewed.

I've been deep in research, lost track of time, and don't even hear my door open. Suddenly I have the prickly feeling I am being watched. I look up to see Asher standing in my doorway, leaning against the jam with his arms crossed. A cocky smile turns up one corner of his mouth.

Holy hell, he's so damn beautiful. Today he's in a custom-made grey pinstripe suit, his silver Tag watch glittering in the florescent lighting. I have to pinch myself every time I look at him to remind myself this gorgeous man belongs to me, *loves* me. It's surreal and heady. I'm not sure I'll ever fully believe it.

As we silently devour each other, the look on his face is one of love and intense longing and instantly, that hot anticipation is no longer about finding a corporate criminal, but how fast I can get him inside of me.

"Hi, baby." His eyes smolder. His voice is low. Raspy. Sexy as fucking hell.

"Hi," I reply gruffly, before I stand and walk toward him, never breaking eye contact. I pull him in and shut the door, pushing him against the hard wood. When I pull his lime-green buttoned shirt free from his trousers, his breath catches.

"What are you doing?"

I say nothing while I unbuckle his belt, unbutton his pants, and separate the metal teeth of his zipper. With each brush of my hand, his cock hardens more. By the time I pull his pants and black boxer briefs down, he's like titanium. When I drop to my knees, taking him inside my mouth for the first time, his head falls hard against the door.

"Fuck, Alyse. Jesus," he rumbles gruffly.

His hand fists in my hair, making my scalp tingle as he holds me steady, guiding his shaft in and out. I grab the base and begin to twist as I suck, lick, and nip lightly. I've never really enjoyed giving a guy oral sex, but I think I could spend the rest of my days between Asher's legs. His taste is clean, masculine, unique and the salty sweetness that hits my tongue on my first taste makes me want to bring this man to his knees daily with my mouth. I can't believe I was missing this all this time.

"So fucking good," he mutters, chest heaving, breathing erratic.

It doesn't take me long to learn what he likes. When I run the flat of my tongue in a particular way right underneath his sensitive underside, swirling up to his hole and back again, his grip tightens, raw instinct taking over.

"Look at me," he growls.

I do.

209

"I'm gonna come in your mouth in about ten seconds. Better stop if you don't want that."

I don't. Stop, that is.

Ten seconds never felt so long...or so short, as I wait for him to make good on his promise, as he always does.

But this time he falls a little short. He doesn't quite make it to ten.

Hot anticipation. It leads to damn good things.

CHAPTER 29

ALYSE

"I THINK I'M READY TO GO HOME," LIVIA ANNOUNCES LOUDLY, TRYING to be heard over the thrum of the music. We have a reserved booth toward the back of this upscale dance club, courtesy of Kamryn, who seems to have connections all over town from what I've heard, but it's still very loud.

"Oh hell no! It's only ten o'clock," Addy quips, throwing back another shot of tequila. Kamryn said she nearly single-handedly keeps Patron in business. I'm not sure I disagree at this point. I've never seen a woman drink as much as Addy and not be falling-down drunk. "This is your bachelorette party, babe. You're staying out until the bars close."

"I'm pregnant, Addy. With twins."

"Yes. You're pregnant, not dead. And you're not even waddling yet."

"Ugh. I can't even drink."

Addy reaches across the table, grabbing Livia's hand. "But you can dance and spend quality time with your friends and sister, which, by the way, you don't do anymore because you're too damn busy getting laid every single night. And I'm not begrudging you for it, because if I had a Gray I'd do the same thing, but damn girl…give your vajay-jay a break. Besides, Gray is out at his bachelor party tonight too, so it's not like he's waiting for you to mount him the second you step in the door."

"Jesus, Addy," Livia retorts.

I laugh hysterically. Addy is one of the funniest, most fiery people I've ever met. I swear she doesn't give a rip what anyone thinks. I love it. The more time I spend with her, the more I like her. She is witty without alcohol, but with alcohol…watch the hell out. She's off the rails. It will take a very strong man to tame her and I wish him luck. He'll need it.

"Please," Addy whines, sticking out her lower lip so far you could set a drink on it.

"Fine. Midnight. That's it."

"I'll take it!" Addy beams like she's won the lottery. "So, babe, how are you liking the city so far?" she turns, asking me.

"I love it." I smile, genuinely meaning it. I absolutely love this vibrant city that's so different from Detroit. Everyone I love is here. I'm beginning to stress about going back to Detroit after I'm done with the audit, because I can't fathom being separated from Asher all week, week after week. After yesterday, I know I'm getting close to finding the culprit, so I may be done with the audit by mid-January at this rate. Sadness tries to settle around me, but a question lobbed my way pulls me back.

"Anyone special showing you around?" Kamryn asks.

Without meaning to, I look at Livia before answering and see the glitter in her eyes. She picks up her water, trying to smother the tugging smile. Of course, Addy latches onto that like a dog with a damn bone.

"Oh my God, there is, isn't there? Who? Who?" She bounces up and down like a five-year-old who's about to be handed a brand spanking new Barbie doll.

"I'm not sure I should say. I don't even know where it's going." It's not *really* a lie. I know exactly where I *want* this to go. Asher's made it very clear he's taking this seriously, even hinting at marriage for heaven's sake, but he doesn't know everything about me yet. I'm still doing the protect-the-heart dance, trying to convince myself not to get fully invested before all of my secrets are out in the open. I've failed at that task miserably.

"Is it someone at CFC? I mean, you probably don't know many other people and Livia says you're working yourself into the ground with that audit."

Yep, dog with a bone.

"Addy, really, I don't want to jinx it."

"Asher runs CFC, right?" Addy looks to Livia for confirmation. She nods, not even trying to hide her smile this time. I throw her a sisterly glare that she's all too familiar with. "Have you met him yet? He's smoking hot, like every other Colloway. Daaauumm, I don't know what their parents did to make such perfect masculine specimens, but I need to get me some of that."

At the mention of Asher's name, my poker face must fail me miserably, which doesn't go unnoticed by the woman to my left who could easily make a living as an FBI or CIA agent.

"Fuck me. It's Asher isn't it? Oh. My. God. You have a Colloway brother too?" she screeches.

"Addy..."

"Holy hell, this calls for a celebratory shot." Addy grabs the bottle of Patron that she insisted the waitress leave at our table and pours three glasses. My head is already buzzing from the one shot I've had and the three glasses of wine I consumed during our painting class in Addy's studio earlier, which is how we started the night. I'm now the proud owner of a beautiful hand-painted canvas featuring water lilies in a pond. It's actually pretty damn good if I say so myself.

"To hotness. May we each get a slice," she announces before we throw our drinks back.

"And where exactly will you be looking for this slice of hotness?" a dark baritone voice drawls behind me, causing me to sputter.

I immediately recognize the owner.

I didn't spend a lot of time talking to Luke, but his sexy drawl is definitely not something you forget. Ever. I may be in love with Asher, but I still appreciate male beauty, and Luke is its walking poster child. Just...wow.

When I turn around, I'm not surprised to see Gray, Asher, Conn, and a few other gorgeous men I don't recognize walking toward us. What I am surprised at, however, is the heat that's now volleying back and forth between Luke and Addy. He hasn't taken his molten eyes from her for a single second. When I turn back to look at Addy, she's gazing at him with the same fire in hers.

Huh.

"Addy," he greets.

"Luke," she replies a little breathlessly. Guess they know each other. I wonder how well?

He briefly looks at the nearly empty bottle on the table before his eyes snap back to hers. "How much have you had to drink?"

"Not really any of your business, hun."

He steps around to the front of the booth, grabbing the bottle quicker than Addy can react. Laughing, he holds it out of reach while Addy yells and tries to pop up over the table to retrieve it.

"I think you've had enough."

Oooohhhh. The sparks flying between these two are so hot I'm worried the booth we're sitting in may catch fire. Asher and his brothers arrive at the table just in time to catch the good part of the show. I'm sitting on one end of the booth and Livia on the other, with Kamryn and Addy in the middle, so Asher and Gray have positioned themselves by us, respectively. Conn and the others stand back, talking to the waitress, presumably putting in an order.

"I paid for that, asshole. Put it back."

"Not on your life, sweetheart." Luke hands the bottle off to a man I don't recognize, but is someone they walked in with. He then reaches in his front pocket and peels five twenties from a wad of cash, throwing them on the table. "Compensation."

I glance over to see Livia and Gray watching the exchange with rapt fascination. Livia's eyes are wide with surprise, but Gray's are glittering with mirth, his lip curled into a smirk.

"Who the hell do you think you are? You do realize there's more booze here, right? I mean, we *are* in a fucking bar. And who appointed you my keeper tonight anyway? Why are you guys even h—"

Addy continues to rant, unable to get out, while Luke watches on, pretending to be unaffected, except I'm not sure how Addy can miss the fire blazing higher and hotter in Luke's eyes with each scathing word.

Like a good tennis match, I volley back and forth between the two. I think the tamer may have just arrived, complete with his bullwhip and chair. Except instead of a fancy tailcoat and top hat, this one brandishes worn black boots, a leather bomber, and faded jeans that mold to his body like they were made just for him.

Hmmm. Interesting.

"Dance with me," Asher rumbles in my ear. I hear the beginnings of the sultry Rhianna singing "Skin" playing in the background. I want to stay and see how this little play is going to turn out, but as I look up into the blue eyes of the man who has brought me back to life again, I don't hesitate to take the hand he's offering, letting him lead me to the dance floor.

They say you can tell a man's skill in the bedroom by how he dances. I don't know who "they" are, and I don't necessarily believe that's true, because I've danced with some guys who the phrase "white man dancing" was coined after and they were good in bed.

Okay, *good* may be stretching it. Decent. They were decent.

But Asher? *Holy balls.* I can absolutely say that phrase is true...and not the "white man dancing" one. He dances like he fucks.

With intent.

With finesse.

With rhythm.

With all-consuming seduction.

As he grinds the length of his body into mine from behind, one hand firmly on my hips, the other running the length of my torso, he has me completely submerged in the sensual spell he's expertly woven.

"You look so damn sexy, baby." His soft lips brush the shell of my ear. His voice is gritty. Wicked. Full of longing.

I place a hand on his roaming one, moving it around to my lower stomach, right above the waistband of my dark jeans riding low on my hips. His hand slips under the hem of my sparkly brown halter-top, caressing my bare skin, before the tips of his fingers slide south underneath the denim.

Heat blooms between my legs and I moan, my head relaxing against his shoulder. People surround us, moving their bodies seductively to Rhianna's suggestive words about stripping your clothes and liking it rough. I'm quite sure the dance floor is very visible from our booth, but I can't find it within myself to give a damn who may be watching. I'll be embarrassed later, I'm sure. But I'll worry about that then.

"Christ, I want you, Alyse. Right here. Right now."

I spin in his arms, drawing his dirty mouth to mine on a groan. "Yes," I mumble against his wet lips, dragging his lower lip between my teeth before kissing him hard. He tastes like whiskey and mint. And sin. This is why I've never tried drugs. I have kind of an obsessive personality. Now that I've had a taste of Asher, he's the drug I will never, ever give up.

Roughly palming my face, he angles my head just where he wants it and deepens the kiss. It's brimming with urgency and dominance. I willingly acquiesce. Placing my hands on his waist, I press our bodies tightly together as he takes what he needs. Pulling back, he searches my eyes as if needing assurance and when I silently give it, he presses one last hard kiss to my lips before taking my hand, leading me through the sweaty, grinding bodies toward the back of the club.

Spotting a door halfway down the first hallway that says "Employees Only," he pushes it open, pulling me inside behind him. I see him take a quick perusal before shoving me against the flimsy wood.

Alcohol and desire-glazed eyes holding mine, he makes short work of the stiff fabric that's the only barrier to our mutual pleasure and seconds later, with my legs wrapped around his waist, he's pushing roughly inside me.

"Fuuuck. I want to live inside your pussy," he pants, pounding furiously, quickly chasing the heady rush we've both come to crave that can only be quenched with each other.

"Then do," I counter, my breath whooshing out with each hard drive.

"This is mine."

"I know."

"Pinch your nipples, sweet Alyse."

I comply with his demand. Pulling up my shirt and my bra cups down, I pinch and twist and knead, watching his dark pools grow darker, hungrier with each tweak.

"Hell yes. So hot." Our eyes lock as he puts his thumb in his mouth, then reaches a hand between us, circling my clit with his wet digit. My eyes want to float closed, but I don't want to shut the doors to my soul that only open for him. "I'm never letting you go. God I love you, Alyse. So fucking much."

"I love you," I pant, so close to the finish line I'm stretching to reach it.

"That's it, baby. Come on me. I need to feel it."

An intense climax hits me hard and fast, the euphoria of it firing through my bloodstream like a rocket fueled with nitrogen. I'm unable to keep my eyes from drifting shut or containing the broken wail that escapes as my pussy contracts around his stiff shaft. I know by the swell of his cock and pace of his hips he's close behind.

"Ahhhh, baby..." He stiffens, his harsh cry chasing mine as he releases inside of me, the hot wash of his seed setting off another orgasm on the heels of the first. His body deliciously shudders against mine and I feel my walls pulsing, milking him dry.

"Alyse, Alyse, Alyse," he pants repeatedly while we're floating down from our sex-induced high. His forehead is pressed against mine, our ragged breaths mingling. My limbs feel warm and liquidy, my heart full and happy.

"I concur," I chuckle.

"I'll never get enough of you."

"You may change your mind."

"Never. You're all I think about. I'm obsessed with you."

"I like your form of obsession."

Chuckling, he presses a soft, lingering kiss to my lips before withdrawing and tucking his still-impressive, semi-stiff arousal back into his jeans. Then he helps me up with mine. I would definitely need to make a bathroom stop.

"Why aren't you guys at the strip club?" I tease, pushing his hands out of the way so I can finish putting myself back together. I had no idea what they were doing tonight and didn't ask because I didn't want to seem like the clingy, jealous girlfriend already. Deep inside I hoped it wasn't that. No woman wants to know her man is getting an intimate lap dance by another beautiful naked woman, although they will almost certainly tell you she was a dog. Oh, and that she wasn't *completely* naked.

Laughing, he grips my waist, pulling me to him. "Jealous?"

No need to deny it.

"No."

But, no need to feed his big ego either.

"Yes, you are. Your eyes are a little green, right around the iris."

I smirk, plucking at an imaginary fuzz ball on his fitted navy sweater. "Don't transfer your jealously issues to me. I couldn't care less if you have some classless whore rubbing her disease-ridden crotch on your lap."

His entire body shakes with laughter. "Oh, Alyse. That mouth of yours."

"You love it."

His smoldering eyes hold mine as he leans down, a hairsbreadth from my kiss-swollen lips. "Yes. It's very talented."

I close the scant distance, showing him just how right he is.

~

AFTER CLEANING UP, I splash water on my face and skate over my disheveled appearance in the mirror, willing the just-fucked look away before I have to go back to join the group, who, no doubt knows what we slunk off to do.

I hear the door open. A look in the reflective glass shows me that Addy just walked in, or more like wobbled in, her high heels now becoming a dangerous weapon in her drunkenness. When she spots me, she winks and a shit-eating grin takes up the space where her beautiful mouth usually is.

Sauntering on unsteady legs, she meets me at the sink. I notice her eyes are unfocused. I wonder if she's managed to get her hands on more liquor in the short time I've been gone or if it's just the half-dozen shots that have finally caught up to her.

"So, you look...satisfied."

I think I could deny it and she'd never remember, but what the hell. I am. Why deny it? "Very," I retort. We both dissolve into a fit of giggles, reminiscent of my high school days.

"I like you, Alyse," Addy slurs a bit.

"Feeling's mutual, Addy. You all right?"

"I'm good."

"Feeling no pain?"

Sadness briefly flashes across Addy's face before she pastes on her happy one again. "Almost." She turns and heads to a stall before I can say anything else. I decide to wait for her to make sure she's okay.

Stepping outside the crowded ladies room, I walk a few steps back toward the club and lean against the wall, closing my eyes. Between the drinks and the sex, I'm suddenly feeling very tired and ready for bed, even though it can't be even eleven yet.

A male voice calls my name and I open my eyes to see Cooper standing in front of me.

"Hi," I say, surprised to see him here, hoping I don't look like I just had a quickie. Damn he looks good in his khakis and blue flannel that's rolled at the sleeves, hanging open over a fitted grey T-shirt.

Every time I lay eyes on him, I travel back to almost eight years ago and it takes me a minute to catch my bearings.

"Hi yourself. What are you doing here?" He takes up position next to me, but keeps a respectable distance.

"I could ask you the same thing. Stalking me?"

He laughs. "If you weren't already taken, I would most definitely be stalking."

"Good to know you're a criminal in training. Maybe I should cut ties with you right now."

Hand over his heart, he says, "I promise I'm harmless. So, you here with your boyfriend?"

"Um, sort of. Bachelorette party for my sister, but the guys showed up a bit ago. I'm waiting on a friend in the bathroom who's a little drunk. You?"

"Just another Saturday night on the prowl."

Now it's my turn to laugh. "Lucky her."

"I hope so," he chuckles and winks. "You free for lunch Monday? I can bring the contract. Promise I won't forget this time."

I think about my schedule and chance it. I can always cancel if Heather has meetings scheduled. "Yeah, that should work. Same time and place?"

"You got it. Say, I'm here with my cousin. The one I own the studio with. I'm sure he'd love to meet you. Do you have a couple of minutes?"

"Uh..." I'm saved from answering when two things happen simultaneously. I look up to see Asher striding at a clipped pace down the hallway toward me and when his eyes flick to Cooper standing beside me, he does not look happy.

I shake my head and grin, which appears to piss him off further.

At the same time Addy stumbles out of the bathroom, nearly falling when her heel catches and she loses her footing. Luckily Cooper is there to catch her before she face plants.

"Thank you," Addy mumbles against Cooper's chest.

Asher stops beside me as this whole scene unfolds, placing a possessive palm on my neck, yanking me close. "What's taking you so long? I was worried about you," he breathes against my cheek, eyeing Cooper the entire time.

"I was worried about Addy. She's pretty drunk, so I waited for her to finish in the bathroom."

"You smell good," Addy tells Cooper loudly, her head hanging back as she loops her arms around his neck.

Cooper looks at me with a smirk, his eyes skipping to Asher briefly before landing back on mine. "Your friend?"

"I'm more than her friend, asshole," Asher corrects gruffly, his grip tightening.

"For the love of Christ, he's talking about Addy. Behave," I hiss. "Yes," I answer Cooper, while elbowing Asher. "Cooper, this is my *boyfriend*, Asher Colloway. Asher this is Cooper Jensen. He's the photographer I hired for Gray and Livia's wedding next weekend."

"Nice to meet you, man. I'd shake your hand, but...they're kind of full."

"Yes, I see that. Nice to meet you, too." Asher actually sounds sincere and I breathe a sigh of relief that this won't turn into some knock-out brawl instigated by my irrationally jealous lover.

"You have beautiful lips," Addy slurs, pressing hers against the curve of Cooper's neck. "Kiss me," I hear her mumble before Cooper laughs.

"Um, where should we take her?" Cooper asks, readjusting his grip on a slumping Addy. He looks amused and not one bit uncomfortable. But who would be with a stunningly beautiful woman in his arms, even if she doesn't have all of her faculties about her at the moment.

"Kamryn's driver bring you?" Asher asks me, kissing the tip of my nose.

"Yes."

"Can you walk, Addy?" Asher leaves me, going to Addy's side. He tries pulling her from Cooper's arms, but even in her drunken state, or maybe because of it, she's strong and clings to Cooper like she'd float away into space without him.

Cooper chuckles. "It's okay, I've got her. Just show me the way."

Asher nods, snaking an arm around my waist. Cooper and I

exchange a knowing glance and wink before he follows us to our booth. About five feet away Luke notices what's going on and jumps up to meet us. The look on his face is reminiscent of a jealous and possessive Asher.

"What the fuck," he practically yells accusingly, taking Addy from Cooper's arms. Cooper's eyes shift between Addy and Luke, his jaw ticking furiously.

Uh oh. I smell testosterone.

"Just helping out. Maybe you shouldn't let your girlfriend get falling-down drunk next time and go off to the bathroom by herself," Cooper spits, his eyes flaring.

Uh oh. I smell a fight.

"He's not my fucking boyfriend," Addy tries saying, but it comes out more like, "Heeessss no me fuckn boooyfrn." Addy then tries pushing out of Luke's hold, reaching again for Cooper, but Luke hooks one hand under her knees and scoops her into his arms.

"Where's her coat? I'm taking her home." Luke's hard glare never deviates from Cooper, just daring him to say another word. Cooper looks to me, calming slightly when I mouth, *It's okay.*

Next thing I know Luke's walking through the crowd, coat draped over Addy, who's now snuggled into his chest, eyes shut.

"Well that was...interesting," Cooper mumbles, his eyes following Luke's back until he disappears around the corner.

Uh oh. I smell competition.

"So, Alyse, nice to see you. I need to get back to my cousin." Cooper doesn't wait for my reply before leaving. Nor does he wait for an introduction to the happy couple he's going to be photographing for an entire day a week from now. And I'm secretly glad he doesn't say anything about lunch before he makes his exit. There's been enough drama tonight without adding to it by causing Asher to pound his chest, forbidding me to be alone in the presence of another man without a chaperone.

I take a seat in the booth, squeezing beside Libs and Asher. I casually watch Cooper retreat, stopping at a high-top table across the room, all the while thinking about the rightness of being with this wonderful man flush to me, arm slung around my shoulder, and how lucky I am to have found him again.

Watching Cooper talk to the man whose back is to me, but who I assume must be his cousin, I feel giddiness bubble inside at the thought that for the first time in years I'm hopeful to have a future that I didn't think was ever possible.

I notice their heads close together and imagine Cooper's probably giving him a play-by-play of the last ten minutes. I decide it's finally time to come completely clean with Asher, shedding my armor, letting the ugly secrets of my past spill. While Asher's managed to jackhammer much of my fortress, I want to demolish the rest myself. I'll brace for the worst, but the truth is, I believe in Asher, so I'll hope for the best.

As I absently watch Cooper, while I plan the right time to find all those damn keys so I can lay my soul bare to the man I've fallen in love with, I observe his cousin's head slowly turn my way.

Our gaze violently collides.

My eyes narrow. My breath catches.

My entire world comes crashing to a screeching halt.

Everything I thought I knew to be true blows up like a nuclear bomb in my face, the fallout just as toxic and deadly.

Across a dark, crowded bar in Chicago, Illinois, almost eight years to the day, I lock eyes with the first man I loved, the man I gave my virginity to, the man I created life with.

The man I thought was dead.

Gears click soundly into place, the noise loud and deafening.

Doppelganger.

Cousins.

CB29 Studios.

Cooper. Beck.

Beck.

Time rewinds.

I hear the horrific sounds of metal crunching.

I feel the pain of broken bones and glass slicing open my fragile skin.

I sense warm blood running in rivulets down my face, into my eyes.

I hear screaming. *Mine.*

I hear silence. *Beck's.*

Tightly woven memories blanket me until there is nothing but darkness.

CHAPTER 30

ASHER

"A<small>RE YOU SURE YOU'RE FEELING OKAY, BABY?</small>" I <small>ASK, RUNNING FINGERS</small> through her silky hair as she lies with her head on my lap. We have the TV on, watching some old western, but I don't think either of us could tell you what's going on. My dad was a huge western fan. Out of the four brothers, I'm the only one who inherited his love of them.

"I'm fine, Asher. Really." Her voice is flat and monotone.

If I hear another goddamn "fine" I may just lose it. She's not *fine*. Ever since she passed out cold last night at the bar, she's been the furthest fucking thing from *fine*.

She claims to have no idea why she blacked out for a few seconds, blaming it on the mixture of tequila and wine. I'm skeptical. She's been distant and quiet and I've barely been able to pull a word out of her since. Something is wrong. Very wrong. Something happened, and for the life of me I can't figure out what it is.

Everything was perfectly fine until Addy was hauled off in Luke's arms and that photographer left. Then shortly after, she's slumped over on my shoulder, dead to the damn world. I've never been so fucking scared than in those few seconds I couldn't rouse her. When she finally came to, she was pale and shivering. The look in her eyes was like nothing I've ever seen.

She was simply lost. Empty.

She didn't say a word the rest of the night, other than to repeatedly tell me she was *fine*.

A panicky feeling is building in my chest, right about where my heart is. It's been intensifying all day. She's pulling away. I feel it. I see it. I sense it down to my very core. Her moat is back and filled to the brim with choppy black waters, her drawbridge firmly up and locked. All the progress we've made at letting me in over these last few weeks has just vanished. I'm standing on the outside of her fortress again, knowing I need a new plan. Knowing I'll have to start all over again.

And I'll do it. A thousand times over if I have to. I simply refuse to let her slip away from me. Not when I know I'm meant to spend the rest of my life with her. I told her I would never abandon her and I will go to my grave keeping that promise. I will never let this woman down like so many before me.

I'm trying not to overreact, but I'm terrified. Truly, utterly terrified that I'm losing her. I want to shake her, force her to spill the secrets she's hiding. I want to open up her damn brain and pull them out myself and then erase them, so all she'll know is the unconditional love and happiness I will lavish on her every day for the rest of our lives. I want her to trust that she's emotionally safe with me, that she can be vulnerable without being judged or condemned.

I'm so distraught I even called Livia from the bathroom a bit ago to see if she had any insight. She claims to be as clueless as I am, but she seems extremely concerned. That's only intensifying my own anxiety.

I can't believe how woven Alyse has become in my daily life in such a short time. I have a hard time sleeping if she's not in my arms. I have a shitty day if I can't see her face before I start it. I'm irritable if I can't talk to her, even by text, several times a day. She has bewitched me completely and thoroughly.

I've been racking my brain trying to figure out how I'm going to keep her here after the audit because after the best blow job known to mankind the other day, she excitedly went through what she'd discovered. When she was rattling on about vendors and fake invoices and bank accounts, I could barely listen to the words. I was completely mesmerized at her enthusiasm and passion and sheer love of her job.

Plain and simple, she's the most incredible woman I have ever known.

Alyse's phone buzzes for the fifth time today. I haven't missed the fact that the other calls have been from the same number, a number I'm not familiar with, and when I hand the phone to Alyse, she checks it, declining the call.

Those little seeds of doubt and worry have fucking rooted and are growing at an alarming pace. But in checking the caller ID this time, I'm relieved to see it's Heather. I grab it off the stand next to me and hand it to Alyse, sure she'll want to take it.

"It's Heather, baby."

She sits up, putting the phone to her ear. The conversation is short. All I hear is Alyse's terse one-word replies. "Yes." "Okay." "Fine." "Sure." "Bye." I don't know why, but it marginally relieves the ache I'm feeling to know whatever mood she's in isn't just directed at me.

"What did Heather want?" I decide to ask a direct question instead of an open-ended one, hoping to get more than one or two words out of her.

"I have to go back to Detroit tomorrow."

My heart sinks.

"For how long? Next week is Christmas. You remember we're spending Christmas Eve and day at Gray and Livia's." Usually we'd gather at my mom's, but because the wedding is just two days later, we all agreed it would be easier to have Christmas here this year.

"I know. I have some new potential clients I need to meet with. I'll be back Tuesday night."

"I hate being away from you, even for a night."

I pull her back into me, lips lingering on her forehead before we resume our previous position.

Before Alyse came back into my life, I would have said nothing would ever be more important than my career and my business and my family. But it's not anymore. Alyse has jumped into my top slot. Permanently. I never intended to find my soul mate, never intended on getting married after Natalie, never intended to have a family.

But now...now the last two are all I can think about. I don't want to be away from her. I've even cut my weekly trips to Detroit back significantly, not at the jeopardy of my business, but because I don't need to be there as often as I have been. I have competent executives who can handle the management of that office without my constant presence.

"I can come with you," I announce before even thinking it through. I'm sure I have back-to-back meetings on Monday and Tuesday that will need to be rescheduled, plus I was just in Detroit last Thursday so I have no need to go back. With the way things seem to be with Alyse, though, I feel like if I let her out of my sight for even a day, I may lose her completely.

Screw work.

"No, it's fine. I have a lot of paperwork to catch up on and will be working the entire time I'm there. It's just one night, Asher."

Fine. There's that fucking word again.

I turn her over so she's now forced to look up at me. I cup her cheek, stroking her supple skin with my thumb. "Are you sure? I can rearrange my calendar, no problem."

Her eyes water and for the millionth time today, I ache to know what's going on behind those sad, desolate, chocolate puddles.

"You would do that for me?"

You don't have to be a psychiatrist or have any mental health training at all to know that Alyse suffers greatly from abandonment issues, but in that moment, the full extent of them hits me like a ton of fucking bricks. She doesn't even feel like she's good enough for me to cancel a few meaningless meetings? No one has put her first.

Ever.

No one.

My heart bleeds for her.

Right then and there I vow to spend the rest of my life making sure she knows how loved and vital and cherished she is. It will take a while for her to believe it, but I'll work tirelessly until she does.

I catch a tear that's escaped. "Alyse…baby, when are you going to believe that I would do anything for you? I would slay dragons. I would walk through hell. I would wage wars. I would lie and cheat and steal and kill for you. I'd break every fucking law and commandment for no one else but you. I am madly, deeply, *unconditionally* in love with you. Your happiness is my first and only priority."

I finally see a ghost of a smile and my Alyse shines briefly through her veil of sadness and watery eyes. Seeing that she's still inside her new coat of protective armor, I feel like I can take a full breath for the first time since last night at eleven-thirty.

"Wow. Dragons, huh?"

"Don't forget the killing. And the wars," I tease, tugging playfully on her lower lip.

That gets me a brief laugh before she turns somber again.

"I have a hard time believing this is real sometimes."

The sadness in her eyes twists my insides into so many goddamn knots I feel like I belong on a fucking sailboat.

"That what's real, baby?"

"You. Us," she whispers.

I tug her onto my lap, so she's cradled in my arms. "Why, Alyse? What happened last night to make you question what we have is real?" I want her to believe in us so badly, but I don't know how.

Until these five strange phone calls today planted a new seed of uncertainty, I've run through every scenario in my head. The only thing I can come up with is my raging jealousy over other men looking at, talking to, or touching her. I know she saw it when she was talking to that photographer in the hallway. I realize I'm being completely asinine. I trust her and I need to start acting like it. I decided first thing this morning to get that under control because my fear is it's pushing her away from me.

For the first time since Conn mentioned it, I'm seriously considering calling Natalie, knowing that conversation won't be as hard as I originally thought. I don't think I've ever experienced real pain, the debilitating kind that would bring me to the edge of despair. I now know losing Alyse would lead me there and I'd never come back. Even with everything Natalie did to me, to us, it's a fraction of the certain agony I would be in without Alyse.

"I don't know what's real anymore."

I don't know what to make of her cryptic response, but one thing I've learned about Alyse is that I need to let her talk about things in her own time. I hate it. I want her to spill the entire contents of her guts now. But the more I push, the more she withdraws. My best approach is to continually remind her that I will be here for her come hell or high water.

"I'm real. We're real." I tip her chin up, snaring her eyes. "My love for you is *real*. It consumes me, Alyse. It burns hot like a thousand suns deep inside my soul and there is nothing that could ever extinguish it."

Her lips turn, but the weak smile doesn't reach her eyes and it's like knives to my heart that she's feeling so lost.

"You're not alone anymore," I tell her, needing her to believe my words are not just syllables strung together, but promises that come from the very center of my being. "I'm here and I'm not going anywhere. I'll carry you, I'll catch you, I'll hold you up when you need it. I'll shoulder your burdens when they get too heavy. You're not alone, Alyse." I cup her face, bringing her close. "You're not alone."

Her eyes refill with tears and they spill over, running down her face. "Asher, I...I love you. So much."

I take her lips in a deep, drugging kiss, pouring every thought and every feeling I have into her, willing her to believe it.

Believe in me.

Believe in us.

Fight for us.

I spend the rest of the night holding her, loving her, and doing something I haven't done in a very long time: I pray.

I pray that my love will be enough to hold her to me. I can't help the niggling in the back of my brain that the walls she's resurrected again have everything to do with the painful past she refuses to discuss.

I just wish I knew what happened to slam them back into place so I can fix it.

CHAPTER 31

ALYSE

YOU KNOW THAT ANXIOUS, GUT-TWISTING FEELING YOU GET WHEN THE walls are closing in on you from all directions and there's not a damn thing you can do to stop them from crushing you? All you can do is sit helplessly frozen, watching as they inch ever closer to exterminating your hopes, your dreams, your very life?

I felt that way when I learned that Beck had died. I felt powerless, weak. My body and mind nothing but a swirling mass of utter despondency for several long months.

I worked hard to overcome my depression. It was a long, difficult road, but I did it and I vowed I'd never let myself get to that place again. No matter what. But since Saturday night, I feel like I've slipped. I'm suffocating. I'm slowly circling that dark pit of despair again and I'm scared. Absolutely terrified.

It's a place I welcomed last time because I didn't know any better. I couldn't see beyond my soul-destroying agony. This time, however… it's not fucking welcome. At all. It's not, because I've found love again. I'm happy and hopeful, but even so I still feel the darkness seeping in around the edges like shadow warriors come to claim my soul so they can feast on it for eternity.

I look down at my phone to see fifteen text messages and four missed calls.

Cooper.

Livia.

Asher.

Asher is smothering me with worry and his anxiousness is washing over me in thundering, booming sprays. But I also feel his love wrap around me like a warm, comforting blanket and I need that damn blanket like a lifeline. It's my only savior in this entire fucked-up situation, because without Asher, I would be hopelessly lost for good. I can only hope and pray he continues to be patient with me as I work to find my way out of this hole I've fallen through. I want to reassure him that everything will be okay, but how can I when I'm trying to understand it myself, let alone explain it?

I'm trying so hard to outrun my past, but every time I move forward, there it is again.

Blocking my path.

Holding me back.

Keeping me prisoner. Before it was just memories, but now…

Beck is alive.

He's always been alive.

I keep replaying that moment, just a second frozen in time. I saw so much, but so little at the same time. I keep telling myself that it wasn't really him, but I know that no amount of pretending will make it untrue. And the fact that I've heard from Cooper multiple times tells me it's not a hallucination.

Beck is *not* dead.

Before I fainted, I saw the moment he recognized it was me. I saw sorrow turn down his handsome features. I saw regret eating him alive.

I anxiously wait, obsessively looking at my watch, my foot bouncing up and down so fast I think I'm shaking all the tables within a six-foot radius. I scan the diner for any signs that I've been tricked.

My heart's racing. I don't why I'm here, why I kept our lunch date, but I guess curiosity got the best of me. I didn't respond to Cooper's texts to confirm that I was coming, but I didn't tell him I wasn't either. I don't even know if he'll show. I think what I need is for him to look me in the eye and tell me he didn't know anything about this. Because if he and Beck played me, I don't know how I'll ever be able to trust another human being again. I don't know how they could have, but who expects her dead ex to rise from the fucking grave either?

I sure as shit didn't.

After I recovered from the shock, the pain set in, fresh and raw and gut-wrenching. I felt flayed to the bone, my heart sliced to ribbons all over again.

Beck's not dead. He's not dead, yet all this time he let me believe he was. He left me to deal with not only my physical injuries on my own, but my emotional ones, too, as well as the loss of our baby. By myself.

He abandoned me in the worst possible way anyone could.

The loom of a shadow lifts my head. I don't realize I'm holding my breath until it whooshes from my lungs at the sight of Cooper. He stands there, sympathy bleeding from his eyes and I know he can't have known. My relief is so great, an involuntary sob breaks free. He holds out his arms. My need for human comfort can't be denied. I stand, let him engulf me, and cry against his cold winter jacket, uncaring that we're making a scene.

"I didn't know, Alyse. Jesus, I swear. I didn't know."

Seconds, minutes, hell hours later, after my sobs subside, he smooths my hair, taking my face between his hands.

"You okay?"

I snort. "I'm nowhere near okay."

He nods, dropping his hands. We sit and just look at each other for several moments.

"You should talk to him," he finally says.

"Are you fucking kidding me? Do you know what he did to me?" I spit, incensed that he would even suggest such a thing. But, of course, Beck is family, so what is he going to do? From the way he's talked about "his cousin," they're very close. Hell, they opened a business together.

I've gotten what I came for. I believe he didn't know about the connection between Beck and me. I stand and turn to leave when a strong hand grips my wrist.

"Alyse, please. Just hear me out."

"Cooper, don't. I just...I can't," I choke. I feel like I'm seconds away from falling into a puddle on the floor, crying myself into a pool of tears until I drown. I kept it together all day Sunday, but today, seeing Cooper, it's a completely different ball game. He lets my arm go and I start forward, making it about ten paces until his next words stop me mid-step.

"I didn't realize you were *that* Alyse."

I slowly spin on my heels. "What do you mean '*that* Alyse'?"

"Will you sit down while I explain or do you want to invite all our new friends to join?"

I look around to see that a dozen sets of eyes are intently watching our exchange, so I huff, walk back, and sit.

"What do you mean '*that* Alyse'?" I repeat, this time getting angrier.

Sighing heavily, he scrubs his hand over his hair several times, messing it up so it stands on end. I try to remain unaffected, but the gesture reminds me so much of Beck, the waterworks begin again. I angrily swipe them away. An undead man who pulled one over on me does not deserve my tears. Or my forgiveness.

"He talked about you all the time, you know."

"No. I don't know, actually. He never talked about *you*. He never talked about anything really, because Beck was about as secretive as the KGB, so apparently I didn't know a fucking thing about him. He let me believe he was *dead* all this time, Cooper. All these years. So, forgive me if I don't believe you. I almost—" I almost killed myself because I didn't want to live without him.

"He was in love with you. He was, Alyse. I...I don't think he's ever gotten over you."

235

"How can you possibly say that, Cooper?" I sneer. "Did he tell you I was pregnant? Did he tell you he fucking lost it when I told him? Did he tell you he drove us into a grove of oak trees, trying to kill us after I gave him the good news that he was going to be a father?"

He looks as heartbroken as I feel. My breath hitches.

"He told me everything, Alyse. Beck was devastated after the accident, but the accident was *not* intentional. Carelessness? Yes. Intentional? No," he says quietly.

I'm so overwhelmed in that moment I don't know what to do, so I put my head in my hands and cry. I hear the scrape of chair legs against the floor. I feel an arm around me as Cooper takes the seat next to mine.

"Why? Why? Why would he do that to me?" I openly weep. "Why would he let me believe he's dead all this time? I loved him. Even after what happened, I still loved him."

His arms tighten. "That's his story to tell. I won't do that to him."

We sit like that for ten, maybe fifteen minutes and this intense, overwhelming need to see Asher unexpectedly hits me. To have him hold me, kiss me, make love to me. I have a four-hour drive ahead of me, but I can't leave town first without seeing him. It's like someone has pulled a thread, just one loose thread that's barely holding me together. The only person who can stop me from completely unraveling is him.

"I have to go." Pulling a tissue from my purse, I wipe my eyes the best I can and stand, looking down at Cooper's seated form. "Do not bring him to the wedding, Cooper. Don't do that to me. Please."

"I wouldn't, Alyse. I won't. No matter what's happened between you and Beck, I like you. I don't want to lose you as a friend."

"How will that work exactly? Our friendship? With Beck?"

"I don't know, but you are both important to me, so I'll figure it out."

I want that, too. I truly like Cooper. Nodding, I lean down, placing a light kiss on his cheek. "Thank you."

"Alyse, please tell me you'll think about it. Talking to him, I mean."

"I—"

"Don't say no. Just say you'll think about it. Please. Not for him, but for you. There are things you don't know. Things you don't understand, and I think if you knew them, you'd see the situation in an entirely different light. He's…well, he's suffered just as much as you have, if not more."

"Doubtful," I mumble as I walk out.

Outside, I stand in the blustery winter wind, pulling my coat tighter around me. While I wait for the little white hand at the cross-walk to indicate it's safe, something makes me turn to my left. When I do, through all the throngs of lunchgoers, I see Beck standing across the street, leaning against a brick building, intently watching me.

My breath is momentarily lost. He's aged into a simply beautiful man.

"I've never loved another person as much as I love you, Alyse. You're my entire life. My world. My future." Beck has tears in his eyes. I wonder what's wrong. He's been more erratic than usual lately.

"Mine, too," I whisper before pulling him down to my waiting lips, trying to seal him to me forever. "Don't leave me, please."

"Never. Never, baby."

I realize that since the front of the diner Cooper and I were sitting in is solid glass and we were by the window, Beck's probably watched our entire exchange. Watched me yell, watched me break. Probably hoped I would want to see him, just waiting for the prearranged signal.

Ever since I saw Asher again months ago, the giddy, teenage feelings I've always had for him have blossomed into undeniable love. A love so deep and passionate, it makes me breathless. I'm so filled to the brim with happiness I feel like I might burst some days. Some may think it's too early, but I don't care what they believe. I know what I feel. It's a love that makes you question all other loves before it and I've found myself wondering if I ever *really* loved Beck at all or if that was something I made up in my young mind.

But seeing Beck again, gazing at me with those dark, hooded eyes, the same ones I fell into the first time I saw him across a coffee counter, I know my love for him was real and true and it's never left. In all these years, it's never faded.

Even from this distance, I still see the love for me swimming in his own eyes.

Guilt eats my insides raw until they bleed. I love Asher with my whole self and I shouldn't be feeling this way about another man, especially one who duped me.

We stare, neither of us shifting toward the other. I can't deal. Not now. Maybe not ever. When the crowd starts moving, that's my cue. I break away and cross with them, hoping like hell he doesn't follow.

Then I make it to my car, point it toward Detroit, and drive. As much as I need Asher, the only thing that will happen if I see him is tears (mine), questions (his), and hurt feelings (both) because I can't talk to him about this yet. I'm not ready. I need time to process something that's come directly out of a fucking soap opera and figure out what the hell I'm going to do with the pile of crap that's now thickly coating the bottoms of my shoes.

CHAPTER 32

ASHER

"Hey, baby. How was your day?"

"Long," she sighs heavily.

"I wish you would have let me come with you. I could be rubbing your feet about now." Or taking away every trouble and every worry and every doubt with my mouth and fingers and cock.

"That sounds heavenly, actually."

Dammit, I should have insisted I go with her. I spent an endless day in a barrage of meetings and I can't tell you a damn thing that was said. My attention was entirely distracted on the leggy, beautiful woman that I'm trying desperately to figure out how to hold onto.

Sandra, my VP of acquisitions and divestitures, was pretty fed up with me by the end of our two-hour planning session. I also agreed to a new marketing campaign that's to start next week, signing off on slogans I couldn't repeat if you held a gun to my head. Guess I'll see what I did when the multimedia ads hit the market.

"What are you doing now?"

"In bed, nursing a glass of wine."

"Are you naked?"

She laughs. I love her laugh. "No. I'm only naked when I sleep with you. Otherwise I'm usually in pajamas."

"The sexy, see-through kind or the grandma kind?" That earns me another laugh which sends a zing directly to my dick. It's now semi-hard at the thought of her wearing something black and see-through. God, I miss her.

"Is your mind always on sex?" she asks, her voice low and sultry.

"Surprisingly, no. Don't get me wrong, I think about sex with you a lot. A. *lot*. But I enjoy holding you in my arms when we sleep or the feel of your head in my lap as we watch TV or cooking dinner for you just as much, Alyse." I'm surprised at how much I mean those words.

"Asher," she breathes.

"I love you, Alyse. So very much."

She hesitates to respond and just those two seconds feel like an hour. "Why?"

It guts me that she keeps questioning how I feel, but it utterly shreds me that she believes herself undeserving of it. "Baby, the better question is why not? You're an incredibly amazing woman. I wish you could see what I do when I look at you."

"So do I," she replies quietly.

"I've never loved anybody more. Calling what I feel for you *love* is an injustice, because it goes so much deeper than that. I have never felt this happy or alive or...whole. I finally know who I am when I'm with you, like I'm the best version of myself, if that makes sense."

"It does," she whispers.

As much as I detest her insecurity, I hate my own more. Dammit, I've been feeling this nagging uncertainty since Saturday night and it's eating away at my insides more and more every minute to the point I think I may be getting an ulcer. I'll probably hold the world record for the least amount of time taken to make my own gut bleed.

"Tell me you love me, Alyse." *Jesus, please tell me you love me.*

"So much I can hardly breathe." Her voice is soft and threaded with amazement, but I also don't miss the underlying tone of sadness.

My entire body sags into the couch in relief. "Baby…you going to tell me what's going on with you? And don't tell me it's nothing and that you're fine. Because neither is true."

"I just…I need some time."

My heart stutters, hoping to hell that's not code for "it's not you, it's me." "Define time, baby."

"Promise me you'll be patient with me. Please, Asher."

"I promise, Alyse."

"I…need to work through a few things."

"Do these things have to do with us?" I ask hesitantly, not at all sure I can stomach the answer, feeling the bleed gush a little more.

"No. It's…complicated."

"Okay," I concede, when that's the very last thing I want to do. I'm not 100 percent sure I believe her. Whatever happened a few days ago is threatening to tear us apart. "But you should know patience is not my strong suit."

She chuckles, teasing, "Really? I didn't know that. What else are you hiding from me? Hair-trigger temper? Secret family? Ugly wart on the bottom of your foot that I haven't come across yet?"

"Well, I was going to wait to tell you this until after you agreed to marry me, but I do have royalty in my bloodline. It may be nine times removed, but royalty is royalty, babe. I didn't want it sway your decision or anything."

"Royalty, huh? You know, I've always been a big fan of crowns and staged social engagements and stuffy dinner parties. If you're really royalty, as you say, it's a definite yes."

The thought of making Alyse my wife has been rattling around in my head since that first night I cooked for her. Nothing has felt as right as being with her. I know it's only been a month that we've actually been together, but I'm almost thirty years old and I've known Alyse for years. Dating for whatever cursory time period people think is acceptable, before marrying the person you know you are meant to spend your life with, is absurd. I know this is right with every fiber of my being. Alyse is my forever.

"Wow, if that's all it took, I would have asked you to marry me already."

Her breath catches. "Asher..."

Before she can say another word or protest, I change the subject to what her day looks like tomorrow and move into a comfortable, easy-going conversation for the next hour.

When we hang up, I realize I had it all wrong. I thought Alyse was sent to save me, but now I know it's the other way around.

We are together because *I'm* supposed save *her*. I can't wait to have her back in my arms where she belongs. Where she'll always belong and I can remind her daily of my love and utter devotion to her.

I feel her slipping through my fingers. My original fear of her hurting me rears its ugly head, spewing doubt and suspicion. I can't let that happen. I *won't* let that happen.

I don't want anyone else besides her. When I picture my future, there's not one scenario that doesn't include her. I don't know how, but I know I'm not letting her go this time. I will fight to the death for her, because she's quickly become my entire world. The only thing that truly matters.

Before I go to bed, I send her a text that I hope conveys I've meant every word I've ever spoken to her.

Me: give a listen to everything by lifehouse

Several minutes later she responds. Her sassy words warm my insides.

Alyse: dominant, romantic, and sappy? i've hit the triple crown

Me: u forgot royalty

Alyse: and egotistical

Me: confidence is not ego, baby. it's just confidence

Alyse: i love u asher colloway

Me: i love u back alyse kingsley

I go to sleep that night alone, but with a smile on my face and love and hope in my heart.

CHAPTER 33

ALYSE

I SIT ALONE IN MY DARKENED APARTMENT, WATCHING THE FLAMES dance across the floor and walls. Swirling the glass of bourbon in my hand, I let the tears flow. Once again I celebrated a holiday with the Colloways, and, once again, I had a ringside seat to their happiness, their closeness, their love, their traditions. While Thanksgiving is all about fun, Christmas is all about giving back.

We spent several hours serving meals to the homeless and less fortunate at the Cathedral Shelter of Chicago, to which GRASCO Holdings is also a generous benefactor. They also don't buy each other gifts, buying toys and clothes that they take to a local women's shelter instead. It was enough to bring tears to my eyes, because places like that and the generosity of people like the Colloways were sometimes the only way Livia and I *were* clothed.

The entire Colloway clan is still upstairs in Gray and Livia's penthouse, but I couldn't take it anymore. I haven't had a second to myself since I returned on Tuesday night. I've been trying my best to pretend I'm holding it together, yet all the while I'm breaking inside. I needed a few minutes alone so I could break on the outside. If I did it in front of anyone, the barrage of questions would return. Questions I have no answers to.

So I told Asher I had a migraine and needed to lie down. Alone. He reluctantly let me, but I expect he'll be back to check on me, and if he catches me crying, I can at least blame it on the fake pain that's supposed to be crippling me. The pain is all too real and it *is* crippling: it's just in my heart, not my head.

Beck is alive. Alive.

The betrayal I feel is indescribable and incomparable to anything else I've ever felt, even when I thought he was dead. But the thing that disturbs me even more is the fact that, after seeing him, those old feelings of love have risen to the surface. And that makes me angry...at myself. Now I feel like I'm the one doing the betraying.

What are you supposed to do with the fact that the person you were in love with...what? Faked his death? Thought having a family with you was so repugnant he'd rather you think he was taking a dirt nap than break things off face-to-face? Who does that?

Why aren't I worthy? Why am I not deserving of anyone's love? Why am I not worthy of anyone's trust? Why did my father not love me enough to sacrifice for me? Why did my mother turn her back on me? Why did Livia desert me for three long years?

This last month with Asher has single-handedly been the best of my life and, until Saturday night, I was even starting to truly believe that maybe I'd found my person. The one who would *really* and *unconditionally* love me, maybe even for the rest of my life, but after seeing Beck, I'm back to doubts and whys again.

Why?

Why?

Why?

No answers. Only questions.

And secrets and lies and hurt and betrayal.

It's a never-ending vicious circle from which I can't escape and I'm tired of it. I want off this self-destructing ride. Anger and bitterness and resentment have taken up permanent residence inside me and I want them gone.

I want to *believe* again.

In goodness and integrity and loyalty.

In dreams and hope and love.

In *me*.

I've been replaying Cooper's words since Monday, trying to figure out what I'm going to do. *"There are things you don't know. Things you don't understand, and I think if you knew them, you'd see the situation in an entirely different light. He's...well, he's suffered just as much as you have, if not more."*

The thought of seeing Beck turns my insides to a ball of knots. I don't think I can hear what he has to say and even if I would consider it, how can I possibly believe a single word? He's let me believe all this time he's been dead, so it's pretty clear he didn't want me to know he wasn't.

On the other hand, how can I move forward with this all this toxic shit swirling inside me like an electrical storm, threatening to obliterate anything and everything in its path? Threatening to ruin what I've tenuously built with Asher?

I think back to the five days I spent in the hospital. I remember little about the first two, because the pain meds made my brain fuzzy and sleepy, but I will never forget the words my father told me on day three while he sat on the corner of my bed holding my hand.

"What happened?" Everything hurts like I've been run over by a truck or dropped from the top of a building.

"You don't remember?"

Remember? There's something trying to work its way into the frontal lobe of my brain, but I can't quite grasp it. The elusive memory hangs in the dark fringes, trying to protect me. "No. I can't..."

"We talked about this yesterday. You were in a car accident, sweetheart. You're lucky to have survived."

Accident? Car? I try to wade through the sludge that is slowing my brain function down. In retrospect, I wish I didn't, because the second the memory slams into me, I am hysterical.

Beck.

Baby.

"Beck, Beck, where is Beck?" I cry.

My father looks angry. The tone he uses when he speaks the words that will ruin my future is completely at odds with the look of pure rage on his face. "The driver didn't make it. Blunt force trauma to the head. I'm sorry, sweetheart."

I'm sorry.

I break. My dad holds me as I soak his shirt with my grief. The entire time, I think the only thing I have left of Beck is our baby. But later that day the doctor asks for privacy. Because I am eighteen, my 'condition' hasn't' been revealed to my family.

"Alyse, were you aware that you were pregnant?"

Even in my drugged state, I don't miss the use of the word 'were.' I nod, not able to speak through the constriction now shutting off my air supply.

She looks sad, delivering her prerehearsed words with just the right amount of sympathy and sorrow. "I'm sorry to inform you that you miscarried shortly after surgery. Oftentimes the trauma..." She continues to talk, but I stop listening to her words. They are all irrelevant anyway. All that matters in my world is gone. Dead, as if it never existed in the first place. As if these past months never happened.

"I'm sorry," she says with sympathy before squeezing my hand, leaving me to my own anguish.

I'm sorry.

I'm sorry.

That phrase has to be the most wholly inadequate one in the entire English language, especially when used in conjunction with death. It's what we say, because there's nothing even created that could possibly ever be sufficient, but it doesn't take away the debilitating pain piercing your very soul. Only time does that, turning that debilitating agony into something you can at least bear without a knifing burn each time you take a breath.

I hear the scrape of the door and quickly swipe the lingering tears, hoping my puffy eyes and splotchy face will be hidden in the darkness. My back is to the door. I don't turn, fully expecting my visitor to be Asher, but it's not.

It's Barb Colloway.

"Hi," she greets carefully, taking a seat beside me. She looks at my face and to my glass. "How's the headache?"

I've never had a migraine in my life, and somehow I think Barb knows I made up an excuse to escape. That makes me feel even worse.

"Lingering," I settle for. It's not entirely untrue. I've had a stress headache for five solid days. "Thank you for checking on me, Barb."

"My pleasure, dear. Asher wanted me to take his spot in their annual game of Monopoly so he could come down and check on you, but I don't play games with my boys. Haven't since they were little."

I chuckle. "Too much testosterone?"

"Something like that," she says with a wink. She regards me quietly for a few moments. "Is it all right if I stay awhile?"

"I think I'd like that," I nod, genuinely meaning it. Barb Colloway is a magnificent woman. I can easily understand how her children love her so much. The first time I ever met her, she was so highly regarded by her kids, even at an age when children don't always appreciate their parents, I expected to see her walking on water. She wasn't, but seemed to walk on air instead.

I can't imagine there's anything that would ruffle that woman's feathers.

"Maybe I can snag a glass of that, too?"

"It's straight bourbon."

"Even better."

"Barb, you badass." Chuckling, I jump up and pour two fingers over ice, handing it to her before retaking my seat.

"I've been known to have my moment or two," she quips.

"Are you excited about the wedding?" I ask after a few moments of silence, because now I feel like I need to make small talk.

"Very," she smiles. "Livia's always been like a daughter to me. She and Gray are perfect for each other. Always have been, so I'm glad to see they're finally getting their happy beginning."

"Happy beginning. I like that."

"I only wish Frank could be here."

"I can't imagine how hard it is for you," I say softly. I refrain from saying I'm sorry, because…well I think we covered that before.

She doesn't reply, but she doesn't have to. The love I witnessed between Barb and Frank Colloway, even the few times I spent with them in my teenage years, was palpable and had an impact on me even then. I wanted what they had. I'd never seen anything like it, not that I had any role models in the 'endless love' category growing up.

We both watch the fire and sip our cocktails in comfortable peace for a while before she breaks it.

"You know, my boys do everything fiercely, but when they fall in love, it's with their whole entire being. They give everything they have, everything they are. Just as they do with everything else in life. They don't know any other way."

My gaze slides to her profile, knowing this conversation has now turned from Gray and Livia to Asher and me.

"I believe once you find that one special person, you know it immediately."

She turns, holding my stare. I'm hanging on every word, wondering what she's going to reveal next.

"I knew immediately when Gray met Livia that something in him had changed. There was a twinkle in his eye and lightness to his step that wasn't there before. Happiness radiated from him at the sheer mention of her name."

She pauses. I realize I'm holding my breath in anticipation. Of what, I'm not sure.

"I've seen the same thing in Asher recently."

I can't help the small smile that curls my mouth.

"I've never seen him as happy as he is with you, Alyse. Not with anyone."

"I'm in love with him," I confess thickly. I haven't told another person, except Asher of course, how I feel about him and now I just blurted it out to his mother of all people. But it feels right. This is a conversation I've imagined having a hundred times with my own mother. Talking about boys and love and heartbreak. I want Barb to know how much I do love her son, even if everything else around me feels like it's falling apart and makes no sense. *That* is one thing I know with absolute certainty.

"But?"

I'm momentarily taken aback. I'm not sure how to respond. Barb has to be one of the most perceptive people I've met. Now I know exactly where Asher gets it. I look down, embarrassed. "No one I love stays around too long, I'm afraid."

"Oh, my dear," she replies softly, taking my free hand. "You know, life takes us exactly where we're supposed to be, even if that road is bumpy and fraught with detours and potholes. I'm going to share something with you that I haven't even told my own boys, but this stays between us, okay?"

I nod, feeling a mixture of anxiety that I'm so transparent and excitement that Barb's about to confide something to me—*me*—that even Asher doesn't know. "Of course."

"When I was young, I loved my mother to the ends of the earth. She was beautiful, smart, and funny. But she was also a free spirit and when I was eleven, she fell in love with someone else and walked out on our family." Her knowing, empathetic gaze finds mine. Of course she knows about my mom. "I later found out she was pregnant with his child and she wanted to start fresh with a new husband, new family. To this day, I still can't understand how a mother could abandon her family as easily as if she were trading in an old car for a new model. My father took it hard and whereas he was once a kind, easygoing man, he became hostile, abusive. Let's just say the last half of my childhood was not bubble gum and cotton candy."

She clears her throat, her personal pain evident even all these years later. "I spent years resenting my mother's betrayal. I spent my entire childhood and a good part of my early adult life wondering what *I'd* done to make her leave. Maybe if I'd helped out more? Maybe if I'd talked back less? Could I have done something different to make her stay? It had to be me, right?"

Her words were mine. My feelings. My thoughts.

"It ate me alive. It ruined every relationship I had. I couldn't let people past that magical protective barrier I'd spun around my heart. Then when I was twenty, I met Frank and we fell madly in love. I knew after my second date that I was going be his wife. After only three months he asked me to marry him, but as much as I loved him, I couldn't completely drop the guards. I tried to sabotage my own relationship, because I was so lost in fear that I wasn't good enough. I made mistakes, Alyse. Big ones, almost unforgiveable ones, and he broke off our engagement.

"It was then that I realized I was about to lose the very best thing to ever happen to me because the past was shackled firmly to my ankles like dead weight, and I dragged it around with me everywhere like a darn prize, using it as a crutch, an excuse. It took me a long time to realize, Alyse, that every person is responsible and accountable for his or her own decisions in life. We may not understand them or agree with them, but it's not our job to."

I'm captivated, sucking in every word of motherly advice like a dry sponge. Barb Colloway had a childhood similar to mine, with a mother who left her, and yet she is the most put-together, open, and loving woman I've ever met. She found the love of her life and raised four wonderful sons.

"We're all imperfect, Alyse. We've *all* had people betray our trust and our love, but it's what we do with that adversity that separates us from the pack. Holding on to bitterness and resentment and anger only holds us back. It limits us in every possible way. In life, in love, in happiness. It's an easy place to stay, but it's also very lonely.

"Forgiveness, however? *That's* hard. Much harder than holding onto our hurts and wrongs and using those to excuse our own actions. It takes courage and bravery to forgive. Oh, but Alyse… forgiveness is freeing. Healing. In both mind and spirit. Forgiveness allows you to thrive and flourish. Forgiveness allows you to shed your burdens and embrace life, short as it is."

I'm letting her insightful words roll around and sink in when I hear a noise in the kitchen. I look over with blurry eyes to see Asher standing there.

"Sorry to interrupt," Asher says sheepishly, gaze bouncing between the two of us. I have to wonder how much he heard. I also wonder if my pulse will gallop with excitement every time I lay eyes on him. I hope so.

I glance over at Barb to see a sly smile on her face. Did she know he was standing there? She pats me on the leg before surprising me and throwing back her drink in one swallow. "I should get going, dear. I hope you get to feeling better."

She's halfway to Asher when I call after her, popping off the couch. "Thank you," I mutter, pulling her in for a hug. "Thank you."

She embraces me as I imagine a mother would. I melt, letting her comfort me, not caring that Asher is watching, not caring that I'm crying again.

"I see how much you love my son. Let him be your strength, Alyse. Besides, I need to grow the number of Colloway women," she whispers quietly in my ear and I laugh through the tears. "Asher, take care of our Alyse."

"I will, Mom." He hugs and kisses her. Then she's gone and I'm in Asher's arms. "What was that all about?"

"Girl talk. Your mom is incredible."

"That she is. Are you feeling better?" With my face in his hands, he searches my eyes, wiping away the remnants of my internal conflict.

"Yes." After the long talk I just had with his mom, I can honestly say that's true. The clarity I need is floating somewhere in her wise words, just waiting for me to reach out and grab it when I'm ready.

His thumb plays with one of the one-carat drop-diamond platinum earrings he surprised me with in bed this morning. My leather jacket to him pales in comparison to his gift. When his eyes snag mine again, they're smoky and swirling with love and blatant desire. "You deserve to be spoiled, Alyse. Every day for the rest of our lives."

The need to be loved by this man is overwhelming. The intense need to *believe* it's all real almost buckles my knees.

"Make love to me, Asher." His name is swallowed as his mouth descends hard on mine, tongues dueling, hands frantic like we haven't touched each other in months when it's only been hours. Then he carries me through his apartment to the bedroom where he spends the rest of the night honoring my request again and again.

CHAPTER 34

ALYSE

"Libs, you need to eat something."

"Oh my God, I can't," Livia mumbles, pacing back and forth in the small conference room that's doubling as a bridal suite. Her wedding dress swishes hypnotically with every step she takes. She lucked out and was able to find an absolutely stunning embellished ivory lace dress with lace cap sleeves, highlighting just the right amount of cleavage. It's flowy and elegant, with a high waist, accentuated by a thick silver ribbon that hangs long down the back. The design is flattering, while at the same time it hides her growing belly. She's the most beautiful bride I've ever seen.

"You haven't eaten anything all day. You're going to pass out when you say your vows. Here, at least eat a protein bar. Get something in your stomach." I unwrap a Kind bar and hand it to her.

She looks at it with disgust. I wave it impatiently, forcing her to take it. She takes a bite and chews methodically while she walks.

It's twenty minutes until showtime. Along with making me her maid of honor, she asked me to walk her down the aisle, which brought me to tears. Everyone else, including Barb, departed about five minutes ago, leaving just the two of us some precious time together before she becomes someone's wife.

"It's not too late, you know. You can pull a runaway bride and I'll cover for you." I wink, knowing that's not at all the issue. Livia's crazy in love with Gray, but she *hates* public speaking. Even though there are only about fifty guests, I'm sure the only memory she's replaying right now is the one from her eleventh grade speech class where she completely froze, forgetting her entire speech on whether students should be required to take mandatory drug tests. She locked her knees and passed out cold, hitting her head on the hard tile floor and needing seven stitches.

"Livia." Forcing her to sit down, I take a seat in front of her. "Don't think about anyone else. Just focus on Gray and how much you love him and your happy beginning. Let him be your strength." I smile, reusing Barb's words.

"Happy beginning. Yeah, I like that." She takes a deep breath, letting it out slowly. "Okay."

"This is what you want, right?"

"With everything in me," she answers immediately. Her eyes water and I squeeze her hands tight, unable to remain unaffected.

"Stop that. You're going to ruin your makeup," I scold, secretly trying to hold myself together so I can help hold Livia together.

"I know," she says, dabbing an escaped tear.

"You are so beautiful, Libs. I'm so happy for you. I know I may not always show it, but I do love you. Very much."

"I love you too, Alyse." Pausing, she adds, "*Everything* I've ever done is for you. There's *nothing* I wouldn't do for you. No sacrifice is too great."

I nod, feeling like the lines she's asking me to read between are blurry and confusing. I'm not sure they'll ever come into focus.

"Our lives have been hard," I say.

"Very."

A wave of need to tear down all the walls I've built between us hits me hard. I know not all of this has been my doing; Livia's kept her fair share of secrets, but so have I. I need to rectify that. I've been doing nothing but thinking about Barb's words for the past two days. *Forgiveness is freeing.* I want to be free. And regardless of whether Livia will ever tell me what happened, I want my sister back. But now is not the time.

"I want to tell you so many things."

She nods, as if she completely understands. "Is everything okay with you?"

I swallow hard. Honesty is so much harder than lying, letting people believe you're fine. "Not really, but I'm working through it."

"Is it Asher?"

"No. My past has risen from the dead," I tell her, not exaggerating in the least.

"Is it a guy?"

I nod, unable to voice the guilty words.

"Does Asher know?"

I let my eyes fall to the floor. "No," I whisper.

"Alyse, look at me." I do. "Take it from me. As much as you think keeping your past hidden will protect your relationship with Asher, it won't. I almost lost Gray for good because I tried to keep mine a secret. Trust me, altruism often feels like betrayal to the other person. Learn from my mistakes. Talk to him before it's too late."

I nod, knowing she's right.

"Do you love Asher?"

"Yes," I respond immediately. "More than I ever thought possible."

"Do you love this other guy?"

My eyes sting and my stomach churns. I've been slayed with guilt for an entire week. "Yes," I whisper. "He was my first love." And so much more.

She squeezes my hands hard. "You need to figure it out Lysee. Asher's crazy about you."

"I know. I know," I repeat. I can't picture my life without him.

Before we can say anything else, Addy pops her head in. "It's time," she whispers excitedly.

With one last look at each other, Livia and I stand and hug.

"Wait, I have one more thing to do before we go," I tell her before rummaging through my bag. When I pull out the Magic 8 Ball, Livia busts out laughing, which was exactly my plan.

"You still have that thing?" she asks.

"Duh. I'll take this to my grave. I think we need to see what she has to say before you walk down that aisle, don't you?"

"It's tradition," she quips.

"Yes, it is." I shake the ball, asking Livia, "Ready to marry the love of your life?"

We're both grinning from ear to ear when we turn the globe over and peer through the milky blue waters as her answer comes into focus.

Without a doubt.

"Well, now it's eight-ball official. Let's go get you hitched, sis." I tell her, hooking my arm in hers as we walk toward the door.

"I love you, Lysee."

"I love you too, Libs."

TEN MINUTES LATER, as I stand to Livia's left holding her bouquet and mine, Asher stands to Gray's right, holding onto the wedding rings. Our eyes never leave each other as Livia and Gray profess their undying love in front of all their family and friends.

"Livvy, angel, you are my light, my hope, my dreams, my future. I'm a whole man only because you're with me. I'm strong only because my strength comes from you. Who knew when I walked into that pizza joint nearly nine years ago and heard your laugh that my life was about to come into focus for the first time. When I saw your face…" Gray pauses to compose himself and tears shine brightly in his eyes as he holds tight to Livia's hands, his words choked when he starts again.

"When I saw your face, I knew I was looking at my once in a lifetime. My greatest love. My *only* love. My everything..."

Gray takes his time, pouring his heart out to his new wife, who's so emotional by the time it's her turn, she can barely speak. The ceremony is intimate, tender, and poignant as they talk about love almost lost and never letting each other go again. By the end, Gray and Livia are both freely crying and there can't be a dry eye in the house. Even through my blurry ones, I see the glimmer in Asher's as he watches me with unmistakable love.

I can't help imagining it's *me* that's standing in Livia's place and Asher in Gray's. I imagine it's *us* telling the whole word that we've met the one person we can't imagine walking a day without.

I imagine my future.

It dawns on me as I stare into the watery blues of the beautiful, loving man across from me, that I've never had my whole heart to give any man. I've always left a piece of it in the past and guarded the rest. When I was with Beck, a part was left with Asher. And now that I'm with Asher, a small part still remains with Beck.

I need my whole heart back, because I'm finally ready to hand it over in the palm of my hand and let somebody else carry it.

On the exact day I thought my life ended eight years ago, I realize that it's only just begun, but I need to put my past where it belongs, once and for all.

Firmly, permanently in the rearview mirror.

Unfortunately, the only way to do that is to confront it head-on.

CHAPTER 35

ASHER

"I DON'T LIKE THAT ASSHOLE," LUKE GRUMBLES, TAKING A LONG PULL from his Heineken, glaring daggers across the dim room.

"Who?" I ask, trying to follow his line of sight.

"That photographer." He points with the mouth of his green bottle to Cooper Jensen, who is done taking pictures for the evening but has hung around to chat with Addy. They have their heads close, laughing. Addy has her hand on his forearm in a flirty gesture.

I saw him talking for quite a while with Alyse earlier and I had to hold myself back from wiping the floor with his face when he hugged her. But as I try my best to exorcise the illogical jealousy that clouds my judgment, I have to say I think Mr. Jensen seems to be far more interested in Addy than Alyse.

And that's good for his longevity, at least as far as I'm concerned. Now from Luke's perspective, it may still be very much in danger.

Between the two of us I think Cooper Jensen should be *far* more worried about my older brother.

"You like her," I state matter-of-factly, thinking back to last Friday night when Luke acted like a hungry lion protecting his kill. I thought he and camera boy were gonna throw down about who kept Addy in their arms.

"Didn't say that."

I smile, knowing he's full of shit. I'm the motherfucking king of jealousy and I clearly see shades of green swirling wildly around Luke's aura, threatening to crowd out every scrap of common sense. "Then why do you care if she's talking to pretty boy?"

"Didn't say I did. Just don't like him." Luke turns to me. "He was hitting on *your* girl earlier."

"They're just friends," I retort. At least I hope that's all it is. Since last weekend, I may have figured out the unknown number calling Alyse all day Sunday belonged to Cooper Jensen. I may have possibly memorized the number and called it when Alyse was out of town on Tuesday. And he may have told me he was calling about the photography contract when he answered the phone.

Maybe.

Yep...motherfucking *king*.

As I take a swallow of my own drink, I watch Alyse chatting and laughing with my mother and my aunt across the room. I can easily picture her as a permanent part of our family and not just as Gray's sister-in-law. My mom has taken a very keen interest in Alyse, treating her as if she's already one of the family. It seems they've bonded on some sort of female level that I'll probably never understand.

This evening Alyse hasn't seemed quite as withdrawn as she has for the last week, but my hold on her is tenuous at best. I need to up my game if I want to keep her. I'm working hard to break down her walls again. I think I'm making progress, but then there will be a setback, like Christmas evening, when I intruded on a clearly private and intense conversation between Alyse and my mother. I heard the end of it, when my mom was talking about forgiveness, but I never asked what she was referring to. I hoped Alyse would offer, but she didn't and I tried not to let that hurt.

"You love her. Livia's sister," Luke says, nodding in the direction to which I'm intently focused.

I nod. "With every part of me."

"Hold onto her then."

"I'm trying," I confess. "You should ask her to dance. You know, the one you can't peel your eyes from," I suggest as the DJ changes from some new pop song I'm not familiar with to a slow, romantic one that I am. Throwing back the rest of my whiskey, I leave my older brother before hearing his response, making a beeline for my lovely Alyse.

I'm tired of sharing her, even with my family. I want one last dance before I take her back to our hotel room and ravage her for the rest of the night. My dick has been twitching all damn evening watching her in that stunning, knee-length navy-blue dress she's wearing. It looks strapless, except for the sheer halter that covers her delicate neckline. The strappy silver heels make her bare legs look like they go on for miles. I want to see her bending over the bed in nothing but those in about ten minutes.

"I'm going to steal my woman back now," I say quietly to my family, holding Alyse's eyes as I hold out my hand. In the background, Ed Sheeran croons lyrics about people falling in love in mysterious ways and loving until they're seventy. I've decided seventy years isn't long enough for me. If I had one wish, it would be for a dozen lifetimes with her.

Setting her hand in mine, the smile she gives me is brilliant and blinding. I want to drop to my knees and beg her to marry me, to bind herself to me forever. Right here. Right now. Instead I lead her out to the dance floor and twirl her in my arms before pulling her close, enjoying her laugh.

With her left arm around my neck, I place our twined hands against my heart and my forehead against hers, swaying gently to the music. There are so many things I want to say, but none of them seem adequate to express what I'm actually feeling.

Watching my brother marry Livia—the woman he spent five years pining away for—was surreal. It made me believe that love really can conquer all. Despite all the odds, they found each other again. The love that filled that small chapel was pure and rare and tangible, and you'd have to be dead inside for it not to choke you up.

I want that. I want *her*. I want her in my arms every single day. I want marriage. Children. Grandchildren. I want an entire lifetime with her by my side. And I want it yesterday. I'm happy for Gray and I can honestly say I haven't been jealous of any of my brothers a day in my life. Until today. He now has everything I want. I won't rest until I get it, too.

Not caring that my entire family may be looking on, I lean down and capture her mouth. She's tentative at first, but quickly gives in to the chemistry that always draws us tightly together. I kiss her softly, teasing her closed lips with my tongue until she allows me entry.

"You're very good at this," she says quietly after I break away and nuzzle her ear, nibbling her lobe lightly.

"At what? Kissing?"

"Kissing. Dancing. Seducing. Everything."

"Alyse," I whisper hoarsely, pulling her as tight to me as I can. "God, I am *madly* in love with you."

"Show me," she implores breathlessly, her words teasing, pleading.

Don't have to ask me twice.

Grabbing her hand, I walk us the short distance to where Gray and Livia are dancing, completely lost to each other.

"We're heading out," I tell Gray, bringing him in for a quick hug. Turning to Livia, I squeeze her tightly as Alyse talks to Gray. "I'm so happy for you and Gray, Livia. You've made him a very happy man."

"Thanks, Asher. That means a lot."

I look away briefly, embarrassed for how I've treated her. "I have a different perspective on things now."

"I know." She winks knowingly. "Take care of Alyse. She's...fragile."

"She's stronger than you think," I reply.

She drops her voice so only we can hear. "I don't want to see her hurt."

"It won't be by me," I promise her. "Enjoy your honeymoon." In about twenty-four hours, they'll be basking on the sunny beaches of the Maltese Islands. "Talk to you guys when you get back in two weeks."

Taking Alyse's hand in mine, I lead her silently to the elevator bank and impatiently wait for a car to open. When it does, I pull her inside and push the button for the seventeenth floor, wishing there were sixty floors in this hotel so I could have more time alone with her. I want to fuck her against the cherry wood paneling until her voice is raw and her body is a twisted mass of want and need.

I stand on the opposite side of the steel compartment once the doors close, not wasting any time.

"Take off your panties," I demand, locking eyes with her.

She doesn't hesitate, dropping a very damp nude thong on the elevator floor beside her.

"Pull up your dress, not quite all the way, and spread your legs." Within seconds I can see her nether lips. *Fuck*. They're already glistening. "Show me how much you want me, Alyse," I growl. I fist my hand to my side to keep from stroking myself.

When I see a finger disappear into her slick folds and come out coated, I close the distance between us. In a flash I'm kneeling in front of her, my mouth sucking her finger clean before latching onto her pussy. She moans loudly, digging her hands into my hair, as I feast on her with single-minded intent—to make her come before we reach our floor. She's so damn responsive. In record time she reaches the peak, crying out my name as her thighs clamp my head tightly, her body convulsing in pleasure.

"Asher, God," she sobs.

She's floating down, her body still trembling when the elevator slow to a stop right before I hear the ding. Placing a smattering of kisses on her inner thighs, I reluctantly rise, pull down her dress and tug her into me with an arm around her waist just as the doors open.

Two college-age boys stand right outside waiting to go down. By the looks on their faces and their gaze at Alyse's panties lying on the tile floor, they know exactly what happened in the forty-five second ride to the top.

I smirk and bend down to scoop them up, stuffing them into my pants pocket as they watch in attentive fascination. *Learn something, boys.*

"Gentlemen, have a good night," I nod, stepping past them with Alyse's hand tucked securely in mine.

"Looks like you already did," one of them joked.

"I'm just getting started," I mutter, not caring if they heard or not. I stop at our room, making short work of the locked door. By the catch in Alyse's breath, she heard, and that's all that matters.

That, and sliding into her silky heat while she's bent over our bed, ass in the air, in nothing but those sexy fucking shoes in...

Five...

...

Four...

...

Three...

...

Two...

...

...

...

Ahhh. Fucking. Heaven.

CHAPTER 36

ALYSE

FOR TWO DAYS I'VE BEEN RACKING MY BRAIN TRYING TO FIGURE OUT how I'm going to meet with Beck without letting Asher know. The night of the wedding, I told Cooper I was ready to talk to him and asked him to text me Beck's phone number, which he did on Sunday. I saved it under B, but I haven't called him yet.

I don't want to see him in public, because I'm quite sure there will be plenty of yelling and screaming and crying. All on my part, of course, and I don't want to have another public meltdown. I definitely don't want to meet Beck at his place, but I can't do it at mine either, because I spend every free minute with Asher and that's simply too risky.

But now that I've decided to talk to him, I just want to get it behind me so I can heal and forgive. Move on. With Asher. So whether it's luck or divine intervention, Asher has an emergency meeting he's been called to in Detroit this afternoon. Some very important client has filed a lawsuit claiming fraudulent behavior from one of his financial advisors, so he needs to meet with the client tonight and then the advisor and his team of attorneys if the client meeting doesn't go well, which he's not expecting.

"I'm sorry, baby. This client has been a pain in the ass for years. I've just been waiting for him to pull some sort of shit like this. Usually I can keep him under wraps with a few expensive dinners and bottles of Scotch. I need to nip it in the bud before it goes public. We can't afford that kind of negative publicity along with this embezzling issue that I'm sure we won't be able to keep under wraps much longer."

"It's okay, Asher. You're the big boss. You need to handle this. I get it. I'll be fine."

"You sure I can't convince you to come with me?" he asks, cornering me against the cold window in his office. His mouth descends to my neck, nipping and sucking *veeeery* persuasively. If I didn't have this thing with Beck hanging over my head, it would probably have worked.

"I can't. You want me to catch your perpetrator, don't you?" For once I have very conflicted feelings about doing my job. Once you find that elusive thread, the rest seems to unravel quickly. In fact, I could probably return to Detroit and finish the audit there, but I won't.

He groans. "I'm not sure anymore."

"Asher."

"Fine. Yes. I won't be back until probably Wednesday morning," he says between kisses.

"Okay," I pant, as he moves his way to the other side of my neck. He pulls down my blouse, his lips lowering toward the cup of my bra. "Oh, God," I breathe.

"When I get back, I'm whisking you away to Mackinac Island for New Year's Eve."

"Okay."

"I need you to suck me with your sinful mouth before I go, baby."

"Now I'm the one corrupting you," I laugh.

"No. You're the one saving me, my sweet Alyse."

His heartfelt words rip the breath from my lungs. He vacillates on a dime between wicked and sweet. It's hard to keep up, but it's exactly what I need, what I crave. It's like he always knows precisely what to say at precisely the right moment to pull me in deeper, burrow further into my heart. As if he could.

He steps away, leaving a wake of fire where his lips have just been and makes quick work of his pants, dropping them to his knees right in front of anyone in the other office buildings who cares to look. Placing his palm against the cool glass, he leans forward, his pulsing, veiny cock jutting straight toward me, looking angry and in need of soothing.

Twist my arm. I guess I'll volunteer.

CHAPTER 37

ALYSE

"DEEP BREATH IN, DEEP BREATH OUT," I MUMBLE TO MYSELF AS I PACE the length of my temporary apartment, waiting for security to call. I hold my hands out. They're shaking. I haven't been able to eat a thing all day. Beck couldn't meet last night, which would have been ideal, but Asher called this afternoon to say he won't be home until Wednesday morning for sure, so I feel comfortable meeting Beck here.

The intercom buzzes, making me jump. "Ma'am, there is a Beck Mercado who says you're expecting him."

I press the talk button with a wobbly finger and answer with an equally wobbly voice. "Yes. It's fine, Sam. Thanks."

The next couple of minutes tick by like hours as I wait for the knock on my door, but when it comes, I stand there, frozen, unable to turn the knob. I think I may throw up.

"Alyse, you there?" a deep, low, disembodied voice comes from the other side of the thick wood. I couldn't make myself call him so we just texted instead and now I know why. Jesus, it's exactly as I remember. Low and gravelly. It makes my heart hurt and my stomach churn. I can't respond. We stand there in silence. "Alyse, I'll leave if you want me to."

"No," I whisper, still not able to make my hand grip the knob and twist, but unable to tell him to leave. I have to do this. I *need* to do this, as gut-wrenching as it's going to be.

"We can't do this through the door. Please. Open up, babe."

I. SEE. RED.

Flinging the door open so hard it bounces off the wall, I spit, "Don't you *dare* call me that. You lost the right to call me *anything* the day you let me believe you were dead."

His eyes drop briefly before returning to mine. "I'm sorry."

I'm sorry. See? Wholly inadequate.

I turn and stalk into the living room, not caring if he follows, but when I hear the door close softly, I know he hasn't left. I feel his presence as much now as the first day we met. I always thought Beck was larger than life. I think that's why I fell in love with him so fast. He reminded me a lot of Asher in that regard.

Too bad I let myself fall for someone who was a complete enigma as well as a devious liar. That's a mistake I haven't made again, because I haven't fallen for anyone in eight years until now. And Asher is neither of those things.

I stand in front of the window, watching the bright lights of Navy Pier, relishing the coolness I feel seeping into my skin and bones. I let it soak in and I store it away. I'll need to be cold to get through this. I need to remain aloof and unaffected. But I'm about ten seconds away from a complete nuclear meltdown.

"I would offer you a drink, but since this isn't a social call, I won't." In the glass's reflection, I can see he's taken a seat on the overstuffed chair facing me. Remorse is written over every feature, every action, the slump of his shoulders.

"That's fine," he mumbles.

"You have ten minutes," I tell him, turning around to face him. I wrap my arms protectively around my middle. It physically hurts to look at him, to be this close. I want to run my fingers over his stubbly face as much as I want to slap it. I want to wrap my arms around him, holding him tight, to feel that he's really sitting here in front of me. But I want to kick him out, telling him I never want to see his lying face again.

Jesus, he's beautiful, and time has only made him even more so. He's wearing a hunter-green sweater that fits his lean, muscular frame perfectly. The worn, dark denim on his lower half hugs him like a glove. His dark hair is shorter than I remember, but it looks good on him. I have to fight not to be drawn into his sparkling emerald eyes like I was from day one. And I'm a god-awful person, and girlfriend, to even think any of those things.

A fresh plunge of guilt injects itself into the toxic, roiling mixture that my emotions have now become.

"I don't know where to start," he begins quietly.

"Let's see...how about we start with the fact that you tried to kill us when I told you we were going to have a baby."

He cringes at my caustic words, but I don't want to take them back. I've been in agony over this for over eight years. I thought I was over the anger and the hurt, but as I stand here looking at him, it's fresh and raw and bleeding. I'm wrapped in it like a living, breathing entity and each second that ticks by it becomes stronger and more venomous.

"Alyse, it was an accident. I...can we not do this with you standing there, lording over me? This is hard enough."

My bark is bitter and spiteful. "You have no idea what I've been through."

I see a flash of anger, which he quickly hides. "Neither do you." His words are slow and measured and full of secrets I'm no longer sure I want to hear.

I turn back toward the window, wishing I had poured myself a very healthy glass of bourbon before I let him in. For someone who doesn't drink that stuff, it's quickly become my numbness of choice this past week. I watch him rise and walk toward me with a slight limp in his step, our eyes connecting in the window.

When he stops behind me, I close my eyes, silently begging for him not to touch me, only I can't force the words past my closed lips. If I feel the heat of his skin on mine, the cool and aloof I'm trying for will disintegrate into nothingness and all that will be left is raw emotion. I'm not sure I can get through these next few minutes with no protection.

"I'm—"

"Don't say you're sorry," I interrupt softly. "Please, anything but that."

My eyes are still tightly shut when I feel his hands on my shoulders, gently turning me toward him. Tears sting and I refuse to open my lids even when he tips my chin up gently. I nervously chew on my lip, trying desperately to hold myself together.

"Alyse," he coaxes. "Please look at me."

I shake my head.

"Alyse." He says my name with reverence and love, and when my watery eyes open and fall into his, I know he still feels those things. "I never wanted it to be like this."

"Then why?" I choke, hanging onto my emotions by the very tips of my damn fingers. A traitorous tear leaks out, running down my cheek. I want to call it back. He's undeserving of it.

He takes my hand, leading me to the couch and I let him. When he sits too close, I push myself back into the corner, getting as much distance between us as possible.

He looks resigned, nodding once at my action.

"I'm waiting," I whisper, arms wrapped tightly around my knees, which are drawn up to my chin. I need to get as many things in front of my heart as possible.

"Before I start, I want you to know that I loved you, Alyse. I still lo—"

"Don't say that. I don't want to hear any of that."

"Okay." He sighs deeply, looking down at his hands. I'm trying to

271

be callous, but the fact that I hurt him guts me more than I want to admit.

He lied to you, Alyse. Be strong.

"This may be hard for you to hear."

"Stop it already!" I yell. "Just tell me the goddamn truth!"

"Your mom is married to my dad."

That old adage, *the truth shall set you free,* pops into my mind. See... this is the thing about the truth. It does not set the *recipient* free; it sets the *teller* free. They can release their guilt because they've finally spoken it out loud. They get to let go of their burden, but then their burden becomes someone else's. There's a reason people keep secrets. It's because they're either shameful or they'll hurt the person you want to protect most.

This couldn't have hurt me more than if he'd held me down and cut out my heart while I watched.

"You're my..." Gulp. "Stepbrother?"

"Sort of."

"Jesus, Beck. What the actual fuck?" I scream, jumping off the couch. Pacing, my hands flail as I rage. "You either are or you aren't. Did you know that when we were dating? Fucking?"

He winces at my vulgarity. "Yes."

I can't breathe. I stop in front of him, pointing to the door. "You need to leave."

"No. You need to hear the rest of the story."

"I don't need to hear anymore." My ears are ringing. "I think I'm going to faint," I whisper before my knees buckle, but Beck is there, catching me before I can hit the ground.

He settles me back on the couch and heads to the kitchen. I hear a few cupboards open as the cotton and ringing in my ears starts to recede. He returns with a glass of water, which I greedily gulp.

"He's my stepdad, actually."

"What?"

"Can I get the story out this time without you freaking the fuck out?"

I glare at him, knowing full well I deserved that jab. "Yes."

"You never talked about your mom, you know. It's like you pretended she didn't exist," he says softly.

"She didn't. She left me. Left her children, her husband."

"She didn't leave. Your father kicked her out. She was a drug addict, Alyse. You probably don't even know that because you were so little. He couldn't take it anymore. Back then your mom was not a good person. She slept around to get money for drugs. She had drug dealers in your house when you were home, putting you in danger. She sold anything she could get her hands on to get her next fix. For all your father's faults, he did the right thing making her leave. It helped her get her life back together."

"You're lying," I choke, unable to believe a word he just said. "I would have known if she was a drug addict. My father would have told us instead of just telling us she just walked out."

Sympathy oozes from him. "It's true, Alyse. Your father was trying to protect you and your sister. He still loved Elaine."

"By telling us she abandoned us? How the fuck does that protect us?" I snarl.

He shrugs. I can tell he doesn't really understand it either.

"I don't understand any of this."

"Your mom got better," he continues. He's now holding my hand. I let him, needing the comfort, human touch. Gravity. "It took her a few years, but she got herself into a program and got clean, but by then your father was the one in trouble with the gambling. She tried to come back and get you girls, but he fought her. By then he was a changed man, bitter. She threatened to take him to court to get custody and he said she'd never win because of her drug history. He was probably right, but who knows."

I swallow down the bile that's burning my esophagus. For the second time in little more than a week, everything I've always thought to be true is a lie. My head is literally buzzing.

"I need a drink." Standing on unsteady legs, I head into the kitchen, grab the Woodford Reserve sitting on the counter and pour myself a highball glass full. Leaning on the counter for support, I take a couple large gulps and several deep breaths.

But the dam that I've been able to successfully keep my tears behind since Beck walked through that door cracks and the first sob involuntarily breaks free as I process his words.

My mom didn't leave me.

She was kicked out.

She tried to come back.

My father wouldn't let her.

My entire life could have been different. It could have been happy. Carefree. Maybe I wouldn't be this fucked-up person who was constantly afraid of getting hurt, so she kept everyone out instead.

My body heaves and shakes and suddenly I'm engulfed in Beck's arms. He's whispering, "It's okay," over and over, but it's not okay. It's not. And I don't know how to make it okay. I don't know how I'm supposed to forgive everything that's been done to me.

After my sobs subside, he leads me back into the living room and settles me on the couch, drink in hand. I stare down into the caramel-colored liquid trying to form all I've heard into some sort of shape that makes sense. I fail.

"Where do you fit into this? It wasn't a coincidence we met, was it?"

"No," he replies softly.

I cry, not even trying to stop it now. My heart is breaking. My soul, crushed.

"My mom married Roberto Mercado when I was just nine months old, but she died of breast cancer only five years later. Roberto adopted me, raising me as his own. Your mom met my stepfather during his campaign for city councilman in Dearborn. She was a volunteer. By then she was recovering and they fell in love and were married when I was fourteen. She wanted you and Livia back, but my father's political career was taking off. He had moved quickly from councilman to mayor and had his sights set on state senator. They were trying hard to keep Elaine's drug addiction under wraps and your father threatened to go to the press if she pursued custody, so she didn't."

I listen to every word, not able to wrap my head around any of it, but I also know he's not lying. Stuff like this happens in movies or books, not real life. *Does it?*

"She always looked out for you and Livia, but from then on, she did it secretly. Even my father didn't know she kept tabs on you. She pulled me in on her clandestine stalking I think mainly so she could use me as an excuse when my father questioned what she was doing or where she was going. We would drive by your house at least once a week and occasionally we would get a glimpse of you or Livia. She told me she even snuck in at night sometimes while you were sleeping and your dad was out gambling so she could just sit there and watch you."

A river of pain pours from my eyes as I remember back to the nights I thought I'd dreamed she was with me. *I hadn't.* She was there.

I want him to stop.

I want him to continue.

I want to be anywhere else but here.

"When I was twenty, my father got the Republican nomination for state senator and won. They moved to Lansing and Elaine was distraught at not being able to make sure you were okay, especially as it seemed your father's gambling had reached an all-time high. And since I was staying back in Dearborn..."

He stops and wets his lips, his stare intense.

"She asked you to keep an eye on me," I supply.

He nods solemnly. "I wasn't supposed to talk to you. I was just supposed to watch you from afar, but...you were too fucking irresistible, Alyse. I couldn't stay away. I think I'd been in love with you for years from afar. I watched you grow up from this awkward, gangly little girl into a stunning, incredible, smart woman who had been given an unfair lot in life but made the most of it anyway. Not once did I ever think of you as my stepsister. You were simply the woman I was in love with."

My mind is reeling with each new confession. My stomach's now agitating like a washing machine in the spin cycle, so I set my whiskey down.

I reach up, wiping the tears away. "They found out, didn't they?" My shaky voice is barely audible.

"Not until the accident."

Once again, he reaches for my hand, twining it in his. I look at my small fingers engulfed by his large ones. I let myself remember the way it used to feel so long ago, skin tingling every time he touched me.

We were both put into an impossible situation, one that would never have a happy ending no matter how hard we would have tried. The bitterness and resentment slowly start melting away at that realization. My eyes lift to find him watching me attentively, waiting patiently.

"What happened after the accident?"

"My dad and your mom were called and they came to the hospital. I was in pretty bad shape. I had five broken ribs, a punctured lung, a fractured right arm in three places and my left leg was completely crushed. I needed a total of a hundred eighty stitches between my arms, head, and torso. I had swelling in my brain and was in a drug-induced coma for two weeks. I guess I went into cardiac arrest five times during those two weeks. I spent three weeks in ICU, but I was in the hospital for eight total."

Then he releases my hand, bending over to draw up his pant leg. I almost lose my ability to breathe.

"Jesus, Beck." I feel positively ill. Cooper's words hit me like a sucker punch to the gut. *"He's suffered just as much as you have, if not more."* He's right. Beck has suffered far more.

"I lost my leg right above the knee. I spent nine months in intense rehabilitation. I was in a bad way, Alyse. I went into a deep depression. I wanted to die. I thought my entire life was over. My father was furious with Elaine and me, and your father was practically homicidal, threatening to press charges. I later found out that my father paid him off to keep him quiet. Fifty grand. But part of the deal was I wasn't to ever have contact with you again and let you believe that I'd died and...I agreed." His voice cracks and I find myself comforting him by squeezing his hand. A smile plays on his lips before they press into a thin line.

"At the time, I thought it was for the best. I didn't even want to live, let alone be with anyone, and I couldn't imagine I could ever be loved by a woman—*you*—with part of my body missing."

"Oh, Beck. It wouldn't have mattered. Not to me."

"I know that now, Alyse. But at the time I couldn't make sense of anything. It took me years to physically and mentally get back to where I was before the accident. To actually *want* to live again. Depression makes you look at things very differently."

"I know," I reply softly.

His eyes are full of sorrow and understanding. "Jesus, I loved you so much. I wanted to marry you, and for weeks I'd been trying to figure a way out of the fucking mess I'd created. To tell you the truth, wipe the slate clean so I could be the man you deserved. But every scenario I came up with ended badly. I needed to tell you the truth to keep you, but the truth would drive you away, and I couldn't bear the thought of that.

"And when you told me about the baby...for a split second, I can't even describe how happy I was, but then reality crashed into me and I felt the bottom drop out. I felt like I'd lost everything before I even had it. I panicked. I drove recklessly and almost cost us our lives. I cost our baby its life and that torments me every fucking day, Alyse. Every. Fucking. Day."

Next thing I know, Beck is beside me, my wet face in his palms. His eyes are wild with torment. "I'm sorry. I'm so fucking sorry. About the accident. About the baby. About not coming back for you. About everything. I know you don't want to hear it, but I am so very sorry, Alyse."

"I forgive you," I whisper. "I forgive you, Beck."

Then his mouth is on mine, his need for me evident. His lips are soft and warm, as I remember. His kiss burns with longing and love as it always did. But this time I also taste regret.

When I saw Beck across the street last week, the feelings that washed through me were love, among so many others, but I couldn't deny one of them was definitely love. But as I feel his mouth on mine now, I know it's not the kind of love that forevers are made of. That kind of forever is with another man.

"Beck," I mumble, placing my hands on his chest, pushing. "Beck, stop."

Hands still frame my face as his forehead touches mine, chest heaving. "It's too late, isn't it?"

"Yes."

His sharp intake of breath cuts me to the quick. "It's him, isn't it? The guy at the bar?"

I nod. "Yes."

"Do you love him?"

"Very much."

He presses his lips to my temple, letting them linger. "I feel like I'm losing you all over again."

His pain seeps into me, battering my heart. "Beck, I—I don't know what to say."

"I'm sorry. I know that's not fair. I'll always love you, Alyse. Always."

"So will I. Just...not in the same way as I once did." I just didn't fully realize that until now. Those chains I've had locked tightly around my heart suddenly break, each link severing permanently from the link before it. For the first time in twenty-five years, I feel whole. Repaired. *Worthy.*

My mom wanted me.

Beck wanted me.

Asher wants me.

"Can I hold you? Please?"

I may not be in love with Beck, but I still care about him immensely. We have a history that can never be erased. I need this for closure, even though I hope that maybe we can be friends somehow. "I'd like that."

Beck pulls me to him, tucking me under his arm and we relax against the back of the couch.

"Jesus, I have missed you."

"Me too."

"I've thought about you every day for the last eight years, Alyse."

"Me too," I confess. "I'm glad you're not dead."

"So am I. Took me a while to get there, but...yeah."

"How did you know about the baby?"

"I saw the marker along the side of the road."

I tilt my head up as he bends his down. "You went to the crash site?"

His eyes soften and the agony I see churning makes me swallow back my tears again. "Many times. Going back there was part of the healing process for me and then...then I just wanted to be close to you and our baby and I didn't know any other way."

"Beck..." I feel immense guilt for all the bad things I've thought about him over the years when he's suffered so much. We sit there in silence, neither able to break away from the other, both of us remembering.

He clears his throat. "So, this guy..."

"Asher," I smile. "Asher Colloway."

"Asher. You're in love with him, huh?"

I nod and his mouth turns down slightly. It tugs hard on my heart.

"Does he know about me? Us?"

"Not yet," I reply softly. But I need to fix that.

"You going to marry him?"

"Yes," I answer with no hesitation. Because now I know there is none. Hesitation, I mean. I want to tell Asher everything. *Everything*. Barb Colloway was right. Forgiveness is freeing. Even through this horrible scenario, I feel lighter. Happier. Finally...*finally* ready to move on.

"I'm glad. I mean, I'm jealous as hell, but you deserve to be happy, Alyse."

"Yes. I do." I grin again and he laughs, squeezing me tighter. "Tell me about my mom."

So he does. He talks and talks and talks until I can't keep my eyes open anymore.

CHAPTER 38

ASHER

I STAND THERE, UNABLE TO MAKE MY MIND WORK THROUGH WHAT I'M seeing.

Bob Everley called me at eight to tell me he was dropping the lawsuit. I gathered through my discussions with Patty, his financial advisor, that Bob's been asking her out for quite some time. She's refused. He trumped up some bogus charges to try to scare her into changing her mind. Needless to say, we won't be doing business with Bob Everley any longer. He can take his twenty mil and have some other firm manage it. Motherfucker.

Even before I ended that call, I was walking to my car, overnight bag in hand. I couldn't stand to be away from Alyse for another second if I didn't have to. No matter that I haven't had but two hours of shut-eye over the last two days. I settled in for the four-hour drive home just so I could sleep with her in my arms. Seems like I can't do anything as basic as sleeping anymore without her.

It's now a little after midnight and I let myself into Alyse's place, knowing that's where she would be. But what I never expected was to see her lying asleep in the arms of another man. The room is dark, but I can make out that it's the fucking photographer.

The words she said in her office that day when I caught Aaron trying to kiss her come rushing back. I believed her then. I don't now.

"I may have a lot of personality flaws, Asher, but adulterer is not one of them. I have never cheated on a man in my entire life. I wouldn't do it."

Turns out Alyse wasn't any better than Natalie and I was right. I have never experienced debilitating pain before today.

My anguish is bone deep and soul crushing. Never mind they're fully clothed instead of naked, writhing on each other. Never mind they're on the couch instead of the bed. The way he's holding her is more intimate than any sex act.

I turn and walk out as quietly as I came, leaving my beating heart on the floor at their feet, bloody and broken, eternal darkness taking up the empty space it left.

CHAPTER 39

ASHER

"Hey, you can use the house tonight if you want. My plans changed."

"What do you mean they *changed*?" Conn asks, skepticism in his voice. I've wanted that fucking house every year for the last five years and now that I have it, I'm giving it up. Yeah, he knows something's up. I'm glad I'm having this conversation over the phone. It would be much harder to lie to his face.

"Just what I said. Something's come up."

I hear rustling in the background and a few seconds later, it sounds like his breathing's picked up. Wow, starting early, huh? "Asher, what did you do?"

That pisses me off. "Oh, what? Because *I* would be the one to do something, right? Not her."

"Well, yeah."

"You don't know shit."

"And you're probably jumping to conclusions, as usual. Jesus, Asher, do you have to sabotage every good thing you have?"

"I'm done with this conversation. Take the house if you want it. If not, fuck off."

I no sooner hang up on him than I hear pounding on my door.

Asshole.

"What?" I growl, opening the door before I walk back to the couch, where I sit with a nice, strong, mostly vodka Bloody Mary. Who the piss cares if it's only nine o'clock in the morning? Maybe this will help me pass the fuck out, because God knows I didn't get even a wink last night as I lay wide-eyed in my bed wondering how this could have happened to me yet again.

This time, however, I will not recover. Pain lances every cell of my body this morning even worse than last night. I'm finding it hard to breathe. To think. To give a fuck about anything but numbing my heartbreak.

"Tell me what happened."

"No."

"I'm not leaving until you do." He eyes my Bloody Mary and then snatches it from my hand before I have a chance to react.

"Prick," I snip.

"Grow the fuck up. What happened?" Conn takes a seat in the loveseat across from me, resting an ankle on his opposite knee.

I stay silent, having no intention of divulging my stupidity over a woman once again to my twin. Fool me once, shame on me. Fool me twice, well...I don't even know what to do with that. What I do know is there won't be a third fucking time. I'm strictly a hit-it and quit-it guy from now on.

"Do you love her?" he asks.

"This isn't about love."

He nods. "I'll take that as a yes. Where is she?"

"I don't know. Probably still in the arms of that fucking photographer I caught her with a few hours ago."

Conn's unable to contain his reaction before masking it. "Cooper Jensen?"

"The one and only."

"What were they doing?"

"Sleeping."

"Naked?"

"No," I reply, shaking my head. It was so much worse than that.

"There has to be an explanation," he retorts. His optimism just pisses me the hell off sometimes.

"You always think there's an explanation, Conn. I stood there quite a long fucking time staring at him holding my woman as they slept trying to figure out if my warped mind was playing tricks on me, but after about ten minutes it finally sank in that it wasn't a goddamn hallucination and I left."

"Without confronting them? Getting answers?"

"No, I didn't confront them. They looked pretty fucking cozy. It's simple, as it always is, brother. I was played. Again."

He's silent for a few minutes. Guess that shut him up.

"Did you ever cheat on Natalie?" he finally asks.

Or not.

"How are you turning this around on me?"

"Just answer the question. You ever cheat on her?"

"No."

"She's convinced you did. She says that's the only reason she turned to this guy was because she thought you were sleeping with someone else and she wanted to hurt you like you'd hurt her."

"I was one hundred percent faithful to her for the entire time we were together, even though she obviously didn't deserve it. I never gave her any reason to think I was cheating. So I guess that's on her then."

"You're missing the point."

Sighing heavily, I play along even though that's the last thing I want right now. I want to drink. I want to forget. I want to figure out how the hell I'm going to move one step ahead, let alone an entire lifetime without the woman who has herself buried so deep inside me I know I'll never be free of her. "What *is* the point, Conn?"

"Assumption. The whole point is she *assumed* something that wasn't true *was*. And she's regretted it ever since. Don't make the same mistake, Asher. Don't *assume* you know what you saw. It could be entirely innocent. Talk to Alyse. She doesn't seem like the cheating kind to me and I think you know that."

He rises and hands back my cocktail before clasping me on the shoulder. "In our entire lives, I've never known you to quit on anything. For years, you even fought for that doomed relationship you had with Natalie. Don't quit now. Fight like the tenacious bastard I know you are. You are meant to marry this woman, brother. I feel it. I see it every time I watch you two together. So swallow your goddamn pride and fight for her. Even if there is something going on with this guy, which I doubt, then fight for her anyway. If you fuck this up because you let your pride get in the way, you'll live the rest of your life under nothing but a mountain of regret. And trust me, that's no way to live."

Then he leaves me alone with my hard liquor and a crushed heart to mull over his words.

CHAPTER 40

ALYSE

MY EYES SHIFT FROM MY COMPUTER SCREEN TO THE CLOCK ON THE wall once again. Five minutes past three. My door is open and I can hear the few people on this floor making their way to the elevator in anticipation of partying the night away. I suddenly wonder what I'll be doing; the prospect of being by myself in a lonely apartment doesn't sound appealing in the least.

I haven't heard from Asher all day. I've texted him three times and called twice, but each call went to voice mail. Each text remained unanswered. I'm sure he's knee-deep with this lawsuit, but I can't help but worry. It's not like him to not at least respond with a quick flirty or dirty message.

Out of my peripheral, I see someone standing in my doorway and my heart speeds up hoping it's Asher, but as I spin around I see it's Tara. "Alyse, I'm taking off. Did you need anything?"

"Uh, no. I'll see you next week then, right? You're taking Friday off?"

"Yep. Have a good holiday." She winks.

"Say, have you heard from Asher today?"

"Yeah, about a couple hours ago. He said he'd be in later to get a few files."

"Oh." I try not to let my face fall, but apparently I fail, because she quickly responds. "He said he's been really busy, so I wouldn't worry about it if you've been trying to reach him." Ever the good assistant... trying to cover up for her boss.

"Oh. No, I'm fine. I...just wanted to run a couple of things by him is all." For being so proficient at lying, I'm failing miserably right now.

"I'll see you later."

"Yep," I mumble, but she's already gone.

I return to my report. Even with my mind elsewhere, it's been a very productive week with Asher gone. I'm practically jumping up and down about telling him what I've found so far. Although I'm not done completely with the audit, I finally have enough documentation to at least suspend the suspect, pending further investigation. I've gone through all the charities and suppliers and found one charity and two suppliers that are not only suspicious, they're just plain bogus. Well, the businesses are legit, the invoices aren't.

The CFO, Edward Reigen, requested all three to be set up. Asher will be less than happy when I tell him the charity approval for Feed My Starving Children even has his signature. In the June board of directors meeting minutes, a hundred thousand-dollar donation was approved, which the new supplier notes indicate, but the money never made it to Feed My Starving Children. Instead, it made it to the bank account of Mr. Reigen. In fact, the invoices for the other suppliers also made it into Mr. Reigen's bank account, which he just opened in February of this year.

No matter how small or large a company is, one thing is the same across them all. The grapevine. It's surprising how much gossip people want to spread about the misery of others. Mr. Reigen, the CFO of CFC for over five years now, has apparently been going through a very nasty divorce and is being put through the ringer by his ex for outrageous child and alimony support. Amanda freely offered that little tidbit up at the coffee pot last week, so I was less than surprised this morning to find that he also owned the bank account that the false invoices were being paid to.

I feel his presence before I see him and lift my head just as he walks through my door. He looks troubled, angry, and something else that I can't quite place. The anticipation that I'd had at seeing him quickly changes to unease.

"Hi," I say. "I was worried about you. I haven't heard from you all day."

Without a word, he shuts the door and sits down across from me.

"What's wrong?"

He starts talking. Slow, deliberate. "I'm going to ask you this one time only, Alyse, and I expect the truth, no matter how painful it may be to say it."

My brows furrow, not liking his insinuation at all. "Ask me what? Asher, what's going on?"

"Are you having an affair with that fucking photographer?"

"What?" I half snort, half laugh. "Who? Cooper? That's ridiculous. Of course not."

"Wrong answer," he says. Rising he starts walking to the door but I jump up and rush over, standing in front of it before he can make it all the way there. He stops right in front of me. His presence is imposing. I've never seen him like this and I have to admit I'm a little scared.

"What the hell is going here?" I demand, arms crossed.

"I think that's my question."

"I don't hear from you all day and then you walk in here accusing me of having some imaginary affair with a friend? What the hell, Asher? You really have a problem, you know that?"

From this close distance, I smell the alcohol wafting off him like he's been dunked in a vat and soaked for a few hours. It's steaming from his pores with such potency, I can almost see it rising like hot vapor on blacktop.

"You're drunk," I accuse.

"Not nearly enough."

"Did you drive?"

"I'm not that stupid, Alyse."

"Asher," I lay my hand on his waist and he flinches so I remove it, trying not to let it hurt as much as it does. "Please. Tell me what's going on here."

"I saw you." His voice cracks. I can tell he's one rung away from falling into an inky black void where I won't be able to reach him.

"You saw me what? You aren't making any sense. Please, let's talk when you're sober."

I start to move away, to let him leave when he slams his body into mine. My back hits the door hard and then his mouth is on mine. It's rough and bruising and not in a mutually I-want-to-rip-your-clothes-off way, but in an I'm-so-fucking-pissed-off-at-you-I'm-going-to-make-you-bleed way.

This is not Asher. Asher is not physical or violent. He's demanding and sometimes rough, but he's never done anything that I didn't like or want. I try to push him back, but he doesn't give an inch, taking, taking, until I'm scared he's going to take something he'll later regret when the alcohol haze wears off. He finally breaks his mouth from mine, and bites his way down my neck, asking me "why" in between hard, painful nips. It hurts...and it's meant to.

"Asher, stop. Please, stop. Please," I beg over and over, my voice shaking more with each escalating plea. It must finally get through, because he does. Leaning his head against the maple wood, his chest heaves and he pulls me to him, squeezing so hard, I almost can't breathe.

His shoulders begin to shake and I realize he's crying. It breaks my heart in pieces to think something has brought this strong man to such a place of despair. His pain is so unbearable it physically hurts me. I stroke his hair with one hand, holding him close with the other.

Air is overrated anyway.

"I love you, Asher. I love you. Only you. Please tell me what's wrong."

"I love you so fucking much, Alyse. I know I love you, because I've never felt soul-tearing agony like I did last night when I saw you in his arms. Why would you do that to me? To us? You're my everything and now I have nothing." The last few words are rumbled on a sob.

Oh shit. Now it's all making sense.

I was emotionally and physically exhausted last night and accidentally fell asleep on the couch with Beck. Something woke me shortly after midnight and I asked him to leave, which he did immediately. And Beck and Cooper look so much alike...

He sags against me, his hard body completely pinning mine.

Okay, maybe air isn't overrated.

"Asher, baby, listen to me. Can we go to your office where we can sit down and I can explain? It's not what you think."

"Never is. Always me," he mutters, not making a lick of sense. I wonder how much he's had to drink and how long he's been doing it. And I wonder why he didn't just confront me last night instead of leaving, angry and hurt.

Suddenly I'm petrified that I may lose him, all because I was too afraid to confess my secrets earlier.

Tears threaten. This is all my fault. Had I just been up front with him from the very beginning, we wouldn't be in this situation right now. Once again, I have fucked up big time. But I push those baby-bitch tears and the emotion down, because right now Asher needs me. I can't help him if I'm a blubbering mess.

He lets me push him back. I manage to get us away from the door enough to open it. I look out into the hall to ensure no one is loitering. Would probably be a bad idea for Asher's employees to see him smashed at four o'clock in the afternoon, even if it is New Year's Eve.

Tucking an arm around his waist, I walk him the short distance to his office and sit him on the couch. His eyes are now heavy and unfocused and he's having a hard time keeping them open, even though he's giving it his best college try.

"Can I have your phone?" I ask quietly, sitting next to him. He reaches into his jeans pocket and produces it. I quickly find the contact I'm looking for and dial. On the fourth ring he answers.

"Hi. It's Alyse. I need your help."

CHAPTER 41

ASHER

I CRACK OPEN MY EYES AND BLINK, TRYING TO MAKE OBJECTS COME INTO focus, trying to remember where in the hell I am and how I got there. It takes me a few seconds, but slowly, events from the last twenty-four hours come rushing back. I wish they fucking hadn't.

I realize I'm in my own bedroom, fully clothed, sans shoes, just like I'd left this afternoon when I went into the office to confront Alyse. I wasn't as drunk as Alyse thought, but I wasn't exactly sober either, so I remember every word spoken. Unfortunately I also remember how rough I was with her. Regret eats at me for the way I treated her. No matter what, she did not deserve that from me. I went there with the intent of fighting for her, but things quickly escalated out of my control. Hurt easily commandeered the reins from common sense.

I sit up, taking stock of how I feel. I lost count of how many

Bloody Marys I had throughout the day. Whatever it was, it wasn't enough. I spent hours stewing over Conn's advice, reliving every single memory I've ever had with Alyse. I ached with the thought of giving that up. Of giving her up. It was excruciating to think of a life without her.

It still is.

Looking at the clock, I see it's almost eleven o'clock. I think I passed out from exhaustion more than the alcohol and had been sleeping for almost seven hours. With the way my body feels, I think I need about seven more, but the need to find Alyse is far more urgent than drifting back into my restless dreamland.

After a pit stop in the bathroom and a quick brush of my teeth, I leave my bedroom and hear soft voices in the living room. Rounding the corner, I see Conn and Alyse sitting on the couch, each with a glass of wine in their hand, quietly talking. The TV is on in the background. With the millions of tons of confetti floating through the air it looks like the east coast is celebrating a brand new year, while I'll be nursing a hangover here shortly. This is not at all what I had in mind for ringing in the year that I had planned to make Alyse my wife.

"Do you think I should check on him again?" she asks, worry threading her tone. At least she still gives a fuck after the way I treated her earlier. That's something.

"Nah. Give him another half hour. Then we can," Conn answers.

"You can go, you know."

"Alyse, I'm not leaving. You and Asher belong together and sometimes he's his own worst enemy. Besides, he needs a good tongue-lashing for the shit he pulled today and that's what brothers are for."

Her smile pulls me forward. I take a few more steps when Alyse spots me and stops mid-sentence.

"I'm glad he—"

Conn cranks his neck following Alyse's line of sight. His lips thin in fury, directed entirely at me, but I don't care. He's right. I deserve it. I quickly shift my attention back to Alyse, drinking the sight of her in, lifting my hand to rub the pain in my chest.

God, I love her. So damn much.

I can't lose her.

"Hi," she says quietly, making no attempt to move. "How are you feeling?"

"Pretty much like an asshole."

"You should. You *are* an asshole," Conn grates. "Did you not listen to a fucking word I said earlier?"

"I did." I listened. I just took a little self-pity detour first.

"You owe me," he says, standing and walking into the kitchen to set his glass down. I brace myself for the "tongue-lashing" he's about to deliver. "Big time. I had to sneak your drunk ass down the stairs and out the back entrance and you cost me a fan-fucking-tastic lay tonight. On New Year's Eve of all nights, thank you very much. All because you were wallowing when you should have been getting the fucking truth like I told you to. Honestly, if I were Alyse, I'd kick your jealous, overreacting ass to the curb. I have no idea what's wrong with my brothers. Book smart, business shrewd, relationship incompetent," he mumbles the last part under his breath.

I ignore the last part. Like he's a damn expert at relationships. "Good thing you're not Alyse then."

Our eyes haven't left each other's and, at this point, I don't know what to think, what to believe, but I know this: I'm going to give her a chance to explain, because I don't just want her, I *need* her. Desperately. And if there's somebody else, as ego bruising as it will be, I'm going to fight for her.

I want her to choose me.

Conn walks back over to Alyse and kisses her on the cheek. "I'll be just a phone call away if you need anything else, okay? I can be up here in a flash." He glares at me when saying the last part. Then he walks to the door, but before he closes it, he drops a bomb that stabs me in the gut like a hot poker. "You do anything to her in anger again and you and I will have a big problem."

I start to ask him what the hell he's talking about when I see Alyse's hand cover the right side of her neck. A wave of nausea hits me fast. I think back to how fury lit my blood on fire when I saw bruises on her arm from Finn. I feel absolutely sick. I am no better than that fucking loser.

"Fuck, Alyse. I'm…Jesus, I'm sorry."

"I'm fine. Conn's making it a bigger deal than it is."

Sitting down next to her, I take the wine and reach behind me, setting it down. When I turn back, I gently remove her hand to inspect the damage I caused. My stomach rolls at the tiny bruises I already see forming. My eyes lift to see her watching me carefully.

"I'm—"

She places a finger to my lips. "Stop. I'm the one who should be apologizing."

My eyes search hers. I can't possibly be mistaken at the love and affection I see. "Pick me, Alyse," I beg, unable to stop myself. I'll get down on my knees and stay there for all my days if I need to. I'll swallow an ocean full of salty pride if it would persuade her to be mine. "Choose me. I don't know how to live without you anymore. I don't *want* to."

"Asher," she breathes with a voice that's beseeching. "There never was a choice." I must look confused because she adds, "There is no one else. There's only you. I'm in love with *you*. I *want* only you."

"But I saw you with him. Last night."

She takes a deep breath, blowing it out slowly. I hate that her eyes shift from mine briefly. "I have a lot of things I need to tell you. Are you up for it now, because it's not a short conversation."

I nod, but I'm not at all sure I'm ready to hear something that could turn my entire world on its axis again.

"Do you remember the accident I was in when I was eighteen?"

"Yes," I reply wondering what in the hell that has to do with the fact that I saw her in another man's arms last night.

"And you remember that the driver died?"

I nod.

Another big breath. I can tell this is hard for her. "He didn't die."

"Okay…" I stretch the word out, getting more confused by the second. "What do you mean he didn't die? And what does any of this have to do with last night?"

"The guy you saw me with last night wasn't Cooper. His name is Beck Mercado. He's Cooper's cousin. He was the driver in that accident. He was my boyfriend." Her eyes sweep down briefly before delivering the killing blow.

"And the father of my baby."

CHAPTER 42

ASHER

AN HOUR LATER MY MIND IS REELING WITH EVERYTHING SHE'S TOLD ME. Her dead boyfriend is alive and is her stepbrother, and his stepdad is married to Alyse's runaway mother.

Both she and this guy have walked through hell and come out the other side. Different people, but they've come out nonetheless. It absolutely shreds me that she was pregnant with someone else's baby, but I would be a hypocrite of epic proportions to ever think differently about her because of it.

As much as I'm seething inside with jealousy, I feel for the guy. He was put in a tough spot. The difference between us is that *nothing* would have kept me away from Alyse. Not a damn thing. Now I understand why Alyse has been so protective of her heart. Why she's tried to keep me out.

"This is all a little unbelievable. Like a fucking soap opera or something," I mutter, scrubbing a hand over my hair. Then I ask the question that I know without a doubt I do *not* want the answer to, but not knowing will eat my gut raw. It's already bled far too much these past two weeks. "Do you...do you still love him?"

The way I saw him holding her makes complete sense now. He's still in love with her. I didn't have to see anything other than the tender way he held her in his arms, even in sleep, to know that. I have to know if she feels the same.

Fuck. I can hardly stand to hear her answer.

She reaches for my hand, and both her gesture and words settle me. "I think a part of me was still in love with the *memory* of him. I'll always care about him because of our history, but I'm not in love with him. I'm in love with you, Asher. *You.* I was wrong to keep all this from you, but it was just too painful to even put a voice to it and after I saw him at the bar that night, I just...I didn't know what to do. What to think. *I* had to understand what was happening first before I could even attempt to talk to you about it."

"I get it, Alyse." And I do. I don't like it, but I do get it. "I understand how hard some things are to talk about." I reach for her, needing her in my arms, my mouth on hers. She stops me.

"There's one more thing I have to tell you."

Her nervousness makes me nervous, too. "You can tell me anything, Alyse. Anything."

She swallows hard. "When I lost the baby and I thought Beck had died, I went into a very deep depression."

"Understandable," I reply softly, aching to hold her to me, to ease her discomfort.

"I...I didn't want to live. I felt like I'd lost everything and I couldn't talk to anyone else about it. Neither Livia nor my father knew about Beck...or the baby. The pain was so vast and so deep; I felt completely and utterly lost. I would lie in bed at night and wish I were the one who had died instead of Beck, instead of our baby. I was in so much emotional pain, I literally couldn't function. All I wanted was to be with Beck and my baby, even if it wasn't in the flesh."

She flashes a look of embarrassment before continuing. "The first time, I took an entire bottle of ibuprofen, but all I managed to do was make myself sick for three days. The second time, though, I got smarter. I took a handful of Cymbaltas and pain pills and as much whiskey as I could drink until I blessedly passed out."

I literally cannot breathe when Alyse pauses, biting her lip. Her gaze shifts away again. This time I don't give her a choice. I pull her into my lap and wrap my arms tightly around her, all the time thinking *fuck fuck fuck*! I could have lost her. Forever. The only woman who was meant for me could have been taken away before I even had her. I squeeze tighter, relishing in the warmth of her body bleeding into mine.

"Livia found me," she tells me quietly. "I'd stopped breathing and she did CPR on me until the ambulance arrived. If she'd been even two minutes later I would have died. After three days in the hospital, my father admitted me to an inpatient psych ward where I spent the next thirty days in intense therapy and another year after that in outpatient care."

My eyes prick as irrational guilt assaults me. None of this would have happened either if she were mine back then. If I'd never let her go.

"Jesus, Alyse. I'm sorry. I'm so sorry you went through all of that by yourself. I'm sorry I wasn't there for you."

"Asher, you have no reason to be sorry. It's just...my path, I guess."

"I should have never let you go. It *is* my fault."

"Stop. It's not. You don't...think any less of me because I had a little psychotic break?" she asks tentatively.

"Christ, why would I, Alyse? I can't even imagine what you were going through. I'm in no position to pass judgment on something that I can't possibly understand. If anything I'm proud of you."

"Proud of me?" she asks disbelievingly.

"Yes. I'm not sure I could have been as strong as you were to get through all of that."

"I wasn't strong. I was weak."

"No, baby." I tilt her face to mine. "A moment of weakness doesn't

298

make you weak. It makes you human. You're here and you're an extraordinary woman. The strongest I know."

Her smile is tired and sad. "After I recovered, that's when I got the tattoo. To remind myself to believe in hope and life and me."

"I figured it was something deep and meaningful," I say, stroking her hair.

"Yeah."

She looks away again, going silent. I have to wonder why she was so nervous to tell me something like this. As far as I'm concerned, the whole dead/not dead boyfriend is a far more important part of what shaped Alyse into the woman she is today.

"Your mother's very wise, you know," she finally says.

"Yes she is," I numbly agree, unable to think about anything but the fact that I almost didn't get the chance to sit here now with her. I could have missed the smell of vanilla in her hair or pressing my lips to her warm temple or the feather of her fingers down my spine as I rock inside of her. My arms tighten. She squeaks so I loosen them, but only slightly.

"She told me that life takes us where we're supposed to be, even if that road is bumpy and there are detours. My road has been hard, but I know it's led me back to you."

"She did, huh?" I smile. My mom is one-of-a-kind incredible, always knowing the right thing to say at the right time. I hook a finger under her chin, tilting her head up. Her gorgeous, misty eyes meet mine. "I wish I had never let you go."

"Don't let me go now."

"Never," I whisper. "Never again." As I stare into the eyes of the woman who single-handedly brought my heart back to life, I can't keep the next words from leaving my mouth no matter how hard I try. I didn't plan on doing this now, but I can't imagine a more perfect time. "Marry me, Alyse."

"What?" she murmurs in shock.

"Marry me," I say with conviction, positioning her so she straddles my thighs. "It doesn't have to be tomorrow or next month or even in six months, but I want nothing more than to be your husband. I want to spend every single day of the rest of my life worshipping you, taking care of you, loving you. I've never loved a single person more than I love you, Alyse, so marry me. Let me spend the rest of my days showing you just how much you are wanted, because no one will ever want you as much as I do."

"Asher…" Her eyes swim with unshed tears.

"Don't say anything unless it's yes."

"No 'yes or no' ultimatum this time?"

"No. Because all I want to hear is yes."

"Okay." A devilish smile spreads across her face, but I'm still waiting to hear only one word.

"Okay? Is that a yes, or is that just an okay?"

"Yes."

"Yes it's a yes, or yes it's just an okay?"

She laughs, her smile bright and happy. Cupping my face, she sobers a bit. "Your proposal was more of a demand than a question. You're very bossy."

My lips curl. "You love it."

"Yes."

"Yes you love it or yes you'll marry me."

After a few beats, she answers, "Yes to both."

"Alyse…" My eyes close briefly before opening and capturing hers. I find myself tumbling into her dark, fathomless pools. I plan on staying blessedly adrift there forever. "God, I love you."

"Show me. Show me I'm yours."

I stand, wrapping her legs around me, my cock pulsing, dying to slip into her wet heat after two nights away. "I'm going to spend the rest of my life showing you. Over and over."

My mouth latches onto hers as I carry her to our bedroom and gladly fulfill *her* every demand this time.

CHAPTER 43

ALYSE

"OH MY GOD, YOU LOOK AMAZING!" I SQUEEZE MY SISTER TIGHT, hardly able to believe how fantastic she looks. She's absolutely glowing. Even in the two short weeks since I last saw her, her belly has rounded out a bit further.

"Soaking in vitamin D for two weeks does wonders for a person."

"Somehow I don't think that a few rays have you glowing like that," I tease.

"You're right," Livia giggles.

"I missed you," I tell her, truly meaning it.

"I missed you, too."

"Liar."

"No, I really did. It was great to spend some quality alone time with Gray, but I'm also glad to be home and able to get back into a routine. Sleeping in my own bed. Spending time with my sister."

Gray and Livia returned from their honeymoon last night, and I've been dying to spend some alone time with her. I have so much to tell her.

"Can I get you anything?" I ask.

"No. I'm good. Thanks."

I pour myself another glass of wine before taking a seat beside her, nerves setting in.

"So are you going to tell me about the blinding rock that's weighing down your left hand?"

I can't help but smile as I gaze at my almost three-carat cushion-cut platinum engagement ring that Asher and I picked out last Friday. In fact, I haven't been able to stop smiling for over a week. He was pissed that the boutique jewelry store he wanted to take me to was closed on January first, so we had to wait until the next day. That was a whole week ago now. "Yeah, about that..."

"About that," she mimics.

"I didn't want to tell you over the phone. I wanted to tell you in person."

She nods. "You look radiant, Lysee. So happy."

"God, I am, Libs. Sickeningly happy. You don't think it's too soon?" I don't. I know with every fiber of my being that Asher's the one for me, but I guess I'm also seeking the approval from the one person outside of Asher who really matters.

My sister.

My friend.

My pseudo mother.

"I think the heart wants what it wants and when you know, you know. There's no magical timetable for falling in love, Alyse. I fell head over heels for Gray the first time I saw him, even though I tried hard to resist his charms."

"Sometimes I don't think it's real, you know," I tell her, my voice low.

"Yes, I do know," she answers just as softly. I sense those secrets I know she's hiding coming closer to the surface.

Our gazes hold for a minute in solidarity. It's time to spill my secrets again, but this time it will be easier.

"I have so much to tell you, Libs."

"Me too," she replies.

I take a deep breath and start my story from the beginning. I tell her about Beck. I tell her about our mother and how our father kept her away. I tell her about the baby I lost. I even tell her about my summer fling with Asher when I was seventeen, which makes her laugh.

Two more glasses of wine and half a box of tissues later, I get one last confession off my chest, so I can start this year completely free. Free from burdens. Free from secrets. Free from bitterness.

Free to be completely happy.

"I've had a lot of resentment toward you, Libs."

She swallows and her eyes water again. "I know, Alyse. I'm sorry."

"I'm trying to let it go, but when you left I felt abandoned. Again. I needed you more than I ever had and you were just...gone." Telling a person you love that they've disappointed you is gut-wrenchingly hard. Let's face it, who really *likes* confrontation? But it's far better than letting that resentment fester deep inside until it becomes cancerous, permanently tainting your relationship.

Rising from the couch, Livia walks to the window. It's snowing, and while I hate the cold and snow, from this height I have to admit the white flakes floating down from the heavens above are peaceful and beautiful. A complete contradiction to how I feel right now.

"I didn't leave you, Alyse. I...saved you."

"Saved me? From what? How could leaving me save me?"

Livia finally sits back down, takes my hand, and reveals yet another bizarre chapter in this fucked-up story that's become my life. She tells me how our father "sold" her to pay his debts, but that the monster really wanted me. She tells me how she was beaten, raped, and lost her baby. She tells me how she almost didn't make it out alive and how Luke/Grant (confusing) saved her.

When she's finished, I almost wish for oblivion.

For years I've had it all wrong.

For years I've believed the worst of every person who's ever loved me.

For years, I've believed I was never good enough.

Every person I thought didn't fight for me or love me enough to stay, sacrificed *everything* for me.

Everything.

Except for one. My *father*.

He didn't sacrifice enough.

CHAPTER 44

ASHER

I'VE BEEN ON CLOUD NINE FOR MORE THAN A WEEK NOW. AND IF YOU tell me that sounds like a chick thing to say, I will tell you I don't give a flying fuck. Within twenty-four hours, I went from thinking I'd lost the only thing that mattered to me to somehow, someway getting her to agree to spend the rest of her life with me. *Me*, the guy who has more personality flaws than I can count. I'm still in disbelief she said yes.

I am the luckiest goddamn man on the face of the planet. I will never take a day with her for granted. I feel like I've waited my whole lifetime for her. In many ways I have.

What Alyse has been through is unimaginable. She's a strong, determined, loyal, and loving woman despite her rough life, but I will do everything in my power to keep her from suffering another day for as long as she lives.

And what Livia went through to save her is almost too horrific to comprehend. I owe her everything, my heartfelt apology being the first thing. She sacrificed more than one person should have to because of the love she has for her sister. I have absolutely no doubt I would not be with my soon-to-be wife had it not been for her selfless act. Alyse had just been through something so traumatic that there's no way she would have survived the hundred kinds of hell Livia had to have endured. I'm ashamed at the horrible things I've thought about her all this time.

I hear the chime of my phone and grab it off my nightstand, smiling. Alyse is out with Livia, Addy, and Kamryn for a few engagement celebratory cocktails, insisted on by Addy, and I have little doubt I'll be the recipient of a mind-melting blow job in about an hour.

Alyse and Addy have quickly become good friends. I'm glad. Alyse has so much to give and anyone who is let into her very small inner circle is precious to her. I guess I also have to accept that both Cooper and Beck are in that circle, like it or not. And for the record, I *don't* fucking like it. At all. But I'm dealing, until I can figure out a way to shove them out permanently. I guess I'm not making too much progress in the jealousy category, but I am trying.

Alyse: want me to pick up that cheesecake u like on my way home

Me: ur all the sweet I need, baby. i plan on indulging later

Alyse: luv u

Me: not more than i do sweet alyse

I set my phone down, not expecting her to respond again, getting back to the task at hand. I'm going through my pile of clothes to take to the dry cleaner tomorrow, making sure all the pockets are emptied. I've lost all kinds of shit because I'm too lazy to clean out my suits. Wallets, money, business cards. So now I take ten minutes to scour my clothes every Sunday night.

Tonight I have a pile on the floor in my closet that includes probably five dollars' worth of coins and nearly a hundred dollars' worth of paper money, along with several scraps of paper.

I'm scooping the scraps up to throw them out when I notice the crumpled up one that Conn gave me several weeks ago now. The one with Natalie's phone number on it. My mother's words, which were meant for Alyse, but that I overheard anyway pop into my head.

"Forgiveness? That's hard. Much harder than holding onto our hurts and wrongs. It takes courage and bravery to forgive. Oh, but Alyse...forgiveness is freeing. Healing. In both mind and spirit..."

I think about Alyse and how she's been able to forgive the wrongs that were done to her. She's even listening to me about possibly meeting her mother. And then I think about how I need to do the same. I need to let my bitterness with Natalie go, once and for all so I can be completely free of that dead weight.

I pick up my phone and dial.

"Hello?" her soft voice chimes through my earpiece.

"Natalie, it's Asher."

"Asher?" Her voice perks up, full of surprise. "Hi. I'm glad you called."

I'm not. "What did you want, Natalie?"

"I—I wanted to see you."

"That's not going to happen." I curse myself for being so short, reminding myself of my purpose. Forgiveness. Move forward without baggage. With Alyse. "But I have a few minutes now to talk."

"Yes, okay. I'd like that. I, uh...I wanted to apologize. For everything that happened."

"Why, Natalie? Why now?"

"Because I made mistakes and I hurt you. I was wrong and I wanted you to know that."

"Why would you do that to me?" I need truthful answers if I have any hopes of ending this conversation with a lighter heart.

Her prolonged silence irritates me. "I was lonely, I guess. You were gone all the time and Rick was just there. And part of me...part of me wanted to get back at you."

"Get back at me? What the hell for?"

"I know there was someone else, Asher. The last few months we were together, you'd call out a woman's name in your sleep. You even said it a couple of times when we were having sex and you were drunk."

I sigh heavily, not wanting to rehash the same shit more than four years later. I'm beginning to wonder if this was such a good idea after all. "Natalie, we've been over this before. There was no one else."

"Then who was Alyse?"

My heart stutters, my breath momentarily stolen by her words. "What did you say?"

"Alyse? Who was Alyse?"

Even though it's highly inappropriate, I laugh, unable to believe what I'm hearing. "Why did you never mention her name to me before now?"

"So it's true?"

"No. It's not true. Alyse was an old friend." A friend I wanted to fuck, but we were never officially more than that. "I didn't see her the whole time we were together, Natalie. I promise you."

"But she was someone you cared about?"

I guess Alyse was buried deeper than I ever realized. "Yes. I never realized that I'd never really gotten over her. I'm...I'm sorry, Natalie." I almost need to say thank you. Natalie's insecurities and inability to effectively communicate kept me from making the biggest mistake of my life, pushing me back toward the love of my life instead.

"I'm sorry, too, Asher." Her voice cracks and I hear sniffling. Now I feel like a piece of shit.

"I guess we both made mistakes," I tell her. I wasn't the perfect boyfriend. Too worried about climbing the corporate ladder, I didn't pay enough attention to Natalie or her feelings or insecurities. This is the first time I ever admitted my culpability for the demise of our relationship, and apparently it's far overdue. I can now see I did my fair share of pushing her right into her lover's arms, even if most of it was unconscious.

"I guess we did. I'd do it all differently if I had to do it over again."

"I know." I can't say I would, because then I wouldn't have Alyse. I'm not sure even if she confronted me about this back then that I'd have tried to pursue Alyse. I would have tried to smooth things over with Natalie. Make it work with Natalie, all the while never knowing my true destiny was waiting elsewhere for me.

I swallow hard before asking my next question, but I'm tired of wondering if everything she said was a lie. "Tell me one more thing. Was it mine?"

She's silent for so long I don't think she'll answer. When she does, I'm gutted anew. "I was never unfaithful to you before that night, Asher. And I didn't sleep with Rick until two months after we broke up. I'm...God, I'm so sorry."

"Good-bye, Natalie," I croak, blinking the sting from my eyes.

"Asher, wait. Are you with someone now? Happy?"

"Yes." I don't tell her it's Alyse, because for some reason that doesn't feel right, even though she deserves to have the knife twisted a bit. She'll think I was lying to her, and it turns out the only person I was lying to all along was me.

"I'm glad."

"Good-bye, Nat."

"Bye, Asher."

I hang up with mixed emotions, anger and relief fighting for dominance, but knowing forgiveness is somewhere deep within me. It will take a while for it to trump everything else, but at least I've taken the first step.

LATER THAT NIGHT, after one fan-fucking-tastic bj and a round of toe-curling sex against the shower tile, I lay entwined with Alyse in comfortable silence. It feels right to finally tell her about Natalie.

"I know I get irrational sometimes about other men looking at you or talking to you, Alyse, but...I can't stand the thought of losing you to anyone else. It makes me fucking crazy. It's not that I don't trust you. I do. It's my own insecurities. I'll try to work on it."

"Okay," she says, lightly running her fingernails over my flank.

"You were right, you know."

I feel her smile against my pecs. "I usually am," she replies saucily. I grasp her side, making her giggle.

"Her name was Natalie." Now I feel her smile fall and her hands grip me a little tighter. "I started dating her when I was twenty-three. We met at the gym when she was trying to figure out how to use some piece of equipment, I forget even what it was now. Anyway, I had just graduated with my MBA and started working at my father's company. In the early days as VP of client management, I had to travel a lot, so I was sometimes gone all week for weeks at a time.

"Natalie was an editor at a small publishing house and she struck up a close friendship with a fellow colleague. A male colleague. I knew they spent a lot of time together when I was out of town, but she swore nothing inappropriate was going on. Only it was, and I was young and naïve and ignored all the signs. She knew how much it bothered me that she spent time with this guy, who was clearly after her, yet she did it anyway. She talked about marriage all the time, as if that would solve our relationship issues and change the scope of my job so I was home more.

"So I decided I would ask her to marry me. In retrospect, I don't know why, because I have no doubt we'd be divorced by now. I had been out of town all week and she was expecting me on Sunday morning, but I ended my meetings early and caught a late flight home on Saturday night instead. I had the ring in my pocket. I had the words memorized that I would say when I got down on one knee. Instead, I caught them in bed together. In my house. In *my* bed."

"God, Asher."

The final piece of my confession sits like arsenic in my veins, slowly corroding me from the inside out. Saying it out loud is harder than I ever imagined.

"And the worst part of it was," I choke on the vile words that I've never told anyone else before. "Two months later she sent me a text. A fucking text. Told me she was pregnant, that it was mine but she'd aborted it because she knew I would never forgive her and she couldn't raise my baby without me. I now know just how manipulative Natalie was."

This whole time, I wasn't even sure if she had ever been pregnant. And if so, I had no clue if it was mine or someone else's. To get through the wrenching pain I'd felt at the remote possibility it was true, I told myself it was a lie. But now I know she was telling the truth. She made a life-altering decision without even discussing it with me first.

"Oh, my God, Asher. That's horrible," she breathes, and I know she understands. While different circumstances, she's suffered the same loss that I have. Then she rolls onto her back, encouraging us to change positions, so I am now lying on top of her.

With my head nestled on her stomach and my arms wrapped tightly around her, she strokes my hair, my back and quietly lets me cry the tears of anguish I've held inside for four long years.

CHAPTER 45

ALYSE

6 WEEKS LATER...

"THANK YOU, detective. I appreciate the update.

"Yes.

"Please keep me informed.

"Thank you."

I listen to Asher's side of the conversation and know it's about the class-one felony charges that were filed earlier this week against his CFO. The total funds embezzled were close to six hundred thousand dollars, occurring over a ten-month period of time and most of it has already been recovered, thankfully.

"What's going on?"

"Reigen posted bail earlier today."

"Well, we knew that would happen."

"Yeah. Still chaps my hide that fucker isn't going to be spending his nights on a cot being someone's bitch."

"Oh, I think he'll get plenty of time to get used to that role. Four to fifteen years, to be exact." I laugh, but he doesn't. He frowns instead.

I turn back to the box I'm packing and we work in silence for the next few minutes.

"Is this box ready to go, baby?"

Every time he calls me that, my pussy tightens. I hope when I'm eighty, it still does. "Did you put the files from the bottom drawer in it?" I ask.

"Yes."

"Then it's ready. You can tape it up." I stand from the box I just finished securing, wipe my brow, and look around. My office is a mess of boxes and paper and...crap. I didn't think I had this much stuff in here. It's amazing what you accumulate over the course of a year.

"Did you talk to the landlord?"

"Yes. He has someone who's interested in subleasing coming through on Tuesday. And Heather has the movers scheduled for next weekend."

"She excited about moving to Chicago?" he asks, stacking the box he just taped up onto another. I admire the flex of his muscles as he lifts the heavy object. He looks delicious today in his black Foo Fighters T-shirt and faded jeans. The need to feel his two-day stubble scraping between my thighs is making me pulse with intense need. I want to strip every piece of clothing from him and have him fuck me against the wall. Hard.

"Alyse?" he asks, bringing me out of my lurid fantasy. Damn him.

"Uh, very. Her sister and three nieces live there, so she's going to stay with them for a while until she finds a place. Her brother-in-law is in the military I guess and is stationed overseas for another three months, so she could use the help."

"I'm glad she's making the move," he says, leaning his fine ass against the nearly bare desk. He crosses his arms, biceps bulging, and smirks as he catches me practically drooling. "Like what you see?"

"You know I do," I retort, eyes silently challenging his.

"When is Tabitha planning to come?"

"She's going to commute two days a week for now until they can sell their house. That may take a while in this market."

He nods. "And Al? What did he decide to do?"

"Who cares?" I say, dropping the tape to the floor as I stalk toward him.

"I care. I want to be sure you're staffed appropriately so you're not working eighty hours a week. I'm selfish like that."

"Wow," I tease, running my hands underneath his untucked shirt, savoring the taut muscles contracting under my fingertips. "We're adding selfish to the ever-growing list of notable personality traits, huh?"

"Yes," he tries to answer, but it comes out as a hiss when my nails scrape his flat masculine nipples. His eyes dip to half-mast. I feel his growing erection against my lower belly. My core tingles, flooding with want. It's heady to know I can bring a man like Asher Colloway to his knees with just a look or a simple touch.

"Fuck me," I whisper, my lips finding the hollow of his throat. I don't know if the movers are still outside in the main lobby or not, but I don't care. Not like I'll see them ever again. And my door is shut, so there is that.

His answer is to twine his fingers in my hair, yank me back, and take my mouth with claiming, branding force. His tongue invades, twisting with mine, our moans and breaths becoming one. My hands roam up and down his sinewy back, scratching lightly while his free hand snakes under my yoga pants and panties, palming my bare ass.

I groan when his fingers slip between my crack, toying with my forbidden entrance. He moves lower, dipping into my wetness before bringing a lubricated digit back, pushing it in slightly. He swallows a long moan that passes through my parted lips.

"I want you here," he murmurs against the line of my throat, nipping his way upward toward my ear. The raw lust in his voice causes ripples of pure desire to implode every brain cell. "I need all of you. Soon, baby."

No one has ever been there. I would never allow it. But hell if that's all I can think about now. "Yes," I grate, my body willingly, submitting to his fervent ministrations. "More," I beg, not able to understand the incredible sensations I'm feeling at such an illicit act. As he pushes in further, my eyes roll back, my breath expelling on a rush, a low curse falling with it.

"You're incredible, Alyse. Fucking incredible."

"Fuck me. Now. Please."

"Baby, you beg so nicely. Makes me so damn hard."

His finger hasn't stopped its relentless assault and I'm so close to coming, it will take one swipe on my clit to send me into the stratosphere. I almost whimper when he withdraws his hand from my pants, but he's quickly peeling off my clothes, along with his, dumping them unceremoniously onto the matted carpeted floor. As usual, his smoky, desire-drunk eyes never stray from mine.

But mine briefly break away when I notice he's stroking himself, circling the angry bulbous head, rubbing pre-come onto his silky soft shaft. *Sweet baby Jesus.* There is nothing fucking hotter than your man taking his throbbing cock into his own hand while you watch. My eyes raise, connecting once again with his stormy ones right before he palms the back of my head, pulling me roughly to his waiting mouth.

"Do you want my fingers, my mouth, or my cock, baby?" he whispers crudely against my kiss-swollen lips.

"Do I have to choose just one?" I pant, my hands now full of toned, taut ass cheeks.

He chuckles darkly against my goose-bumped flesh. "All three it is then, my greedy girl."

Before I can think or respond, the cold metal of my desk bites into the naked flesh on my back, but the warmth of Asher's mouth on my aching sex lights up the only nerve endings that matter.

Two, then three fingers stretch me, thrusting feverishly in and out as Asher's talented mouth devours me, tongue circling and flicking. The instant I feel suction on my pounding clit, I shatter into a million, ecstasy-filled pieces, floating aimlessly for long seconds. I feel nothing but searing pleasure race through each molecule. I never want to leave this wonderland of sheer euphoria.

Dimly I become aware that I'm being lifted and pleasure crashes into me once again when I'm slammed down onto Asher's thick, hard cock. He stills for a few seconds to let me adjust to his size. My legs dangle over the edges of my guest chair, which luckily for me doesn't have arms. I always hated that...until now.

His hands snake under my arms and up my back, gripping my shoulders from behind. God, I love the way he completely dominates me, while putting me on a pedestal at the same time. It's sexy as hell.

"Ride me, baby."

I tilt my pelvis and roll my hips slowly back and forth, wanting to draw out his bliss.

"Yes, just like that. You're a goddess, Alyse," he moans. I tighten my walls, silently rejoicing in the swell I feel as he nears his own release already.

"Fuck, I love the way you feel clenching around me."

"Keep talking," I beg, loving every naughty word. I clench again and gasp when he leans me back and picks up his pace, driving into me harder and faster. Just the way I love it. The way I need it.

"Come, sweet Alyse. Come undone around my cock."

As I watch the pleasure rise in his blue eyes, almost like the tide, darkening and swallowing them, I've never wanted to simultaneously stave off an orgasm and have it wash me away at the same time. But his own moan of desire, combined with the slight bite of his teeth on my neck unravels me completely and I explode again headlong into pure, uncontrolled bliss. Asher's grip tightens seconds before he follows, groaning as his own orgasm takes hold. I feel his release deep inside.

"When are you going to marry me?" he asks as we lay against each other panting, recovering from our mind-bending expression of our passionate love for each other. His fingers feather slowly across my back. I sigh in contented happiness.

This is a conversation we've had several times since New Year's

Eve. "I'm moving my business to Chicago and moving in with you, aren't I?" And I even did it without a pros and cons list, because the only thing on that list that matters now is that's where Asher is.

I declined Asher's proposal to buy my business. I need to build its success myself before I can ever think of selling, and Asher's already done so much to help with referrals that I've had to hire two more auditors to keep up. GRASCO did have some extra office space that I'm renting for a steal though, so I'll be close to Asher every day.

"My mom's not too happy we'll be living in sin," he jibes and we laugh, knowing it for the lie it is. Barb Colloway is over the moon thrilled that son number two is heading down the aisle soon. She's made it pretty clear she wants loads of grandbabies. Sooner rather than later. Asher agrees.

"Well we don't want Barb upset, do we?"

"No, we most certainly do not."

"I always wanted to get married on a beach," I say quietly.

"Then that's what you'll get, Alyse." He gently sits me up so I'm looking at him. He's still tucked inside me and I feel him growing thick again. "I'll give you everything you want."

"You already have," I say, smiling, running a finger down his cheek. "You've given me you."

"I want to give you my name, baby. I want everyone to know you're mine."

"I'm already yours. You're an incredible man." I lean forward to kiss his lips.

"Because of you. Now…a date?"

I've already looked at the calendar, trying to plan a date that will be after Livia gives birth, so they can travel. I can't get married without my sister there. "July twenty-fifth."

"July twenty-fifth? That's months away," he groans, beginning to thrust his hardness slightly, causing my eyes to float closed.

"We need to wait until after our nephews are born and I need time to plan. Find the perfect beach. Buy a dress. All that girlie stuff," I pant, starting to lose my grasp on coherent thoughts, because all of my attention is now diverted south and focused on the way Asher's cock is sliding slowly in and out of my very moist sex, each glide reigniting the sensitive nerves again.

"Okay. July twenty-fifth. Then you'll be forever mine." He grabs my hips and begins to drive into me slowly this time, his eyes daring me to stop him.

As if.

"I already am," I tell him on a pleasurable sigh. "I already am."

EPILOGUE

ALYSE

ONE DAY LATER...

"You doing okay?" Asher asks, hand in mine, even though it's shaky and clammy. He's my strength. My rock. My steady.

No. "Yes."

"Are you sure you don't want me to go in with you?"

No. "Yes."

"What about you, Liv? You holding up?" Asher catches Livia's eyes in the rearview mirror. I turn my head to see she looks about as sick as I feel and she's clutching Gray's hand about as hard as I'm holding Asher's.

"Good. I'm good." She's not.

Asher slows his SUV in front of a nice apartment building in Dearborn. We all sit there in silence, nerves thickening the air to almost claus-trophobic levels. I pull at my turtleneck, wishing I'd worn something that didn't threaten to choke the life out of me, because my own body is doing a stellar job of that on its own. My stomach churns wildly and I'm pretty sure I'm seconds away from having to open the door to vomit the meager contents of my stomach onto the snow-covered blacktop.

"You girls don't have to do this, you know," Gray announces. "We can come back another time when you're ready." Then I hear him add quietly, "I don't want you to put any stress on the babies, Livvy."

"The babies will be fine, Gray. They're strong like their daddy."

"No, they're strong like you, angel. I want to go with you," he murmurs.

"I need to do this by myself. Please. You'll be right out here if I need you, right?"

"I wouldn't be anywhere else."

"Let's do this before I change my mind." As if I haven't done *that* fifty times already on the thirty-minute drive here.

We all open our doors, mine with a shaky hand, and within ten seconds Asher has my face in his hands. I grab his waist, holding on for dear life, trying to stop my body from shivering with anxiety. "I love you, baby. I'll be right here waiting."

"Thank you for doing this. I know this isn't...ideal."

The pained look on his face kills me. "I'm not gonna lie. I don't like the fact that he's here and I have to stay outside, but I'm handling it. I trust you."

I nod just as his lips descend on mine. "You're mine," he reminds me.

"Only yours," I mumble as his mouth takes mine again in a posses-sive display of ownership.

Forcing myself to break the lip lock, when all I want to do is spend the day getting lost in Asher, I turn to see Livia waiting for me, Gray's arm protectively around her waist.

"Ready?" she asks.

"As I'll ever be," I sigh.

She holds out her hand to mine and with a look back at our sexy men, we take the first steps toward the meeting I've been both anticipating and dreading in equal measure.

Beck was the intermediary to set up this little one-hour meet and greet with our mom. It surprised me to find out how close he and my mother really are and that she asked if Beck could be with her for moral support. Apparently at least she's been a good mom to someone, and yes, as you can see I still have a little resentment securely stored inside. Forgiveness doesn't happen all at once, but once you start the process it becomes easier.

Elaine and Roberto Mercado divorced two years ago, and according to Beck, the crux of their issues are currently about thirty steps away from her front door. After our father's death, Roberto still didn't want her to have anything to do with us. I guess she couldn't live with that, but she never took steps to make it right either. Considering all this time apart from us, she was afraid of rejection. I try to put myself in her shoes. I suppose I can see where she's coming from. I've been afraid of rejection almost my entire my life, so I try not to condemn her decisions.

I'm hoping this can be a new beginning, the next step to healing, to forgiving. To leaving the last of my past hurts behind me, because I have never been happier than I am now. I don't want that last little bit of resentment weighing me down. It's still a heavy burden on my soul and I want it gone.

I feel like I've found the other part of me. My heart and soul are both finally whole in ways I never thought humanly possible. Asher has healed me in ways he'll never truly comprehend, but I also give myself credit, because *I* am the only one who can make the choice to be happy, to forgive. To live. He just finally gave me the reason to *want* to.

Our feet stop moving. We now stand at my mother's closed burgundy door. Livia gives my hand a quick squeeze. I twist my head to look at her. Her smile strengthens me.

Even a month ago, I wasn't ready for this, but Asher kept persistently convincing me I needed to keep my mind open to *possibilities*. He's right, of course. Look how his persistency turned out for us.

"What's Magic Eight have to say?" she asks, making us both chuckle.

"Cannot predict now," I reply immediately, having every answer burned into my memory. I want to be optimistic that this will be the first step to building a relationship with my mother, but I also want to be realistic. I'm only human after all. Still in need of protecting my fragile heart.

"She's never steered us wrong."

"Nope. Never," I quietly reply, remembering how Asher's fate was suspended in the balance of a few shakes that first night.

With one last smile, I take a deep breath, raise my hand, and knock. Several moments later, the door opens and I'm looking at me, just an older version. I'm looking into my eyes. Watery, scared, chocolate-brown ones. I see Beck standing behind her in my peripheral, but am unable to tear my stare away from the woman standing in front of me to acknowledge him.

Then I break.

"Hi, Mom," I choke, tears spilling over my lids in rivers.

Suddenly Livia and I are enveloped in her arms, all three of our bodies shaking from not-so-silent sobs, and all my faded childhood memories come rushing back in living color.

Her voice, her smell, her love wraps me in its warmth, comfort, and motherly embrace, and I decide that this is the only time that Magic 8 has ever failed me. Within ten seconds of setting eyes on my mother again, I know the answer to the question I asked her before I came would be decidedly different now.

Me: *Is this a new beginning?*

Magic 8: *Without a doubt.*

MUSICAL INSPIRATION

My musical inspiration for writing *Undeniably Asher*:

"Everything" by Lifehouse
"Dirty Little Thing" by Adelita's Way
"Lay Me Down" by Sam Smith
"Take Me Over" by Red
"One and Only" by Adele
"Beautiful" by Akon
"Halo" by Beyonce
"Hold Me Now" by Red
"Give Me a Sign" by Breaking Benjamin
"This Time It's Different" by Evan's Blue
"Set Me On Fire" by Flyleaf
"Marry Me" by Train
"All Falls Down" by Adelita's Way
"Thinking Out Loud" by Ed Sheeran
"So I Thought" by Flyleaf
"Skin" by Rhianna
"Lost" by Red
"Not Alone" by Red

Other works by K. L. Kreig, all of which can be found at Amazon: amazon.com/author/klkreig or through her website at klkreig.com. Also, check out her merch store on her website and order a signed, personalized paperback while you're there!

The Colloway Brothers series:

Have you met the other brothers yet? All available now!

Finding Gray (FREE Novella)
Forsaking Gray
Undeniably Asher
Luke's Absolution
Destination Connelly

"This series is absolutely amazing. Brilliant. Intense. Passionate. Suspenseful. K. L. Kreig really brought her all when she introduced us to the Colloway brothers." ~ **Renee Entress's Blog**

"The Colloway brothers are some of the most swoon-worthy, panty-soaking, endearingly flawed men in contemporary romance today. They are full of grit, intelligence, and sex appeal that will leave you breathless and begging for more." ~ **Rachel Caid, Author of the Finding Home series**

Time Stamps (*Standalone*)

Time Stamps, my father called them. Significant milestones to the seemingly mundane. But those stamps are finite, pre-determined. And eventually our allotment runs out. (Time Stamps is a BookFest Spring 2022 First Place Romance winner and is available now!)

"It was beautiful, quirky, wonderful, romantic, and funny. It was so tragically heartbreaking, cruel, and unfair. It was life. Time Stamps has left such a deep long-lasting impression on our hearts through the magnificent story of love told by K.L. Kreig." ~ **TotallyBooked Blog**

"I know it's early to call it, but I think I've just finished my book of the year. This book is beyond amazing. It's one of those that will leave a stamp on your heart. I'm wrecked and broken; I'm lifted and buzzing. I don't know what to do with myself but that's the best way to feel after a book, isn't it?" ~ **Reviewer, Karen Cundy**

Finding Me Duet:

Lost In Between (Book 1)
Found Underneath (Book 2)

The Escort. The Playboy. The Contract. And my one rule: Never fall in love with the client. Start today with Lost In Between, or download the complete Finding Me duet with an exclusive bonus scene.

"KL Kreig nailed it! The perfect, heart stopping ending to a fantastic duet, Found Underneath is everything you hope it will be and so much more!" ~ **KL Grayson, USA Today Bestselling Author**

"Forget Christian Grey, forget Gideon Cross, forget Jesse Ward .... Shaw Mercer is it for me!" ~ **Reviewer Ana Rente**

Black Swan Affair (*Standalone*)

I'm in love with one brother, but marry the other out of spite when he betrays me by marrying my sister. Now we're one big happy fucking family. Start the 2x USA Today bestseller and the 2017 Kindle Book Review winner now.

"OMG what did I just read? This book… WOW!! It's been years since I read a book straight through. Yes, seven hours I was glued to the pages of this book. A yo-yo of emotions that left me breathless with every scene. *Black Swan Affair* is a must read!!" ~ **Nashoda Rose, NYT and USA Today Bestselling Author**

"I was rapt from the first page, consumed by its every word, and I still cannot stop thinking about it. This rare gem of a story is a top recommendation from me." ~ **Natasha is a Book Junkie**

The **Regent Vampire Lords** series:

Surrendering
Belonging
Reawakening
Evading

She's just an ordinary girl with extraordinary powers. And when she comes forth in a missing persons case, she finds herself the center of unwanted attention in a world she knows nothing about. Start this spicy paranormal series today with Surrendering.

"If you like J. R. Ward, Sherrilyn Kenyon, or Kresley Cole, you'll love K. L. Kreig. This series just got even better! Books like these are the reason we, the reviewer, should be able to give six stars!" ~ **L. A. Wild, Author, Chance The Darkness**

"This author has done it again. I was captivated and transported into the story right from the first chapter. A truly fantastic vampire book with romance, suspense, twists and turns, keeping you on the edge of your seat all the way through." ~ **Hooked on Books Forever Bookblog**

LUKE'S ABSOLUTION EXCERPT

Enjoying the view of her toned bare thigh with each step she takes, courtesy of that nice high slit in her dress, I watch her sashay over to where I'm leaning against the bar. She orders a Corona Light from the bartender, tapping her perfectly manicured pink nails against the cool granite while she waits.

I've been watching her with that jackass photographer for the last hour, getting progressively angrier by the minute, but not quite understanding why. She's smokin' hot, yes, but I have absolutely no claim on her. Not that I wouldn't mind a little sample. Or fifty.

Confusingly, it's the same reaction I had when I saw her in his arms last Friday night. The urge to introduce his face to a cement wall was so great, had she not been drunk off her ass, I may not have been able to resist.

She'd be a handful for any man to juggle, no doubt both in bed and out, and picture boy, Cooper Jensen, isn't even close to enough man for her. It will take a strong hand to control her, make her submit, and God himself help me, that's all I've thought of since I laid eyes on her for the first time months ago. I want to hear her raw voice sobbing my name while I have her pinned helplessly underneath me. Who knew that Eric's sister was so fucking sexy? Probably why he kept her under wraps all those years ago.

Addy Monroe is like a wild horse. Untamed, full of fire, even feral if you get her riled up enough. I had a small taste of that last weekend after Gray's bachelor party when we stopped by the bar where the girls were and I saved her from herself by confiscating their almost empty bottle of Patron. Every heated word she spat tugged straight on my cock, and by the time I left with her passed out in my arms, I was stone cold hard. Let's just say it was a long fucking night all around.

I want her. Not that I *deserve* her. She's untainted, unlike me. I have so many fucking stains, industrial-strength cleaner couldn't remove them all. But I'm not looking for a relationship; I'm looking for a good fuck. I'm looking for oblivion.

Liar, my conscience loudly whispers.

Fuck off, I tell him, even louder.

I discreetly adjust my hardening dick. "No tequila tonight?" I feel the smirk on my face, but don't know if she sees it or not, because I'm trying to refrain from looking at her as I will my own body into submission.

"Unrequited love sucks, doesn't it?" she replies instead with a bite before taking a sip of her beer straight from the bottle. I love a woman who isn't too prissy to drink her alcohol from the actual container it's served in. More than that, I love a woman with a smart, feisty mouth.

"I have no idea what you're talking about, sweetheart."

I flick my eyes over to see hers stray to Gray and Livia across the ballroom and her lips upturn in a sly smirk. "Whatever you say. I'm pretty much the subject matter expert on that shit."

She turns and leans her back against the bar, mirroring my stance. We're both silent, watching the happy newly married couple with drinks in our hands. The more I think about what she said, the more it plain pisses me off.

Yes, I care deeply for Livia. I have for years, but no one can possibly understand what I watched her go through and what I had to suffer through myself.

And even if Livia could have been mine, I know her heart will always belong to Gray. I could never interfere with that. Wouldn't. Besides, I've done enough to my family without intentionally trying to steal my brother's girl. I do have a few shreds of decency left that I'm trying desperately to hold on to. They're wound so tightly around my fingers they're cutting off the circulation, but I'll be damned if I'll let them go.

Regardless of what Addy may think, I'm genuinely thrilled for them both, because after what she's been through, *no one* deserves happiness more than Livia. But fuck, I won't deny watching them get married today was hard. Harder than I thought it would be, and it's not because I still want her. I gave up on that notion years ago, even if my heart didn't quite get the memo.

No...it was hard, because the love that hovers above them like a bright golden halo is sickening. What's even more sickening is that as I watch them, I'm envious. I want *that*, but the logical part of me knows I'll never have it. I push those feelings of optimism that keep bubbling to the surface down deep into the muck again. I may have moved past the worst times of my life, but in no way do I kid myself that I'm worthy of a woman's love and more importantly, acceptance for who I am and the things I've done.

So tonight I need to forget.

About Livia.

About my tainted past.

About all the things I now want but will never get.

And I think Addy Monroe is just the woman to do that, even if it can only be for a few minutes. My dick hardens painfully whenever I set eyes on Livia's best friend, one of my best friend's, Eric's, little sister, and I have to be honest...she's the only one who's stirred it for quite some time now. I've wanted this spitfire since the minute I saw her shaking the tits and ass God so graciously blessed her with at the bar when I first came back to Chicago in September to protect Livia from our sordid past.

"Maybe fifteen minutes in the back will wipe that smirk off your face," I whisper as I lean sideways toward her. In my peripheral, I see her head turn to me.

"Wow, a whole fifteen minutes, huh? I think I'll have to take a rain check on that offer, Rico Suave." She spins on her heels to walk away from me.

Oh hell no.

Next thing I know, her body is pressed against mine, held in place by a firm palm to her neck and another circled around the trim waist I've wanted to squeeze all night.

Sweet Jesus and Mary, she feels fantastic. I have to suppress the groan that wants to escape from somewhere deep inside, because it would give her too much power over me and control is what I need to wrestle from her, inch by agonizing inch. My lips are at her ear, grazing the tender flesh with each word I rasp.

"Sweetheart, I can spend the next fifteen *hours* lavishing untold pleasure and blissful pain all over and inside every single inch of your delectable body until you beg for me, *cry* for me, to stop."

The way her breath hitches has my cock pleading to ram into her over and over. Uncaring who may see, I release her waist and grab her hand, bringing it between our bodies, forcing it to my shaft with mine on top. Guiding her, I squeeze, moving our twined fingers up and down the length of me. She moans and my eyes close at the image of sinking my cock slowly between her red-glossed clever lips.

Nipping her lobe harshly, I grate, "Let's start with that smart mouth of yours, shall we?"

BABBLES...

I was doing my final proofread of *Undeniably Asher* and decided to completely blow up this section. This is off the cuff and unedited, so forgive any missing or misspelled words, or punctuation errors. I suck at commas.

This is my fifth full-length novel released, but I've actually penned seven now, and have already started on my eighth and ninth (which will all be releasing in 2016). The thing that's different about this book, though, is it's personal for many reasons.

There is a lot of me between these pages. A lot of truth mixed in with fiction. I leave a little bit of myself behind in every novel I write. For example, the bike story Alyse told Asher in Chapter 18? True story. It happened. As was the lie that my sister and I told our mother about crashing into each other on swings. Uninventive, but we were like ten, so cut me some slack. And last year, our family went bowling and played laser tag on Thanksgiving Day. It was my first time (not bowling, but I do suck at that, too) and I had no idea how to put on the vest or work the gun. And yes I hid in the corner for a while because I was getting smoked by my son and husband anytime I moved. It was a complete blast so guess what we'll be doing next Thanksgiving?

I put a little of myself in all my female characters. My sass. My independence. My strength. My humor. But the thing about this book in particular is that Alyse is probably the closest character to myself that I've written so far. Alyse's mother abandoned her. *My father did.* Alyse has a hard time letting people in. Really in. *Ditto.* Not many people see my damaged murky depths, because I show them only what I want them to see. Just like Alyse. But unlike Alyse, I loathe math. I'm more of an English gal myself. I didn't have a Magic 8 ball growing up, my daughter did. I loved that thing. But the feelings of wanting to be loved unconditionally by someone? Needing your gravity? Those were mine.

Why are you telling me this? you're asking yourself. Because until I started writing, I never really thought about these things when I read. I never understood how much of themselves an author leaves behind on each page. I'm not talking about their blood, sweat, tears, frustrations, Cheetos and wine stains. I'm taking about how many real tidbits they tell us if we'd only listen. And sometimes how shallow the well is they need to dig into to capture the right emotions for their story. We show little glimpses into our soul. You just need to look hard enough to find them. I read every book with a different set of lenses now (okay, so they're readers. Don't judge).

Finally, I need to address the dedication of this book in case you missed it. My brother, Rodney, committed suicide several years ago. It devastated our family and that never goes away, no matter how much time passes. If my mother is reading this, she'll probably not make it through to the end. He left behind a wife, a child, shattered parents, siblings and countless other friends and family. In the book I talk about Alyse struggling with severe depression and attempting suicide not once but twice. I haven't personally hit this low but I will admit to thinking about it a long time ago when I was also young and didn't understand life better, so that's where I pulled those emotions from (if you've made it this far, you have a glimpse into me most people do not). There are a lot of people that struggle with depression and thoughts of suicide. They affect so many people, not just the victim. It's a shame this isn't discussed more. It's something that *should* be talked about, needs to be talked about, not held inside. If you're at this low, or you know someone who is, there *is* help. In the U.S. please call the National Suicide Prevention Lifeline at **1-800-273-8255**. I'm sure there are similar other resources in other countries that can be found through a quick Google search.

Now onto my thanks and gratitude. This time I'm not going to name every person who's had a hand in this book, because, let's face it, this section has already gotten *waaaay* out of hand. Friends, family, bloggers, authors, editors, formatters, proofreaders, pimpers, etc: if you had a hand in this, you know who you are and you know I thank you from the bottom of my heart. I am nothing but grateful for your belief in me.

I loved writing this story. It turned out better than I thought it would when I started. I hope you enjoyed reading it. I love these brothers more and more with each book I write. Thanks for taking this journey with me, for buying my book and supporting an author you love. Whether that's me or not, your support of your favorite authors cannot be overstated.

If you like this book, ***please*** tell your friends, your neighbors, shout it from the rooftops. Hell, tell people you don't even like! The best thing you can do to support an author you love is word of mouth and LEAVE A REVIEW on Goodreads, Amazon or wherever. Even one or two sentences or simply rating the book is helpful for other readers. Reviews are critical to getting a book exposure.

ABOUT THE AUTHOR

This is the hardest part...talking about myself.

I'm just a regular ol' Midwest girl who moved to the South (Tennessee) and now understands the slight "Bless Your Heart" really means. I've fallen in love with yoga and Jess Sims from Peleton. I don't do as much running as I used to, but I still eat, and I still love carbs and there is still a love-hate relationship with my ass and thighs. Mostly hate. I like a good cocktail (oh hell...who am I kidding? I love *any* cocktail). I'm a huge creature of habit, but I'll tell you I'm flexible. I swear too much. I love alternative music and in my next life, I want to be a badass female rocker. I still hate, hate, hate spiders, telemarketers, liver, acne, winter, and loose hairs that fall down my shirt (don't ask, it's a thing).

And at fifty-two years of age, I also have a new love. Her name is Vienna Faye. As parents, we love our children deeply, but the love you have for your grandchildren is more, somehow. It's indescribable. And she is spectacular, just like her mother. If you follow me on Instagram, you'll see her once in a while, and I'll bet you agree!

God has blessed me in so many ways ...and I know it.

If you're a stalker, the first step is to admit it. After that, you can find me in the usual social media sites: Facebook and Instagram. Also give me a follow on BookBub, TikTok, Goodreads or Amazon, all of which I use with irregular frequency. Truthfully, if you want to reach out, email (klkreig@gmail.com) is the best way as I check that every day and I respond to every single one.

In this day and age, with so many great authors and so many new releases, it's challenging to keep up with it all, so if you don't want to miss when my next book is releasing, sign up for my newsletter found on my website at klkreig.com. Promise, no spamming and you'll only get it when I have something important to say, which isn't often.

Happy reading.

~ Kelly

Made in the USA
Coppell, TX
27 August 2023

20851234R00204